A CRUEL KIND OF

Beautiful

MICHELLE HAZEN

BOOK 1 OF THE SEX, LOVE, AND ROCK AND ROLL SERIES

Cover Photos used with license by Shutterstock

Cover Design by M. Fairbanks, Fresh Design

Edited by Katie Golding and Sheila Athens, Author Accelerator

Copy editing by Keyanna Butler

Printed and bound in the United States of America

First Edition

ISBN: 978-1975889876

Dedicated to

NAOMI DAVIS

Your faith in this book triggered so many amazing events in my life,
and even more that haven't happened yet.
You've already read a few hundred thousand of my words,
and you'll read a million more before I find a way to express
how much it means that you always believe in me.

Table of Contents

Chapter 1: MEET UGLY

When the newspaper broke my window at four in the morning, I didn't stop to think about the fact that I was wearing sweats. Not thin, make-your-butt-look-cute yoga pants but old school sweats: cuffs cinched tight around my wrists and ankles like rib-knit shackles, plus deflated airbags of material sagging at my crotch and knees.

This is definitely something I would have considered if I'd known I was going to open the door to biceps like his.

Turns out my renegade paperboy isn't a boy at all; more like six feet two inches of pure man-candy. With his fist raised to knock, all his muscles stand out in exquisitely stark lines, and I'm definitely not staring. Or maybe I am, because he takes a step back and drops his hand, brow furrowing.

"Shit," he says. "*Shit.*"

I quirk a brow. I'm five foot flat on a good posture day, so it must be the atrociousness of my sweats that's putting the fear into him.

"Don't tell me this was a revenge window-breaking and you got the wrong house." I nod toward my neighbor's place. "Did Mr. Schmelzly steal your girl or something?"

His eyes dip below my collarbone for a second, but I'm not exactly worried about my lack of a bra. This sweatshirt is so baggy I could be packing the curves of Santa Claus or Kim Kardashian under here and he wouldn't be able to tell the difference.

"I wish I could claim it was revenge. More like a total failure of motor skills." He grimaces. "I'm so sorry about your window. They give us a half day of training, which felt like four hours more than anybody should need, but right now, it's looking like I could have used five." His shoulders hunch as he gives me a sheepish look.

My annoyance melts, and I offer, "In your defense, it was the Thrifty Tuesdays paper. Tuesday has some serious heft in tampon coupons."

"Plus, the supplemental entertainment section." His face relaxes into a smile. "If it'd been a Wednesday, you might have been safe. Here, can I at least help you clean up the glass?" He steps forward.

"Uh..." I hesitate, surprised that he's offering to do housework. Not to mention he probably has another twenty miles to pedal to finish his route, because who the hell gets newspapers delivered these days? Though I guess if anybody did, it would be this neighborhood, where I'm the youngest by four or five decades. Not exactly the iPad generation.

"I'm sorry, you probably don't want a strange guy in your house who just broke your window. Trust me, I'm not a serial killer or anything. If I were going to kidnap you, I'd like to think I'd be a lot smoother about the whole thing."

"Good to know. There's nothing I hate more than an inept kidnapper."

His eyes lighten at my response. "That doesn't seem fair. Shouldn't you hate successful kidnappers more? There's the ride in the trunk and the whole ransom debate...it's probably a real pain."

"Nah, people love successful kidnappers. Because Stockholm Syndrome." A smirk tugs at the edge of my mouth. "Shouldn't you be convincing me to trust you, not defending kidnapping fails?"

"Right. I'm batting a thousand this morning, aren't I? Sorry again." He blushes, actually *blushes.*

He's like a walking sex dream with close-shaved hair and a cologne-commercial jawline, and I have no idea how a guy can be this hot without a trace of cocky to go along with it. Abruptly, I realize I've been holding those delicious dark-chocolate eyes for longer than I have any right to when I'm dressed like somebody's Aunt Melba. I step back to let him inside.

"No problem. I promise by the time we work the glass out of my shag carpeting, you'll have worked off every debt you've ever owed."

He glances down as he steps over the threshold, then sucks in a sharp breath. "Your feet!"

I follow his line of sight. There's some chipped green polish on my toenails, but nothing that requires an exclamation point. Though now that I look closely, there are a couple of tiny blond hairs growing on top of my big toe. Gross. Do people tweeze toe hairs? Is that a thing?

"You don't have shoes—are your feet cut?"

I prop one hand against the wall and lift my foot to check for blood. "Nah, I'm set." I don't bother to check my other foot. He's close enough now to weigh in on my toe-tweezing dilemma and frankly, his was not an opinion I had hoped to poll.

"Here." He hops to keep his balance as he pulls off one of his sneakers and hands it to me.

I consider this trophy, tipping my head. "Um, thanks?"

"Put it on." He flushes, though this time I'm not sure why. "If you tell me where the dustpan is, I can start picking up the big pieces while you go get your shoes."

Bouncing on one foot, he removes his other shoe, wobbling for a second so his shoulder bumps into mine. He blushes again at his clumsiness but earnestly pushes the other one of his Cadillac-sized Vans at me, waiting until I put them on.

Now I have clown feet.

I peek up at him, my lips losing a battle with a smile that's pure are-you-for-real-right-now?

His eyes fly from his Vans up to my face, his gaze snagging on my lips. "Uh…"

A year ago, a look that hot from a guy like him would have been the Holy Grail of my dating existence. But now, he's more like the picture of Ian Somerhalder that Granna once taped to our vacuum: something pretty to look at while you clean, and nothing more.

I shrug, wishing the movement could shake off my goosebumps. "Give me a second to grab my own shoes and I'll be right back."

"Um, yup. I'll just be here, then." He folds his hands in front of him, but the corner of his mouth twitches irrepressibly upward. "Researching successful kidnapping techniques on my phone, so you'll trust me."

I choke on a laugh. "Yeah, because that's not creepy at all."

Except as the smile spreads across his face, lighting his eyes, it really isn't. I've known the guy for five minutes and if a real criminal burst through the door, I'd probably jump behind him.

Besides, we already know he can do some real damage armed with a newspaper.

"If you hit expert level before I get back, I want my cut of the ransom," I call as I slide-waddle my borrowed shoes across the crunch of outdated carpet and splintered glass. Each one of his puffy skater shoes is as long as both my feet put together, and I have to shuffle along like an old lady or risk them falling off. If my bandmates could see me now, I'd never hear the end of it.

When I get to my room, I shove a dark strand of hair back into my messy bun, ignoring the small, hopelessly female part of me that wants to search for a hairbrush. I kick off his shoes in favor of a pair of pretty ballet flats, then glare down at my feet. I peel them off and stuff my feet into a heel-squashed pair of slippers. My subconscious definitely cannot be trusted.

After Andy and I broke up, I set my Facebook status permanently to Single and dropped my makeup into a bottom drawer. I'm done putting my ass on the line—or into a set of Spanx—to impress a man. So instead of primping, I hook two fingers into the back of the stranger's Vans and carry them into the living room.

"The trash can is in the kitchen," I call out, "but if you want to do some heavy lifting, my behemoth of a vacuum cleaner is in the hall closet. We call her Bessie. Well, and a few other names I probably shouldn't mention if you happen to be religious. You'll see why once you—" I break off as I round the doorway and realize I'm talking to myself.

I glance at the huge sneakers in my hand, then up at the rest of the room. My guitar still sits in its stand, my crate of semi-collectible records resting next to my antique turntable. Everything that might interest a thief is still here, but of my walking sex dream, there's not a trace.

He's just gone.

MICHELLE HAZEN

Chapter 2: DISAPPEARING ACT

I kind of forgot to be upset about the window when it came with a chocolate-eyed, blushing newspaper deliveryman. Unfortunately, now he's MIA, leaving me with an abandoned set of Vans that don't fit me, a giant hole in my house, and a new song eating a matching hole in my brain at a truly inopportune moment. Sitting back on my heels, I drop another shard into the dustpan and glance at my phone to check the time.

"Come *on*, Danny." If my friend doesn't show up before Western Civ starts, I'm going to have to choose between my attendance grade and leaving my house with a convenient burglar's entrance in the front wall.

Sighing, I give up on the glass for the moment because it seems to have set up shop inside the shag carpet. I dump the full dustpan into the kitchen trash, whacking it against the side of the plastic bin in an attempt to block out the lyrics playing through my mind. When my band performs, the drums are my jam, but when I write our songs, I don't always start with the percussion. I just get it however it wants to come, and when it plows in this fast, I'm pretty much useless until I finish writing. If I try to drive somewhere, I'll end up in a part of town I don't recognize or stopped mid-street at an invisible stoplight.

When my life actually gives me the time and space to grab a guitar and work it out, the experience is phenomenal. Music never sounds as good as it does when the muse is feeding it straight in through my bones. Not Zeppelin, not Jack White, not even Hendrix.

But on a day like today when my schedule holds two classes, a shift at the bar, and three pages left on a research paper due by eight a.m. tomorrow? Music is just a bitch.

Hurrying down the hallway, I rip the elastic band out of my hair and shoot it in through the bathroom door. The mass of deep brown falls over my eyes and I blow it out of my way, some of the lighter, sun-bleached strands catching in my eyelashes. My brush rests on a hall table and I snatch it up, taming my hair with one hand as I shimmy out of my horrific sweats.

Ever since I was a kid, I would kick off my blankets and wake up shivering before morning. Eventually, I had to give up and go to bed in something a little warmer. Turns out, the tight cuffs on old-fashioned sweats don't leave as much room for a draft to squeeze in. Highly convenient, though they're awful looking and I didn't start wearing them until after I stopped caring about looking cute for a boyfriend.

By the time Danny strolls in with a bag of Cheetos, I'm wearing unzipped jeans and I'm half-in, half-out of a black tee shirt with a picture of a zombie garden gnome on it. All I need is to pull the shirt over my right arm, but I'm busy scrawling on a vodka bottle with a Sharpie, sketching the shape of the melody so I can capture it long enough to make it stick in my mind.

"Hey, Jera? Since when do you drink vodka?" My best friend and bassist plops onto my bed with a protest of metal springs. He tosses a Cheeto up in a perfect arc that ends with the snap of his teeth.

I blink down at the bottle. "I don't. Actually, where the hell did this come from? Did Jax leave it last weekend?" Jackson Sterling, the lead singer of our band, has been known to hit the hard stuff pretty darn hard when he's in a certain mood.

Danny tips his head toward me. He's all messy black hair and vivid eyes, his arms decorated with spare, inky twists of art that complement every bulge of muscle without ever obscuring. He's the only tattoo artist I've ever met who doesn't believe in full sleeves, and I can't imagine anyone ever disagreeing once they've seen his arms—or his portfolio.

"Any booze left?" he asks.

"Nope," I lie. The bottle holds about an inch of liquid but if I'm forced to watch him drink cheap vodka with Cheetos before eight in the morning, I might barf.

My hair is at least partially brushed, so I wind my hair up on top of my head and stick the Sharpie through it, then finish getting dressed.

A Cheeto crunches as Danny goes back to considering the ceiling, crossing his unlaced boots at the ankles. I glance down at him, the weirdness of my morning calming a little at the sight of his eyes—the familiar gold-green hazel that's a darker version of my own. Between that and the way we've picked up each other's gestures and expressions over the years, people often mistake us for siblings.

Then again, that could just be the bickering.

"You're the best house guarder in Portland." I bend to leave a smacking kiss on Danny's cheek. He grimaces at the sound and selects another cheese-flavored snack as I sweep up my messenger bag. "I owe you one."

The crunching ceases. "Pizza?"

I wrinkle my nose and trot down the hall. "Only if you don't insist on putting pineapple and potato chips on it. Again."

Danny's a vending machine vegetarian. No meat, but he's not into fruit stands and farmer's markets, either. He subsists entirely on items that can be deep fried or bought from gas stations. Somehow, he still has a flat stomach with just the hint of a six-pack to it, though in seven years I've never seen him do a sit-up.

Life? Is not fair.

I nab my keys and slam through the side door, the books in my messenger bag thumping together when I swing it over my shoulder and hit the garage opener. I kick a leg over my bike, and coast out from under the still-rising door.

When I inherited this house from Granna a little over a year ago, I meant to tear up the shag carpet and bag the avocado green curtains, but it never happened. I did manage to line the whole garage in Auralex foam to make a practice space for my band, but the rest of the house is still more suited to doilies and Precious Moments figurines.

I gave up on a lot of things when Granna died, and decorating was one of them. But the house is conveniently located only a mile from campus and today I'll be much less likely to get myself killed if I bike instead of drive. Mostly because the drums start hitting behind my ears with the first stroke of the pedals and then I'm lost in a haze of music.

By the time I lock up my bike on the Portland University campus, I have two more lines of lyrics and the kind of restlessness that leaves me feeling like I don't really live inside a body anymore. It is days like today when I think I might not be cut out for college.

What I need is a crappy job waiting tables and nothing in my life but space to fill with songs I invent. Unfortunately, that's what Mom is afraid of, and it would make Dad a little too proud. Besides, when I don't have a song that's begging to be written, I like going to class.

But right now, my fingers tingle with the gravitational pull of chords I need to play and I don't care about anything but writing them down. When the flow of students bottlenecks in the doorway, I grind my teeth until they start to move again, then beeline for an open seat, clawing my notebook out of my bag.

As soon as I open it my mind goes completely, cursedly silent. I hiss a four-letter word and slump in my seat.

Without the gleam of the muse's magic to distract me, the classroom looks dull, like I'm seeing it through the washed-out lens of a daytime soap opera. Cheap blue upholstery on the stadium seats, and centuries-old news waiting to be transcribed into two hundred dutiful notebooks as we all fulfill our general grad requirement.

Shit, I need to call my homeowner's insurance. I pull the marker out of my hair to jot that in my notebook where notes and lyrics should have gone. I haven't called the insurance company since I switched Granna's policy into my name, and I can't look up the number until I can remember their Super Generic Insurance Company Name.

I stare past Dr. Marcus's podium to the wall of windows beyond him. Today sucks.

Outside the glass, the October sun sends glowing fingers through the morning fog as a girl darts after a Frisbee. I wish I were playing Frisbee. Or my guitar, or Jax's PlayStation. Anything but trying to figure out if insurance covers newspaper-related window fatalities, and what I'm going to do with the set of dude's shoes my vandal left behind.

Frisbee Girl hurls her disc, taunting me with her freedom. Except she flubs the release so it wings a sharp curve backward and catches in the branches of the tree outside Dr. Marcus's windows. The professor doesn't seem to notice, clearing his throat before he calls the class to order. Which is when I see *him*.

My walking sex dream has changed out of his newspaper delivering clothes, but I'd recognize those biceps anywhere. He jogs to the rescue, jumping to grab the lowest branch and chinning himself. He holds his weight with one arm as he nabs the Frisbee, then drops back to the ground and hands it back to its owner.

It has been—I check my phone—an hour and eighteen minutes since he took off from my house, barefoot. That shoots to shit any notion I had that he left due to an emergency rather than a sudden attack of do-not-want-to-pay-for-window-itis.

"Yikes, you too, huh?" the girl next to me murmurs.

Outside the glass, Walking Sex Dream gives a distracted smile to Frisbee Girl and hurries off in the other direction. I stop scowling at him, and glance over at my classmate. She has reddish hair in one of those ponytails with a smooth bump in the front, and as weird as that would look on me, she's kind of pulling it off. Her eyes sparkle as she gives me a knowing smile.

I shake my head as I try to catch up. "Sorry, what?"

Bumpy Ponytail Barbie leans back in her seat. "No need to be embarrassed. Jake Tate's body leaves a trail of broken hearts everywhere he goes, and it's even worse for the few of us who've actually managed to *talk* to the guy."

I snort a laugh through my nose and throw her a sidelong glance. "I take it you know him, then?"

"I can't believe you don't, considering everything. I'm Cleo, by the way. It's Clementine but that's too long, and Clem?" She shudders. "Not so much."

Dr. Marcus has already started into his lecture, but with a couple of hundred bodies in the room, he doesn't even notice our whispering.

"Jera. Nice to meet you." It comes out as automatically as a sneeze, my Granna-honed manners covering my innate lack of tact. "But what do you mean, 'considering everything'?"

She tilts her head toward me and says in an undertone, "During freshman year, Jake was the big man on the baseball team. Starting pitcher by his second semester, their number one recruit, cushiest scholarship and living stipend, all the extras. I heard they were going to buy him a freaking *car*."

My eyebrow lifts, and I wrestle it back down. I am not interested. Unless of course he wants to use that cushy living stipend to buy me a new window.

Cleo darts a glance toward the professor before she continues in a whisper, "Then, end of spring term comes, and rumor has it there was some crazy drama with his family. Suddenly he's not at any of the parties, somebody else was pitching all the games, and the search

20

committee was pulling every kind of string to tempt a new pitcher to transfer to PU mid-year."

Big deal. He played baseball and now he doesn't. I'm a little curious what kind of family problems make you quit a Division I baseball scholarship, but it's not like we're buddies, so what do I care? Though now I understand how he put so much velocity behind a simple newspaper.

"What was the drama all about?" I hear myself ask.

I am excellent at minding my own business.

Cleo purses her lips. "I don't really remember. Too bad though—the baseball boys are a blast, and he was some lovely eye candy at the parties." She smiles. "Plus, nice hands. He caught me once, when I was doing a kegstand and dipshit Eric stumbled and dropped me."

"That's cool," I mumble.

So he's a jock. My ex-boyfriend, Andy, was on the lacrosse team, so I know the stereotypes about jocks are mostly bullshit. It's not that they're all self-centered. It's just that with one to three practices a day, they're busy as hell.

Of course Jake Tate would have somewhere more important to be this morning. On the other hand, what could have been so urgent that he couldn't wait for me to get back so he could make an excuse and reclaim his shoes?

"So..." Cleo's expression is halfway between sly and curious. "Did he ask you out or something? How do you know him?"

"I don't." Decisively, I flip to the next page of my notebook. "I don't know him at all."

Chapter 3: NEGATIVE IMAGE

I swing a leg off my bike, balancing on one pedal as I glide toward my garage. My fingers tap against the handlebars, the underlying beat to my new song already as solid as the concrete of my driveway. I drop my bike and step up to key in the door-opening code when my hand freezes halfway there.

When I left, there was a gaping hole in my house, the rising sun glinting off the lines in the shattered glass. Now, there's a piece of plywood nailed neatly across it.

Dry grass crunches under my Chucks as I cross the lawn. I can't believe *Danny* fixed my window. The last time I saw him drive a nail, it was just to hold some cables out of the way in our practice space, and it was so crooked it didn't even manage to do that for long.

I lift one hand and touch the head of one of the nails. They are big but each one's sunk deep and true, with no dents in the wood from missed hits. A professional job. Did Danny hire someone to fix it? If so, it seems like he would have called, because no way would he have the cash to cover it. He doesn't get paid until Thursday, and money is one of the many things that escapes Danny's notice. Which is why he rarely has any.

I pull my phone out and check the voicemail to see if I missed a message when I was in class.

The only voicemail on the list is Andy's, nearly twelve months old. A pang drops emptily down through me and I click off the screen. No answers there.

Retrieving my bike, I let myself into the garage, then the house. "D?" I call out.

The plucked bassline from a Red Hot Chili Peppers song is my only answer. I follow it to the living room, frowning at the ground when I get there. The glass is gone, and the normally mashed shag carpet displays the electro-shocked buoyancy of having been vacuumed by all four horsepower of Bessie's oversized engine.

Danny coaxes another note out of his bass, tipping his head back to look at me. Without the window, the living room is dark as a cave, lit by a single lamp glowing in the corner.

"You didn't call Dad to board up the window, did you?" My tone is tight, but I can't really help it. I may not have paid for this house, but it's mine now. I can take care of it without my daddy's help.

"Nah," Danny says. "Guy showed up with a sheet of wood. Put it on the window, asked where the vacuum was. I told him, and he vacuumed."

"What guy?" I dump my messenger bag onto the floor. "Was it someone we know?"

"Nope." He looks back to his bass and plays a quick little flurry I've never heard before. It tickles at my ears, but I refuse to be distracted.

"Seriously? You let a stranger with a hammer into the house?"

"I got him your hammer out of the garage. But he brought his own nails."

I exhale a curse that imaginatively connects the anatomy of three different animals. "What did he look like?"

"Like a dude."

I prop my hands on my hips. "Are you even human, Daniel? You weren't curious? You don't even want to know why my window is broken and strange men are wandering in with nails and no hammer?"

Danny shrugs. "Hey, I forgot to say earlier: if you want to get that tattoo you've been talking about, I have a shift at Negative Image in two hours and we got in some Tahitian black ink this week that would be perfect."

I groan through my teeth, but it doesn't matter that Danny doesn't remember a single identifying characteristic. It had to be Jake Tate. And he was in here while I was stuck in another class and then an interminable meeting with a professor about my project for Music Composition II. It sends an uncomfortable little thrill through me to think of a guy that hot moving through the private spaces of my house.

"He left that." Danny points to the coffee table with the toe of his boot, his untied laces swinging.

I snatch up the plain envelope, thick with several sheets of paper inside. Is it a note? An apology, or an explanation of his bizarre disappearance?

"How's the song you were working on earlier?"

"Finished most of it in class." I flip the envelope over to find it sealed.

"You write the bassline?"

I glance up, surprised he would even ask. "No. Of course not." I can write for bass, but I can't write for *his* bass, any more than I could reproduce the tattoo designs that bleed from his fingers: so beautiful people beg him to transcribe them permanently onto their skin.

The front door swings open, the creak of its ancient hinges the only warning I get before my dad strolls in. "What happened to the front window? Wild band party?"

"Orgy," Danny says.

"You don't have the square footage for a decent orgy. It's no wonder you guys ended up breaking shit."

25

I roll my eyes and stuff my mystery envelope into the back pocket of my jeans. "Jesus, Dad, could you *be* more embarrassing and inappropriate?"

"Answer: yes. Don't tempt me." Dad glances over at the window again, his eyes narrowing on the hole in the center of the shattered glass. "Danny," he says. "I have a sudden and intense need for coffee. Consider it this month's management fee."

I grimace. What was I thinking letting my dad manage our band? Not that he isn't a brilliant manager. He's the best, way too good for a local group. But he's my *dad*, and how teenybopper is that? Besides, every time he uses his connections to get us a new gig, I feel like we're wringing the last drop of currency out of his band's old glory days. I don't want my name to be a prefix for "the daughter of Hank McKnight."

"Yes, sir." Danny sets aside his bass and swipes his keys off the coffee table. "You want anything from Starbucks, Jera?"

My father shakes his head. "You know, more of—"

"More of your dollar stays in the community if you buy local," I finish. "We know, Dad. Though I did happen to notice that your real estate company is part of a national—"

"Brewed Awakenings it is," Danny interrupts before we can really get going. "Coffee or tea?"

"Latte. Thanks, D. You can take my car if yours is low on gas."

He nods and digs in my messenger bag, standing with a faint snap of keys against his palm.

Dad doesn't reach for my guitar in its stand, the way he usually does after two minutes in my house. Instead, he waits for the door to close behind Danny, then drags the piano bench out and sits across from me. "Jera, was it Andy who broke the window? You can tell me the truth."

"No, Dad, jeez!" I haven't seen Andy in over a year. I never told my family he moved away after our breakup, because saying it out loud makes my stomach churn.

Dad hmphs, and I can't tell if he believes me. He knows I've got a checkered history with the opposite sex, but I didn't bother to inform him of my new motto: look but don't touch. Because once I touch, sooner or later we'll make it to bed, where neither one of us ends up happy.

"Andy's not violent. What you saw of him, at the end, that wasn't him." It was what our relationship turned him into. I look away. "The paperboy broke the window. It was just an accident."

Dad frowns, following my gaze to the fat newspaper on the side table. "You get the paper delivered? Why would you waste trees on a newspaper I've never seen you read?"

I pick at a loose thread on the piping of the loveseat. "Granna paid for a bunch in advance and they don't give refunds." And I might have re-upped. Once. Maybe twice. It's always been a constant at her house: the newspaper on the front porch, smelling of fresh ink and new paper, wilted a little at the edges from a smattering of rain. So much has changed since she died but not that. "Hey, what are you doing here in the middle of the day? Shouldn't you be selling houses or something?"

He ignores my question. "You ought to get serious about Danny," he says. "He would never pull the kind of crap Andy did after you two broke up."

"Andy had every right to be upset. And stop holding your breath on the Danny thing. I've told you a hundred times: we're not having sex, we're not together, and we're not going to *be* together."

"Jera, you're with the guy every day of the week, and I know how often he sleeps over here. Are you just worried if you call it dating, it might affect the band?" Dad lifts an eyebrow. "As far as I can tell, Jax is too busy with his own love life to get jealous about yours."

I curl my knees up onto the couch, finger-combing my hair moodily. Dad is about two miles down the wrong track, but it's not like I can explain to him about the far more complicated reality of why I stopped dating. Since I'm stuck with platonic anyway, why wouldn't I spend my time with Danny? He's got his quirks, but he accepts everything exactly how it is. Even me.

"There's nothing to be embarrassed about," Dad says. "A healthy sex life is a big part of a successful relationship, and if the sleepovers are any indication, you and Danny already have that."

I can't stand the worry in Dad's voice. It's only one shade off from disappointment, which folds me like a house of cards. I hold up a finger. "You have one second to change the subject to something utterly unrelated to Danny's penis, or I'm going to kick you out before he gets back with your coffee."

"Fine, be grouchy. But Mom's been wondering why you don't bring your boyfriends over to meet her anymore." He stands up. "Anyway, I got distracted by the window, but that's not why I'm here. I have news."

Chapter 4: **THE MYSTERY OF 37**

The quick bleat of my VW Bug's pitiful horn sounds as Danny pulls in.

"One sec. I gotta go out and give Danny a hand," I tell my dad, grateful for the interruption. I need an extra second to brace myself for whatever he has to say, especially since it's almost certainly news about my band. It's the most important thing left in my life, and after losing Andy, and then Granna, I'm full up on bad news for the year.

I swing through the door and jog down the sidewalk toward the driveway. Danny grins up at me, sun glinting off his retro sunglasses, and his black hair in nearly atomic disarray from the wind. I laugh when I realize he took the top down on my convertible for the five-minute drive to the coffee shop.

"Apparently, my father's dirty mind never quits," I say when I get close enough. "I had to set him straight about us. Again."

"Ah, really? I kind of love freaking him out with the idea of my dirty, tattooed hands all over his precious only daughter." Danny passes me the two coffees from the cup holders, retrieving the last cup from where it was propped between his thighs.

"He's more hopeful than freaked out. He's worshipped you since the day you outplayed Bear."

"Hank likes me. But I only outplayed his band's old bassist." Danny bumps the car door closed with his ass. "If I could show him up on the guitar, he'd hand over his wife with full blessings. When we auditioned Jax and he opened with that crazy fast solo, I swear I caught Hank drafting your betrothal contract on the back of a Safeway receipt."

"Still, I'm fairly sure chlamydia is not in the future he envisions for me, so Jax is out."

Danny takes a sip of his tea and gives me an uninflected look that somehow manages to make me feel catty as hell. "Jax always flies safe."

I turn back to the house. "Please don't enlighten me as to how you know that." If Danny's decided to tag along during our lead singer's legendary sexcapades, I'd rather not hear about it.

I try to juggle the cups and turn the doorknob at the same time, and Danny takes one from me just as it begins to spill. "Jax is a good guy," he insists.

"I know that." I duck inside. "I spend more time with him than most wives spend with their husbands."

"Yeah, but I don't think you—"

"Large latte!" I put on a smile to smooth my interruption as I nod to Danny to pass over the drink. Whatever he was about to say about Jax, it is almost certainly not something I want to discuss in front of Dad.

Danny swipes his face against his shoulder to push his sunglasses up onto the top of his head, then passes a cup to Dad.

I reach over to straighten the sunglasses on Danny's head, mouthing, "*Later,*" so he knows I'm not just being an asshole and cutting him off from whatever he wanted to tell me about Jax. He shrugs and takes a seat on the couch.

"So, is the news a gig?" I ask, trying to be positive. "Is it at The Basement again?"

I can't quite meet my dad's eyes, because I don't want to look ungrateful, but The Red Letters have been playing the same three crappy dive bars forever. At some point you cross the line between working your way up, and realizing for you, there is no up because you're only Dive Bar Good. My band is getting perilously close to that line.

"I mean, it's a decent-sized venue. It's just…"

"That every breath you take for the next three weeks tastes like stale Keystone Ice?" Dad pops the top off his coffee to blow across its surface. "Trust me, I know. Their ventilation system probably hasn't been updated in twenty years."

I pick at the lid to my latte. Why does he have to remind me that his band played all the same venues first? I already know the staff at The Basement remembers him, that they're comparing The Red Letters to The Heat every time we perform.

He takes a sip and winces when he burns his tongue. "You know, while I've got you two here, I really think we should talk about hiring a keyboardist to lay in a track or two for the new album."

"For the last time, we do not need a freaking keyb—" I pause, squinting at him. "You're stalling. What's going on?"

His eyes twinkle above his coffee. "Well, it just so happens your poor old dad scraped up a gig for you. At a little music festival I like to call Things That Go Bump In The Night."

I shriek.

I'm not proud of that reaction, but at this moment, I am not dignified either. As clearly evidenced by the caffeinated-koala impression I proceed to execute, leaping on my dad as he laughs and swings me around the living room and doesn't say a blessed thing about the chiropractic bills I probably just cost him.

When he sets me down, I run both palms over my totally numb cheeks, and then my hair.

"As an opener, right?" I ask him, eyes huge. "Or one of the side stages, maybe?"

31

"An opener..." He taps a finger to his lips, pretending to consider. "If you consider being the top billed band for the pub crawl an opener, then yes."

Danny's still sitting down but nodding...and nodding, his smile growing with every second.

Bump In The Night is the biggest off-season music festival in the Pacific Northwest, and while playing as an opener on the main stage might be a bigger crowd, the pub crawl bars are more intimate venues. That means it's easier to get the audience stirred up, and if we do that, we can draw in the crowds passing on their way to the other bars. Including, hopefully, the record label scouts who swarm to this festival.

I grab Dad and press a near-assaultive kiss into his cheek. "You're a band-management genius. I have to call Jax. He's going to tattoo your name on his ass when he hears this."

Dad laughs as I pull out my phone and speed dial. I bounce on my toes, grinning over at Danny, but it goes straight to our bandmate's voicemail.

"Jackson freaking Sterling!" I yelp into the phone. "The sky is falling, the birds are singing, and I have the best damn news of your life. Call me. Call me, call me, *call* me!" I hang up.

Dad, still smiling, glances toward the door. "I should head back to the office. I was showing a house to a client a few blocks down and I wanted to see your reaction in person."

Danny jerks to his feet, holding out a hand. "Thanks. Uh, thank you." He pumps Dad's hand a few too many enthusiastic times, and I can't hold back a snicker.

"I'll call you tonight and we'll talk details." Dad goes to let himself out.

Danny looks at me, blinking like he's still trying to process what just happened. I shake my head, grinning hard enough for both of us. "Holy shit."

My best friend chuckles, the sound a little lightheaded. "Hey, breaking a mirror is supposed to be seven years of bad luck. Maybe breaking a picture window is the opposite."

Reminded with a jolt, I reach in my back pocket and yank out the envelope, eyeing it with even more nerves than the first time I saw it. There's no way it contains anything good. Dad's news probably just ate up my next decade's share of good karma. I need to go cure some hamsters of AIDS or something to stock back up.

"And the Oscar goes to..." Danny prompts as I continue to stare at the envelope clutched in my fingers.

There's a bounding, sparkling sensation deep in my belly that has nothing to do with our upcoming show and everything to do with knowing this envelope came from Jake Tate's house. Maybe even from his bedroom. And I'm officially not thinking about that.

I rip open the envelope. Instead of notebook paper, there are bills inside. I leaf past them, but there's not even a scrap of paper on which a note could be written. Okay, well, money's good, too. I guess.

Danny retrieves my notebook out of my backpack and flips from the back until he finds the lyrics and chord notations on the last used pages.

I count the money. Thirty-seven dollars.

What the hell? Not enough to pay for the window but not a nice round number for a payment against the full amount. What is the significance of the extra two dollars? Emotional damages? Rental fee for use of my hammer? A poor substitute for the nude picture I maybe sort of wish it was?

Maybe since Jake quit the team and lost his scholarship, he didn't have enough money to pay for the whole window and was too embarrassed to admit it. It makes sense—in my experience, family drama usually comes along with bills. One of the reasons I moved in with Granna instead of living in the dorms was because her insurance wouldn't approve home health nurses until the very end. Whatever

Jake's family faced, it left him chucking newspapers instead of baseballs.

Unless none of this is about budgets at all and he just ran off because he caught on to my bicep-ogling ways and he thought if he paid at least a few bucks, maybe I wouldn't contact him again for the rest.

My toes curl in my sneakers as an image of soft brown eyes flashes through my mind. It's just that…he seemed nice. Of course, Andy was nice, too. And handsome. I am not about to get sucked into second-guessing another guy's actions, trying to decide what he's thinking about me. What matters is what *I* think about me.

I toss the envelope onto the table and lift my guitar out of its stand. "Come on, let's see if we can finish that song before we both have to go to work."

Unlike men, music has never let me down.

Chapter 5: THE COMPLIMENT OF GLUTEN-FREE SOUP

I'm strolling down the canned vegetable aisle when my Friday afternoon decides to kick me in the teeth.

"Excuse me? Hi, um…"

The familiarity of the voice behind me thrills my skin with goosebumps. I've never seen Jake Tate in this store before. Did I conjure him with my guilty daydreams about his biceps? I stumble, then recover, checking the way my arms are placed on my cart to be sure they feel natural and not too stiff. Good? Good. I have successfully proven my ability to ambulate and wildly fantasize about strangers at the same time. Next step: get a life.

"Not sure you remember me… Jacob? With the newspaper, and the window?"

I turn around, and my smile falters as his brightens a notch. Sweet baby Jesus riding a duck, he has beautiful cheekbones. And I'm wearing an old Audioslave tee shirt I swiped from Danny.

I flick my hair back over my shoulder, irritated with myself. I wear whatever's comfortable these days, but apparently I still haven't broken my habit of thinking about my looks in terms of men's approval. He's the vandal—I'm not the one who should be worried about making a good impression. "I don't think we got around to names. But yeah, I remember you. What with the disappearing act and the mysteriously appearing board and the tip you left, it'd be a little hard to forget."

As soon as I say the word "tip" his jaw flexes and he looks down.

"I am going to pay for it," he says in a low voice. "It's not like I thought thirty bucks would be enough, it's just that I—"

"Thirty-seven." I figure he should get credit for the seven extra bucks, but he jerks a single solemn nod, as if he's taking responsibility for a crime, and I cringe. That came out sounding all wrong.

"It was everything I had on me that day, and I thought you'd rather have a down payment instead of waiting until I could get it all."

"No, no, of course!" I hesitate, trying to choose my words more carefully this time so I don't make him feel any worse. Of course a guy considerate enough to board up the window wouldn't just drop a few bucks and run. My eyes fall as I think and then I realize he doesn't have a cart—just a handheld basket with a single can of gluten-free lentil soup.

My own cart sits accusingly between us, the pile topped with kale, organic tomatoes, extra creamy Mocha Almond Fudge ice cream, and oil-free acne wash. I reach in and casually bump the kale over until it covers my face wash, wishing it were a sleek bottle of Products for Beautiful People Who Don't Need Products. I swear, grocery shopping is way too personal to do in public. The last time a cute guy stopped to talk to me in here, my basket was headlining anti-fungal cream.

"Payments were very thoughtful, and I wasn't dogging on the amount or anything." I shrug one shoulder. "It's just that if I were going to pick a random amount I would have gone for forty-two."

"Right." He grins. "The answer to everything."

He got my Hitchhiker's Guide to the Galaxy reference. A smile tugs the corner of my mouth up.

"I should have scraped up another five bucks to be witty. Live and learn." He heaves a sigh that jumps my eyes up to his, which is definitely a mistake. I don't know if it has to do with the gentle color or maybe the tiny lines of worry at the corners but...he has the kindest eyes I've ever seen. And it absolutely murders me.

I clear my throat. "Well, thank you for boarding up the window, Jake."

"Jacob. Some people call me Jake, but..." He exhales. "Call me Jacob, please."

I like that better—the name matches his eyes instead of his letterman jacket shoulders. Except I shouldn't be thinking about either of those things. "It was nice to officially meet you, Jacob, but I should get going." I lean into my cart and head down the aisle.

"Hey, hold on a sec."

For a second, I consider pretending I don't hear. This man calls up every flirtatious impulse I have, and silence would be easier than corralling my conversation into the "platonic" zone. I mean, it's not that I particularly love being single, but I definitely like myself better when I'm not twisting myself up in knots to please a guy. Also, I'm up to T-minus eighteen months since the last time I ruined someone's life. Not too shabby.

"I never caught your name," Jacob says, matching my stride.

"It's Jera." I flash a quick, polite smile. *See, Granna, I'm not totally a lost cause.* "Jera McKnight." Part of me braces for the inevitable "What kind of name is that?"

Jake brightens instead. "Jair-ah." He spaces out the syllables. "Am I saying it right? That's a cool name."

I shrug. "Hippie parents, you know. It happens."

"Don't they normally go for the New Age ones, you know, Rainbow and Aura and all that?"

My lips quirk in spite of myself, and I peek up through my lashes at him, leaning on my cart. "It's a freaking acronym. Come on, if that's not hippie, what is it? OCD? Bureaucratic? Irresponsible?"

His eyes go vague as tries to puzzle it out. "Oh God, why did you do this to me?" he mutters. "I'm not going to be able to think about anything else all day."

"Jimi Hendrix, Eric Clapton, Roger Waters and Art Garfunkel," I rattle them all off in one well-practiced breath and he grins, nodding along with every famous musician that I list. "It took my dad until I was two to confess to my mom what it stood for. She just thought it was pretty."

"It is."

Breath, meet lungs.

As I try to manage my own response, his eyes flick from my face to my hair, which is still drifting long and wavy from the rain I biked through this morning. My pulse ticks up at his interest and yeah, I'm so over riding that particular rollercoaster. I scrape my hair back into a strict knot, then dig one-handed in my messenger bag for a pencil to skewer it with. Jacob's gaze follows my fingers with a flicker of disappointment.

"I won't get paid again until next week, but maybe I could do some chores around your place, work off a little of my debt in the meantime." He clears his throat and shifts his basket from one hand to the other.

"Nah, the house is in good shape," I lie, my pulse thrilling to the Diet-Coke-commercial-like images of him shirtless on a ladder: nailing on fresh shingles, or fixing that wheezing rattle in my ventilation system. "The money is no big deal, really."

"Can I be honest?"

No. Christ, no. "Sure." At the single word, the trepidation in his eyes abruptly matches the trembling in the pit of my stomach, and I hate to see him look so nervous. I smile to cover it, for both of us.

"Hey, if you can't make a confession in front of the canned beets, where can you make one?"

Relief rebounds into his face and he says, "I'm about to the point where I'd sell a kidney to take back that window. I'm glad I got the chance to meet you, but I don't want you to think that I..."

"What, that your best pick up line is vandalism?"

His grin debuts back into the canned vegetables aisle and it's possible that I might dissolve into a semi-liquid state right here, puddling amidst the Veg-All and the lima beans.

"Actually, while we're being honest, that very well might be my best pick up line."

"Oh?" I manage.

Flirtatious I can handle. Confident I can walk away from without a hitch in my step. But sheepish? How am I supposed to give the cold shoulder to sheepish?

He peeks back up at me and his smile goes crooked. He rests a finger across his lips. "Don't tell."

My resolve lies, tattered and gasping, under the wheels of my grocery cart.

"No worries," I rush to assure him. "It's covered under vegetable aisle privilege. Lawyers and doctors have nothing on us."

"So, can I..." He edges out of the way of a passing cart. "Help you shop? To work off my debt?"

He is killing me. Absolutely killing me.

"Don't you need to get your own things?"

"Nah. I mean, it can wait." He shifts, then considers the rows of pickled beets. "Actually, I sort of saw your car. In the lot."

"How do you know what my car looks like?"

"It's parked in your driveway every morning when I deliver your paper."

I consider face-palming at my own stupidity.

"The vines...the cool spiky ones on the bumper, you know? I haven't seen them anywhere else. Did you pay someone to do them?"

I drop my eyes, looking only at the kale. Kale is safe. Clean. Moral. "No."

He pauses for a beat.

"I guess I didn't think Sharpie would last so long on a car." The basket jiggles in his fingers. "Or that anybody would be brave enough to just go for it. Permanent ink, you know? On metal." He sounds wistful. "Not that I think you'd screw it up or whatever. It's just that…"

It's just that permanent is so damned real.

"Yeah. I know." I clear my throat. "I didn't do them myself, though."

The main thing Danny had to be trained for when he became a tattoo artist was how to deal with people's indecision. He just couldn't fathom how someone wouldn't know what images they wanted their bodies to showcase for all the uncountable decades to come. Sharpie on a car bumper doesn't even register on his commitment scale.

"So, what were you looking for?"

I startle. "Excuse me?"

He tips his head, his smile lopsided. "As your personal shopper, ma'am, I'm going to have to ask you to be a little more specific."

"Uh, corn?"

Jacob smiles as if I've said something amusing. "Okay, can do."

As soon as he turns away, my fingers start plucking at my shirt, and I slam my hands back onto my cart. My body has gender role issues: I've got tomboy arms, all corded muscle and agile, tree climbing shoulders, but somewhere along the line, my bra size filled out from "adequate" to "obvious" and my hips traced themselves into a line more suited to 1950s dress catalogs than to pipe-legged skinny jeans. I used to dress to play up my best features and hide my worst, but I gave all that up a year ago. Now, I throw on whatever's convenient because I need my body to run and drum and dance, and I love it for doing all those things. It doesn't have to please anybody else, not anymore.

I hate Jacob a little bit for making me so conscious of my appearance again, even though he hasn't done a thing wrong.

He adds a can of corn to my cart, and when he looks up from that to my face, tingles expand warmly across my skin.

Crap, what's wrong with me? I'm not doing this again.

"You know what? That was it." I yank the pencil out of my hair and snap a dark line across the last item on my shopping list, holding it up as proof. "The last thing I needed." My hair tumbles down around my shoulders, drawing his eyes.

I duck my head, stuffing the shopping list into the messenger bag at my hip, then shove my cart down the aisle toward the cash registers.

He comes along as if he didn't recognize my brush off, and I bite my lip. I really don't want to hurt his feelings, and I'm not sure how to make myself clear without being rude. Sweetly shy guys like Jacob don't usually pursue me.

When we round the aisle, Jacob replaces his lentil soup on an end cap of identical cans directly across from the door, avoiding my eyes. An achy kind of heat licks down my whole body as I realize he only picked up the can as a prop after he saw my car and decided to fake a grocery shopping mission. And then proceeded to blow his own cover by not buying the soup and telling me he came in here to talk to me.

I'm starting to think guys like Jacob don't usually pursue *anyone*.

He folds the handles of his basket and half-jogs to the front door to put it back on the stack. I push my cart into line, placing a bright rack of magazines between me and the temptation to watch the man returning to my side.

He arrives just as the conveyer belt in front of me turns over an open spot, and he starts unloading my cart: cans and bottles first, then cardboard boxes, then the more delicate items on top. This guy has obviously been doing his own shopping for a lot longer than the first couple of years of college. Is he older than me?

"Hey, you don't have to do that." I grab the last couple of items and put them on the belt.

"I don't mind helping." He pushes my cart through to the end of the check stand and unfolds my wad of mismatched reusable bags.

I shift, at a loss. It seems oddly intimate, letting him handle my shopping bags. Especially since he blurted out that he felt guilty for being attracted to me because of how we met. What signal am I sending by letting him bag my groceries? Is this one of those things like on *Seinfeld* where "going up for coffee" is not at all about beverages, caffeinated or otherwise? I'm totally letting him "bag my groceries" right now, aren't I?

Damn it, I'm like a grocery store slut.

"Miss?" the cashier says, possibly not for the first time. "That'll be $64.12."

Yeah, and I thought *that* was going to be twenty bucks cheaper. So much for a quick run to the store.

Jacob's head comes up. His hand twitches toward his back pocket but then he blushes and looks away.

I swipe my card, take my receipt from the cashier, and Jacob and I step away from the counter as if we do our shopping together all the time.

"You know, I've nearly blushed at my grand total a time or two, but this is definitely the first time someone else has." I risk a sidelong glance in his direction.

Jacob swings the cart around toward the exit doors. "My dad was Iroquois and Puerto Rican, Mom was Norwegian/Irish. Blushing is kind of a genetic lottery I lost."

Yeah, that makes sense. I've never seen anyone with such gorgeous olive skin tones be able to turn so startlingly red.

The doors whoosh open in front of us. The sun has weaseled its way through the thick clouds for a moment, and wisps of steam rise from the damp pavement as my cart rattles its way to my VW under Jacob's guidance. Apparently, he's walking me out now, which is a shade more intimate than just talking in the store. I shouldn't lead him on, but is there any non-jerkish way to repossess your grocery cart from someone?

"I liked the vines," he says out of nowhere, pushing the cart to the front of my car. Somehow, I'm not surprised he knew the trunk of a VW Bug isn't in the back. "I didn't mean to make you think I didn't."

Warmth pulses in the very center of my chest and I stop next to him and use my key to open the trunk.

"Like I said, I can't take credit for them. But thank you." I straighten. "A good friend did them for me. There's something about the smoothness of the curves contrasted with the thorns that's always caught my eye."

His lips tip upward, brown eyes glowing lighter out here in the sunlight, and I snap my mouth shut before I bore him half to death. Something about that gentle smile of his makes it way too easy to keep talking, but it's not like he cares what I think about the shape of vines, for crying out loud.

He moves before I do, turning to lift my bags into the car. I scoot to help him and the last bag is loaded in seconds. He shuts the trunk and then turns to me, stuffing his hands into his pockets. "Any chance you'd let me buy you a cup of coffee, since you won't let me work on your house?"

No, no, no. Please do not ask me direct questions to which I must say the word no. I can only be around a man like this if I can keep him securely banished to the Friend Zone. But if he notices my attraction to him, he's going to expect me to act on it, and both of us are going to end up an ugly kind of disappointed.

I wrap both hands around the strap of my messenger bag, my toes curling in my leather flip-flops. "I really sh—can't. I have ice cream in the car."

"Okay, but it's rainy, so it might last a while. Besides, today, I have two hours before I have to be anywhere, which practically makes it a holiday." He takes his hands out of his pockets and smiles, just a little. "I can't think of a better way to spend it than with someone else who knows a towel is the most important thing you pack on your spaceship."

Another Hitchhiker's Guide to the Galaxy reference, heaven help me.

"I…" *Say no, you idiot. No is safer.*

"It's just coffee. If you want. And I'll make it up to you if the ice cream melts."

I bite my lip. He really does seem sweet, and there's no reason to punish him for my baggage. Hanging out is fine as long as I stick to my golden rule: I won't change a thing about me to appease anyone's expectations. As a friend, he's safe to take it or leave it as he wants, and that way, I can be me without hurting anyone.

Jacob tips his head, as if he can sense me wavering. "Please?"

Chapter 6: JUST COFFEE

The room is scented with coarse ground, dark roast coffee beans and it hums with voices. I close my eyes and inhale, my face softening.

"What?" Jacob asks, a smile lifting his voice.

When I open my eyes, he's turned around in line, his back to the list of choices printed above the bar and his head bent so he can see my expression better.

I don't glance away when my heart picks up speed, because this isn't a date, and I need to stop letting the sight of Jacob catch me off guard. When Jax first joined the band, I could barely do more than stutter in his presence until I got used to how pretty he was. This part will pass, and if I like spending time with Jacob after that? Then we'll *actually* be friends.

"I used to work in a place like this," I say. "I still get a twitch when I hear the sound."

"What sound? The milk foamer thingy?"

"Nope. Wait for it." I hold up one finger and mentally count down the seconds because it never takes long. On four, we hear the vigorous *thump thump thump* of a filter banging against the rigid side of a trashcan and I smile. "The coffee shop percussion section." He laughs and I sigh. "I always loved the scent, though."

I tilt my head up as I pretend to scan the menu I know by heart. Jacob only had his bicycle, and I was in my car, so we ended up at generic chain coffee shop across the parking lot: pretty much a carbon copy of the franchise where I worked from ages sixteen to twenty, despite Dad's truly limitless bitching.

"Where do you work now?" Jacob asks.

"A bar." I flash a self-deprecating smile. "I'm still slinging drinks, but at least I'm free of the endless mountain of used coffee grounds. What about you? Is delivering newspapers your only calling?"

I bite the inside of my cheek after I say it, because probably he doesn't want to talk about baseball, or why he left it. It's just that athletes are achievers at heart. Andy was amazing but a little intimidating, too, with his volunteer work at the hospital, and his O-chem books that almost outweighed my VW, and yet he only played midfield on the lacrosse team. As the pitcher, Jacob would have been the king of the team, and PU is in the top echelon of college baseball. A guy like that wouldn't quit anything easily.

Then again, I quit a lot of things last year and ended up better off. I wonder if Jacob might know a thing or two about that.

He looks wistful for a second, then scratches the back of his neck. "My calling, huh? More like a way to pay the rent. I make a few bucks on the paper route, fix people's cars on the side—if you ever lived in the dorms, you probably saw my fliers—and then I have an hourly gig on campus whenever I'm free, with the art department."

The barista greets us as we step to the head of the line, and Jacob turns away to fumble his way through the vocabulary lesson necessary to order a drip coffee at a kitschy espresso joint.

I try to keep my face expressionless as I process what he just told me. I've seen the art department's advertisements, and as far as I know, the only paid position they offer is for anatomy models for the figure drawing classes.

Clothing is not, shall we say, useful to the goals of the program.

I barely manage to gather my concentration in time to order, and the barista's fingers fly over the register. "That'll be $5.90, please."

This time, Jacob doesn't blush when he goes for his wallet, but he catches sight of me digging in my messenger bag and frowns.

"Just coffee," I remind him. "The 'just' implies I pay my half."

"When I said 'just' I didn't mean for you to take it like I was cheap." He removes a five and a one from his deeply scratched leather wallet.

I have to smile at that, even as I enjoy a little guilty thrill at dropping my money back into my messenger bag. If I let Danny buy me coffee, it shouldn't be a big deal to let Jacob do it once, too. The thrill fizzles when he hesitates, then removes another dollar to push into the tip jar, leaving the cash slot in his wallet empty. He quickly puts it back into his pocket.

I step back from the counter. "Hey, I should have mentioned earlier: the window is getting fixed today and I don't actually need you to pay for it." I dig the envelope containing his thirty-seven dollars out of my messenger bag, where it's been sitting since he gave it to me. "The insurance company's waiving the deductible as part of their customer loyalty program, since the house has been under the same policy for twenty years."

He takes the envelope hesitantly, even though I saw how empty his wallet was. "You're not in trouble with your landlord?"

"I am my landlord," I say, and then our order is up.

Jacob tucks the envelope into his pocket and picks up our drinks, passing mine over as he gestures for me to lead the way. I pick a pair of chairs tucked into a corner behind a support column. It sucks trying to hold a conversation while pretending I can't hear the people eighteen inches to either side of me at their own tables.

"You own that house?" He lifts an eyebrow. "*All* of that house?"

I kick a glance up at him as I settle into the overstuffed cushions of the armchair. "Um, should I answer that?"

"Doesn't seem like your style, is all." The glint in his eye is the only indication that he's having trouble biting back his reaction to my bile-colored shag carpeting and décor that falls on the un-trendy side of the vintage spectrum.

"I inherited it about a year ago." I say it quickly, trying to dodge the squeeze in my chest that always comes along with having to explain this. "My grandma was sick and I ended up moving in and helping her for a couple of years before she got bad enough that hospice took over."

"Wouldn't you have been just in high school then?" He sounds impressed.

"It was the summer after graduation." I tug at my shirt, a little uncomfortable because people react weirdly when I tell the story. Either they think I'm some kind of saintly do-gooder, or they think it's nuts that my parents didn't do it for me. Nobody ever hints at the truth: that I was good company for her, but maybe she would have been better off with real nurses. "It's not like I was living with some old crazy lady or whatever. Granna and I were really close. Even when she was pretty sick, we'd watch *The Daily Show* and *The Vampire Diaries* together. She had a huge crush on Matt Davis."

Jacob smiles, a sad tilt to it that makes me wonder what he's thinking about. He asks, "Matt Davis?"

"An actor." I glance down at my coffee, a smile easing some of the tightness in my lungs as I remember some of the ribald comments Granna would make about him.

"It's nice that you got that time with her," Jacob says in a low voice. "And amazing you could keep up with your classes and everything."

I snort. "Keep up is a bit of an overstatement." I slipped to 2.94 one semester, and my mom was convinced I was headed for a future as a busboy. "I didn't sleep much. Bottomless coffee at work definitely helped."

A buzzing sound interrupts our conversation. Jacob startles so hard he almost spills his drink, then digs a phone out of his pocket. "I'm sorry, I really need to check this." His eyes are already on the phone.

I nod and look away to give him privacy, because he said that with the urgency of a doctor on call. Most college students treat every phone notification like a crisis, but not quite to that level.

I turn my cup in my hand. Then again, this is exactly what people do in college. They procrastinate their homework to go hang out with new, interesting people on not-really-dates where every word of fairly ordinary conversation seems to sparkle, the tang as different from normal syllables as champagne from still water. The thought holds more than a little nostalgia for the days when Granna was still alive and Andy and I used to do stuff like this.

"Sorry. It was nothing." Jacob lifts up to put his phone in his back pocket, and as soon as his gaze comes back to my face, he cocks his head. "What's that look for?"

"I don't know. Just…it's been a while since I've hung out in a coffee shop like a regular old college kid. It's kind of nice." I look down, picking at the cardboard sleeve on my cup. Why did I just tell him that? Now I sound like a loner for whom going out for coffee is a major event.

"I know, right?" His eyes warm as he starts to chuckle. "These days when I get to campus, I feel like I'm at a costume party and I forgot to dress up. If it weren't for the tuition bills, I'm not even sure I'd still qualify as a college student."

"Oh, come on, you're not that far out there." According to Cleo, not too long ago he was at the white-hot center of social life on campus. "What constitutes normal? Playing Frisbee in the quad? Drinking beer while upside down? I bet you're great at both of those."

He shakes his head. "I'm out. No Frisbee this term."

I raise my eyebrows, and decide not to mention the one I saw him rescue out of a tree the day we met. Then again, he wasn't really playing. "Oh, that is a problem, then. You're skating on the edge of weirdo territory, Mr. Tate."

He nods. "Warned you."

"I think there are alternate qualifiers for the non-Frisbee oriented. Have you, by any chance, tried to drink an entire gallon of Carlo Rossi wine by yourself?"

"Sadly, I have, and there are pictures of me playing soccer on the roof of the Earth Sciences building to prove it."

I draw a tally mark in the air. "Okay, have you swam in a decorative fountain, preferably at night?"

His mouth twitches. "Are you going to resurrect your ice cream excuse if I say yes?"

"This is strictly for scientific purposes, sir."

"In that case, I may have."

"Okay, you're officially a college student."

"Was," he corrects. "I haven't done any of that crap this year. But what about you?"

"Sadly, the same." Even if you dress like a punk rock cat lady who gives zero fucks, attending college functions makes avoiding dating exponentially harder. Plus, neither of my bandmates run in those circles, which makes it easier to forget I ever did. I lift my coffee cup in a toast. "We're a couple of has-beens."

"Nah. Look at us. We're doing a decent impression right now."

I take a sip to hide my smile. It's sort of nice to know he's feeling out of practice at all of this, too.

Jacob takes a drink of his coffee. Looks at it with a completely straight face. Takes another sip. "This is terrible."

I laugh. "Come on, people come to coffee shops for the espresso and the company. You can get drip coffee at a 7-11."

"Good point." He sets his cup aside. "So be good company and distract me. Tell me something really juicy, like your favorite band."

"I like your idea of 'juicy.'" I grin. "But it might be quicker to ask which bands I don't like. I don't listen to much country, I guess."

"How do you not like country? The lyrics apply to pretty much everyone. Besides, it's catchy."

"I'll start listening when their instrumentation reaches the level of proficiency of their hairdressers."

Jacob laughs. "Music snob. I should have known. Portland is full of them."

"If you grew up listening to my dad's friends dissect music, you'd start getting pickier too, I promise. And now that you've said all that, you *know* I have to ask."

"Nope." He relaxes back into his chair and kicks a foot up to cross his opposite knee. "There's no way I can tell you my favorite band. It'll ruin this whole thing."

"What whole thing?" I tilt a gesture between the two of us with my cup. "This is 'just coffee' and you already admitted your coffee is terrible. So this whole thing is already a loss."

"Yes, but my favorite band is non-negotiable."

I hold up my hand. "If you don't want to come out of the closet with your love for MC Hammer and One Direction, that's fine with me. I'll let you keep your dirty secrets."

"That's very generous of you."

"But you at least have to tell me your major."

He wrinkles his nose. "Can I lie?"

I pretend to consider. "Yes."

"Business."

I make a loud buzzer sound. "Game over, try again."

"What? You said I could lie."

I laugh. "I'm in Finance. We share a building with Business, and I've never seen you in there."

"Finance? Come on, I didn't say *you* could lie."

"Wait, are you stereotyping me?" I scowl.

"Name five Finance majors whose living room contains a guitar, a piano, and the Beatles' *White Album* on original vinyl. Go ahead, I'll wait."

"Seriously? You went through my records?"

"That one was on the top of the crate!"

"You didn't have time to wait to get your *shoes* and you had time to pigeonhole my educational choices based on albums you were ogling without invitation?"

He winces and rubs the back of his neck. "Yeah, that must have seemed really weird, huh? While you were gone, I got a call about a...kind of a family emergency. I had to go."

I bite my lip, glancing down at my coffee. What sort of family emergency leaves you scared enough to take off on a bike, barefoot? Maybe similar to the kind that kills your athletic career and makes you feel like an imposter amongst other students. I don't know how to ask, but I'm dying to crack the basement door on his past, to peek inside and find if his reasons for keeping his distance from campus social life are anything like mine.

"Though I admit, before my phone rang, I was considering braving the broken glass in my socks to check out your record collection."

Okay, so we're not going there. Fair enough, I'm practically a stranger, and I know how much I hated talking about it after Granna got sick. Instead, I say, "Paige L'Marche."

"What?"

"She's the only PU Finance major who owns *The White Album* on vinyl."

Jacob shouts with laughter, and the group of girls crowding the register turn to stare at him. A tall redhead's eyes linger, and I'm tempted to stick my tongue out at her. Yes, he's hot. Yes, he's here with me. Well, kind of.

"To be fair," I relent, "I'm only a Finance minor. Majoring in Music Theory and Composition." I was a double major, but after I crashed and burned at pleasing everyone, I thought I might try out pleasing myself, so I dropped Finance. A semester later, I missed it, so I picked it up again, but just as a minor.

"No shit? You write what, symphonies? The whole thing?"

"Modern concentration, not classical. So, more rock songwriting than Beethoven."

"Seriously?" He's unabashedly staring at me now. "Can I hear one of your songs?"

My eyes go vague for a second as I focus on the music playing over the speakers in the ceiling. The current song is by the Satan Pigs, so no way it's piped-in satellite. This is local radio, which is something you'd only see in chain coffee shop in Portland, maybe Seattle, probably Nashville. Our people sip indie albums right along with their fair-trade dark roast.

"They're playing a local station. If you wait long enough, one of my band's songs will come on. 'Out of Order' or maybe 'Wilderness.'" His eyes go round, mine dropping as I smile a little. "Fair warning, though, you may have to wait two or three days. We don't get that much play."

"Do you sing?" His gaze falls to my lips.

"Not on those songs."

I really want to tell him about the radio interview the band has scheduled for next week, but if we're just hanging out it's not like I should even *care* about impressing him, and he doesn't know me well enough to be excited that this is a big deal for my band. I change the subject instead.

"Hey, don't think I didn't notice your dodge. You didn't tell me your major."

"It's engineering." He reaches across to massage his right shoulder, a ruddy hue touching his cheekbones.

I scoff out a laugh. "You're a nude model and you blushed over engineering?" As soon as the words are out, I freeze. He didn't actually say he was modeling, he just mentioned that he worked for the art department. And yeah, obviously my dirty mind was going there anyway.

Jacob shrugs. "I'm not like a *model* model. The art department just needs visible muscular structure to draw. I do a little freelance for artists around town, too. Pay's good and all I have to do is sit still."

"Okay, but you still have to be naked in front of a whole bunch of strangers. That sounds way more embarrassing than admitting you're learning how to build a bridge." He looks suspicious, so I try to reassure him. "Engineering is perfectly respectable, Jacob."

"Coming from a music major, I can't decide if that's an insult."

I scoff. "Music majors are just snooty to engineers because they're secretly math phobic."

"Not you, apparently, with that finance minor."

I roll my eyes. "My mom does mortgage financing, and she's determined that if I ever make some money at music, I'll know how to manage it. If you met my bassist, you'd understand: he's exactly the kind of oblivious guy whose accountant would run off to Guam with all his cash. Plus…" I make a dismissive sound. "I'm weirdly good at it."

"I don't think it's weird," he says quietly.

I shift in my seat, realizing he's hardly looked away from me the entire time we've been in here. I like that, way more than I should. God, my hormones are like idiotic little lemmings, forever tugging me toward the cliff that is the male gender. Or maybe it would be more accurate to say I'm *their* cliff.

My messenger bag interrupts, playing the theme from Psycho.

"Do you need to get that? It sounds dire."

"It's my alarm. I have to go." I push out of my seat and gather my bag. "I've got Digital Music Production in half an hour. I'm going to have to fly to put my groceries away if I want to make it on time."

Jacob rises. "I could come along and help. It'd be faster."

"Except you're on your bike and my car doesn't have a bike rack." I make my way toward the exit. He reaches past me to push the door open and waits while I slip through. How long has it been since somebody other than Dad did that for me?

"It's no big deal to help. I'll jog back here and get my bike when I'm done. It's barely three miles."

That is not sexy.

Not.

Sexy.

"No, it's okay. Thank you for the offer, though." I hold out my free hand. "Can I have that?"

Without question, Jacob hands over his coffee. I drop it into the trashcan outside the door and keep walking.

"Hey!" He's half-laughing as he jogs to catch up.

"That was not coffee." I pass him my whole milk, half-a-shot-of-walnut latte. "*This* is coffee."

He takes a quick sip, not looking away from me until the last instant, and then stares down at the cup. "God. That is not just coffee... What *is* that?"

"Magic." I toss him a smile and goodbye wave, ignoring the tug in my chest as I start to unlock my car. This is no big anything, so what does it matter if I don't know when I'll see him again?

"Can I say something?"

I close my eyes for one tiny scrap of a second, and against my better judgment, I turn back. "I should really go. I'm going to be so late."

"I own the entire collection of The Beatles on vinyl: every record they ever released. Plus every one from Pink Floyd and all but one Led Zeppelin. Mostly because my little brother managed to lose it."

My eyes are as round as greedy gold coins. I have no idea why he just told me that, and I don't care. I want that collection, want to shoot it into my veins and roll naked in it and drown in the gorgeous, classic sound of song after song brought to life by the needle of my beloved antique turntable.

As I swallow to disguise the watering of my mouth, Jacob laughs. "That's exactly what I thought your reaction would be. Which means you definitely have to come over and listen to them."

I'm missing one record of Pink Floyd's The Wall, and I haven't been able to listen to the album straight through ever since, except on MP3, which is about as satisfying as looking at a postcard of a Rembrandt. But this sounds dangerously like a date.

"Or, actually, why don't we go to your house?" Jacob says quickly. "I saw you had a turntable, and your place is nicer than my crappy apartment anyway." When I still hesitate, he goes on, "I know I busted your window and ran out on you like a barefoot lunatic, but I promise I'm not always that awkward." He pauses. "Tuesdays and Thursdays, yes, but I'm usually okay on Mondays."

Damn, why does he have to be so sweet about it? "Look, Jacob, I don't think it would be a good idea for us to get involved. Because I can't..." I look away. I could tell him all the many things I'm no good for, and that would end this conversation really fast.

"Look, it's okay if you don't want anything serious. Honestly, that might be a better idea for me anyway."

So *that's* what this is really all about.

I start to laugh. Granna's probably doing back flips in her grave at my manners but I can't help it. He couldn't have picked a worse girl to proposition for a friends with benefits package. Though at least he finally made it easy for me to turn him down.

"Yeah, thanks but no thanks. I'm not in the market for a boyfriend, and I'm nowhere near volunteering for a casual fuck."

His head jerks back. "Jera, when I said nothing serious, I meant we should hang out as friends, not that we should—"

"Oh, God." Both my hands jump to cover my mouth. Now he knows I was thinking about sex, and he wasn't thinking about sex, and I look like a horny predator who talks about hooking up in the parking lot of the Stop N' Shop. "I'm so sorry. Can we please forget I ever said that?"

Jacob stuffs his hands in his pockets. "No, it's my fault if I made you think I was trying to get you to..." He clears his throat. "I guess maybe other people don't actually listen to music together, and so it sounds like a line, but I really meant—"

"Yes, that's fine. Records are fine," I blurt, because I'd say anything to stop his awkwardly earnest explanation of how giant my ego is that I thought he was hitting on me instead of just being friendly.

"Okay. Tonight?"

I grimace. "I have dinner with the parents tonight. I swear, that's not an excuse, I really do."

"Sunday?" He still looks mortified. I am such a jerk.

"Yup, Sunday, okay good." I just wave and jump in my car, because if I keep apologizing, I'm only going to make it worse. Which I then proceed to do, by popping the clutch and killing the engine right in front of him. I'm pretty busy avoiding eye contact and babying my shitty transmission, so it's not until I pull out into traffic that I realize what I've done. I've invited Jacob Tate over to my house, to listen to beautiful music together. Alone.

This is so not going to end well.

MICHELLE HAZEN

Chapter 7: THE BEAVER INCIDENT

I step over my discarded jogging clothes, still damp with sweat, and hitch up my towel as I head toward the closet. Dinner with my parents tonight is going to require a step up from my usual jeans and tee shirt. For some reason, Mom thinks the way I dress now is proof that I'm depressed.

Squatting down, I reach into the back corner of my closet, where I keep the pile of my clean underwear. I used to keep them in my top drawer, folded in colorful, matching sets as my training bras gave way to padded demis and then underwires to support my expanding bust line. After my high school boyfriend, Brayden, I just dumped them from the laundry basket to the floor.

I snatch up the first underwear I touch and yank them on, the plain cotton as rough as the memory of the infamous panties that started all my problems with men.

Brayden never actually broke up with me. Instead, the day after I gave him my virginity, I arrived at school to a rumor that he'd found better lays in the frozen foods section, and our school mascot's statue wearing my panties on his face.

Rather unfortunately, our mascot was a beaver.

The panties weren't half-bad: turquoise with a hopeful border of purple lace. I'd bought them especially for the occasion so the elastic wasn't even sagging yet. It was just that when Brayden positioned them on the beaver, he put the crotch facing out, and it was not clean.

There was no blood, of course. I couldn't find them once the deed was done, because apparently Brayden hid them to keep as his trophy. Instead, there was a faint white film hardening the fabric and proving that at one point in the process, I must have been enjoying myself. If I did, I don't remember it.

Cold water drips down my shoulders, and I pull off my towel and scrub at my hair before I drop the towel and snatch up a bra.

The worst part was that up until Brayden broke up with me via beaver, I had no idea there was anything wrong between us. I still don't know if I was some kind of bet, or if his friends teased him about me and he threw me to the wolves, or if he just wanted to look more worldly. At the time, I really thought he liked me.

After that, I started paying better attention. It turned out that people were giving me tons of cues about stuff they didn't like about me. I started to notice peoples' slightly curled lips, or sometimes a certain stiffness of tone. Report card eyebrow raises from my mom, and sighs from my dad during our music lessons. The way Granna would exhale through her nose when she was worried I was making a bad decision. Once I was looking, I saw the signs of disapproval everywhere, so I started trying harder in an effort to drown them out.

I snap the hangers of my favorite clothes aside and dig deeper for an outfit that won't make my mom worry. She's almost certainly going to ask if I'm seeing anyone, and since running into Jacob this morning, boys are already way too much on my mind.

I push past neat khaki skirts and buttoned blouses that are nearly five years old: relics of the beginning of the people-pleasing era when I started doing my homework earlier, practicing the guitar longer, not piping up at lunch unless I was certain I had something that would make my friends laugh.

When my fingers catch in fishnet, I snort and start to laugh. God, I'd forgotten about all that phase. I finger the black, ripped drape of fabric that I think is supposed to be a shirt. Yeah, boyfriend problems are so not breaking news for me. You'd think my mom would get a clue and stop asking after all these years.

Exactly one day post-beaver, Brayden showed up to school with a limp and a nose so swollen it was encroaching on his eye sockets. Danny's destroyed right hand didn't make it hard to trace the culprit. He scored a full week's suspension for that stunt, but the only thing he ever said to me about it was, "Some guys are just dicks."

I figured he was right, so I didn't join a nunnery. Instead, I got a subscription to Cosmo, helped myself to Danny's collection of Playboys, and began the process of educating myself so my next lover couldn't compare me to a refrigerated tilapia fillet. I had read my way into a thorough sex education by the time I met Tyler, but he still broke up with me when the imprint of his carpet was still fresh on my knees. Turns out it's not enough if they're having fun, you have to look like you're having fun, too, or it's weird. Lesson learned.

With my next boyfriend, I paid even more attention, trying to anticipate what he liked so I wouldn't get caught off guard again.

I flick past the black fishnet creation. That one was for Nix and his slam poetry nights. Next is a J. Crew sweater that I wore when I was dating Corey and hanging out with his friends at the mall. I shove the rest of the clothes to the side with a sigh and just grab a plain tank top.

It didn't matter how close I watched or how hard I tried. Sometimes I got tired of them first, sure. But if I liked a guy enough to stick around, they'd get bored of me and dump my ass, no matter what it was clad in at the time. I was batting a big fat zero with the opposite gender by the time college rolled around. Then I met Andy. He was blond, and fun, and thought me being in a band was the coolest thing ever. I fell hard and figured love would solve all my problems.

It so didn't.

I step into a pair of jeans with snakes sketched up both outer seams, tangled and knotted together, their opened mouths hissing with fangs. Thankfully, Jacob doesn't seem to have anything in mind for Sunday besides music. Considering that my heart tries to turn itself inside out every time I look at him, it'd probably still be safer to cancel, but I don't have his number. Besides, the thought of all the vinyl he mentioned...I'd hang out with Adolf Hitler for a shot at a record collection like that.

I just need to stop thinking about the expert way Jacob bagged my groceries, his hands quick but always aware of the fragility of some items, the dangerous weight of others. Or the way he blushed when I said "fuck" as if that word was jarring in contrast to whatever he was actually thinking in that moment. Which should be my reminder that before he comes over on Sunday, I need to grow some boundaries. Friends are definitely not supposed to daydream about one another.

Grabbing my messenger bag and stepping into ballet flats, I head for the door. By the time I pull into my parents' driveway and shut off the car, I'm a little bit late, but hopefully they won't notice. I hurry a little bit going up the sidewalk, just in case.

"Hey, Mom," I call as the front door slams behind me. I toe off my shoes by the old coat tree, soothed by the familiar sight of its scratched wood and over-laden hooks. I drop my bag next to my shoes and breeze through the living room to the kitchen, catching Mom in a quick side-hug since her hands are buried in a bowl full of raw chicken pieces. Her hips are softer than they were when I was a kid but my arm still fits around her slender waist. If I want to be in the shape she's in when I'm her age, I need to start liking running a hell of a lot more. "Need some help?"

"Thought you'd never ask. Your dad wanted kabobs. He knows how long it takes to get everything on these darn little sticks, and suddenly *poof*, he has a late showing of that house on 10th." She rolls her eyes at me and I chuckle. "Plus, he just texted me an emoticon that was shooting itself in the head, so I'm thinking that means the client's a talker and he's not going to be home to help with the barbecuing either."

"Bummer." I brush a strand of hair away from her face for her, since her hands are busy and the bun she wears for work is starting to slip. A few years ago, that bun would have been a perfect match for my own sun-streaked brown but a few more threads of gray have crept in since I started college.

I grab a mushroom and pop it into my mouth, then head for the sink. "You want to do bell pepper slices or squares?"

"Squares. Did you wash your hands?" she asks just as I'm reaching for the faucet.

I roll my eyes. "I am washing my hands, right this absolute second. Believe it or not, I've somehow managed to keep from poisoning myself in the three years I have been doing my own cooking."

"You didn't wash your hands before you ate that mushroom," she points out. "Are you sticking around after dinner? I got the *Les Mis* DVD from Netflix just in case you had some extra time this week."

Guilt needles through me. "Mom, I can't. Homework." It's true, but I still feel like a jerk.

My mom is kind of a freak as far as band wives are concerned. She doesn't even own a single freaking MP3. She loves movies, though, so she's always palming me off on my dad to go to concerts while she tries to bond with me over musicals. Ever since I outgrew Disney, I haven't had the heart to tell her I kind of hate musicals.

She gives me a sidelong look, skewering some more chicken on a wooden kabob stick as I set up a fresh cutting board and a bell pepper next to her.

"Regular homework, or are you starting to get behind because you're doing too many radio appearances and rehearsals to get ready for this music fair?"

"It's a festival, Mom, not a fair, and so far there's only one radio appearance scheduled." I rip out the seedy part of the bell pepper and toss it into the trash. "Bump In The Night is big, but it isn't exactly Lollapalooza."

Her lips purse with disapproval like she heard everything I left out of that statement. "Jera, it's amazing that you got this festival spot. Hank told me all about what a great opportunity it is for the band. But when the show is over, school is still going to be there, and your professors aren't going to let you turn in work whenever you get around to it."

"I'm not behind! I'm just...busy." Busy rehearsing, that is. Every spare hour the band can scrounge together is about to be spent in my garage, which means until the festival I'll be doing all my homework at night and sleeping will become a teensy bit optional. Which would make a pretty good excuse for cancelling on Jacob. I bite my lip. Listening to records is almost like research for our show, if you think about it. Pink Floyd was the master of the narrative set list.

"Okay," Mom says dubiously, as if she can scent the stretching of the truth on the air. "I just don't want to see you putting all your eggs in one basket. The music world is tough, you know that. Even if you do get a foot in the door, it's not like they have a 401-K."

My mother, ladies and gentleman. A cliché for every occasion.

"That's not really a problem." I flash her a tight smile. "I'm just going to sell my body, get a little cash for if I don't happen to be good enough to get a foot in that door."

"You know I didn't mean it like that. You three have been working so hard and I'm *so* proud you got a place in this show." She bumps me with her shoulder. "I told all my friends on Facebook about it."

I start threading bell peppers onto sticks, my smile softening. "Somehow, I'm not thinking our sound profile is quite their speed, but thanks for the free publicity."

"So," Mom says, and I can practically *hear* the dot dot dot. "Are you bringing a date to the show?"

I bite back a groan. I'm not in the mood to do this with her today. "Nope. Still not seeing anyone. Just like the last forty times you asked."

"What about Andy?"

MICHELLE HAZEN

Chapter 8: REQUIEM FOR A RUBBER CHICKEN

I damn near stab myself with a kabob stick. "What?"

"I just wondered if you two were keeping in touch." Mom doesn't look up.

Did she find out he left school? Or is she just being her normal level of nosy? "Uh, no. Andy and I broke up. Not talking is usually part of that package."

"I know that, but…" She smiles. "Do you still have that rubber chicken he got you? I remember the day I came over to visit and its neck was sticking out from under a pile of textbooks. It freaked me out but you just laughed and said Andy was always doing that: stashing the chicken around as if furniture or dishes or something had just fallen on him and squashed him. You thought it was so funny and I figured any boy who understood you so well must be…" Mom trails off.

The bell pepper suddenly seems cold against my fingers.

That rubber chicken lives in a box on the top shelf of my closet. I kept it, and the voicemail, and I know what my mom was about to say. She thought Andy was maybe the one for me. A wave of irritation shivers up my spine, mostly because I thought he was, too.

Mom sighs. "Well, I guess it doesn't matter. Anyway, he was nice. I don't understand why your dad hates him so much."

Of course she doesn't. We never told her about the night when Andy was drunk, shouting and crying outside my locked front door, and I had to call Dad to make him leave. Granna was so sick by then that she slept straight through all the yelling, thank God. It was also the last time I saw Andy. I don't know if he dropped out or transferred, and I really hope it was the second because it makes me ill to think I was the reason he left Portland University. But that night wasn't until weeks after our quiet, anti-climactic breakup.

I finish the last skewer of bell peppers and set it on the tray, grabbing an onion and slicing into it.

"It wasn't Andy's fault," I tell my mom. "We both tried really hard. It just…didn't work out." I just wish I didn't have quite so many vivid memories of *why* it didn't work out.

A door slams somewhere else in the dorm, and I nuzzle my face into Andy's neck and inhale. He's sort of sweaty but beneath it is the clean, sporty scent of his soap from the shower he took right before I came over. I leave a kiss in the soft hair just behind his ear and catch my breath as he slides another finger inside me. He takes that as encouragement and pushes deeper, and I'm glad he can't see the quick grimace that crosses my face. I'm still kind of dry, but when he nudges my thigh, I shift my legs farther apart for him.

"Slow, okay?" I murmur.

He pauses, then resumes the push and retreat of his two fingers at a more measured pace, reaching up with a thumb to prod at the top of my sex. My face twitches again and I have to force my legs to relax, but he's on the right track so I let out a little sigh so he'll keep trying. He brushes a kiss over the pulse in my neck and my arms tighten around his back. The next time he moves his thumb, excitement flickers up through me. I hum a muted moan and my head falls slack on the pillow. Andy's breath hitches at the sound and his fingers shove harder, which shocks my eyes open.

His alarm clock rests on his desk right next to his bunk, and I blink at the numbers. Crap, less than twenty minutes before his roommate, Zach, is going to be back from class. I close my eyes and focus on the feel of Andy's sleekly muscled back beneath my hands. I try to bring up a scene from the steamy novel I was reading last night. His fingers feel wide and foreign and I can't concentrate. I curl my hips, hoping he'll get his thumb in on the action again, but he doesn't take the hint.

Twenty minutes is enough if we get started right now, except then I'll have to ask him to get the lube out of the drawer, and I can't take the look on his face when I have to suggest that.

"Maybe we could try, um, if you used your mouth. Just for a minute," I whisper.

He makes a sound I don't know how to interpret, but he withdraws his fingers and I'm ashamed at the twinge of relief that follows.

Without meeting my eyes, he scoots down on the twin bed, kicking a stray pillow out of his way. I wriggle farther up on the mattress to make room, crunched into half a sitting position against the bookcase crammed in next to the bunk beds. He settles in, and when he lays his tongue against me, I exhale and my shoulders ease, even though the edge of the bookcase digs into my arm.

My breaths get shorter but then he moves and it's good but not…

"Honey, higher…just a little higher."

He stops altogether and my eyes start to come open but then he complies. I sneak a glance at the alarm clock. Fourteen minutes. I can feel myself relaxing a little, and decide that's good enough.

I manufacture a throaty moan I hope doesn't sound too overdone, and tug at his shoulders. "Now, Andy. I need you now." My face flushes. He said he likes it when I talk that way, so I just hope he's turned on enough he won't notice if I'm not exactly pulling it off.

He reaches back and tugs open the bedside drawer to get a condom, blond hair falling carelessly over his forehead. The sheets bunch as I slide down on the bed, running a hand over his arm while he covers himself. Is he into this? He's turned away from me, so I can't quite see his expression. He moves back and settles between my legs. I wrap my arms around his neck again, lightly scratching him with my nails in a way I know he likes. Where our bodies meet, there's just pressure, like he's not lined up right, and when he moves his hips forward, it kind of hurts.

"Sorry," he mutters. "We were messing around so long, and would you mind...?"

"Of course." I agree quickly, because he just did it for me, so even if I'm not really in the mood for that right now, I owe it to him to make the effort. I grab a quick kiss as we switch places on the bed and he ditches the condom, tossing it toward the trash can by his desk. The clock stares at me before I turn to kneel in the space between his thighs. Eleven minutes. I really wish Granna's health were better and I could get my own place. Even a single room in the dorm would be more privacy than we have now. Andy has practice tomorrow, and I have band rehearsal the next day, so this is our only chance for a while.

I lick my lips and take him into my mouth, trying to ignore the faint tang of latex that still clings to his skin. I hate doing this when he's not hard, which I guess is stupid because that's the whole point, really. But it puts this small, squirmy feeling in my stomach that's the furthest thing from sexy, and until he starts to swell I feel so awkward, like I'm doing everything exactly wrong. I guess he was probably feeling the same thing, or he'd still be excited now, too.

I smooth my hand over his hip and try to remember how much tongue he likes. Jeez, I'm thinking way too much. I need a fantasy that doesn't involve the way the springs of this cheap mattress are digging into my kneecaps.

By the time I get Andy worked up enough to get into another condom, we have six minutes. He hugs me and rolls me beneath him, and I take the opportunity to lick my fingers and swipe them down below, hoping that will be enough. He enters me quickly and I have to wriggle to adjust before I wrap my legs around him, making a small noise of approval to spur him on.

He tucks his head into my shoulder and starts to thrust. I tilt my hips, searching for that angle he sometimes hits that gives me more sensation. I move one leg and he stops. "What's wrong? Are you okay?"

*"No, no, it's good." I smile and put my leg back where it was. He props himself up on his hands to get more leverage and then—*thwack!—*his head raps against the underside of the bunk.*

"Shit!"

"Oh no, I'm sorry! Are you okay?" I reach up to cup the back of his head and he shakes me off.

"I'm fine, hey, it's fine." He drops back to his elbows and kisses me. I try to concentrate on the slide of his tongue, on the way his kisses normally whirl my head and make me forget about school and music and literally everything but his lips.

His thrusts are shorter now and I wonder if he's getting close. He abandons my mouth and squeezes his eyes shut, his face creased almost like he's in pain. I hug him tightly, wishing the heat of his chest against mine was enough to press the hollow feeling out from behind my ribs.

The condom is drying out, and it's starting to chafe, so when he stops, at first I think that's why. He's motionless and for a second I'm afraid to breathe, not sure if he finished or if something's wrong, and not wanting to admit I can't tell the difference. But he mutters a curse and then an apology. When he pulls out, I can tell it's not the condom that's having the problem.

"Sorry. I just...can't today." He twists away to sit on the edge of the bed.

71

I curl my legs to the side and sit up, the mild soreness between my thighs nothing compared to the chill beneath my skin. Wrapping my arms around him from behind, I lay my cheek on his back, which is a little tacky with sweat.

"Hey, honey, it's no big deal, okay? We didn't have much time today." I try for a teasing tone. "Just wait until I get my hands on you this weekend."

He doesn't move.

Someone laughs in the hall, and then a synthetic explosion from the video game playing over Jay's ludicrously oversized speakers, two doors down.

Andy drops his head and pulls off the condom, chucking it toward the trash can. I pretend not to notice when the condom doesn't quite make it and slaps against the plastic trash can before it slumps onto the linoleum floor.

"It's getting worse, Jera."

My heartbeat seizes, and I let him go and move to sit at his side. "Hey, I don't mind, seriously. I was having a good time. Next time I'll, you know, play with you a little longer. Zach said he was going home this weekend anyway, so we'll have this place to ourselves."

His room is a tomb compared to the normal sounds of dorm life beyond. I wish I had put on a playlist, even if we can never agree on what music to play.

"It's not only this time, and you know it. You're always stopping me, telling me to do it this way, do it that way, and I can tell, Jera. I can tell it's not working for you."

I drop my head and press a kiss to his shoulder, tears biting at the back of my eyes. "It's just hard for me to get all the way there. It always has been, and I swear it's better with you than it has been with anyone else. Andy, I love you." Which is exactly why this hurts so much. I always hoped my issues were temporary, that as soon as I found someone I cared about enough, it would just...work.

He shoves off the bed, my hands falling away. "Do you love me? Really?" When he turns on me, his familiar eyes are angry and so, so hurt. "Because I was with girls in high school and they didn't have any complaints." He shoves off the bed, grabbing his boxers. "I never went soft with them. It's like you—"

It's like my problems infected him. He doesn't have to say it.

His sheets feel like a stranger's hands on my breasts and I throw them down, turning my back on him as I find my panties and jerk them up my legs, not even caring that they're inside out. I can't stand knowing what he really thinks when he looks at me.

"Jera..."

I fasten my bra and spin it around, sticking my arms through the straps. It's the scratchy, lacy one and as soon as I get home, it's going in the trash.

"Don't say you didn't mean it." I push my foot into my jeans and kick at a twist in the fabric until I make it all the way through. "We both know you did."

It makes me ache everywhere, how much I want him to hold me right now, to offer even the smallest scrap of comfort. I shove my hair out of my eyes, my jaw set against the lump in my throat as I look for my shirt.

"I really didn't. It just makes me feel like shit when I can't please you, okay? Don't be mad, Jera. We can...we can keep trying, okay? I don't want to lose you."

My shirt appears in my line of vision, Andy offering it like a flag of truce he's not sure I'll accept. My shoulders slump. I take the shirt and mumble, "Thanks," as I turn it right side out again and pull it on.

This isn't his fault. The issues all started with me, and I don't have any right to take it out on him when he's trying to help me get over it.

I turn back and try a smile, smoothing my hair. "Look, let's go somewhere this weekend, get away from the dorms. I'll spring for dinner at that Chinese place you like." I swear they make all their food out of jellyfish and mayonnaise, but I'll eat ahead of time and just say I'm not hungry.

"Can't. I've got an away game this weekend."

"Want me to drive up?" I pick up my messenger bag and sling it over my shoulder. I'll have to beg somebody to take my shift at the bar, and get Mom to check in on Granna, but he's worth it.

"I don't know." He glances away. "We usually sneak out of the hotel to party after the game. If you're at the game, the coach will be watching for us to pull that and I'll get shit for ruining it for everybody." The doorknob rattles and Zach's key scrapes in the lock.

I shift my weight, my inside-out panties uncomfortable beneath my jeans. "You'll be back Sunday, though, right?"

"Uh-huh. I'll call you. I'll have a lot of homework after being gone, though." Andy bends to kiss me on the cheek, and I lift my eyes briefly to his face—both of us looking, checking to see if we're still okay. He's the first to look away.

I smile brightly. "Yeah. Sure. Maybe we can get Chinese after you're done studying. Or something." I don't want to keep trying to negotiate a date that he'd actually be excited about, not with his roommate here to witness all the awkward. I slide past Zach as soon as the door opens, and flee down the hall, hoping he doesn't know what we were just doing. And if he does, that he won't realize that's why Andy's suddenly not so excited about hanging out with me this weekend.

The faucet shuts off as Mom finishes washing her hands, and she comes over to give me a longer hug now that she's raw-chicken-free. She's no taller than I am, but she stands on her toes so she can press a kiss to my forehead. "Well, keep an eye out for a date for your concert. Any boy would be lucky to have you. Remember, there are plenty of fish in the sea, sweetheart. You don't have to keep the first one you catch."

I bite back a sigh. She said the same thing after Brayden. I never stopped fishing, never stopped trying new bait, a new flick to my casting strategy. With Andy, it finally seemed to be working. But the harder I worked at our relationship, the more uncomfortable he was around me, in bed or out of it. By the time we broke up, he was as messed up as I was. I'm never going to risk doing that to another man, or to myself, but my mom doesn't need to know that.

I manage a strained, but fond smile. "Not that you're biased or anything, Mom."

"My daughter is perfect." She picks up the tray of skewers and heads for the backyard. "So perfect she doesn't even have to be asked to set the table anymore."

"Obviously, I get my subtlety from your side of the family." I smirk, moving to open the patio door for her.

"Your brains, too." She winks.

I pause in the doorway for a minute, my fingers curling hard over the handle as I watch her turn on the propane and fumble with the barbecue lighter. She may have been joking with that "perfect" line, but I know my mom loves me, even if I'm not always exactly who she wishes I was. "Maybe I'll stick around for *Les Mis* after all. I can do some of my homework during the movie."

The burner lights with a whoosh and Mom looks up, a smile brightening her features. "Yeah? As long as you're sure it won't put you behind, that would be nice."

"It'll be okay." I've got a to-do list a year long, but these days, I'm in college to learn, not to kill myself over graduating with a golden tassel instead of a blue one.

After Andy and I broke up, I turned back with renewed energy to taking care of Granna, to school and the band. By the time Granna died, I was so tired that for the first time since I was sixteen, I couldn't muster the energy to care what anybody thought of me.

Giving up was such a relief.

I'm happier now, even though it means choking down my parents' occasional disapproval and avoiding adding people to my life, since they all come with expectations I can't live up to. Some nights, though, even suffering through one of my mom's musicals is easier than facing the emptiness of my own home.

Chapter 9: ONE OF THE GUYS

"Come on, you were a half-beat behind there, *again*," Jax groans at Danny.

I wing a drumstick at Jax and it bounces off his elbow, clattering to the garage floor. "Don't yell at him! You're going up an octave when you're supposed to drop it down, so no wonder we can't follow."

"Yeah, because if I don't, there's no contrast and the whole song sounds flat." Jax stomps over to snatch a bottle of water off one of the amps in the corner of our practice space.

I groan. As soon as I opened my eyes this morning, I started wondering when Jacob would come over. That pissed me off so much that I threw on the dorkiest shirt in my closet and called my friends over. I have a life, thank you very much, and I'm not about to mope around waiting on some guy. Except now all Jax wants to do is argue.

"We just went over this in my class last week," I inform him. "If there's too much contrast in each verse, the song doesn't have its own signature. It doesn't hold steady anywhere long enough to distinguish itself in people's minds."

Danny ignores us, shrugging out of his bass and walking over to push up the garage door and let in more air.

"Hey, Jera, do you remember the part where I was performing music before you even *applied* to your snooty little college?"

"Hey, Jax, do you remember the part where you pulled your head out of your ass, because I was right?"

He snorts. "Okay, but for this song, fuck your fancy degree. Our music is all about contrast."

"If he wants to try it different, we should try it different." Danny turns around and I squirm on my stool under the look he hits me with. Maybe I am too hard on Jax.

Danny scoops up my lost drumstick on his way back across the garage and tosses it to me. I catch it, twirl it, then sigh. "Fine. Go as high as you want on the next round. I'll back the drums off a touch so it doesn't sound so angry and we'll see how it goes, okay?" Jax nods, and then a second later he can't hold it back and he grins. I point my drumstick at him. "Don't even start. If it doesn't sound brilliant, we're back to my way, yes?" I wait for Danny to slip into his bass, and then I rip back into the song.

When we finish, Danny grunts. "That shit was way better."

"Traitor."

"Don't be an asshole, Jimi," he says, cheating by using my nickname, pulled from the acronym of my name. He knows I can't be mad at him when he calls me that. "You liked it better, too."

I sigh. "True." I peek over at Jax, but he's fingering silent chords on his guitar, not even looking at me. "Jax, did I die and go to heaven, or does being a year older than me make you so mature you don't even need an 'I told you so'?"

"Why do you think Bump In The Night waited until two weeks prior to book us?" he asks without raising his head. "I mean, we sent our demo tape in months ago."

Danny and I swap a look.

"Another band probably cancelled," Danny says, voicing the thing we'd agreed not to tell Jax unless strictly necessary.

The singer's fingers slow and then sag against the frets of his guitar.

"Oh, come on," I burst out. "You're seriously going to whine about the fact that we weren't their first choice? It's a freaking fantastic opportunity, Jax."

"I know," he mumbles.

"What are you going to do?" Danny asks. "Turn it down?"

"No. Hey, no." Jax blows out a breath. "Sorry. It doesn't bug you, though?"

"It did at first," I admit, pushing back the nibble of doubt that wants me to stay up all night practicing. I refuse to get neurotic and ruin all the fun of music again. "But watching you angst is helping immensely."

He narrows his eyes, pulling a gum wrapper out of his pocket and flicking it at me. "You," he announces, "are not a good person."

The wrapper bounces off my chin, and I point my drumstick at him. "Who's the bad person now? Littering is a federal offense in Oregon, *Mister* Sterling. If you don't pick that up, Captain Planet's going to swoop down and give you a spanking, and I have it on good authority that he uses a salmon."

Danny snorts. "How can something be a federal offense specifically in Oregon, Jera?"

"Since 1937, when we started developing a system of cooperative federalism," answers a voice from outside the garage door. "Which provides for the individual implementation of federal statutes on a state by state basis, with allowances made for the concurrent enforcement of local amendments to statute."

I sit up straighter, my eyes following the voice to a form with broad shoulders and fidgeting hands, backlit in the cloudy sunshine filtering through the haze of this morning's rainstorm.

"Uh, hi." Jax rakes his dark blond hair back out of his face, frowning. "Were we playing too loud or something?"

"No!" Jacob and I say at the same time, and then the words all fall apart as we start to talk over each other and he pauses, flushing, and gestures for me to go ahead.

"He's not a neighbor. This is my friend, Jacob." I clear my throat. It feels weird to call him that but since he's here, I guess that's what he is. "This is Jax, and I guess you already met Danny when you came to board up my window."

Danny straightens from unplugging his bass, nodding at Jacob. "Hey."

Jacob returns the nod and then takes Jax's extended hand, shaking it firmly. "I didn't mean to interrupt your rehearsal." He looks to me. "Should I come back later? You didn't tell me what time to come over, so..."

"Now is fine." I shrug and Jacob's eyes drop to my shirt, which says, "Como se llama?" with a picture of the farm animal on it. Because nothing says "just friends" like bad llama puns.

It takes a second for Jacob to read the caption, and then all his uncertainty cracks apart into a delighted grin. "Nice."

I bite the inside of my lip to hold back a smile. "You know, if you don't want people to know you're a nerd, you may want to avoid using phrases like 'cooperative federalism' and laughing at llama puns."

He scoffs. "Who doesn't like llama puns?"

My smile escapes into a full-on grin, but then I remember my band is still here, and I didn't exactly tell them I was expecting company. "What do you think, guys? Are we done or should we take another run at 'Broken Sidewalk'?"

Jax shrugs. "I only had time for one more song anyway. I've got a session booked with a new personal trainer this afternoon. I should head out."

"Say it a little louder, Jax. I don't think the Tri Thetas heard you."

He smirks. "Oh, I don't know. They tend to listen mighty carefully when I talk." I groan and he laughs. "We're going to practice again tomorrow, right? Gonna have to be after five, because I'm running out of personal days at work."

"Five-thirty it is."

"Cool." Jax gives my ponytail a tug that leaves it crooked, and saunters out. I scowl after him, then glance at Jacob. He stuck his hands in his pockets, and the light from the open door highlights the line of his jaw as he checks out all the band's equipment. He's every bit as distractingly handsome as he was in the grocery store, except with my drum kit set up around me and music still pulsing through my veins, I don't get that stomach-dropping feeling of panic, like he might make me forget everything I am.

Danny snaps his bass guitar case shut and turns to me. "Jera, can I talk to you?"

It takes me a second to pull my eyes back to my friend. "Hmm?"

"Alone?" Danny's hair is blasted up on the right side as if he fisted a hand in it without thinking. Uh-oh. That's not a good sign.

Jacob shifts his weight.

"I'll just be a minute." I give him the side-eye. "Don't even think about playing with my drums."

"No, ma'am." Jacob gives my kit a covetous look. I snap my teeth playfully in his direction and push up off my stool, taking the side door that leads back into my house.

Danny stalks right on my heels all the way to the kitchen, like he's riled up about something. There's only one reason he'd have a problem with Jacob, though, and it's absurd.

"All right, O'Neil." I turn and prop both hands on the counter behind me. "Is this the part where, out of jealousy, you confess your deep and undying love for me and promise that you know me better and will therefore treat me better than any other man alive?"

Danny pauses on an indrawn breath, lines of confusion crinkling beside his eyes.

I throw my arms around his neck and pucker up. "Oh, just kiss me already!"

He knocks my arms away. "Jesus, Jera, are you drunk?"

Maybe a little bit. On the rock and roll I love and the reminder that I hang out with lots of pretty boys. The novelty of their looks fades after a while, and with friends, I can be myself because we never get to the stage where I'm guaranteed to disappoint. Jacob doesn't have to be any different from Jax and Danny, and that realization makes me almost giddy.

"Are *you*?" I turn to dig in my snack drawer for some jerky. It's all gone, so I settle for peanut M&Ms, popping a blue one in my mouth and crunching noisily. "What was all that dramatic, 'I must speak with you' bullshit? Did you just now remember you let him take off with my hammer or something?"

"Hey," Danny says, his voice sharp and serious.

I freeze, a red M&M halfway to my mouth, and he takes a step closer.

"You didn't tell me you were *dating* the guy who broke your window." Danny drops his voice. "Look, I don't care if you two had a fight or something. Any guy who would do that just because he was angry is a piece of shit."

I guffaw so hard the red M&M pops out of my fingers and rolls across the floor to ping off Danny's shoe.

His shoulders are clenched tight and ready under his shirt, and when I bend to go after the candy, he actually grabs my arm to stop me. "Jera. I'm going to get rid of him. You should wait in here."

I throw up my hands. "Oh, for the love of—" I give up on the red M&M and tap the bag on my hand, coming up with a mere yellow. I eat it anyway. "He's the paperboy, Daniel, and it was an accident. Oldest story in the book. We didn't even know each other when it happened, and we're not dating. Christ, have you missed the last year and a half of my super-single life or what?" I wrinkle my nose. "It's a little concerning that both you and Dad thought I would date the sort of guy who breaks windows on purpose. Apparently, I'm so boring you two feel the need to liven up my reality with a little fantasy."

The lines in his forehead start to ease as he gauges my expression, evidently comforted by whatever he sees there. I twirl the bag of candy closed and drop it back into the drawer.

"Don't worry, D. He's just a friend. No bodyguard duties required." I pat him on the shoulder and then brush past on the way to the front door.

Jacob's leaning a shoulder against the outside wall next to the garage, a little stiff like he didn't know where to wait. I leave the door open for Danny, and it slams behind him as he ducks around me, munching on a handful of M&Ms he stole out of my drawer.

"You working late tonight?" I call after him as he detours to grab his bass from the garage.

"Yeah." He opens his car door and pauses. "You stopping by? We still have a little of the Tahitian black ink…"

"Don't save any on account of me. I might come over to the shop and study there for a while, though. Text if you want me to bring dinner."

"'Kay." Danny takes another look at Jacob before he slides into his car, freshly-minted caveman instincts apparently satisfied for the moment.

I don't need to bribe him with pizza—he'll be over it by the time he hits the end of the block. Still, Danny worried is almost as sweet as it is annoying. I'll probably bring pizza.

His engine turns over and as the car pulls away, I swivel to face Jacob.

"Everything okay?" He glances toward Danny's taillights.

"Yup. Apparently, I just needed a minute so my friend could interrogate me about whether or not you and I are in a volatile and potentially abusive relationship."

His brows rise. "I'm not sure if I should be flattered that he thinks you're with me or offended that he thinks I'm dangerous."

"Offended seems safer." I glance away, shoving away the self-conscious tingle his wording coaxed up out of me. "So. Please tell me you brought your record collection, and it's extensive enough you need help to carry it inside."

"You could say that."

I make a show of fanning myself. "You keep teasing me like this and we're going to have a volatile and potentially abusive relationship."

Jacob sweeps a hand toward the curb. "See for yourself. I'm curious to find out what effect my record collection has on the definition of our relationship."

I shoot him a glance that's half-warning, half-gauging if he really meant that the way it sounded. But he only smiles innocently, not a blush in sight. So help me, I can't tell if he's just that sweet and oblivious or if he's way more sly than I'm giving him credit for.

I turn back to the street, glancing around for his car. It has got to be some incredible restored something-or-other with a 6-mpg, mega-billion-horsepower engine. That's what mechanics drive, right? Or maybe a hot motorcycle that will be an excuse for public spooning at some point in our future. The car right in front of the house, though, is a junker that might even be older than Danny's. Most of it is a rust-flaking brown, except for the passenger door, which is robin's egg blue. I grin as I cross the lawn toward it. I bet that thing is almost as loud as my VW Bug.

I peek in the window, looking for his records. The backseat is littered with snack food wrappers, random tools, and a milk crate full of textbooks, a whirlwind that's somehow left the side behind the passenger seat completely untouched. That's weird.

But then Jacob pops the trunk and when I see three big, beautiful boxes of records, I forget about everything else.

Chapter 10: ICE CREAM SUNDAYS

Jacob has been here for hours and we haven't even gone through a tenth of his collection. We're just lying on our backs on the carpet next to the turntable, the notes of The Beatles' *Norwegian Wood* wafting over us like a dream I wish I could have every night. I'm pretty sure this is the most ideal use of a Sunday ever.

Well, at least the best one that doesn't also involve bacon.

"I'm in love," I sigh. "Not just with Paul, God bless his bedroom eyes, and not just with John, who I love strictly for his brain, but—"

"As far as I can tell, you're deeply in lust with Ringo and you can call it whatever else you want, but I know raging hormones when I see them."

I laugh, my back bowing up off the ground with the force of it, and Jacob shoots me a sidelong glance.

"What?"

"Nothing." I choke a little on the words, and the irony. "Inside joke. It's nothing."

"Wait, shut up, quick, shut up," Jacob interrupts. "I love this part." We both hold a respectful silence for the ending and then he lets out a sigh that's not too far off from mine. "Okay, yeah. The

Beatles are pretty amazing. They are solidly my third favorite band of all time."

I roll up onto my elbow. "Third? *Third?* There are about a trillion yuppie women with Pilates-toned triceps who would be happy to tear you limb from limb for a statement like that."

Jacob opens one eye. "Should I start running now?"

"Depends. Who's your second favorite band?"

"You ought to know, considering they're your ringtone."

"The Black Keys?" I smile. "I guess it's a good thing you like the ringtone, since my dad has been calling like a jealous girlfriend all morning. Sorry about that, by the way."

"It's no big deal." He sits up and reaches to swap out the record. "You guys must be close, huh?" His tone is almost wistful. Maybe his father's a dick, and that's part of the family drama he was dealing with last year.

"Dad's the manager for my band. He's having a micromanagement freakout about this show we have coming up. I swear he's not usually this clingy."

I roll onto my back, linking my hands over my belly. How does Dad manage to embarrass me even when he's not even here? It's like a superpower.

"No fair changing the subject," I say. "I'm dying to know what band could possibly top The Black Keys *and* The Beatles."

"The non-negotiable kind." Jacob reclaims his spot on the carpet beside me. Just then, "Something" starts to play, and he smiles and shakes his head. "Of course this song would come on right now."

"Okay, a non-negotiable band that attracts you like no other has before?" I paraphrase the lyrics, and movement flashes in my peripheral vision as he looks over at me.

"Something like that," he says.

I rub one bare foot over the other, running options through my head. "My previous forecast was Radiohead with a chance of

Mumford and Sons, but now I'm thinking…it's Taylor Swift, isn't it? I'll hand it to you. Girl has gorgeous hair."

"Because great music is all in the hair."

"I guess her voice isn't half-bad, either." I sneak a glance over at him.

He's relaxed with one hand tucked up under his head and those gorgeous lashes resting against his cheeks as a smile plays across his lips. "Ask me for a favor."

I frown. "Um, did you mean *do* you a favor?"

"Uh-uh. *Ask* me for a favor."

I consider this. "Why, exactly?"

"Because I want to hear one of your songs, and I've been listening to the radio nonstop but they haven't come on. If I do you a favor, then I can ask you to sing me a song."

His eyes are closed so I don't bother to hide the pleasure that tingles through me at the request. "Okay, what kind of favor can I get out of you?"

"Well, I'm pretty good at throwing a baseball. If you need a baseball thrown, I'm your guy."

"Hmm, low on baseball needs currently. What else have you got?"

"I can fix most things on a car as long as it's not too new and it doesn't require a hoist. Oh, and I'm excellent at reading books out loud with funny character voices."

"Now that's tempting. I've got a lot of accounting reading to do and it could seriously benefit from funny character voices. But I also have a slipping clutch that Mom hasn't had time to look at…"

That gets his head up and eyes open. "Your mom normally works on your car?"

I nod. "Grandpa was a master mechanic. Never made much money at it, but he scraped together enough to get Mom to college. Which is why she's almost as good with cars as she is at mortgage finance." She tried to teach me when I was younger, but I have the attention span of a fruit fly for mechanical things. Not that I'm about to admit that to Jacob.

He drops his head back to the carpet with a groan. "God, that's hot."

I smack him in the arm. "Gross! That's my mother you're speaking of."

"Sorry, but it is an objective fact that chick mechanics are hot. Chick mechanics, chick motorcycle riders, chick drummers..." He ticks them off on his fingers.

Okay, that was definitely flirting. I glance away and push myself upright, curling my legs beneath me as I flip through the closest box of records. It puts an ache deep in my belly to know he has a thing for drummers. That is the last thing I want to be thinking about when all six feet plus of his flawless muscles are stretched out on my floor in front of me.

As long as we were lying with eyes closed, absorbing the music together, I was okay. But now my skin heats and the fabric of my jeans seems suddenly coarse against my inner thighs. All my circuits are set to go, and yet I know if I were to draw him up to his feet and lead him back toward my bedroom, it would be a disaster. I've never had trouble with attraction. Just relationships and everything that goes with them.

I swallow, tongue scraping the dry roof of my mouth.

"Animals," he says without opening his eyes.

I nearly choke. "Sorry, what?"

"Play The Animals next. I have a thing for the chord progression in 'House of the Rising Sun.'"

I put my hands to work searching for the album, because they obviously don't know what's good for them anyway.

"So, I don't mean to be creepy or anything..." Jacob begins.

"But you're wondering if my mom is free for dinner sometime?"

"What?" He snorts. "Oh, no. Though if she has a trick for removing stripped-out screws, I'm all ears. What I was going to ask about was the show you had coming up. Are the tickets already sold out, or is it still open to the public, by any chance?"

My fingers pause on the records. He actually sounds…interested. Andy loved to tell people his girlfriend was in a band, but he was so tied up with sports and his premed classes that he only ever made it to three of my shows, and he never seemed that into the music itself. "I, uh, I'll have to check and see if there are any tickets left." As if Dad and Jax wouldn't both be blowing up my phone if we were sold out. I clear my throat. "Okay, I seriously can't find The Animals anywhere. Are you sure you own that one?"

He scoots up next to me. "No, I do. Some of these aren't in their original sleeves." He pretends to duck away from me in fear. "You're not going to go all purist on me, are you?"

I narrow my eyes. "Just don't consider mixing up *my* sleeves, buddy."

"I got a lot of these from my dad." His fingers flip through the records with the speed of long familiarity. "So some of the missing sleeves are his fault."

"Does your family live here in town?" I ask, and he fumbles one of the records and has to go back and check its label again.

"Yeah." Jacob clears his throat. "We grew up in Beaverton, which is pretty much Portland, but my little brother and I share an apartment a few blocks from campus."

"Does he go to the Stink, too?" I ask, using the unofficial nickname for PU.

"No, Ben just turned eighteen and he's kind of deciding which direction he wants to go right now. In the meantime, he works at AutoZone, which is nice for me because of his employee discount on parts."

"But he's living with you because it gets him out of the house, right? It's kind of painful doing college with your parents breathing down your neck and all." I nod toward my phone and roll my eyes.

His eyes flick up to me, then back down as he reaches across to massage his right shoulder—his pitching side. I wonder if he's got old injuries that still bother him. "Yeah, uh. Look, we don't have to get into it or whatever but my parents—they're uh…"

My stomach drops. I'm not sure what he's going to say, but I can feel how bad it is.

"Car crash." His Adam's apple bobs, but he doesn't look up at me. "Last year."

"Both of them?" I whisper, cold raking over my skin. "At the same time?"

He nods and my heart thumps once, so hard it almost hurts, and goosebumps appear all across my body. I try to picture getting a call and hearing Dad was gone. Just gone; no goodbye, no second chance, nothing. And the first person I would run to would be Mom, but what if she wasn't there, either? My whole family dead while I was just going about my business, listening to records or something and not knowing everything had changed.

"But that's…" I sputter, "that's *bullshit!*"

"Yeah?" Jacob's eyes jump back to mine, and then they crinkle at the edges as he starts to chuckle, shaking his head. "Yeah!" he says louder. "It *is* bullshit."

I draw my knees up, hugging them as I use one palm to try to rub the goosebumps away through my jeans. "What about your brother? You said he was eighteen, and if the accident was just last year…" I swallow, my brain darting across the idea of how short a year really is. "So did you end up raising him when he was a minor? I mean, are you his guardian or whatever?" My eyebrows lift. "You said it was crazy that I kept up with school when I was helping Granna out, but she's an adult. I can't imagine being responsible for a teenager."

He stares at me for a second. Was that rude? I meant that it was impressive but maybe that's not how he took it.

Jacob glances down, rolling his right shoulder and shaking out that wrist. "Our older sister, Hayden, was technically his guardian.

She's got a job and she's married and everything. She would do anything for Ben, but they're exactly the same kind of stubborn and without me there to buffer, they don't get along so great. After two months of that, I swapped my dorm for an apartment and Ben moved in with me." Jacob scratches his ear. "I wouldn't say I'm raising him, but it's tough because we're all on our own now. When Hayden can't make the minimum payment on her credit cards, or her husband is driving her crazy, or Ben wrecks his car, there's no one to bail us out but each other."

The pressure of so many responsibilities feels all too familiar. "So is that why you..." I break off, remembering I heard about his baseball career mostly through rumors.

"Is that why I quit the team?" He smiles a wry, pained smile. "You can say it. It wasn't my family's fault, though. That was all me."

His fingers pick at the corner of one of the album covers and I have to stop myself from covering his hand with my own. It might turn this into something it's not, and it probably won't do anything to ease the pain he must be feeling, having to re-live all this.

"You don't have to—"

"No, I don't mind. I hate dancing around people knowing about my parents." He takes a breath. "A lot of things changed after the accident. My coaches and the team were really supportive and everything, but I couldn't just ride the bench until my head was back in the game. I'm the pitcher."

I don't miss his use of the present tense. Some things you can't erase. I could put down my drumsticks tomorrow and I would still—always—be a drummer.

"Doesn't that make it worse?" I hug my knees. "I'm not a huge sports fan, but I know you don't get good enough to play Division I ball—much less be the starting pitcher—unless it's something you really love. When everything else was so shitty, why give up something that made you happy? Besides, if you had to get three jobs to make up for the scholarship and stipend you turned down, it's not like you have more time now."

"It was complicated." His voice is quiet. "And things were, yes, shitty. At the time."

"Yeah," I agree, not wanting to press him if he doesn't want to talk about it. "For real."

We sit for a moment, letting the record spin out.

My mind keeps returning to Granna's funeral, with the one-size-fits-all eulogy the priest gave her, and how angry I was that he didn't know her well enough to realize how little it described who she was. I wonder how close the date of her funeral was to Jacob's parents' accident, and if they're buried in the same cemetery.

I bounce to my feet. I've got to stop thinking about this or I'm gonna bawl, and I'm an ugly crier. I hold out a hand to Jacob and he looks up, his eyes clouded for a second as if he was pretty far away, too.

"Ice cream," I state, and he lays his hand in mine, still appearing confused. I grasp his wide palm and try to pull him to his feet, which really doesn't work because I weigh about as much as his right thigh.

Fortunately, he's too polite to let on, so he stands up as if I helped. "Why ice cream?"

I start tugging him toward the kitchen. "Because I feel like shit and it's going to take me a lot of empty calories to get back on track." Guilty lines appear next to his eyes and I've got to nip that right in the bud, so I keep my voice light. "Don't worry, Sparky, you're not on the team anymore, so you don't have to watch your waistline."

At that, a smile appears, and he starts to chuckle. "Good point."

"We are also probably going to need to bust into my emergency M&M supply, because life is *bullshit,* which means I don't get to meet your folks to see where you got all those great baseball-throwing and story-reading genes. So, you are going to tell me a fact about each of your parents for every bite we eat. If we don't feel better after that,

I'm calling Jax over so he can use the wisdom of his advanced years to teach us the proper way to make Jaeger floats."

Jacob's stopped in the doorway of the kitchen, not even pretending to let me lead him anymore. But instead of letting go, his hand clings to mine. His eyes warm with a light that tells me I made the right gamble with hoping he'd want to talk more about his parents, not less.

"I think I would like that," he says, very quietly.

My heart stumbles over something in his tone, but I'm in full cheering-up mode now, so I only wink. "I wouldn't make any promises just yet. The only kind of ice cream I have is mocha almond fudge that melted once and was refrozen, and you don't even want to know what that tastes like in a Jaeger float."

Jacob starts to laugh, really laugh, and the sound makes me smile. He's a good guy, and I don't know why I was so skittish about spending more time with him. He even wanted to come to my concert.

My whole body tingles at the idea but I'm not sure I should risk it. I've gotten better at ignoring all the small clues that I'm disappointing people, but when it comes to my music, my band? Those are sacred. And yet the steady warmth of Jacob's hand in mine makes me think that this time, it might be okay.

I let his hand slip from mine and busy myself getting out silverware, my eyes on the drawer. "You know, I might be able to dig up one more ticket to my show. If you want."

"Are you serious?" Jacob takes a step forward. "Because I want. I want, bad."

MICHELLE HAZEN

Chapter 11: **TO BE RECOGNIZED**

"Guys suck." I drop my head back against the wall of the radio station and sigh. The hallway we're waiting in smells like scorched Ramen noodles. "Men are like beautiful agents of Satan, spreading insecurity and misery throughout the world."

"You know we're guys, right?" Jax asks. "Don't be sexist."

I click on my phone again, and Danny swipes it out of my hand and shoves it into his pocket. "You wouldn't hate guys so much if you didn't spend so much time over-thinking our text messages. We type shit. The same shit we are actually thinking. End of story."

"Yeah, stop being such a girl about it," Jax says.

"You know I am a girl, right?" I elbow him. "Sexist." I cross my arms and stare at the wall across from me. Ancient concert posters line the radio station's hallway, their corners curling up underneath the thumbtacks that keep them on display. I've read them almost as many times as Jacob's texts.

Danny so doesn't know what he's talking about, because not all guys just say what they really mean. If they did, everything would be so much simpler. I steal my phone back out of my best friend's pocket, and he just shakes his head as I scroll back to the four-day-old texts from Monday.

We've got a problem.

You can't come to the show? That's ok. No worries. :)

Why the fuck did I add that happy face? Like, yeah, I love it when you ditch me after practically begging for an invitation. No problem. Let me just sing a quick chorus of Shiny Happy People.

No, even worse. I was telling my little brother about it, and as soon as he found out you were the drummer, he stole my ticket.

Uh-oh. That is a problem.

Brilliant, Jera. Hilarious.

Now he wants a tattoo. Question: Is there any part of his anatomy you definitely do not want your name across?

Elbow. I couldn't stand to have my name associated with the ugliest part of the human anatomy.

Damn, the elbow was his first choice, and you don't want to know the second.

I smile, picturing Jacob's deadpan perfectly. I read his next text.

I have a plan. I was thinking if we could keep him from seeing you onstage with your drum kit, we might be able to keep him from falling in love in the first place. I noticed the venue is a bar. He's only eighteen—is the venue going to allow all ages on the night of the festival?

I stared at this text forever when it first came in. It's sorta flirty, but then I've made the mistake of thinking Jacob was flirting before and been wrong. What's with all this stuff about his little brother anyway? Was he planning on bringing him along? Is he not joking around and his brother really has a crush on me? In the end, I decided I was sexually frustrated and overanalyzing, and just sent the simplest answer.

Sorry, we're part of the pub crawl night of the festival. No kiddies allowed.

Ah, he'll be crushed. Maybe he can watch it on YouTube or something.

He sent nothing but more chatty, jokey texts for three days and then this morning it got weird:

Hey, something came up. I'm going to try really hard to make it to your show, but I can't promise anything yet. Will let you know for sure when I know.

I put away my phone. Yeah. I must have gotten a hundred texts like that from my ex. It wouldn't even be surprising that Jacob was flaking on me like every other guy, except that he's so painfully charming up until this point. Well, screw him. The good thing about being out of the dating world means I don't have to put my heart out there where anybody can kick it. I can stay right here, with the two guys in my life I can always count on.

On my right, Danny has his hands clasped behind his head, studying the ceiling as if the patterns in the acoustic tile are swirling themselves into new tattoo designs in his mind. On my left, Jax leans forward, elbows propped on his knees so that his jiggling leg makes his whole body rattle like an old, gas-guzzling Chevy.

"I just don't get why, if your uncle could get us this interview, he couldn't get us the list of questions ahead of time," Jax says.

I pick at the peeling sole of my combat boot and reach deep for my patience. Jax is the perfect front man, with a face that could sell a billion albums and a voice like foreplay, but until you give him an audience to perform for, he's a hot mess.

"First, Bear is my godfather, not my uncle, and he didn't get us the interview," I say. "This radio station is one of the sponsors of Things That Go Bump In The Night, so they're interviewing all the bands. Bear just got us the time slot right before the festival headliners, so anybody who tunes in to listen to PhantAsmic's interview is probably going to catch a snippet of ours."

"And second, they don't *have* prepared questions, douchebag," Danny says. "This is KKSX, not MTV. The guy probably just makes it up on the spot."

"What's with the name?" Jax says. "'Bear' is kinda cutesy for an '80s rocker."

"His given name is Grizlane." I drop my voice a little. "Sometimes a nickname is a gift, Jax, and if you value your limbs, do not tell him I told you that."

Jax's knee jiggles harder, his big hands clamped together so every knuckle stands out. During the day, he works as a logistical something or other at UPS, which only feeds his compulsion for details. He pretty much gorges on checklists all day and then girls at night, the kind who'll sleep with anybody who can play "Wish You Were Here" with a soulful look on his face. Give him a task or an audience of any kind and he comes to life like you just stuck a quarter in his back, but ask him to sit still? Well, maybe just best not to ask.

Reaching over, I pat him on one broad shoulder. "Just pretend you're on a date. They don't give you a list of questions for that, and you do just fine."

"I *know* what women want, Jera."

"Modesty?" I ask tartly.

"Radio wants the same thing girls do." Danny's hands remain loosely linked behind his head. "Charisma and confidence. Just talk about the music."

Jax snorts. "Yeah, and Jera's all charisma over here." He plucks at the sleeve of my faded pink Race for the Cure 2009 tee shirt.

I slap his hand away. "It's a *radio* show, not a TV spot. Besides, charisma is a state of being, not a characteristic of your wardrobe, Mr. Kettle Black." I aim a look at his brown UPS uniform shirt and clear my throat.

"What are you, twelve?" But despite his bluster, I've got him laughing now.

I reach over and tousle his wavy, dirty-blond hair so it falls forward, brushing the line of his jaw. "That sounds like a challenge to give you a wedgie. Don't tempt me, Sterling. I'll go atomic on your ass."

The studio door opens and we stop mid-bicker to jump to our feet. A short guy smiles up at us—well, at Danny and Jax. I'm still a few inches below eye level, even for him.

The interviewer wears pleated-front khaki slacks that bag at the ankles and a hoodie unzipped over a shirt that says "It Takes a Viking to Raze a Village."

I step forward with a smile. "Hey, Martin."

Surprise lights his eyes, and I realize he didn't connect my band name to me. It's not like I really know the guy, I've just been to a couple of barbecues at Bear's house when he was there.

"Oh hey. Jeri, right?"

"Jera." I shake his hand.

He winces. "Sorry."

"No worries. Thanks for having us. This is Danny, our bassist, and Jax, lead singer and guitar." I gesture the introductions and Martin shakes everyone's hands so fast it's almost rude.

"We're just on a quick commercial break." He ushers us into the studio and points us to seats. "There are only two guest microphones, so you'll have to share. We had three but I was interviewing this lady about her permaculture classes last week and she busted one." He makes a face. "Farmers."

"No worries. I think we can handle microphones." I wink.

"It's in the blood, right?" He laughs as he skirts a bank of sound equipment to take his seat across from us.

Oh, so it's going to be one of *those* interviews. The ones that are more about who my dad is than what kind of music we're making. I grimace. We've only been featured a few times: in the *Willamette Week*, *Portland Mercury*, and on a couple of blogs. Almost all of them wanted to talk about The Heat more than The Red Letters, and I can never tell if they think we're measuring up or not.

The first band I started, in junior high, sounded like a cover band for the keyboard-heavy signature of The Heat. By high school, I was trying to sound like anything *but* my dad, but I would still practice until my fingers bled, trying to earn more than an indulgent smile from his old bandmates. Now, I play the hell out of the songs that appear in my head, and tell myself that's enough.

From the sound booth, Bear waves at me, and I grin and wave back. His long, graying ponytail tangles in the collar of his shirt as he swings his chair away from us and hits a button. My pulse picks up. This is exactly the kind of distraction I need today, and I love the rubber scent and vaguely electronic bite of the air in a studio. It always makes me feel like something incredible is about to happen.

"So, it's a pretty short spot," Martin says. "I'll introduce you all, we'll play one of your songs, couple of questions, and then you're out of here." He pops on a set of headphones and adjusts his microphone, which is suspended on an adjustable arm hanging down from the ceiling.

There are three microphones in front of our table but one is pushed up out of the way, a sticky note dangling from it that says, "Fix me!" Jax commandeers one of the two working microphones, and after Danny shows no interest in following suit, I take the second and put on a set of headphones so I can hear what's going out over the air. I chew on my bottom lip, wondering if Jacob might be listening since I told him this station sometimes plays our songs.

"Is PhantAsmic coming in here?" Danny eyes a smooth stain on the edge of one of the office chairs that might be old gum. I poke him with a set of headphones, gesturing for him to put them on.

"Nah," Martin says. "They're phoning in. They're on tour and won't be in town until the night before the show. Ready?"

We don't even get a chance to nod before he un-mutes his microphone. Nerves flutter in my stomach as he begins his intro.

"Welcome back, folks. You're listening to KKSX, home of the loudest music in the greater Portland metropolitan area. Today we have some special guests to start your weekend off right. They are one of the young and very talented bands that will take the stage at Things That Go Bump In The Night—sponsored by KKSX—which, as everyone knows, is the best Halloween music festival around. Though, awkwardly, this year it's not on Halloween."

He gives a dry chuckle and I wince. He's probably had to do that bit a million times this month in promos.

"Mark your calendars, friends, and this weekend we'll get you into the Halloween spirit early. If you're good, we'll even still let you wear a costume. Now, I'm excited to introduce..." He glances down at his printed schedule. "Jackson Sterling, Jera McKnight, and Danny O'Neil of The Red Letters!"

We all say a quick hello.

"And from their second, self-released album, this is the song that's been heating up the airways lately. They call it 'Out of Order.'"

This song has been getting a little play on two of the local stations, but this is only the third time I've heard it over the air. It gives me a thrill when Danny's bassline stomps into my ears, unvarnished and alone for just one beat too long so you start to get uncomfortable before my drums kick in and Jax's voice, raw and urgent, drops the first line. It's provocative, but we maybe should have gone with something catchier for the lead single on the album. Hooky, like Adele, but hardcore, like **AVA**. I wonder where Jacob's favorite band falls on that spectrum.

I swallow and push the thought aside as I glance over to check on my nervous bandmate. Now that he's got a microphone in front of him, Jax sprawls in his chair, everything from his loose muscles to mussed hair giving the impression that he just finished having fantastic sex. The corner of my mouth kicks up. Even straight from work in his UPS shirt, Jax always manages to look like an ad for the kind of jeans your mother would never buy you.

The song is over before I'm ready, three deep drumbeats blasting out at the end gauged to leave your mind vibrating, wishing for an easy fadeout.

"Well..." Martin gives a little unnerved chuckle. "That's not exactly your mother's hit single, is it?"

Jax laughs, deep and slow, and damned if it doesn't almost make *my* nipples hard. "Depends on the mom. I think you might be surprised."

"It seems like a song about hopelessness is an ironic way to start a career."

My skin prickles with irritation at Martin's comment. Before I can take a breath that will carry words I will no doubt regret, Jax says, "It's a song about the one part of yourself you wish you could change. I think that track's catching on because it's pretty hard to find a person who couldn't identify with that, whether they want to admit it out loud or not."

"But you admitted it out loud," Martin says. "What spurred you to write the song?"

Danny stiffens and dodges a quick glance my way, but I don't correct Martin's assumption.

At first, it was tough to write songs that worked for Jax. I wasn't going to be singing them so I couldn't exactly write a lament to my bra size or bash my ex-boyfriend's morning breath in B minor. But I figure all really good songs are written like a mirror: anybody who looks sees themselves in it. And if I do it just right, what they see is the truth.

"What would I change about me?" Jax scratches the back of his neck. "Give you about thirteen to start. You got a pen?"

Martin laughs, his eyes lifting at the corners.

"Honestly though, you'd have to ask Jera. She's our go-to songstress." Jax props his arms on the table in front of us. "I can sing her lyrics because they get to me, but she's the only one who knows what's behind the songs, and most of the time, Martin? She's not telling."

I'm barely holding in a grin as Jax settles back into his chair. He always smoothes out for the actual interview, but he's selling the heck out of us today.

Martin turns to me. "Jera? What about you?"

"Things about Jax that I would change? Oh, that's a whole different song." I duck closer to the microphone. "It's got a killer drumbeat, though."

Danny smirks and everyone else laughs.

"We're running out of time for this intriguingly reticent new band," Martin says, "but I promise you will *not* want to miss seeing them live." He rattles off the venue information for our show tomorrow. "After this break, we'll be talking with PhantAsmic, electronica and rock visionaries that are coming soon to a stadium near you."

He cuts to commercial and hits the mute button for our microphones. Reluctantly, I take off my headphones and set them on the table. Wow, that was over fast.

"Nice job, folks," Martin tells us. "Always leave them wanting more." He stands up and we follow suit, but before he can finish taking off his headphones, he frowns and pauses to listen, pulling over a second microphone that is probably wired into Bear's sound booth. "Are you serious? Okay, yeah. No problem. Just let me know when you have them on the line."

Martin looks up at us.

"Is there any chance you guys have an extra few minutes to spare? PhantAsmic is running a wee bit late. I could fill the spot with music but—"

"We can stay," Jax interrupts, and I nod enthusiastically. Danny just shrugs.

"Great!" Martin smiles. "Back on in two minutes. Follow my lead and we'll fill the extra time just fine, okay?"

We grab headsets and seats again, my heart pumping at the idea that we're about to double our exposure today, plus we're fully stealing the audience that will have tuned in for PhantAsmic's highly-publicized interview slot.

Martin goes through his whole intro again and then says, "So, over the break I happened to discover an interesting fact about our enigmatic guests, The Red Letters."

Danny slumps a little farther in his seat. I swallow a sigh and straighten my back, because I know they're about to flog the famous-dad angle again, and I don't want to look as annoyed as I actually am.

"Jera McKnight, drummer and songwriter for The Red Letters, is actually the daughter of Hank McKnight of the old-school, hard-rock sensation, The Heat."

I try to scrounge up a smile, suddenly hoping no one I know is listening.

"For those of you too young to remember The Heat, The Simpsons, or anything else good and holy in this world, a quick reminder…" Martin says, "The Heat was one of Portland's very own that blew up quick in the late '80s, did two huge international tours and then disappeared, to the horror of loyal fans everywhere."

It's a kind summary, because they hardly disappeared. My dad's band got pissed at their record label, bought out the rest of their contract and tried to go independent, which in those days was little better than a quick leap off a tall cliff. They couldn't get distribution and outside of Portland, basically no one has ever heard of their two self-released albums. They tried for a new label, but by then their following had faded. They couldn't find a company who was willing to take on a band that was known as inflexible and hard to work with.

Dad is a real estate agent now, but The Heat didn't quit playing locally until they lost their lead singer to cancer when I was in high school. I still remember how they seemed to speak to each other through their instruments, their fingers fast and almost supernaturally precise. How Dad's forehead would crease when I couldn't get my transitions as smooth as his.

"Jera, what was it like growing up in a house with such a dedicated musician?" Martin asks.

My fists clench under the table as I deliberately glance away from our interviewer. I don't have to watch him and rate myself by his opinion. I gave up on that crap, and if he doesn't think we're as good as my dad's band, or if he doesn't like us, that's his problem.

I take a breath and tell him the truth. "Well, Martin, it was kind of a pain in the ass."

Martin laughs, but Jax sends me an alarmed look.

"Dad started me on the guitar when I wasn't even big enough to hold it, which I hated because the strings hurt my fingers. So then it was on to the piano, which was painfully boring." I shudder. "It wasn't until I met Danny that I really got into music on my own terms and asked for drumming lessons for Christmas."

Dad may have taught me to play, but Danny taught me how to love it. He didn't follow any rules, and he never took any lessons. From him, the night-toned twang sounded like something more essential than air, more real than time. Listening to him, I realized that rhythm drives everything. I bought a set of drums, and with the sticks in my hands, I learned to translate the pulse beneath the skin of the world around me.

"When did you two meet?" Martin prompts, sending a glance at Bear's sound booth. Bear shakes his head and the interviewer returns his attention to me.

"That would be in eighth grade, when Danny was puking in the girl's bathroom."

A faint smile flickers over Danny's face. He leans forward and steals my microphone. "Thanks for sharing that, Jimi."

"Anytime." I stick my tongue out at him for using my nickname on the air, and Martin's grinning again.

"So was Jackson in the next stall down?"

"Nope." I snag the microphone back. "We met Jax in the auditions we held after our second band broke up." That one fell apart because Caitlyn, our guitarist, decided yearbook editor would look better on college applications. "That was, what? Three, four years ago?"

I make it sound like a question, but it's actually kind of a sore spot. Jax is a year older than we are, and he played his audition not realizing the other two band members were still in high school. After we chose him and the truth came out, Dad had to do a lot of fast talking to get him to try playing a couple of songs with us. But once he did, not one of the three of us could have walked away.

"And The Red Letters were born. . ." Martin finishes. "Since we have a few extra minutes, why don't we share a virgin-to-radio cut off your new album?"

Jax slants a quick look my way, excitement vibrating beneath his lazy smile. The boy has a taste for fame. I wish I knew for sure how he will handle it if we ever do hit it big.

Martin pauses to listen to something Bear's saying in his headset. "This one is called 'Don't Ask My Name.' Before he hits play, can you give me a quick inside lane on this song?"

I want to slam my head against the table. Please, not this song.

The lyrics are two-faced: they sound like they belong to Jax, singing about how he just wants to be in the moment with all these beautiful girls, but they always interrupt with wanting all these details about him. What it's actually about is my love affair with music and all the things that keep getting in the way, including my history-laden last name.

No way am I saying that on the radio, especially not with Dad listening, even if I *could* do it in a sentence.

Danny claims the microphone just as my silence is starting to become noticeable. "Funny story: she wrote half the lyrics to this song on my shower curtain. Little tip? Never leave a Sharpie anywhere Jera McKnight can get her hands on it."

Great, and now everyone who is listening—including maybe Jacob—is going to think we're sleeping together. Whatever. People can think what they want.

Martin laughs. "There you have it, folks, The Red Letters. The next big thing and the terror of shower curtains and girls' bathrooms everywhere. Now, here's 'Don't Ask My Name.'"

As we pull off our headsets, Jax's voice explodes onto the air, and I have to hold back a proud smile so I don't look like an amateur.

Martin grins. "That was some good radio. Nice to start our festival publicity off with an interview that doesn't make me want to duck out for a coffee."

"Happy to be of service. Thanks for the extra spin," I say.

"Anything for Hank's daughter." He rises to shake my hand again. "You're making some decent music, Missy. Keep it up, okay?"

"Will do." Something about the tone of his voice tells me that we just got a serious compliment, and my pulse kicks up. I blow a kiss to Bear in the sound booth, and he winks, miming a phone to say he'll call me later.

We stroll out of the radio station, and it's an effort not to start skipping as I pass the receptionist. As soon as we hit the parking lot, Jax slings an arm around me and starts to swagger, the sight tugging a smile onto Danny's lips.

"Look, I'm sorry about all that stuff about my dad..." I begin, but Jax shakes his head.

"Doesn't even matter. Not today."

He's beaming in a way that is totally unaffected by the light rain misting down on the pavement, and I'm right there with him, so excited it feels like my body is straining with the effort of keeping all of me contained. Never mind who heard that interview or what they thought of it. My songs are on the radio, and they sound *good.*

"And that's what it feels like," Jax announces. "That, my friends, is what it's supposed to feel like."

MICHELLE HAZEN

Chapter 12: TEN THOUSAND HOURS

Our venue is empty.

Okay, there's a bartender, but he's paid to be here. I take a breath and peek around the curtain to check one more time but all that greets me are empty seats and the accusing expanse of the scratched-up dance floor. Off to the side, my mom's set up with a white wine and her iPhone ready. My dad leans against her table, a video camera bag dangling off his shoulder. While I watch, she rolls her eyes, lips pursed against a smile, then he leans forward a little, saying something else. She laughs, bobbing her foot absently as her shoe dangles from her toes.

I grimace. An event where only your parents show up is almost worse than being alone. When they try to cheer you up, every syllable in their too-perky voices says they're feeling your failure right along with you. It doesn't help that as much as she hates to see me unhappy, I know Mom would be relieved if a disaster gig convinced me to give up the band. She hates the music industry after the front row seat she had to my dad's roller-coaster ride of a career. And as proud as Dad says he is of me, I know he was playing bigger shows than this when he was my age.

I let the curtain fall shut. It's the first time we've played at a venue that could even afford a curtain, much less the gorgeous light system Jax keeps fidgeting with.

"Jax, you're going to break something. Chill." I snatch the clipboard out of his hand, every item on it already checked off and then X'd for the double-check. "Do I need to put our lucky song on?"

He glares at me. "I'm fine."

"Okay, but you don't have to brag about it," I tease, because I know it will cheer him up. He is looking pretty good, but then he probably spent more time in front of a mirror than I did. And admittedly, tonight I logged a little mirror time.

Since it's a special occasion, I curled my hair, the light and dark streaks winding in dramatic spirals around my face. I went all out on my top, too, with a black tank made entirely of crisscrossing straps of thin mesh and chunky metal buckles. It's enough layers to be opaque, but thin enough to breathe once I get really moving. I even played a rehearsal in it to check the buckle placement. There was an unfortunate show in a sparkly top last year that left me with some kind of sequin road rash everywhere my arms rubbed while I played.

The outfit is exactly what I want to be feeling—tough and maybe even a little bit sexy. I'm determined not to let anything on the other side of that curtain ruin my night.

Jax smiles, but it's weak, so I yank my phone out of my pocket, unwind the earbuds from around it, and nestle them into his ears. When I click on my phone to select Macklemore's "Ten Thousand Hours," there are no new messages. I'm not really surprised. If Jacob was going to text to confirm he was bailing, he would have done it hours ago.

Jax drops down to sit on an amp, my phone dangling between his knees as he closes his eyes to listen to the music. I hope this does the trick. Our lead singer puts on a great strut for the pretty girls but he's a squishy-hearted little nail biter underneath.

When I turn around, Danny's the one sneaking a look around the edge of the curtain. I raise my eyebrows. "Et tu, Brute?"

"He's not here." He turns, his hazel eyes tight at the corners.

"Like I care," I sputter. Then I remember I didn't tell him I invited Jacob. "Wait, who's not here? The CEO of Tower Records? Pretty sure he RSVP'ed for the second half."

"Your 'friend' Jacob. Figured he'd turn up if you had a gig this important." Sometimes Danny gets an edge before a show, like he needs to get laid, or maybe punch someone. Today is definitely looking like the second option.

I cross my arms. "You look like a girl when you air quote, you know that?"

"You look like a girl, too." He stares me down, and suddenly the eyeliner and lip gloss I slicked on feels very heavy. "For the first time in about a year."

"It's a big show. I didn't want to play it wearing one of your hand-me-down shirts, so fuck off."

He crosses the stage and takes my face in his hands, reminding me that I might have put on a tiny bit of foundation, too. Which he is now smudging. "Jimi, I'm going to say this one more time. Andy never came to your shows because he was an asswench." He glances at Jax, who's still got earbuds in and his eyes squeezed closed. Danny drops his voice anyway. "It's not because you did anything wrong."

I blush hotly, grinding my teeth at his implication. Andy pulled away a little after we started sleeping together, yes, but even before that, his schedule was always packed. When he did squeeze in one of my shows, the best he could do was nod along a little behind the beat. When it was over, he'd paste on a smile and tell me that no, hard rock wasn't really his thing, but the concert was great. That was the only word my non-music-literate ex could ever come up with. We were so…great.

"You always think people are judging you, being disappointed in you, but they're not, Jera." Danny frowns. "Probably not even Andy. Idiot just had bad taste in music."

"Yeah, let's definitely talk about this five minutes before our biggest gig ever." I stalk toward the edge of the curtain and the bar beyond it, deciding my no-pre-show-drinking rule is stupid.

Danny slips in front of me, crowding me back away from the edge of the stage. "If this guy doesn't show up, he's an asswench, too, and I will buy you a beer for making it through another day asswench-free. Deal?" He holds out his knuckles, and I scowl at him.

"It is definitely not your hand I want to bump with my fist right now."

"Hit me, then." He doesn't budge, his voice low. He just stands his ground, knowing every humiliating thing I'm thinking, and I know he'd take a punch or even ten if that's what I needed to feel better.

I exhale, and hug him around the waist instead, leaning my head against his chest. It's stupid, it's *so* stupid and I blame romantic comedies. Somehow I really thought Jacob would show up at the last minute.

The hollow little feeling that leaves beneath my heart has me holding onto Danny twice as hard. "I really tried not to give a shit this time," I mumble into his shirt. "Why can't I stop doing this to myself?"

Danny's muscles twitch beneath my hands. It's a sore spot for both of us, ever since junior high. If I like somebody enough to stick around, sooner or later they start getting irritated by the same things about me they used to think were cute. They get offended when I zone out into a song I'm writing, or they're annoyed by how fast I talk when I'm nervous, or they think I'm secretly in love with Danny. I've seen dozens of girls do the same thing to my best friend. They line up to get in his bed but then they start wanting him to wear nicer clothes, and talk about his feelings, and not spend every weekend in my garage. Sometimes, he tries for a while. Mostly, he doesn't.

"Ass," Danny says. "Wench."

Jax jumps up off the amp. "Quit screwing around, you guys. Let's do this." He shoves my phone at me. Through the earbuds, I thought I heard my text message alarm chime, but now there's no time to check.

"We can't play yet. There's nobody here." I let go of Danny and leap for the curtain, peering around it. "Okay, there are like fifteen people here." I've played smaller shows than that, but this place is so big, the audience looks like ants sprinkled into a football stadium.

"It's twenty after posted time. We can't wait anymore." Jax grins at me. "You know what turns a crowd into a party?"

"A keg?" I ask weakly.

"Music." He jerks his chin at the pulley ropes to the side of the stage. "Danny, get the curtains. You guys stay behind them until I call you."

"Uh, there's not exactly a side stage," I remind him. "There's like a foot of space back there."

"So spoon. You're both skinny." Jax runs a hand through his hair, deliberately mussing it, then blows into a cupped hand, checking his breath.

Danny heads for the curtain pull. "Man, that microphone cares if you sound pretty, not if you smell pretty."

"Maybe that's why your girlfriend is so grouchy all the time." Jax shrugs into his guitar and points at him. "The full presentation is always important, D."

I crowd up next to Danny as he starts to crank the curtains back. "You're seeing somebody new? Why didn't you tell me?"

He blinks. "Why?"

I roll my eyes. "I have got to get some female friends in my life."

As the curtain parts, Jax takes a step into the gap and rips a distorted chord that blazes through the room, quieting the hum of conversation.

"Hello, Portland!"

The curtains are almost all the way open, and I can tell we're not going to be able to fit behind them. How embarrassing is it going to be when the audience sees us trying? Screw waiting on Jax's master plan.

I stride into the lights. Somebody catcalls and Jax sweeps a hand toward me even though it could just as well have been meant for him. With a grin, he says, "Why yes, now that you mention it, gracing the stage tonight is our lovely drummer, Jera McKnight!" He lifts his voice at the end, and it pulls a few more yells out of the scattered patrons, heads turning away from the bar and toward us.

I stop and milk it for a minute, posing and waving, laughing like it's a big joke and blowing a kiss at the crowd when the whistles break out again. Bowing, I take a seat behind my drums. It's starting to fill up. There might be twenty or more nursing drinks at tables now.

"And just to even things out, our homely bassist, Danny O'Neil!"

Danny comes out and grabs his instrument out of the stand. He lifts the strap to his bass over his head with a quick, tight movement that makes it look like his body is one tall stretch of muscle. He takes a step forward, shoving a hand back through his careless black hair, the angle of the lights above leaving his face in shadow. He doesn't do a thing more, but a table of girls in the back goes crazy, squealing high and loud. Clapping follows them and spreads across the whole room.

"I am Jackson Sterling." Our singer comes in at just the right time with the applause so it sounds like they're doing it for him. "We are The Red Letters, and we're here to kick off everybody's favorite music festival, Things That Go Bump In The Night!" He raises his arms and the few people in here start to cheer.

Jax is such a natural, at all of this. Some people play a guitar like they're punching the keys on a typewriter but he plays like he wants to give it an orgasm. Give him the only stage in a deserted country and he would still *own* it.

But then the sound dies down, and the dance floor is still empty, a smattering of people standing around the edges with hands curled around their drinks as if they're not ready to leave them just yet.

Jax doesn't even appear to notice. He starts to talk to the crowd, joking with them and using the rhythm of his voice to relax the tension of an obviously empty room.

These awkward few minutes at the start of a show always remind me of a blind date. When you don't know the audience, and you're not sure if anybody will dance, or even bother to clap at the end of a song. Before it starts, you can never be sure if the chemistry is going to mesh.

Which is why I'm a drummer. As long as I make each performance just about the music, I'm okay. Jax actually has to work at getting our audience to have a good time, and if I put that kind of pressure on myself, I'd go crazy.

I do one last sweep for Jacob, but all I see is my dad getting ready to film the show for YouTube clips, and I mess with my drumsticks to cover the unsteadiness in my hands.

I just hope this show turns out to be something worth recording.

A drop of sweat runs down the line of my spine, and another trembles at the brink of my eyelashes. The music burns in me now, torching every tendon and vein, my muscles a sacrifice on the altar of speed. I don't even exist except in my lyrics transfigured by Jax's deep voice, my heart pounding a rhythm my drumsticks amplify for the rest of the packed room.

More people trickled into the bar with every song, and now bodies cushion the room, no bare bits of dance floor left exposed. All the colors of their clothes are a canvas I only half notice behind the rise of my drums, the pulse of lights ricocheting off my cymbals.

A change in the movement of the crowd catches my eye in the middle of the fourth song; a set of broad shoulders interrupting the surge of dancers, then a quick flash of a familiar face. Jacob claims a space right up next to the stage, and I skip a beat, my drumstick catching the edge of my drum instead of its taut skin. He's here. Oh my God, he actually came.

Danny glances over when he hears my glitch, but I'm already back in the rhythm, my sticks bounding over brass and skipping across my toms. Jacob grins up at me, his face alight with excitement, and when the song finishes, he waves. I wave back, smiling, and it's not until Jax turns away from the microphone that I realize he already introduced the next song. Belatedly, I count us in.

After those first two fumbles, I hit my stride, and the longer Jacob watches, the better I play. He somehow picked just the right spot so I can see him in the gap between two of my cymbals; his face always in my peripheral vision no matter which end of my kit I swivel to hit. He dances to some songs, but mostly he watches, leaning forward with me every time I bend to my microphone to sing backup, like he's afraid he'll miss something in a room lined with speakers. He laughs at Jax's onstage antics, and bobs his head in perfect time to Danny's bass.

One song disappears into the next, all of them a blur of Jacob's face and the galloping beat of my drums. Nothing has ever felt so perfect.

My arms scream and I can't feel my fingers. I push harder, gulping air as I rocket the rhythm toward the gut-wrenching finale of my favorite song. Danny's hanging easy, adjusting on the go so he can drop every deep note just where we need it, and then Jax howls the last line and we all break off at the same instant, the silence hitting like its own emphasis.

The crowd explodes.

People stand four deep around the bar and all the doors up front stretch open so our music can blast out into the street. I barely noticed the rest of the room once Jacob arrived, but we must be over capacity. The bouncer won't let anybody else in, even though there are a few dozen stragglers listening from the sidewalk.

I swipe the sweat off my forehead and steal a look at Jax. He got way too into the last song and now he's as winded as I am, gulping water. On the last swallow, it goes down the wrong tube and he chokes, water droplets flying from his mouth as he turns away from the crowd. *Shit.* I duck out from behind my drums and go to him.

"Hey, you okay?"

"Fine," he manages, before exploding into coughing, bracing his hands on his knees. His face is red from more than choking, and my chest twinges for him. This is so not in tune with the sex god image he's been building through the whole show, and I know how hard he's probably going to take it. More importantly, he'll need a break to calm his throat, but there's no way I'm wasting this kind of crowd energy, or giving anybody a lull to decide if they want to check out the rest of the pub crawl bands.

I lay a hand on Jax's back as he finally sucks in a breath, panting. "Take five. Danny and I can do our one duet."

"Nah, I'll be okay." He straightens, combing a hand through his hair to get it from thrashed back to gloriously tousled. His neck stiffens as he holds his breath to keep from bursting into another coughing fit.

I tilt my head, pouting. "Come on, I've been dying to do that one in public ever since everybody went crazy for it over at Jimmy T's." It's not just the water going down the wrong tube that's got him breathing hard, I can tell. My pulse has already slowed down, while he coughs into his hand and dashes more sweat off his cheek. This is a longer set then we've ever done before, and I force myself to run at least four days a week. Jax rides a desk and lifts weights, which keeps him pretty but doesn't do much for the cardio.

"You sure you're ready? You guys didn't rehearse that one."

I smile. "We're ready. Come on, let's show these guys we've got some range." I beckon to Danny. He frowns, but I mouth the name of the song, and his lips kick up at the corner. He nods.

Jax backs away from the stage with a flourish of his arms that redirects all the attention toward us, and Danny pulls his microphone stand up next to me.

Jacob strains right to the edge of the high stage now, a grin breaking across his face as I adjust the microphone stand down to my height. I wink at him, mouthing, *"You owe me..."* because he promised me a favor if he could hear me sing. He's getting lucky tonight, because it's rare for me to take center stage. This song isn't even on the normal set list because it's so different from our other stuff. And because I won't let Jax perform it.

Most of the time, I like that Jax's voice, his identity, is the shield between my soul on a piece of staff paper and all the strangers' ears it pours into. But this song is about Danny and me, and it wouldn't be right for anyone else to sing it.

Jacob's eyes warm when they touch mine, and I hold them even when nerves waver in my belly. A lot of guys get weird when they see how close I am to my male best friend. When I invited Jacob to see my band, though, I promised myself I was done making apologies. This is who I am, and if he doesn't like it, the exit is clearly marked. Besides, if there's any part of me I will never be ashamed to show in public, it's Danny.

Ducking my head closer to the microphone, I murmur, "Looks like a few of you boys need a slow song if you're gonna have any chance at getting lucky tonight. But don't worry, I've got your back."

Laughter ripples through the room and the between-song buzz dies down. "This one is called 'My Air.'"

I inhale, and the whole room goes so silent I can hear the traffic outside. When Danny plays a single soft note to key me into the song we created together, any hint of nerves is long gone. This, I can do.

I look over at the guy who has helped me clean up after every party I've ever had, and I begin to sing.

After we close the door
Kill the light and toss the key
We don't need them anymore

What would we be searching for?
Every corner wears the shape of you
From my ceiling to my floor

Feels like you live inside me
And you always find me

Toward the end of the first verse, the bass comes in, soft and inevitable. Danny watches me and never plucks a string until after I take a breath, so the sound vibrates out into the crowd like it's all coming straight out of my chest.

But there are days when this room is too small
And my heart's got no room to beat
'Cause with you seeing me, yeah seeing everything
Sometimes I can't remember how to be

When I first wrote this song, I worried that Danny would be offended by that verse: by the idea that sometimes, you can't really find out who you are until you're completely alone. I should have known better.

When the refrain comes, Danny leans in and starts to sing with me.

But I just don't know what I would do
Without you breathing my air
I don't know what I could do
Without you breathing my air

His voice carries mine, just like his bass did, shading in all my edges until every note is more distinct.

I don't look at Jacob. This moment is too raw, and nobody's ever understood this part. How music and Danny are all tied up with me, so if he died and I went deaf, I wouldn't just change, I would end.

Whatever I meant to say
Is on your lips before I speak
Like it's yours to take away

But whatever you steal or break
It's worth less than you here with me
So it's all yours to take

As much as I don't want to care, I can't stand not knowing Jacob's reaction. I finally drop my gaze to the front row, and he is rapt. There's not a hint of jealousy in his face, though his eyes run deep with emotion. I can't hear the street noise anymore, and the bartenders stand motionless, not a single order coming in.

No, I just don't know what I would do
Without you breathing my air
I don't know what I could do
Without you breathing my air

The finish spills out flawlessly, Danny's voice and bass a texture that wraps around me and whispers over every one of the upturned faces in the audience. In the front row, Jacob's eyes slip closed, his body poised like he's drinking every note in through his skin. It's the way I always listen to a new song: like it's a poem, a code. A prayer.

The whole room comes to its feet in applause, but I don't wave to them this time. That one wasn't for them. It was for me, for Danny. And maybe a little bit, for Jacob. Honesty thrown down like a gauntlet he just stepped over, like he didn't realize it was supposed to be a challenge. As if he never needed that song to be anything except what it was.

As I look out at the crowd, my body hums like a note perfectly struck and I can't help but think of Jax's words from yesterday. Maybe this, tonight, is how it is supposed to feel.

Because playing music alone is fun. Playing to a crowd is invigorating, their energy feeding your own. But playing to a crowd that includes someone who likes me *and* the music? It feels like something so lovely, I'm not sure I could ever get enough.

MICHELLE HAZEN

Chapter 13: A CRUEL KIND OF Beautiful

When I stomp the pedal for my bass drum at the end of our set, the sound hits me like applause. The crowd starts to hoot and scream, and it spreads throughout my whole body, creeping into that place way down deep where you always know if what you're doing is crap, or if this time, it's really fucking good. I ditch my drumsticks and stand up, soaking in their excitement through every inch of my skin.

Oh yeah. Me and this audience are gonna be besties. We're gonna roll up in Barbie Princess sleeping bags on the living room floor and roast s'mores over the kitchen burners and stay up all night giggling about Justin Bieber's abs.

Well, maybe not that last part.

I look for Jacob, and for the first time, he's not front and center. It throws me off, like his face has become my touchstone in the insanity of this packed bar. I look over at Danny. He's shrugged out of his bass and he tosses me a glance like, *"Um, what now?"* and I've got no freaking clue. Jax clings to his guitar, but we've already played two encores and you don't *get* encores with bar gigs. It'd be like taking a job cleaning toilets and asking if you can bring your butler.

Danny makes the decision for all of us, coming to pull me out from behind my drums. He gives me a little twirl across the stage as we head off, and excited whistles spike up through the applause.

When we get offstage, Jax turns with a whoop and reaches like he's going to pick me up but some girl dodges in between us and kisses him. I've never even seen her before, but Jax must have. He responds immediately, his tongue delving slow and deep as he translates the post-performance charge into pure pleasure.

I turn away and run my hands back through my hair, scraping my scalp with my nails. I'm not ready for this night to be over yet. I want to get back onstage, to take the words I scraped out of the darkest parts of me and howl them straight into a microphone. The sound guy queued up a sexy, thumping dance beat, and it's calling to me. I need to *move*.

I look around, but Jacob's nowhere in sight. I shove away the pang of loss that I didn't get to talk to him before he left. Danny comes up behind me and bends to my ear. "Fuck taking down. I'm gonna dance. You coming?"

It's the only way I get on a dance floor these days, with Danny's chest at my back a signal and a shield between me and every man in the crowd I no longer dare to want. But with this energy crackling up through my body, I know even that will end with me feeling achy and dissatisfied and lonelier than ever. I shake my head.

Danny slings an arm over my shoulder and hugs me into his side. His ribs deflate under an exhale that was probably a sigh. Just then, Jacob fights his way through the knot of people in front of us, and my face explodes into a smile that exactly matches the one shining on his.

"Hi!" Jacob shouts over the music.

I'm not sure, but I think I hear Danny chuckle. He gives my shoulder a squeeze before he steps forward, offering his hand to Jacob, who shakes it and yells something that looks like some form of congratulations. Danny leans in to Jacob, but he has to shout to be heard in here, so I catch it when he says, "Glad you showed up after all, friend." He smiles at me, a simple curve in the strobe-lit darkness of the room. Then he disappears onto the dance floor, leaving me alone with Jacob.

Nerves nibble at the edge of my buzz. How are we supposed to transition a brand new friendship from hanging out in front of my record player to a bar pumping with the sensual throb of dub step?

Jacob closes the space between us. He shakes his head as he looks down at me, his eyes alight in a way that matches everything amazing about this night. "Dance with me."

I read the words on his lips more than I hear them, and it's exactly the right thing to say, because I can't stand still. Not now, maybe not ever again. Grabbing his hand, I pull us into the crush of bodies, slick with sweat. Tonight the dance floor is awash in blood-colored light with spears of crystal white and Wizard of Oz green, adrenaline sharpening everything. Jacob sticks close despite the surge of the crowd that's so thick it's more like a mosh pit than a dance party. He leans back on strangers, trying to buy me a little bit of space. That works until I almost lose sight of him, and I decide I'd much rather have him too close than too far away. I reach out and grab his dark button-down, hauling him in tight to my chest.

The lights sketch shadows beneath his cheekbones and jaw, and I wonder if he's blushing. I start to move to the music, and the first time his hips nudge mine, it feels good and I remember that giving up guys wasn't supposed to be about being alone. It was supposed to be about being happy instead of making myself miserable trying to please everyone else. Besides, it's too crowded in here for him to misinterpret it if I enjoy an extra touch or two, for my hand on his hard-muscled side to be anything but holding onto a familiar body in a tide of limbs.

Somebody bumps Jacob, and his hand comes down to cover mine like he's afraid he'll lose my touch. The line of his belt burns into my palm, his hipbone hard underneath. I catch my breath and look up at him. He smiles and shouts something. I have no idea what it was, but I like the easy light in his eyes, the way he doesn't lose his rhythm when we're jostled by the other bodies around us.

He lifts his hand off mine, and my knuckles are cold when he goes. I hate to lose the link of touch between us. It feels like a free pass, like as long as we're touching, reality can't intrude and nothing we do is wrong. But then his hand cups the back of my neck, keeping us close and leaving my arms free to follow the beat as we dance. Our eyes lock in the darkness for a long second. I'm not sure he's breathing.

His fingers flex on the back of my neck, and I can all but feel how it'll be when his lips crash against mine. Except then he lets me go, catching my hand and spinning me so my back is to his chest. My hips settle into the crease of his, and something firm nudges my ass.

He doesn't grind into me, just keeps dancing, and awareness ripples across the entire back of my body. I want to feel that again.

Instead, his knuckles skim up my spine, then his palms trace my arms as he steps forward again. Our hands rise together into the air, fingers brushing together but not quite holding as our shoulders swing one way, then the other. I didn't think he'd be this bold, but every one of his touches is an invitation, not a demand. He never grasps or holds, and yet I find myself leaning into every brush of his skin against mine, hoping for more.

I need to see his expression, need to know if he's feeling that pull just like I am, so I turn to face him. His arms are there as soon as I do, cradling me so close that I get one more tantalizing brush of the hardness behind the fly of his jeans. His eyes gleam midnight dark in the flashing lights. They never leave my face, even when I see him swallow hard. Energy floods through me, and I can't remember a thing about playing it safe. I don't know if the beat grounding me is his heart, or mine, or maybe just the bass from the speakers. Right now, I love them all.

His hands are gentle and his body is rough, and I want *more*. I edge closer, and his thigh slips between mine, but even the press of his jean-clad knee isn't enough to soothe the heat building at the center of me. Just for a second, I let my forehead rest against the front of his dark shirt, and it jumps beneath my touch as he sucks in a breath. His palms melt down my arms.

It's too much, all the possibilities stampeding through my head, thickening the air between us. I'm so thirsty my tongue sticks to the roof of my mouth, and my body becomes a thousand degrees of heat, all burning at once. I can't think right now. I need to get some air, but I don't want to let go of this moment of perfect understanding, where everything is allowed and our world is made of all the same songs.

I lift my head and nod toward the bar but even as I do it, my hand inches toward his. As soon as one of my fingers brushes his, his hand jumps to grip mine. He doesn't let go when he turns toward the bar, and inexplicable relief expands through my throat. He never has to shove, because people move out of his way. I follow along in the wake of his broad shoulders.

I'm not sure what we're going to say to each other now. If he felt that shift, like I did, or if after a whole year of existing on only battery-operated touch, my hormones just roofied my brain. Maybe to him, that was just normal, everyday dancing.

In the end, I don't have to figure out what to say, because as soon as we get off the dance floor, people swarm forward to talk to me. It takes like two weeks to get to the bar, and I can't hear half of what they say, but I love the excitement in their faces. I even give an *autograph.*

I actually laughed at first when the girl asked me, and then felt like a total asshat when I realized she was serious. None of us had a pen and so I had to plow all the way over and borrow one from my *mom.* I'm fairly sure that's undignified enough to take all the shine off the whole thing, but right now I can't even consider feeling bad. About anything.

After a quick stop at the bar, I weave through people, sucking delicious ice water through my straw as I lead Jacob toward the front. He got all weird and twitchy when we went to order, so I just got water and he got nothing. Straight-edge? Drinking problem? Doesn't matter; nothing can puncture my mood as we pass the open archway to the foyer of the club. It's quieter out here, the couple of standing-height tables deserted as everyone collects by the bar and dance floor. Cold air rushes inside when the bouncer lets in one more person. Jacob leans back against the wall, dropping his head back as he lets out something like a laugh all knotted up in a groan.

I finish my water and leave it on an empty table, still riding the wave of all those fans' excitement as I grin at Jacob. "So, did you like the show?"

"Ah, hell." He laughs again. "I thought you guys would be good, but I didn't know you'd be that good."

I narrow my eyes and snort. "Thanks a lot, buddy."

He shakes his head. "You have no idea, and I have no words. It was just—" He pushes off the wall as he focuses completely on my face. He looks incredible in black, the fabric echoing the classic darkness of his hair and eyes. The man would rock a tux like an Armani model.

I came out front to cool off but instead warmth eases through me, melting all my sharp edges. Jacob showed up for me. I watched his face through every song, and I could tell he didn't just enjoy it, he *heard* it. He heard me in every chord I wrote, every word that was supposed to be disguised by Jax's throaty voice. I don't even know how to contain that knowledge, and my skin throbs with it like my whole body is a bruise of longing.

"When you sang that duet with your friend, and I really got to hear your voice for the first time..." Jacob falters into silence, and then he swallows. "Okay, remember my non-negotiable favorite band? It's Norah Jones."

My brows pop up. "Wait, what?"

He blushes a little. "Yeah, I know, everyone always laughs. But her voice just makes me feel..." He hesitates. "Like everything's going to be okay, you know? I've never found a voice I loved as much as hers until I heard you sing 'My Air,' and you said it so perfectly about what it's like to not be able to imagine life without someone, even though sometimes you wish—"

I kiss him.

I don't think about it, I don't even realize I'm moving closer. I only care about his lips. As soon as they touch mine, the air groans out of him and his hands come up and settle on either side of my face. I relax into their warmth, and his thumbs brush my cheekbones while the tips of his fingers stroke the strands of my hair. In that second, we're back on the dance floor all over again, and it's safe here.

When his tongue slides against mine for the first time, tingles echo all the way down my body, the muscles deep in my belly clenching. *This* is what I was yearning toward with every beat as we danced. This is what scrambled my thoughts and stole the breath out of my lungs. It wasn't the music, or even the heat of all those people around us.

It was him.

Jacob draws back just enough so I feel the loss before his mouth begins soothing mine all over again. Everything is so sweet and hot and fucking perfect, it isn't until my palm flattens against bare skin that I realize I've slid it beneath his shirt and *shit.*

I pull back, my wide eyes bouncing between his. He chuckles, low and deep and delighted. "I know, right?" he says, as if in agreement.

He cups one arm around my back and I close my eyes, terrified at how much I want to melt back into its strength and feel what it would be like to really be held by him. I need to remember that I don't do this stuff anymore, because this is the kind of thing that gets the word "tease" thrown at you like a hollow point bullet.

Jacob tucks my hair back behind my ear. "Okay, now you pretty much have to become a rock star and marry me." My eyes pop open and he grins. "Just so we can tell everybody our first kiss was because of the song that made you famous."

I jerk away, combing my hair frantically back as if that will put the last few minutes in order. "Jacob, I don't—"

He holds up his hands, his smile weakening. "Hey, I was just kidding. I promise I'm not going to start picking our future dog's names or anything."

"I have to go." I pat my pockets. Phone, lip gloss. No keys. I need car keys, stat.

Jacob blinks at me. "Hold on, Jera, you kissed *me*. Did you not want to...do that?"

As if I needed the reminder that it wasn't him who slipped. Of course it wasn't. The nicer the guy, the faster I screw it up because I try to be as good as them, as popular, as artistic, as sexually confident. Doesn't matter what it is, because I never measure up. Which is why I need to get out of here, except my keys are still up on stage along with my messenger bag. *Shit.* Whatever, my parents are probably still here, and they have a hide-a-key under the bumper of their Subaru Outback. I'll take their car, and sort out the police reports later.

I head for the door just as the bouncer opens it for someone, and I have to dodge to avoid getting hit in the face. Jacob catches my arm, pulling me over to the side.

"Hey, wait. Talk to me." He dips his head, trying to get me to look at him. "If I did something wrong, or if you didn't like that as much as I thought you did, just say so. I just...sometimes I forget to watch myself with you. But I didn't mean to freak you out and if I did, I'm really sorry."

Feet shuffle against the hard floor, and a buzz of conversation enters the foyer. I so don't want to be having this conversation, here or anywhere. I can still remember the shrinking sensation I had before the show, when I thought he wasn't going to show up. I don't want to bare myself to a man I care about, just to watch the interest leach out of his eyes night by excruciating night.

I won't put myself through that again.

I glance away and he says, achingly, "Jera…"

"It's nothing you did." I duck out from under his arm. It puts me farther from the door but it also puts me far enough away from Jacob so I can pretend to forget the way he smells like trees and open air and everything clean and beautiful. "I told you, I'm not looking for anything but a friend right now. That's all I want, all I can give you."

His eyes darken with hurt. "I'm not an idiot, Jera. I see the way you look at me. You don't want to be just friends any more than I do. I know you're not dating anyone and you—" He spreads his hands. "I thought you liked me."

I suck in a hard breath, guilt sucker-punching me straight in the chest. "I like you just fine, okay? As a—"

"Don't even say it. Look, I'm not in the greatest place to be dating either but that doesn't change how I feel. So give it to me straight, because I actually want to know. Why can't we?"

I've got no room to deflect, or even to misinterpret. He's asking for everything, and if I'm a mess about relationships, I'm a disaster wrapped in a plane crash when it comes to sex. How can I tell this *nude model* I'm such an ice cube in bed that my partners go cold right along with me? I'd rather tell him I have freaking AIDS. I glance at the door. Herpes, maybe? Would that be a less embarrassing lie?

He shoves his hands into his pockets, muscles flexing all down his arms. "I know you have a lot going on, with your music and school and everything, but why can't we at least try? I think we might be a freakishly good match. Like how you like the blue M&Ms best but I like yellow ones, and you said you thrash really bad in your sleep, but I could sleep through a tsunami."

If I thought my hands were trembling before, it's nothing compared to now. He's so damn sweet and I can't stand the thought that someday he might start to hate me, the way Andy did.

"Everybody's life is complicated. I—" He hesitates and changes tack. "We could make it work. We could."

I don't realize I'm shaking my head until his face falls. He pulls his hands out of his pockets, takes another step closer, and I nearly break for the back exit. Somewhere behind us, someone coughs.

"Did someone hurt you?" he says hoarsely. "Please tell me no one hurt you, Jera."

It's the gentleness that does it, because now I know what pain looks like in his eyes, and I never want to see it again. I'm quivering like my sins are crying out of my body all at once and then between one breath and the next, I just...snap.

"No one hurt me!" I explode. "I hurt people, Jacob, *I* do. You want to know why we can't date? Because yeah, it'd be great for a while. We'd laugh and fool around and you'd go to my shows but in the end it would just hurt more. It can't go anywhere after that, because I'm fucking *frigid*, okay? Do you really want a girlfriend who's bad in bed? Maybe you like me now but I promise it wouldn't last long after that."

And it's a mercy, really, because I don't have to watch Jacob's reaction after all. I'm crying too hard to see it. He only takes the briefest of instants to process all that before he speaks, ducking his head so his words are just between us.

"Is that what you've been worrying about? Jera, there's no way *you* could disappoint me in bed." He takes a breath but instead of explaining what he meant, he just shakes his head gently. "We're not even there yet, okay? We'll take it slow and I can tell you right now that wherever our relationship goes, we're never going to do anything you don't want to do."

He sounds so much like Andy did in the beginning that the tears blind my eyes all over again. And I know, I fucking know sex isn't the only thing I screw up with guys. But it's the red, beating heart at the center of everything I've got no clue how to solve.

"Yeah, maybe that's how it would start." I pull my phone out of my pocket, ripping out the earbuds and punching the buttons that pull up my voicemail. If I'm going to disappoint him anyway, I'm going to do it right now, while we're both still clothed. "But you want to hear how it ends?" I slap my phone against his chest. "*That's* how it ends."

I leave my phone behind and walk out of the bar without keys or a wallet or even a coat, escaping toward the parking lot while Jacob listens to Andy's recorded voice saying he can't perform with any girl now, not just me. Telling me he doesn't even feel like a man anymore, and he doesn't know how he's supposed to live out the rest of his life like this.

And it is all my fault.

Shit, it's freezing out here. Portland in October usually isn't bad, but my sweat-dampened tank top offers no protection from the cold wind whipping past the tall lampposts that light the parking lot. Where did my parents park, Canada?

A hand touches my goosebumpy arm, and a sob sticks in my throat. No, no, no. I can't face Jacob right after he heard Andy's humiliating voicemail. I rip my arm free and keep going.

"I'm sorry. Miss?" The voice is deeply uncomfortable. And it does not belong to Jacob.

I shove tears off my face and allow myself one quick sniffle before I turn around.

It's a man wearing a sharp-collared dress shirt, looking both calmer and older than the rest of tonight's crowd. To his credit, his hairline is only receding a little. "That was an incredible show you played tonight."

At any other time, that compliment would have made my whole week. "Thanks." I manage something in the neighborhood of a smile and turn back around, scanning past Priuses and a metric shit-ton of identical Subaru Outbacks. With my luck tonight, I'll steal the wrong white Subaru with its keys hidden oh-so-sneakily under the bumper and it'll end up belonging to someone who isn't genetically required to forgive me.

The man steps into my field of vision again. "Hold on a second. Could I buy you a drink, so we can talk?"

Seriously, Grandpa? You're gonna hit on me right *now*? I only turn back halfway, my eyes still scanning the rows of cars. "Sorry, I have to get going."

He grimaces. "This is obviously a bad time, and I hate to bother you, but I can't find either of your bandmates."

Of course he can't. Jax always vanishes for a while after shows, and Danny's almost as bad. I know exactly where they disappear to. Even if I don't always know who they disappear with.

"I didn't want to leave without talking to someone from the band, but you seemed, um, busy." He clears his throat.

Was this guy standing there, waiting to talk to me when Jacob and I had our blowup? I remember that awkward cough in the foyer. My face burns. Great. I finally get a fan eager enough to follow me outside and I shout out that I'm frigid. A fact he will probably plaster all over the internet tomorrow. Could this night possibly suck any worse?

He takes a card out of his pocket and offers it to me. "We can talk later, if another time would be better. I'm Rob Righetti, with Amp Records."

Oh shit, oh God, I just gave the brush-off to a freaking label scout. Jax is going to dismember me.

"Now." I gulp. "Now is great."

"I liked your set." Rob smiles, holding up the two CDs we had for sale at the bar tonight as evidence. The top one is our latest self-release, the cover featuring an artsy black and white picture of Danny's right hand on his frets, the focus on the bass clef tattoo on his index finger. "We'd like to hear more from you."

I nod. Yes. I will play him all of the music. Right now.

"Do you have a demo of anything you haven't released yet?"

"Yes, yup. Three songs." They're not exactly recorded yet but I will do that immediately, in this parking lot, if it means getting them in front of a real record label. The wind gusts and I shiver and hug my arms over my chest, cupping his business card in my hand so I won't crease it.

"Is that bass and voice duet included in the three? I would very much like to hear that one with some studio balance added." He glances at his watch. "I'm so sorry to gab and run, but I've got a plane to catch. Send me those three songs and the duet as soon as you can, and we'll talk more after I give them a listen."

"Yes, I will absolutely do that. Thank you so much. I'm uh— sorry I was busy earlier." I wince.

"No big deal." He winks at me. "Emotions always run hot in the music industry. Send me that demo, okay?" He walks away, shoes quiet on the asphalt.

I gulp in a deep breath. A chance at a record deal. My wildest dream dressed in a pin-striped collar with no tie, right after I just put my heart through the wringer for another guy.

This is a sign. The timing is so perfect it can't be anything else. I'm never going to be able to have a relationship. But I can have a band, and maybe I can fill myself up with music until I hardly notice all the other empty spaces anymore.

It's just that every time we finish a set, it leaves sensuality pumping through the room, like rock music is the air that sex needs to breathe. For the last couple years, it's been a taunt, a Catch-22. I can perform the music I love, thrive on doing what I'm better at than any other thing in the world. And yet the aftermath always reminds me of the thing I'm worst at, the most intrinsic way I'm defective.

135

I stare down at the business card in my shaking hand with tears still drying on my cheeks. There's no doubt it's a brilliant, crazy world we live in.

It's just a cruel kind of beautiful.

Chapter 14: RACCOON GNAWED ROMANCE

What do you do after the best and worst day of your life?

Apparently, you listen to everyone in your life nag you with eighteen different iterations of "What did the label scout say again?" and then you go to work.

One single shift and a double. Sixteen hours straight in the studio to nail four songs. Two skipped classes you don't mention to your mother. Several hundred ignominiously borrowed dollars from your father to pay for said studio time. Add all that to putting up with a lifetime's worth of muttering about how the only song specifically requested was the only one that didn't include his voice, and maybe it's understandable if you end the weekend by attempting to strangle your lead singer with a dish towel.

When the record label calls to set a meeting after only two days, it's worth it. Everything is worth it, and I hate that even in the midst of the best news I've ever had, I can't stop thinking about Jacob. Most nights, I stay up writing songs with Danny just so I won't have to go home and face the darkness of my own windows.

By Friday, I'm so exhausted I don't even remember going to sleep. One minute, I'm going cross-eyed trying to concentrate on my homework while I count down the seconds until our meeting with Amp Records, and the next I wake up with freezing legs and pain bulleting through my back. An abandoned textbook and an afghan cover my chest, the bottom of the blanket kicked onto the floor.

I stretch my neck, wincing at the kink it always gets from sleeping on the tiny couch, with its armrest that's just a couple of inches too tall for comfort. Afternoon light streams through the shades on my brand-new window, but if a sound woke me up, I hear no trace of it now.

I lift my textbook and peek at the page number to check how far I got. Not far enough. Groaning, I drop the book back down and rub my eyes. I have a deathly feeling there will be a quiz on these chapters tomorrow. I'll just lie here for another minute and then I'll take a shower and get ready for the meeting. I pull the blanket back up over my legs. Granna's old afghan has a comforting weight to it, all the yards of yarn cuddled around my body. I don't even realize I've started to doze again until a shuffling sound outside the door rouses me.

Who would be out there so close to the door without ringing the bell?

My heart lurches and I'm suddenly fully awake. Every day since the concert, Jacob has left something on my porch. The first morning, he returned my phone, hiding it under my newspaper so no one would steal it. He erased Andy's ancient voicemail and left a new one in its place. I stared at Jacob's name gleaming on my screen, every letter curved, gentle with no sharp edges, and I knew without a shadow of a doubt that if I listened to his voice, I'd crumble. I'd go chasing after him and pretty soon, I'd be ditching band practice to work on cars, spending Friday nights with his old baseball teammates instead of Jax and Danny.

The best way to keep from losing myself again is to keep from trying altogether.

I just wish he'd stop tempting me. The second day after the concert, he left me another voicemail, two text messages, and knee socks with drums all over them. The third day, soup.

Gluten-free lentil soup.

It was the only item in Jacob's grocery cart when he was pretending to shop so he'd have an excuse to run into me. I tried not to read too much into that but really, what else could it have meant? It's not like he's concerned about me needing a low-carb, high-protein diet.

Except what kind of guy would realize the symbolism of something like that, and even if he did, how could he have known I took note of what was in his basket before he put it back?

Something scratches from outside, then something almost. . .crunchy. What the hell is Jacob doing? Is he waiting out there?

I rub my eyes, grimacing. "Yeah right, Jera. One kiss and he's camping on your doorstep, for sure."

Obviously, I need some caffeine to help rein in my fantasies. Still, I'm not imagining the sounds from outside. They are distinct, and distinctly bizarre.

I toss away the one corner of the afghan that still covers me and retrieve the textbook that dropped between the cushions, marking my place before I lay it on the floor. Combing my fingers through the tangles in my hair, I pad over to the door and squint through the peephole.

Nothing.

I lean my forehead against the cool wood of the front door. There's no way it's anyone but Jacob, even though it's way past newspaper-delivering time. I texted him once, to say thanks for bringing back my phone, and sorry, for everything. I don't dare do more, because I don't want to lead him on and I already proved I'm not capable of being just friends. But it's only been a week, and every part of my body is sore from the effort of not responding. From pretending it will stop hurting as soon as he stops trying. As far as he knows, he's making no progress. But when I'm up late, my willpower melts with the stroke of midnight and I end up typing his name into Google.

He is, possibly, the only student enrolled at Portland University who doesn't have a Facebook page or Twitter account, and I still haven't located the pictures of him drunkenly playing soccer on top of the Earth Sciences building. Mostly, the world has taken notice of him through the sports section. I've read the articles about different baseball games so many times that I know his stats by heart, even though I still haven't worked up the motivation to Wiki my way into decoding them. I know enough to understand he could have had a career in the major leagues without even a passing glance into a college classroom. There are articles about his parents' car accident but that feels too morbid, so I haven't opened those.

A scrabbling noise from outside yanks my head up. That sounded like *claws*.

I undo the lock and open the door. Something disappears into the bushes with a flash of movement but I don't catch what it is, because my attention is too focused on the. . .thing. . .on the porch.

Next to my newspaper is something white and chunky, with smears of darker liquid clumped into the wreckage. I edge a little closer, squinting at the white stuff. Some of it is melting and yes. . .okay, that's ice, but what is the rest of this junk? Against my better judgment, I pinch a little between my fingers and it crumples easily. Styrofoam.

I drop my hand, mystified as I stare at the wash of destroyed Styrofoam and ice stretching across my concrete stoop and down both steps.

Then I notice a slice of chocolate-covered almond in the midst of the melting goo. The pieces start to make sense all at once, and a smile breaks across my face.

Jacob told me he was going to make it up to me about the ice cream that liquefied in my trunk while we were in that coffee shop. I refroze it and we tried to eat it when he brought his record collection over but it was pretty gross and we made do with M&Ms instead. He must have decided to follow through on his promise. He bought a foam cooler, filled it with ice, and nestled a half gallon of mocha almond fudge in the center.

I start to laugh. Somebody forgot to tell dear Jacob that in this neighborhood, we have raccoons. And they happen to be quite fond of grand gestures that involve mocha, almond, or fudge.

Still grinning, I go to get the trash can from the kitchen. When I get back, I find most of the carton in the bushes with the edges nibbled and a lot of ice cream still left inside. I pick it up gingerly, wondering if you can get any diseases from touching raccoon-licked cardboard.

A glimpse of pale yellow catches my eye as I go to drop the ice cream into the trash. I pause, setting down the trash can so I can turn the carton in my hands. The yellow is a miraculously undamaged Post-It note, stained with flowerbed dirt and drips of melted ice cream. In cramped boy-handwriting and blue ink it says: *Ice cream for your thoughts? There's more where this came from if you're willing to make the trade.*

I stand there with the gnawed carton of ice cream, my slept-on hair standing up in at least three of the cardinal directions, and yesterday's poorly-fitted shirt starting to slip sideways on my shoulder. And I have never felt more *wanted* in all my life.

He came to my concert. Not only that, he understood my music. My thumb traces his note, as if I can feel him through the lines of his handwriting. I lean against the doorframe and exhale.

God, what am I supposed to do? I'd be a thousand times safer with some tattooed bad boy than I am with a sweet, thoughtful guy like Jacob, because he makes me want to *try* again, and I don't think I can survive any more failures when it comes to men.

Swallowing against the lump in my throat, I take the garbage with me when I retreat inside. I need to take a shower and get to this record label meeting, because I think music might be the last safe thing left for me to care about.

Chapter 15: BUYING LOCAL

A mp set the meeting to take place at an upscale restaurant boasting only locally-sourced food. As we're waiting for the hostess to find our party, I lean over to Danny.

"Do you think it's a bad sign they don't recognize the irony of meeting in a local foods restaurant to talk about picking up a local band and taking it international?"

He only smiles. "I think if they give me a great big stage and let me play my bass on it, I'll find that a damn good sign, Jimi. That's what I think."

"Right this way…" The hostess gestures with a sweep of her hand and we follow her to a round booth in the back. The label scout is already waiting, wearing a slim, hipster blazer with another open-collared shirt, accompanied by a woman with blond hair done in a style that's trying a little too hard to be casual.

The woman looks up and beams a smile at us. "Hello! Hello, hello." She stands up. "So nice to see you all. This is Rob Righetti, from the A&R Department."

Rob nods at me and smiles. My stomach twists as I remember the awkwardness on his face when he stopped me in the parking lot. This meeting would be intimidating enough but spending the whole thing second-guessing what he overheard of my argument with Jacob? Stab me now, please.

"I'm Kari Nichols, from the PAR department." She must have seen the crease forming in my forehead because she adds, "That's Public and Artist Relations. Most places just call it PR, but here at Amp, we believe it's not just the public's opinion of you that matters but the *relationship* we want to build between our artist and their fans. I know, I know, it's a tall order for one little acronym." She giggles.

Dad laughs along with her, too heartily, and I cover my wince with a smile. I've been dreading this part ever since I got the call about the meeting. The part where we introduce ourselves and everybody realizes I brought my daddy along.

Kari enthuses all the way through the introductions, though it throws her a little bit when Rob recognizes Dad's name and she doesn't. I have to admit, I enjoy watching her try to prompt Rob into dropping Dad's band name without directly asking what it was. Plus, it distracts everyone from the awkwardness while we all do the bouncy-slide move to scoot into the giant round booth. A move that sucks extra for me, because Jax made me wear a skirt.

"So." Kari folds her hands on the table with a click of her sparkling rings, and leans forward. "We love your music. We *love* it!"

Rob smiles. "Your demo is getting passed all around the company. Even the secretarial pool was fighting over it."

My shoulders tighten. Did he tell anyone what he overheard? So many of those songs have to do with what I went through after Andy and I broke up, and anybody who knew that would interpret them much differently.

"Your hooks are addictive without being cheap, and your instrumentals are top-notch." Rob nods. A tingle of excitement breaks through, and I peek over at him.

"Not to mention that voice!" Kari pretends to fan herself, and then points a flirty sidelong look toward Jax. "I love it," she says again. "I *love* it!"

"Well, thank you, that's really good to hear." Jax gives her a smile whose panty-dropping powers are probably short-circuiting work productivity all the way to the Washington border. I take a sip of water to hide my smirk when Kari's eyes widen.

"And your lyrics..." Rob stops and he curls his fist in front of him, as if he's about to pound it on the table to make a point.

I find myself holding my breath in spite of myself.

"Your lyrics..." he says again, his tone awed.

"Yes, your *lyrics*!" Kari beams.

My eyes narrow and Danny's knee bumps mine under the table. Shit.

It's not just me, then. These people sound kind of fake. Does Rob even remember our show? Did Kari hear the demo at all? But he chased me down in a parking lot, and they set this meeting so fast. Somebody must have really liked it, right?

"I'm glad you enjoyed it," Danny says. "If you remember—did you have a favorite song?"

"'My Air,'" Kari answers without hesitation.

Oh hell, please don't say that in front of Jax...

At the same time, Rob says, "'Delilah.'"

The waitress interrupts to take drink orders. I shoot a glance at Jax and his smile is as plastic as I've ever seen. Jeez, why can't he be happy for all of us? We're a band. We're supposed to be in this together.

While the waitress is still taking drink orders, Kari starts talking over her to say to Jax, "Oh, yes, 'Delilah,' too."

The waitress raises her voice. "I'm sorry, did you say Dr. Pepper or Diet *Pepsi?*"

"It's nothing short of brilliant delivery of top notch lyrics," Kari says, and Jax holds perfectly still, absorbing her every syllable. "Especially the one line at the end where it hints the women may be just as lost as the men. That they know not what they do and all their sins come from a place of misguided innocence. I love it," she adds. "I *love* it!"

I glance at Rob, then down, hoping nothing in those lyrics rang a bell with him after overhearing me yell to the whole damn world that I was frigid. But then, who cares what he knows? These record execs can quote our lyrics after *two days*. Suddenly, I want to pause this entire meeting so I can sneak a quick fist pump, shout, "Take that, bitches!" and possibly drape myself in a feather boa.

Danny's hand fumbles for mine under the table. He ends up grabbing just my wrist and the base of my thumb, and he holds on so hard I almost flinch. My heart flutters as I realize he's excited, too. Maybe more excited than I've ever seen him. I try to fold my fingers down enough to squeeze back, but don't get there before he lets me go and takes a placid sip of water.

"We think your music has so much potential," Rob says. "With a little guidance, we think you guys could be groundbreaking."

"Right, of course." Dad nods. "It's so important to young musicians to have the help and support of knowledgeable industry professionals such as yourself."

Um, what? Am I having a nightmare in which my iconoclastic dad became a kiss ass?

"And they have *you*, of course," trills Kari, who didn't even recognize his damn name.

"You guys had some ideas for our new album?" Jax's face is very neutral.

"Well, just brainstorming, really." Rob pushes his water aside so he can rest his elbows on the table. "It's obvious you guys have already thought about breaking out of the bounds of traditional rock and roll. I bet you've been talking about adding a keyboardist, maybe a little synth sound to offset your classic rock guitar roots with a modern flair."

I will not glare at my father in a professional meeting.

I will not glare at my father in a professional meeting.

I will not glare at my father in a professional meeting.

I will not... but what the fuck? Did he *tell* them to bring up the damn keyboardist? We do not need a keyboardist.

"I mean, I can already *hear* you guys hinting toward that modern edge." Kari leans in closer. "I really think a synth could bring that intention around to completion."

What in the ham sandwich did she just say?

"It's not that we haven't played with the possibilities of a synthesizer." The calm in Danny's speech manages to project the idea of politeness, despite his words. "It's just that we prefer a classic rock interpretation. Little bit of blues influence, contemporary lyrics. That is our sound."

Aaand...bitch slap, wrapped in a flaky pastry crust. My best friend is such a badass.

He nailed it though—it's not that we hate synthesizers. It's more that in today's market, a synth is just a gateway drug, and then you start sampling and looping until your entire song is two lines of lyrics and a catchy beat. I'm not interested in making repetitive garbage. Is that what we're going to have to do if we sign this deal?

"It's so early in your career, though." Rob raises his eyebrows. "I mean, you always want to leave yourself room for artistic growth, and the market is exploding right now with new uses for synthetic sound."

Kari laughs. "Right, right! You're *artists.* The worst thing you can ever do for your creativity is to pigeonhole yourselves."

"It's like what Hendrix did for the guitar." Rob looks to Dad for support. "Old instrument, all new potential."

So wait, they want us to be "groundbreaking" by following an existing trend? Do they need a freaking dictionary?

The waitress comes back with drinks and we order food, though my stomach is in such turmoil right now, I can't even consider eating.

When the waitress leaves, Kari leans forward again. "Let's talk about 'My Air.'" Kari drops her hand from where she was toying with her necklace. "It is an absolutely unique addition to your repertoire, and one I found personally very touching."

Let me guess. She loved it. *Loved* it.

"Jera's a very talented songwriter," Danny says, the plain honesty in his voice clashing with Kari's too-frequent changes in inflection. "We're lucky to have her."

Oh jeez. I'm like one big mood swing today, and I'm wearing eye makeup. Not ideal if Danny's going to be sweet.

"She's also quite a talented singer." Rob looks between Jax and me. "Have you ever experimented in your live shows with swapping back and forth between female and male leads for different songs?"

"Not much at this point, no," Jax says. "Don't you think that would be confusing to an audience? I mean, it's a totally different sound. Her voice is—" He glances at me. "No offense, Jera. You've got a hell of a set of pipes but they don't sound very rock and roll."

I quash a sudden desire to give him an energetic poking with my fork. He just *had* to cut me down in front of these two executives who were complimenting my sound. What pisses me off even more is he's right.

Dad and I have talked about it in exactly those terms before. I have a very feminine, singer/songwriter voice. A voice for love songs, not for the kind of heavy-hitting, bass-forward songs I like to write, and I can't exactly pull off the throaty growl that made **AVA** a rock goddess.

"Most rock bands have a soft song or two on each album," Rob says. "Even rappers hire female vocalists to sing backup for contrast."

I bite the inside of my lip, not wanting to speak before I'm sure what side I'm on. It would be fun to sing a little more, change it up a bit. I just don't want Jax to get all fidgety because he thinks I'm trying to steal his glory. He's so much more confident in the spotlight than I am, and a pro when it comes to handling a crowd.

"We'd love to hear a track where *you* and Jera do a duet." Kari turns her full wattage on Jax. "You two together could really light up a stage."

"There are several songs where she sings backup for him," Dad says. "They came out beautifully."

"Maybe we could change up the mix, bring Jera's part forward," Rob says. "And her voice would work really well with the synth. A smooth slide, if you will." He smiles. "These are all great ideas, folks. It's nice to work with a band where it doesn't seem like their last album was everything they had to put on the table."

My hand falters as I reach for my soda. These are pretty much all their ideas, not ours. Though I guess the change with "My Air" was mine, and I do love how that song came out. Whatever Danny says, the brilliance of it is in his bass playing, in the way he times everything and pitches each note just right so his deep voice supports mine without overpowering. Crap, I should have said that when we were talking about the song.

"I think this creative partnership could be a really positive collaboration," Dad says. "Your label has a talent for developing some truly exciting artists, especially in the last few years. The Red Letters are looking for a label that can guide them toward building a following without being confined to the tried and true paths."

Jax is watching him, nodding along, and my nose twitches. I have to hand it to Dad, that statement was like refrigerator magnet poetry made out of terms from all the bullshit business-speak the Amp execs have been oozing. Is Dad buying in or is he making fun of them?

Never in my wildest dreams did I think I'd be sitting here at twenty-one with an actual record label, but if I stand up for our sound, will they walk away?

"I assume you brought a preliminary version of the contract?" Dad settles further into his seat.

"Of course." Rob turns to the briefcase sandwiched on the bench between him and Kari. He passes out copies and I flip through mine.

I have no idea what most of this means. Probably because I should have been looking up record deal terminology this week instead of pictures from Jacob's old baseball games. But then, does it matter? We're so lucky to have any kind of offer, and I want somebody who can help me take my music to the next level. If Amp can do that, I'd sign anything they gave me. The problem is, I can't tell right now *what* they want from me.

Danny nudges me, and I realize it's probably really rude to read through the contract in the meeting. I move to put it in my messenger bag, then remember Jax vetoed that particular wardrobe accessory. Folding the paper, I tuck it under my leg.

The waitress brings the food. The rest of the meeting passes in a blur of flattery and exciting but non-specific talk about stadium shows and the droolingly fancy recording studio we'll be using to record our first album with Amp.

I keep my mouth closed until we get out of the restaurant, into the car, and Dad puts it in gear to back away.

"Am I the only one who is freaking out here?" I explode. "I mean, what was that? Was that good or bad?"

"Did they actually listen to our songs?" Jax twists to face me from the front seat. "Or just 'My Air' and 'Delilah'?"

"Did they *like* them?" I grimace. "Or was that all just blowing smoke?"

"They liked them," Dad says. "Or they wouldn't have set up the meeting in the first place. You have to understand, these guys are really busy, and they listen to a ton of new bands every week. The fact that they can remember the names of two of your songs is a positive thing."

"Okay." I sit back and take a breath. "Cool. So what about the contract? Does it totally suck? Do we negotiate? *Can* we negotiate?" Longing aches in my throat every time I think about the studio they mentioned. It's horrible wanting something this much and having so little control over how it will turn out.

"Will it scare them off if we push back?" Jax asks. "What was all that stuff about changing our sound? Do they want us to be completely different, or were they talking just a small thing here or there?"

"Does that go in the contract?" I ask Dad. "Can we specify our amount of creative control? How would you even quantify that? Do we need a lawyer?"

He turns on his blinker and watches the traffic coming the other direction. "We already have my lawyer, and he's well-versed with entertainment contracts. I didn't get a chance to look at what they gave us but my guess would be it's pretty bad. You're unknowns right now, so all the bargaining power is theirs. They want you enough to offer, so we've got that, but they can walk away at any time. You have no idea how many other bands they might be courting."

I try to dry my palms against my bare legs. "What about the music? Do they want us to change it? How much? I always hoped to work with a record label that could help us expand, but the ideas they were throwing out weren't exactly clicking with me. I mean, I wouldn't mind singing a little bit more but Jax is the voice of the band."

"Right." Jax blows out a breath. "I guess we could use a little synth, but I don't want to go electronica."

"No synth," Danny and I say in unison, then glance at each other.

"I told you a keyboardist would expand your range," Dad says, "and you know if you're serious about making a career out of music, you're going to have to make compromises."

My fingers clench on my seatbelt. I know he wants me to have the career he couldn't, but this is *my* band. "A keyboardist is a big compromise because it'll change our sound entirely. I was thinking about violin, maybe even electric violin, but I don't know anybody else who plays and I haven't had time to set an audition. Do you think they'll let us try out a violin?"

"Look, this is your first album," Dad says. "You won't have full creative control, no matter what they tell you and no matter what the contract says. It's their label. They decide what they put out with their name on the back."

"Yeah, but it's our name on the *front*." I lean forward against my seatbelt. "Can't we ask how much they actually want changes and how much of that was just tossing around ideas?"

Dad shakes his head as he pulls out into traffic. "They'll never give you a straight answer. They want you to sign, and they'd rather manipulate than negotiate. It's the reason my band quit our label. They'll make the answer sound like whatever you want to hear, but they always get the final say. That's just how the game is played."

"We can't walk away from this deal." Jax shoves a hand through his hair. "I'm warning you guys, though, I'm not going to let them push me out."

"Nobody's trying to push you out, Jax." I rub my eyes. "This isn't all about you, okay?"

"Easy for you to say. You're the one they were fawning all over in there."

I take a sharp breath to argue, but Dad cuts in. "Hey, the flattery is just part of the game. On all sides. They liked all you guys or they wouldn't be here."

"Danny, what do you think?" Jax twists to look back at him.

My best friend is sitting calmly like he always does, one ankle resting across his opposite knee. But he's wearing his good shoes—the shiny ones I haven't seen him put on for anyone since graduation—and his eyes are dark and pained.

The only sound is from the traffic outside as Dad drives and we all wait.

"I don't know," Danny says. "I just don't know."

Chapter 16: SURPRISE

I power down on the pedals of my bike to make it over the last big hill, and I consider whether I might be a bad person. Because I'm wondering if Jacob left me anything new after his heart breaker of an ice cream present yesterday.

My street seems longer than usual, my legs heavy from lack of sleep. I was up all night on my laptop, playing with adding keyboard effects and synth to our old songs with my bedroom door locked as if Danny might be able to hear me from clear across town.

The last thing I can handle today is another perfect gift from Jacob, when I'm already teetering on the edge of compromising everything about the life I've spent a year building.

He's never stopped calling, and I had to set the ringer to silent to keep my fingers from itching to answer. No matter what tricks I use, though, there's a certain feeling I get when his name appears on my screen: a hit of pure excitement and guilt all at once. Lovely and ugly and addictive as all hell.

Yeah, I'm probably a bad person.

Admitting that doesn't keep me from indulging in my new favorite game, starting by looking away from my front door when I coast up to my house on my bike. The builders were too cheap to put a roof over the tiny cement stoop and its two steps, so instead they pushed it in under the main roof of the house, making a little cubbyhole set in from the outside. This means I can put away my bicycle in the garage, walk around to the front, and savor the reveal of whatever surprise he left me like I'm slowly opening a birthday present.

Today my prize is... Christ, it's Jacob. He sits with his back against one wall, legs stretched out and crossed at the ankles, his head resting against the doorjamb. He doesn't move when I come into view, and as I edge closer I realize he's asleep.

I hug my arms around myself, the flush of heat from my bike ride starting to give way to the damp chill in the air. Jacob is wearing a long-sleeved cotton tee shirt, and it's late October with storm clouds throttling the sky. How is he warm enough to sleep?

I swallow, hesitating. If I wake him up, we'll argue. It's inevitable, because I can't say yes to any question he's here to ask me. I'm not naïve: I know Andy and Jacob might not have the same reaction to my issues in bed. But even if Jacob didn't lose confidence in his own ability to please a woman, sooner or later he'd want more from a relationship than I can give him.

Still, I can't leave him out here in the cold.

"Jacob." I almost flinch at the sound of my own voice. "Jacob, hey, wake up."

No response. He must be exhausted. I wonder if something went wrong with his family again, if that nebulous "something" has been keeping him too busy to sleep.

I take a step and speak a little louder this time. "Jacob!"

Nothing. Wow. I take a steadying breath and tell myself that touching his arm to rouse him is the only polite thing to do. I crouch down, the curve of his shoulder fitting gently into my palm, and for a second I forget I'm supposed to be waking him up. I love how warm he always is.

It's a stupid thing to be fond of, someone's body temperature. You may as well get misty-eyed over their toenail shape. Except Danny's always so hot it's a little intense, and Jacob's a more soothing kind of warm. Like a hot bath, or chamomile tea.

I call his name again, and shake him a little. Even when his head lolls against the siding of the house, he doesn't budge. Fear fists inside my chest. Is he drunk, or on some kind of drugs? I check his pulse. It's strong and steady, so I grab both his shoulders and pull him away from the wall, half-shouting his name.

He blinks, eyes soft and vague with sleep, but a smile spreads across his face when he sees me. "Oh, hey."

I let go of him and sit back on my heels, exhaling a breath that sags my shoulders just as the first drops of rain splatter the sidewalk. "Jacob, what are you doing?"

He glances around, stretching his back with a wince. "Waiting for you. I guess I misjudged your class schedule a little bit."

"You were so out of it I had to take your *pulse*. You scared the hell out of me!"

He reaches over and massages his right shoulder, and his eyes fall hazily toward his knees. "Sorry. I'm kind of beat. Must have dozed off. What time do you think it is?"

"When was the last time you slept?"

He blinks, then scrubs a hand over his face.

"That's what I thought you were going to say." I push to my feet, holding a hand out to help him up.

He unthinkingly accepts my help, and his weight nearly topples both of us. He catches me, blinking again. "Sorry."

I pull my keys out of my bag and open the door. "Come inside. You're not even fit to bike right now."

He follows me all the way to my room before he pauses, tentatively touching a hand to the doorframe.

"You need to sleep. And to be honest, my couch sucks." I nod toward my bed, which is—thank God—actually made for once.

"Jera..."

I can't meet his eyes. He takes a step into my room and I clear my throat, edging around him toward the door. As I grasp the doorknob, I risk one glance at him.

Jacob searches my face. "You'll still be here?"

I want to tell him my answer can't be any different when he wakes up, that we obviously can't keep it platonic and we're doomed to failure at anything beyond that. But he looks so tired, so I just nod and close the door softly between us.

Shrugging off my overloaded messenger bag, I leave it in the kitchen and go out through the side entrance to the garage. Rain mists onto the pavement outside the rolled-up door, and I head out into the drizzle, scanning until I find Jacob's bicycle propped in the bushes beside the front door. Its wheels squeak as I walk it inside so it can dry out, his handlebars much higher than my own when I prop the bikes up together.

My drums beckon from the corner, promising me a clear head: all the emotions aching through my body cleaned out with the beat of an honest rhythm. Except I don't want to wake Jacob. I hit the button for the garage door and go back into the house, kicking off my shoes so my steps will be quieter.

If he's been too busy to sleep, he probably hasn't been getting enough to eat either. I suppose it would send all the wrong signals if I made him some soup before he left. Gluten-free, totally platonic soup.

I fall into a chair at my kitchen table, dropping my head into my hands with a grimace. Who am I kidding? Like putting him in my bed wasn't already sending the wrong signal? But I can't drive him home because his bike won't fit inside my car, so I at least need to make sure he's rested enough to safely negotiate the streets. I've been trying to protect both of us by staying away from him, but I think in his current state, traffic is definitely the greater danger.

I take a deep, cleansing breath, but I can't stop thinking about him on my porch, waiting for me for hours. The hard concrete of my stoop is so uncomfortable it would keep most people from dozing off but not Jacob. Most times I've seen him, he's been riding the near edge of exhaustion from all his jobs, school, and playing quasi-parent to his little brother, too.

He's a shining example of everything I used to try to be, only he's not crumbling under the pressure the way I did. If I'm around him, I don't know how I'll keep from slipping into my old patterns.

I honestly don't know what it is about me that chases guys away. If they'd stay if I were the Kama Sutra Queen, or if it has to do with me wanting to talk music longer than any of them, or maybe it comes off as clingy when I try to enjoy their hobbies. I don't know why I can have orgasms when I'm alone but never—not once—with another person in the room. Maybe I'm just not built to connect to someone else, physically or otherwise.

I pick at one of Granna's old flowered placemats as the sound of the synth from last night plays through my head, jarringly out of touch with the classic chords of the guitar beneath it.

Would it be worth it to try again instead of attempting to ignore everyone else's opinion of me?

For Jacob? For Amp Records?

Is there any way to have either of them and still hang onto the things about myself and my music that I've come to actually like?

Jacob and I already have more in common than I did with most of my boyfriends, and we have the same sense of humor. Maybe with a guy like him, I wouldn't have to make myself over into something new to keep him interested. But even if that went okay—and it's a great big if—nothing past platonic has ever worked out for me.

It's not that I dislike sex: at its worst, it's uncomfortable and lonely. At its best, it is vibratingly, achingly frustrating because I can get so worked up without ever getting the release at the end.

Maybe I could fake it.

The worst of the trouble with Andy started when I told him I was having a problem. It's not like he even noticed on his own. Jacob already knows about me, but the first few times we were in bed together, I could act like I was having a hard time. Then I could pretend to have some big breakthrough and just fake all the orgasms after that.

Girls do it all the time.

I sigh, kicking the toe of my shoe against the linoleum. There I go again, acting like something I'm not to make a man happy. I shake my head, exhausted with the whole situation, and seeing no new solutions. My homework is waiting, and the best idea is just to distract myself from the fact that for the first time in a year, my bed's not empty.

Attempting to remember what I have due in the morning, I reach down to pull a notebook out of my messenger bag, and my eyes stray to a piece of paper stuck between my salt and pepper shakers.

It crinkles between my fingers as I pluck it out, and I unfold it onto the table. It's one of Danny's pencil drawings of a tattoo idea, incomplete. I make a mental note to get it back to him in case he wants to put it in his book.

I used to think the clients who used the tattoo books in Negative Images were weird. Who would go in, wanting something permanent, and not know what it was?

Then again, I've seen the incredible things Danny makes to put into those books, hoping they'll be the right thing for somebody. What if you started looking, and you found something so beautiful you could never have imagined it yourself?

What if you didn't want to give it up?

I close my eyes and press the heels of my hands hard against my lids, my brain tired past the point of words. The floor creaks under my feet as I stand up and move down the hall toward my bedroom, every step closer to him one more I shouldn't be taking.

The door is ajar, even though I'm sure I closed it. My face softens, because of course it is: that's what we've been doing all along. I close the door in his face and he pries it back open again.

When I lay a hand on the door, its hinges creak but Jacob doesn't stir. His ship-sized Vans lay crookedly on the floor like he laid down and barely managed to toe them off before he passed out. He's lying on his side on top of the covers, one elbow cocked up beneath my pillow and his sock-clad feet looking strangely vulnerable against the old quilt I use as a bedspread.

He chose the left side, and I always sleep on the right, but I refuse to read too much into that. Instead, with my chest aching, I crawl up onto the bed and lie down where I can watch him sleep. So close I could lean forward and kiss his cheek.

Strangely, with him right in front of me, the churn of my brain quiets; the doubts and worries and endless guilt finally pausing as if his napping has declared a general holiday. The rain funnels out of the gutters and into the lawn with a soft whooshing, but it's raining so softly I can't even hear it on the roof. Just now, the quiet of my house is almost peaceful.

I let all the air slide out of my lungs. When his scent rides in on my next indrawn breath, I let go for the first time in a long time.

MICHELLE HAZEN

Chapter 17: **TERRIBLE BRILLIANCE**

Jacob wakes up gently; his body still relaxed into my bed. His eyes focus on me, and a slow smile unfolds across his face.

I keep my hands tucked beneath my cheek, and I don't smile, don't move. Just watch him with eyes full of everything I'm afraid I'm messing up right now, just by daring to be exactly where I want to be.

He reaches over and touches my hair, rubbing a bit of it between his fingertips.

"How did the meeting with the record label go?" His voice is scratchy and pitched low. "Danny told me you've got one interested."

Of course he talked to Danny. And of course Danny didn't think to mention it.

Jacob's question isn't the one I expected, but it feels right somehow. As if this is a routine that's just been waiting for us to step back into it.

"The meeting was...confusing. And flattering. And scary as hell."

He nods, his slight beard stubble catching on the cotton cover of my pillow. "Yeah."

"Jacob, I don't think this will work. And I don't want to hurt you."

"I know," he says.

Those simple words dagger straight through me, fear clear and bright inside my head. Maybe he's given up.

It's safer if he does, so we don't have to suffer through all the failures that will come if he doesn't. So why am I still afraid?

"I miss you." He's lifted one of the sun-streaked pieces of my hair over his fingers, and now he smoothes his thumb down the strands. "You let me into your life for just one week and I miss you like you wouldn't believe."

He lays my hair down, draping it over my wrist, and then he touches my bottom lip with one finger. Goosebumps leap at his touch.

"If this is about sex, here's the thing: I like sex. Every kind of sex. And I can make it unbelievably good for you." He says it without a hint of a blush, and no trace of arrogance. The temperature of my skin rockets up.

I swallow to combat my suddenly dry mouth. I really, really want to roll him on top of me and forget that no matter how hot he makes me, I'll be left panting and straining and unfulfilled at the end.

I want to pretend I don't know better.

"This isn't a romance novel," I tell Jacob. "It doesn't work like that. You can't just put on some Barry Manilow and call it making love, and be so gentle with me that my head explodes into a rain of fireworks. I tried all that, and it sucked."

I push up to sitting, my eyes darting away from him as I rub one hand down my opposite arm. I hate how ugly it makes me feel to talk about this stuff.

"No matter how excited I get, I can't finish. My ex tried to help me get over it, and it only made the whole thing worse for both of us."

"Look, I get that. I listened to that shitty voicemail he left you. But it doesn't have to go that way, Jera. Did you know that seventy-five percent of women have trouble experiencing orgasm through vaginal sex? Only fifteen percent of women have the same trouble once additional stimulation is provided." He sits up too. "Have you tried toys? Even just a little booster like a vibrating cock ring? What about fetishes?"

I blink, at a loss.

"Fetishes can be really unique, and they are often biologically based," he explains. "Not linked to trauma or anything weird. They're incredibly powerful. You could have an insane gummy bear fetish or something and just have no idea that's what you need to get excited. Have you read much erotica?"

My cheeks burn and if my mouth isn't hanging open, it's only because I'm too shocked to move.

"I might have done some research," he admits.

"Oh really? I thought I accidentally hit play on my *Sexual Dysfunction for Dummies* audiobook. How are you not blushing right now?"

"Lots of stuff embarrasses me, I guess, but not sex." He shrugs. "And it's important to you. Of course I want to know as much as I can. Besides, I'm an engineering major. Taking things apart and figuring out how they work is kind of what we do."

That pulls a reluctant smile from me, because that is insanely nerdy but also sweet, and more than a little embarrassing. I don't even want to see all the ways I've besmirched his browser history.

"Why not experiment?" His gaze drops to my lips. "I'll try anything you're interested in."

I bolt to my feet and pace across the room. "It's not a challenge, Jacob. It's my life, my body."

"I didn't say do it right this second," he protests. "I'm just saying, if sex is why you're turning me down, I think we can work that out."

When I whip around for another lap, he's on his feet and standing right in my way.

"I told you before that I don't know if I can keep up with my life and a relationship, too. There are some things I can't change." He catches my shoulders, his warmth comforting through my shirt. "But I want to be in your life, Jera. Whatever that takes."

"I—" Shit, shit, shit. "Jacob, I can't..."

His face brightens as he sees I'm wavering, and he says, "Then I won't either."

"Wait, what?" I can't think with his thumbs stroking my skin like this. I shake my head to clear it.

"If you can't orgasm, I won't either. Then neither of us will be leaving the other one behind."

I laugh half-bitterly, but when he doesn't join in, I shake my head. "Right. That sounds like a line you use to get a dumb girl into bed."

"Or it's kind of brilliant. No orgasms at all, at least not when we're together. It takes it off the table entirely, which means there's no pressure." He smiles down at me.

"More likely you'll end up all sexually frustrated and grouchy, and we'll break up over that instead."

His eyes are gentle and his smile never falters. "Try me."

It's like the contract with Amp: he's offering everything I want, and that makes it so hard to remember that there's a potentially fatal flaw at the heart of both deals.

I want to say yes. I want to melt into his arms and let him stroke all my problems away, and I know it will just do the opposite. I cross my arms, and tell him the truth. "Look, I suck at sex, and I kind of suck at relationships, too. Every time I'm really into a guy, I try so hard to make it work that I totally forget who I am, and then he dumps me." I rake a hand back through my hair. "Maybe it's just something about me, because that record label says they're crazy about our music, and they want to change everything about it. So far, I hate their ideas, and I was up all night, trying them anyway." I blow

out a breath. "It's every guy I've ever dated all over again, and you—
"

I gesture at him, not even sure how to explain that he's too perfect. What I really need is a guy who leaves the toilet seat up and forgets to call his mother and is sometimes snippy with me because he's tired. Not one who brings me beautiful metaphors of gifts, and who wants to listen to Iron Butterfly's drum solo even more times than I do. With a crappy guy, I wouldn't feel pressured to watch him to see if I'm living up to everything he is, everything he might want.

Instead of trying to tell him that, I switch tactics. "You keep saying you shouldn't have a relationship, so why are you even here?"

His Adam's apple bobs, and for the first time since he woke up in my bed, his confidence falters. "I…" His shoulders tighten, and I can all but see the wheels in his engineer's brain cranking to life. But a long moment passes, then two. A chill of dread is starting to creep along my fingers before he finally answers. "I can't help it."

My breath explodes out, the relief turning it into something like a laugh. "What? Jesus, with a pause that long, I thought you were about to confess something about wanting to make a lamp out of my skin."

He doesn't laugh, his eyes dark and still as he watches me. "You're right. I shouldn't be chasing after you. I've got a ton of family responsibilities I didn't have a year ago. A girl like you deserves somebody who can put her first, and as much as I want to, I can't promise you that. I can't even take you on a decent date, because the only jobs with a flexible enough schedule for me don't pay worth crap and I'm pretty much always broke." The tiny lines of sadness are back at the edges of his eyes, and it's almost like he's asking for my forgiveness. "I know I shouldn't, but there's something about you. I can't…help it."

This man. Dear God, this man.

"Neither can I," I whisper.

He takes a step closer, and when I don't move away, he lifts my hair back over my shoulders, the strands brushing over my neck seeming like a caress just because he's the one moving them. "Are you saying yes?" Guilt and hope war in his eyes, and I know he must see the same thing in me.

"One condition."

"Name it."

"You let me make you some soup before you have to go."

He exhales and then lays a kiss, very softly, on my right cheekbone. Even that small touch sends a flash of heat through me so fast I'm left lightheaded. I never had a prayer of telling him no. Not in person. Not when he touches me like that.

"I have a condition, too."

Nervousness twists under my breastbone. "Okay. Please tell me it doesn't involve exotic sex toys."

"The fact that you look worried tells me you have a lot to learn about sex toys. Don't worry, though, this is perfectly innocent. If you get to make me soup, I get to make you dinner." He straightens and takes a deep breath. "At my house."

My eyes narrow. "Why'd you say it like that?"

His gaze flicks away, and then he puts on a quick smile. "Well, once you see my apartment, you might be overcome with lust and want to experiment with exotic sex toys. I'm just bracing myself."

"I think I can probably resist Casanova Apartment."

His grin is white teeth and pure delight, and it goes to my head like the roar of a mosh pit crowd. "We'll see."

Chapter 18: CRACKED PAINT

Jacob lives on the far end of a boxy, cinderblock apartment building, with trees growing so close around the walls you can barely tell what color it is. I've raised my fist to knock twice, and lost my nerve the same number of times.

I haven't seen him since we struck the infamous no-orgasm deal, because it's taken us nearly a week to schedule our dinner at his house. He had to change the day once, he was busy on Halloween, and I sort of stalled on finalizing the time. Possibly because I was freaking out a little bit.

How do you make polite dinnertime conversation with your new boyfriend when he already knows you're a dishrag in bed? More than that, how do you begin the flirting and making out phase of a relationship when you've already decided you won't go all the way?

I can't explain it, but somehow our pact makes all the things we *can* do seem less limiting and more…tantalizing. The tease of all those suddenly un-forbidden acts renders me incapable of looking Jacob in the eye, which is why I still haven't knocked.

I turn around, not sure if I'm headed to pace around the block or hyperventilate in my Volkswagen, when I'm distracted by Jacob's car sitting at the curb. The passenger door is a cheerful, unabashed blue against the rusting brown of the rest, like the wink of an inside joke. Not an inch of it is the sleek, sporty red you'd think a star athlete would drive. I smile a little bit, looking at it. He invited me here, and despite the jokes he made to cover it up, I get the idea that it was a big deal for him to invite me into his home. The first step to being worthy of that trust is probably not fleeing at the sight of it.

I turn back around and knock. His door needs paint as much as his car does, and it must be as thin as a Post-It because I can hear it clearly when he yelps, "Wait, don't leave! I'm not wearing clothes yet."

"Jacob," I call through the door, "Casanova Apartment is flirting with me already. Get that thing under control before I have to bust out the pepper spray."

"Damn it, Apartment," he bellows. "Get your shit together, man!"

I chuckle, smiling at the cracked taupe paint on his door. It's kind of a nice color, I decide.

It takes him an extra second, but when he swings the door open, he's sporting damp hair, a wide grin, and a shirt that says: "Engineers Do It With Precision."

"Why am I not surprised?"

"Because you already know I love pun shirts, and also I have no dignity?"

My held breath comes bursting out on a laugh.

His eyes flicker to my outfit and he blows out a breath. "Wow, you're not going to go easy on me, are you?"

"What?" My shoulders curl automatically inward as I glance down. My battered brown bomber jacket doesn't totally hide the fact that I'm wearing one of my nicest tops: a cream-colored tank swishing with a bunch of asymmetrical, lacy layers. I also couldn't resist trading in my combat Docs for ankle boots, but I dressed it down a touch with jeans that Danny swirled with Celtic knotwork in black Sharpie.

"How am I supposed to look like a gentleman if I'm staring at you all night?"

Pleasure tingles along my scalp and I pull my shoulders back. All week, I swore to myself I wouldn't get nervous and start second-guessing myself just because we're dating now.

"Better get creative, Tate." I sweep past him into the apartment and drop my messenger bag by the door. "Especially since Casanova Apartment is about to sweep me off my feet with an insatiable desire for exotic sex toys."

"Any second now, I'm sure." He closes the door with its peeling beige paint.

The tiny living room is decorated in Vintage Craigslist Mismatch, and the only thing on the walls is an old Pink Floyd poster with naked women's backs painted like the covers of each of the band's albums.

"Sorry I made you wait. I had to grocery shop so you wouldn't have to eat ramen with hot dogs, and I forgot to factor in time for a shower. Which I definitely needed."

I note the absolute lack of clutter and fresh vacuum marks in the carpet, plus the dried smears on the coffee table that show he dusted with a wet rag instead of furniture polish. "You factored in time to clean."

The corner of his mouth crooks up. "This morning. I had class this afternoon, and I figured I could get away with starving you, or maybe having to show up sweaty from biking, but you'd probably head for the hills if you saw this place the way Ben usually leaves it."

When we danced at the club, he'd been sweaty, the drops glistening on the muscular column of his throat. There was something about the smell of it that made me want to bite him. Suddenly, I wish I would have shown up early. Bite-ably pre-shower early.

"So...what's for dinner?" I ask, too brightly.

"Spaghetti and garlic bread, if that's okay." He leads the way into the narrow kitchen, more like a hallway than a whole room. A wood-grained laminate table and four chairs sit in front of a sliding glass door that displays a miniature back yard.

"Do I qualify for the grand tour of Casanova Apartment, or are you afraid this is all I can handle?"

"Actually, this is pretty much it, plus bedrooms and a whole lot of cars outside that are waiting for me to find time to work on them, including my sister Hayden's Jeep, which I've got to do as soon as the part comes in tomorrow." He gives me a rueful look. "That's why the parking situation sucks so much. My neighbors pretty much hate me right now."

This place is so sparse they might have just moved in, and I glance around with a twinge of disappointment. I don't know what I was hoping for—some kind of insider clue maybe, to a side of Jacob I haven't glimpsed yet. Then again, maybe he wouldn't leave that out in the open. I wander toward the other side of the house, trying to look casual. "What about your room?"

Jacob jolts a step forward, as if he's actually going to grab my arm to stop me. "Um, no." Something about the look on my face must make him realize that was an odd reaction, because he amends, "Maybe next time. I, ah, didn't have *that* much time to clean."

"Okaaay…" He probably bulldozed everything he didn't want me to see into that one room. Like that doesn't make me crazy curious or anything. What would a guy like Jacob have to hide? Engineering schematics he's been studying for fun? Really kinky pornos? He did seem to know an awful lot about fetishes.

"Can I get you something to drink?" Jacob asks quickly.

I slide my hands into my back pockets, peeking out the back door at the totally un-punctuated stretch of grass. Not even a patio chair in sight.

"A beer would be nice." Nice doesn't cover it after the week I've had. A beer, a meal I didn't have to cook, and the chance to sit down without my neck bent over a textbook I don't want to read? Bliss, with chocolate sprinkles.

"We don't really keep any beer around. Sorry. We have water, and..." He opens the fridge and bends, rummaging inside. "Orange juice, apple juice, chocolate milk." He pops his head up again. "Gatorade?"

"A bachelor pad with no booze on the premises?" I pull out a chair at the table, humming a few bars of the *Twilight Zone* theme. "So when do I get to meet the younger brother slash roommate who was going to tattoo my band's name on his..." I give a little two-note whistle and bob my eyebrows.

Jacob chuckles nervously and closes the fridge. "Actually, I should probably explain about that before Ben gets home."

I gasp. "Oh my God, he did it already? Tell me he at least has a big dick, or the guys are going to be so disappointed our band name is all over it."

Jacob grimaces. "Not exactly."

"Not exactly as in he *does* have a small penis?" I let my gaze drift down toward his fly. "We're definitely entering third date confession material here, Jacob."

Jacob crosses his arms over his chest and arches an eyebrow at me. "Where *was* this flirty girl when I was trying to talk you into hanging out with me? I think I like her."

I flush, focusing on shrugging out of my leather jacket. "I haven't dated in...um, kind of a while." I toss him a small smile as I hang it on the back of my chair. "I'm just starting to shake off the rust."

"Me too, actually. I had the same girlfriend all through high school. No one at all for the last year, obviously, after everything happened with my parents." He goes quiet for a second, tilting his head. "So did your dry spell possibly have something to do with the guy on that voicemail?"

My pulse jumps. We haven't talked about the voicemail since I shoved it in his face and wow, yeah, I wouldn't exactly have outed the most shameful moment of my life if I thought I'd ever see Jacob again. He's still here, though, and he seems determined not to let the issue become something that we have to tiptoe around. The least I can do is match his honesty.

I lift my eyes to Jacob's. "Him, and my non-stellar track record with dating."

"Look, I don't know the guy," he says, his voice low, "but I do know if he's blaming you for 'ruining his life'? It's probably because he doesn't want to take responsibility for his own problems."

"Yeah well, Andy wasn't the only one in the relationship." I glance away. "And he certainly wasn't the only one who made mistakes."

Jacob crosses the kitchen, and a gentle finger touches my chin, tipping my face back up to his. "I respect that you say it was half your fault." He gives me a crooked smile. "I don't *believe* it, but I respect it."

Something light flutters up through my chest and I clear my throat. "Well, I don't believe that small penises run in your family but I can respect it if that's what you need to confess."

"Try two notches less embarrassing and you're there." He straightens up. "Thing is, we don't have any beer in the house because I'm not really of age for a couple of months." He winces. "I made up all that stuff about Ben being nuts for your band so I could find out if the bar was going all-ages for the festival. That's also why I was so late. My friend, Cody, said he could get me a fake ID, but he didn't come through until the last minute. I almost had a heart attack when you wanted something to drink, because the bouncer barely glanced at the fake, but I was afraid the bartender would call the cops on me. I definitely can't afford to get arrested right now." He pauses. "Plus, you said something about 'no kiddies allowed' and then I really didn't want to tell you."

"You're twenty?" I don't know why it seems so odd that he'd be younger than me, even by only a few months. I shake my head. I had no idea how much trouble he went to just to see my show. "Jacob, you know I was just kidding when I said that. You could have told me you couldn't get into the bar."

"Not a chance. I meet a hot girl who is in an *actual band,* she invites me to their *actual concert* and I say, sorry, I'm too young to ride that ride?" He makes a face. "God, that sounds lame."

I grin, peeking up at him through my eyelashes. "You are *so* different than I pictured you."

He snorts. "Than you pictured me when? When I blew out your front window with my incredible athletic coordination?" He scrubs a hand over his face, groaning as he leans back against the kitchen counter. "It's because I told you I was majoring in engineering, isn't it? You thought I was this smooth, really witty dude and that cashed me in, didn't it?"

By the time he's finished, I'm laughing too hard to answer. He seems nothing like the Jake Tate that the gossip mill knows.

And maybe I don't need to peek at whatever secrets he swept into his room to get a glimpse of the man he really is. When I first met him, I thought he was Jake Tate, hottie baseball player who set my hormones to singing. Devoted to his family, straight A's in math-heavy engineering courses, he's the kind of boyfriend you bring home to your mom wrapped in a red ribbon. But *Jacob,* with his painful blushing and love of vinyl albums and the fact that he grins at the bad pun on my shirt and not the boobs underneath? That kind of guy is more like a present made just for me.

As it turns out, Jacob is an amazing cook when it comes to delicious, savory-sweet pasta sauce, but falls way short when it comes to how to deal with the pasta underneath.

After the second pot of ruined noodles, my growling stomach and I tried to teach him the throw-the-pasta-at-the-ceiling trick to help decide when it was done cooking. But then we ended up boiling the third pot into oblivion because Jacob insisted that getting it to stick or fall down was all in the throwing style, which led to forty minutes of comparing wrist action and noodle length and extensive theory testing.

His little brother, Ben, came home halfway through our clinical trials when the ceiling was raining spaghetti back down at totally unpredictable intervals and the floor looked like the final exam for a Hazmat cleanup class. I had an excuse all queued up, but then Ben gave me a very teenagery raised eyebrow, which of course led to me throwing a piece of spaghetti—with unimpeachable wrist action—right in his face.

Apparently pitching genes must run in the family, because that kid was hell on wheels in a spaghetti throwing contest, though after all Jacob's hints about "family issues" I half-expected Ben to pull a knife. He seemed like an okay kid, though, his worst trait a blond flop of emo bangs that I had a hard time taking seriously. He retreated to his room instead of eating dinner with us, which is probably for the best since we were headed for WWIII-levels of edible warfare.

In the end, Jacob and I had to cannibalize a couple of boxes of mac and cheese to get enough pasta for our spaghetti, but at least we didn't go hungry.

After that, we started watching *Napoleon Dynamite,* but it took us forever to get through the first half because we had to pause it for Jacob to tease me every time the grandma's house in the movie had similar '70s decorating elements to my house. Then we started debating the soundtrack choices, which led to a long spree of contentious YouTube music videos. Plus, he had to replay the scene where Uncle Rico hits Napoleon in the face with a steak so he could explain why it was a terrible throw and a purely lucky hit.

174

Now I'm falling through a blistering hot sky and I'm sick with the knowledge that I won't survive the impact at the end.

I jerk awake, my knee coming up and whacking the front of the couch, my hip aching where I hit the floor.

"Jera?"

I puff a few strands of hair out of my face and blink. The only light comes from the menu screen on the TV. The air is still tinged with the damp flour scent of pasta, and Jacob's head pops over the edge of the couch to look down at me. Sitting up, I wince at the stiffness in my back. "Crap, did I fall asleep?"

"You fell off the couch." When he sits up it jogs my groggy brain to wonder exactly what position we were lying in before I rolled off the edge. "Are you okay?"

"Ugh, other than needing about a solid year of uninterrupted sleep?" I wave a hand and then reach up to take out my crooked ponytail, beginning to finger-comb it back into order. "It's fine. Not exactly the first time I've rolled myself off the side of something."

"You weren't kidding about being a sleep thrasher, were you?" He winces. "Guess I need a lower couch."

I clear my throat, looking down as I wrap an elastic band around my ponytail. Did he doze off at the same time as I did? Or did he lie down with me and *then* pass out? Somehow, the order of events seems excruciatingly important here. "I should go. God, what time is it?"

He reaches for me and my breath jags but then he just picks up his phone off the coffee table behind me. "Three. You shouldn't drive all sleepy, though. You can just—" He glances toward the hallway where the bedrooms are, then pushes up to standing. "I'll drive you home."

I raise an eyebrow. I pegged Jacob as a "you take my bed, I'll take the couch" kind of guy. "Don't worry about it. I'll want my car tomorrow anyway, so I'll drive myself."

He frowns. "Yeah. But it's late."

"It's just my driveway to my door, and I come home late all the time." I smile. "Besides, I'm the youngest person in my neighborhood by decades. If someone tries to mug me, I'll just take their walker and run away." I get up and wriggle my feet back into my boots, then gather my jacket from the kitchen.

Jacob walks me to the door, and even though it only takes a few steps to cross his apartment, I'm painfully aware of how close he is behind me. If I had been too sleepy to drive home, that is certainly *not* a problem now.

"I had a good time tonight," he says.

The deep rumble of his voice teases my skin and I have to close my eyes and swallow before I can trust myself to answer. "Me too."

I pull open the door and turn back to say goodbye. Our eyes lock, and the entire street behind me holds its breath.

Is he going to go in for a goodnight kiss? If he does, there is just no fucking way I'm going to behave myself. We'll probably end up on the floor, and his little brother is sleeping in the other room. I want to know what Jacob's chest feels like under that corny tee shirt, but I'm not sure I really want to start into all my sexual baggage on the first date.

He leans against the doorframe and reaches up to scrub a hand through his hair, leaving it endearingly tousled.

"I know it didn't work the first time, but I've got some in the freezer, so..." He tries for a smile, but it comes out lopsided. "Ice cream for your thoughts?"

"I..." I gaze up at him, hugging my arms across my chest, and I hate this tentative person I've somehow become. "I like you. And a lot of things would be easier if I didn't."

His eyes flicker. "Yeah," he says. "I know." He lifts a hand and his knuckles trace the line of my cheek. Slowly, and with an odd sense of finality, like he's memorizing it. "Jera, I should—" He takes a shuddering breath, and his gaze jumps back toward his bedroom.

"What?" I'm almost afraid to ask. "What should you do?"

His hand drops. "Anything but this," he whispers, and his lips claim mine. His hands shake when they come up to cup my jaw. In his kiss, I can taste every bit of the longing that's vibrating through me, too.

My hands settle on the sides of his faded leather belt, thumbs curling slightly underneath to hold him closer. I don't know his "why not" and he doesn't know all of mine, but God help me, I don't want to be anywhere else right now.

When our lips part, his eyes drop to my mouth. He's breathing harder than he should be, and he steps back about a hundred years too soon. "Drive safe," he says gruffly.

I need to move. Move or speak. Or even, magically, both at the same time.

"Okay, goodnight," I squeak, very much like an idiot.

I walk to my car, I open the door, I sit down. Once I'm shielded from his view by about six older-model cars in various states of disrepair, I melt into my seat. My head hits the steering wheel with a soft thump as I gulp air I have no physical excuse for needing in these quantities.

If *that* was our first date, how on earth am I supposed to hold it together through a second?

MICHELLE HAZEN

Chapter 19: FORBIDDEN FRUIT

At the rate I'm going, Britain's empire is never going to crumble. I've been on the first page of its dissolution for at least half an hour and I'm still not sure what caused it. Gnomes, maybe? Or snails. They're hell on gardens, and Britain had a lot of gardens.

At least Jacob seems to be making decent progress on his reading. He sits on one end of my undersized couch while I lounge on the other with knees up and my textbook propped on them. Jacob tucked my bare feet under his jeans-clad thigh to keep them warm and his thumb strokes absently over my ankle while he reads.

I need to put a bag over his entire body if I want to finish this chapter before Christmas.

He warned me that he didn't have time for a girlfriend, and it turned out he wasn't joking, so about half our "dates" are doing homework together. He's always rushing off to his sister's house or another of his jobs. He's so busy I would think he was making excuses, like he wasn't actually that into me or he was hiding a terminal illness or something, but even when we're not together, he always finds time to text me something that makes me laugh.

Every time he's working when I have a second to relax, I have to fight the niggling itch that says I ought to be doing as much as he is, that I should learn to fix cars so I can help him or get some volunteer work or put up my mom's Christmas decorations. When I blurted that to Jacob once, he kissed my hair and said when I feel that way, I should write another song. According to him, that's a better contribution to the world than trying to Tetris my Mom's ridiculous Nutcracker collection into fitting on the mantle.

We've only been dating for two weeks, and I'm not sure how long it will take to get used to the way he kisses me as if everything is okay, as if I could never disappoint him. Every time he does it, my body loosens a little bit more, like exhaling after you've been holding your breath nearly forever. It's almost too easy to be around him and forget the bright red line that we haven't crossed yet.

Except tonight, for once, Jacob doesn't have to rush off to tutor anyone or fix anybody's car or rescue Ben from whatever trouble always has him calling at odd hours, needing Jacob to come home. I just want to relax, try to get a little homework done, and enjoy the quiet comfort of my boyfriend's presence.

The problem is, when I look at him, I can't help but wonder if it *would* be different with him. If he knows dirty, sensual tricks that Andy never dreamed of.

I swallow. I need a cold shower. Or an ice bath. Or a brain transplant, possibly for one that's a little cleaner and more focused on Britain's imperial overstretch.

Admittedly, thinking about European history—or even sex—is still better than dwelling on the issues with Amp and the band.

I gave up on adding synth to our old songs, because I couldn't find a single mix I didn't despise. Instead, I threw myself into talks with Amp about what else we might do with the new album. Dad was right—it's a lot of positive-sounding promises and hard to grasp what it will really look like. Then Rob, our A&R liaison, got the flu. The delay has my dad popping Rolaids like breath mints, but I'm relieved for the extra time before we move forward into whatever our musical future is going to be.

Jacob's eyes drift away from his book, thoughts of my career growing indistinct as his eyes climb higher along the stretch of my mostly bare legs.

When he realizes I'm already watching him, he blinks and reddens ever-so-slightly, and I wiggle my toes underneath his thigh. "I don't think my legs are on the syllabus for the 'strictly homework' date we are supposed to be having." I narrow my eyes playfully at him.

His hand moves a little higher, only to my calf instead of my ankle, but my muscles jump beneath his palm and tingles run up beneath my skirt.

"You have beautiful legs. It's pretty impossible not to notice," he says simply.

Heat flushes over my skin. Maybe I need to make an excuse to go to the kitchen so I can cool off.

He has all night, this time. There's nothing to keep us from falling asleep in my bed instead of on my uncomfortable, miniaturized couch, pretending to watch a movie just so I have an excuse to curl into his chest while his fingers trail through my hair.

We should really hang out at his house on his bigger couch, but somehow we always end up at mine. So we won't wake up Ben, he says. I'm starting to think he can't afford a bed or something, because after all this time, I still haven't been inside his room.

If I asked him to stay, just to sleep, he would agree in an instant and never push for more. But I can't imagine lying next to him and not wanting to let my hand go exploring across his chest, my leg hitching up over his hip, my inner thigh brushing the waistband of his...what? Jeans? Would he sleep in jeans? Maybe boxers? Or God save me, boxer *briefs*?

His thumb makes a tiny circle on my calf, and when his eyes come back to mine, everything tightens with a jolt like he just slipped his fingers inside my panties.

"I, um, I'm going to get something to drink. Do you want anything?" I close my textbook and start to swing my legs off the couch.

"Wait a minute." He shoves the textbook off his lap and catches my hand. "Did I say something wrong? I didn't mean to make you uncomfortable."

I'm such a jerk. We're officially, definitely dating, and yet I flee as soon as he gives me a compliment. I look up, which is a mistake. His eyes are dark and concerned, and every time I look at them I just want to lay my head on his shoulder and call a time out. From everything.

"No, it was really sweet." What a stupid way to put it. I love how when he says something nice, it never sounds like a line. It sounds like he's stating a fact and that makes it so much harder to ignore. I smile to soften my inadequate words. "I'm just thirsty."

He glances down, his fingers toying with mine. "Can I ask you something?"

"As long as it's not about the British Empire, and if it is, I might need a multiple choice."

Jacob looks up, and he's not laughing. "Are you afraid of me?"

"What?" I rear back a little. "No! Why would you say that?"

He ducks his head, pressing his lips to my fingers. The silence aches between us, but he doesn't answer me right away.

"Because sometimes you look like I terrify you." He takes a breath, straightening. "And I hate that."

I exhale. "No." I'm shaking my head and that's not enough, so I squeeze his hand, still holding mine. "That's not it at all."

He waits, but when I don't explain further, he releases my hand. "I should get going." He gives me a smile as stiff as his shoulders. "Lunch in the caf tomorrow?" He stands up and grabs his book, turning toward the door.

"I'm picturing you naked," I blurt.

He looks over his shoulder at me and one side of his mouth tips up. "Wait, what?"

As much as I'm trying to be honest, my mind is full of truths that would be far too embarrassing to explain. For instance, that I can't look at him without wanting to touch every single inch of his body. Possibly repeatedly. And I know I'm not going to get off, and that would only raise my sexual frustration to fire sale levels, and yet my dry mouth and eager fingers don't give the slightest hint of a damn about that.

"I, um, when I look at you like that." I shrug, biting the inside of my lip. "That's what I'm thinking. I just…want things. I know that's not where we're at yet, but I think about it. Kind of a lot."

His crooked smile has become a full-on grin.

I should probably not have said that out loud.

"Look, I don't want to go there," I mumble, shifting on the edge of the couch.

He drops to one knee in front of me, abandoning his book on the floor as he ducks his head to catch my gaze. "Go where, Jera?"

Since lately I have nothing resembling dignity, my voice catches when I admit, "I'm not ready to start messing this up."

Jacob leans forward and nuzzles his face in beneath my hair, but I can hear the smile in his voice anyway. "You are so far from messing this up. You have no idea."

He hides a kiss just underneath my earlobe and then stands in a smooth movement and goes to the front door.

I take a breath because I don't want him to leave, not really. Not at all. But he doesn't open the door. He flips the deadbolt, and then he drops the blinds.

Oh. My. God.

He reaches behind his head and pulls his shirt off, fabric tugging up and off every velvety, lickable line of muscle I've longed for and fantasized about and touched through shirts and jackets and everything that has shielded his body from me until this very moment.

"What, um," I say hoarsely, "are you doing?"

Jacob toes off his shoes and turns around. Sweet Santa Claus stuck in a snow globe of cocaine, his chest is even better than his back. "I take off my clothes a few times a week for art students who just need three credits and the ability to draw a realistic quadricep muscle. I would infinitely rather take off my clothes for you."

He walks over to me and I have not the slightest notion what he's done with his shirt. Did he drop it into the Grand Canyon? Transmogrify it into a teapot? Who the hell knows?

He takes my hand and pulls me to my feet. My Western Civ text hits the floor with a thud that sounds vaguely surprised.

"No expectations." Jacob starts to walk backward down the hall, tugging me along with him. "And no worries." He smiles so sweetly it makes me feel even dirtier for every thought I'm having about him right now. With his free hand, he unbuckles his belt, the metal clinking in the quiet of the house.

I need words.

Morals, willpower. An entire continent full of ice and possibly a Bible.

But first, I need words.

"Jacob…"

Damn it, not *that* word.

He pulls me through the doorway of my bedroom and abruptly switches direction, pressing my back against the wall next to the door and stepping in. The metal of his unfastened belt buckle is cool where it catches the hem of my shirt, pressing into my exposed skin.

My lips are parted and he touches a kiss to the bottom one, then the top. And then he claims my mouth so softly that I shiver and sink into the reassurance of it, wishing everything between us could be as patient, as easy as this.

After not nearly long enough, he pulls back and rests his cheek against my temple, the subtle scratch of a five o'clock shadow awakening my skin. "You're worrying," he whispers. "About what will happen, about how much you want and if that's too much or not enough. I don't want you to worry. I want you to *know* it's okay."

When he says that, I want so much to be normal. For him, even more than for me. But it's never going to be that easy.

Jacob takes a step back and flicks open the button on his jeans. "When I model, I spend half the time wishing I would have put on more deodorant because the lights are really hot, and the other half of the time scared to death I'm going to pop wood."

My laugh bursts out a beat late, because I'm watching him so closely, his words didn't process right away. "Wait, has that happened?"

"I plead the fifth." When that makes me laugh even harder, he narrows his eyes in a mock scowl. "It's not funny. Especially not to the other guys in the class, I promise."

"So is that what you're doing?" I lean against the doorframe. "Modeling for me?"

He shakes his head. "Nope. I'm saying I don't want to be. I like the idea of taking off my clothes just because you want to see me." He smiles. "As for getting hard, yeah, well, that's just going to happen. Especially if you keep looking at me like that."

His zipper goes down and every trace of laughter in my body vaporizes instantly into steam. Holy crap, this is such a bad idea. With an easy movement like we've done this a million times, Jacob kicks off his jeans.

Boxer *briefs*.

The clingy black fabric immediately sets my mind into advanced algebraic equations. Before I can finish extrapolating the potential implied by the bulge in front into an exact 3D mental model, he takes them off.

Off.

MICHELLE HAZEN

Chapter 20: A SMALL DEATH OR A GOOD ONE

All Jacob's clothes are on my floor, and he lies back on my bed, tugging a pillow over to prop up his head.

My body tingles with the possibilities of all his bare skin in the same room as mine. I press my fingertips into the wall behind me, because it is the only thing in this entire moment that feels real.

He watches me. His dark eyes are always so kind that sometimes it makes it easy to overlook the immense, analytical intelligence behind them, but right now, there's no missing it. I'm afraid he can see everything I'm thinking.

"You said you're frigid," he says, "but right now, you definitely want something."

His cock flexes, thickening as he waits, and he doesn't make a single move to hide it.

"Do it," he says, his voice going a little hoarse. "Whatever you want."

Is he freaking nuts? Just *do* whatever I'm thinking? Anything I might be thinking? To him? Right *now?*

My feet are apparently a lot more certain about my decision than I am, because they're carrying me over to the bed. God, he's right, because I want. I want so many things.

I wiggle out of my shirt and shrug it to the floor. An odd, tugging tension runs just beneath the surface of me and it leaves me reckless, nearly dangerous.

My punked-out leather skirt is held on with a series of complicated buttons and straps. I have to look down to get it off, so I don't get to see Jacob's reaction but I sense his eyes following along with every movement. When I reach behind me and pop the clasp on my bra, his breathing jumps. I look up and my eyes snag on his as the straps slip down over my shoulders. The bra falls, the lace whispering along my stomach as it drops to the ground.

His Adam's apple bobs. When he flattens a hand on the bed to push himself a little more upright, his fingers are shaking.

I meant to strip all the way, but now I'm overcome with the totally insane urge to comfort him, and I sink onto the bed still wearing my panties. I move up his body and it's all smooth, warm skin sliding against my breasts as I hug him.

His arms come around me and he holds on hard, his head ducked with his cheek against my hair, his heart pounding against my chest, and our skin heating more by the second.

My thigh settles over his, and the hard press of his erection nudges into the crease of my hip, his heartbeat throbbing there as well. All I'd have to do is shift a few inches to straddle him, pull my panties aside and push the thick stretch of him inside me. I'm so ready—worlds past where I'd be after a whole afternoon of fooling around with Andy.

I can already imagine the roll of Jacob's abs beneath me as he begins to thrust… But then we'd hit that crucial moment when he'd be getting close and I still wasn't there and I'd have to fake it. The squinched-up face, the sounds, trying not to be overdone and yet not so quiet that he would doubt it was really happening for me.

I love the honest vulnerability of his uneven breath against my hair right now, and I don't want to lie to this man, not for anything.

"Jacob, I don't want to have sex today," I whisper into his neck.

His hips twitch at my words, the smooth head of his penis rubbing against my side. I shift restlessly, longingly, the hair on his legs rasping against my inner thighs in a way that's very distracting.

One of his big hands cups the back of my head and he hugs me a little tighter. "I know," he whispers back. "That's okay. That's good." He kisses my hair. "Take a shower with me."

For some reason this strikes me as funny. "You want to take a *shower*?" I pull back a little and flick a glance toward his lap. "Really?"

He reaches up to brush a strand of hair out of my face. "There are a lot of sensual things that aren't sex. It's okay to enjoy them, too."

I raise my eyebrows. "That sounds like a ploy you use to get a dumb girl out of her panties."

He grins. "Wear your panties, then. I don't mind. They're cute as hell."

I squirm a little, glancing away, even though that was the reaction I was hoping for when I went shopping last week. Today's set are low slung, slick black satin with a triangular dip of electric blue lace in both the front and back. It's stupid to hold a grudge against pretty underwear for the rest of my life just because one guy was a jerk, and Jacob Tate would never steal my panties, for a trophy or any other cruel reason.

"Okay, then." He smiles with a hint of a wince to it. "I'll start the water. In a minute. When I can walk again."

I bite my lip and glance down. His erection swells under my scrutiny. "Jacob, the deal we made…if you wanted an erm, exemption…" My hand rests on his abs and I let it wander a few inches lower. "I would understand."

He shakes his head. "Nope. A deal is a deal."

189

"Isn't that going to be a little painful?" I peek up at him through my eyelashes.

In response, he strokes a hand over my hair and lazily down the whole length of my nude back. My breath stutters and I settle closer into his side without thinking. "Does that feel good?" he murmurs. I nod, a little confused.

He reaches down with his free hand and drifts his fingertips over himself. My eyes widen and when he touches his swollen tip, my vision blurs a little.

"That feels good, too." Jacob kisses my forehead. "You worry too much, sweetheart. Do you want to turn on the water for us, or would you rather do something else?"

"No, a shower sounds…nice." I climb off the bed, the air colder now that I'm away from his skin. I fight the urge to cross my arms over my chest. I've never thought of myself as a particularly modest person, but with Jacob, it feels like an entirely new kind of naked.

And yet when he smirks up at me, his eyes are happy and soft and I decide being any kind of naked with him is probably okay.

More than okay.

I duck through the door into the master bathroom and reach for the faucets.

The mattress creaks as Jacob calls after me, "Oh man, tell me you don't have one of those teensy little shower stalls!" He pauses, and when he speaks again, it's from the doorway behind me. "Or actually, tell me you do…"

I adjust the water temperature and turn around, hugging my arms around myself because I'm a little cold. "How about a tub and shower curtain combo, with a side of dancing Grateful Dead bears?"

He tosses an admiring look at my colorful shower curtain. "Perfect." He takes a step forward, and he's still blatantly erect. "C'mere, you look like you're freezing."

I hesitate and he tilts his head in question, so I take a breath and go to him, settling against his chest as he rubs his hands up and down my back to smooth the heat back into my skin.

"I have to admit, it's been a while since I've held a conversation with somebody openly sporting a hard-on."

"You see why I didn't want to let this bad boy loose in the figure drawing class?" Jacob clucks his tongue. "He's such an attention whore."

I choke on my laughter, shaking my head at him as I pull away.

The curtain rattles as I step into the tub, trying not to be self-conscious as I tip my head back into the water. He follows me in, his gaze running down my entire, slick body.

I reach for the shampoo just to have something to do with my hands, and he nabs it from me with a quick, neat movement. "No fair stealing my job."

He twirls a finger in the air for me to turn around and I do, feeling silly for still wearing my soaking wet panties. I mean, it's not like they're hiding much, but I don't want to just strip them off now, because I'm not sure what signal that would send.

Are my panties now the flying flag of the platonic shower? Can this *be* a platonic shower when every drop of water on his pectoral muscles is already tattooed on my memory like my new favorite kind of Braille?

Better question: why would I even *want* a platonic shower with pectorals like those?

His blunt fingers slide into my hair and start to massage my scalp, and I forget about flags and showers and even pectoral muscles, sighing my pleasure into the warm water raining against my chest.

He washes my hair like a pro, not a drop of conditioner getting anywhere near my eyes, and leaving me tingling with pleasure like I just spent the day at a spa. I let out a small breath as he strokes soap up my legs and down my arms, in wide circles over my back and gentle, playful ones over my belly. He eases the rigidity out of my

191

body until it feels like all the tension in me has pooled into the few places he's not touching, the ones clamoring louder and louder for even an accidental brush of a wrist against sensitive flesh, the momentary bump of a finger over soaked satin.

I turn to face him, trying not to let the frustrated longing show on my face. This is the best shower that's ever been taken, nationally, internationally, or otherwise, and I'm not going to let my screaming libido end it early.

"My turn?" I hold my hand out for the soap.

He pauses, his wet hair spiky and almost black, eyes seeming darker against the backdrop of white tile. With the hint of a smile, he hands over my bottle of body wash. "Okay, but fair warning, I may ask you to stop."

I arch an eyebrow at him. "Did you just give me the 'no means no' speech?"

He licks his lips and laughs a little breathlessly. "It might sound more like a begging for mercy speech when it happens, but yes."

"Fair enough." I start with his arms: dessert first in case he stops me early.

His skin feels divine with the soap sliding underneath my palms, but his muscles are a little tight so I stop and knead them for a moment.

"Would you judge me if I said my crush on you started with your biceps?" My words drift on the hint of a laugh as water whispers down onto the porcelain of the tub.

Jacob's eyes open, gleaming with amusement. "Seriously?"

I nod, and bite my lip against a grin. "Oh, it was bad. When you knelt down to check my feet for glass, I was having full-on Cinderella fantasies."

He shakes his head. "No way. With me wearing that old ripped-up shirt and sweating like a hog and having just broken your living room window?"

I just smile, my hands savoring every last centimeter of his chest. I make it down two ripples of abs before I start to get lightheaded and have to make an emergency retreat around his ribs to his back. This turns out to be a mistake because his cock slips smoothly against my stomach, and I press closer without thinking, the hard swell of him trapped between us.

He sucks in a quick breath and braces his hands on the tiles behind me, letting me decide how close I want us to be. I move, barely an inch, just to feel him. I want him lower, want him to dip his hips and press inside, soothing the clench of empty space inside me.

I reach for more soap, and then tilt my head back to look at him. He's fully panting now, eyes closed and shoulders tensed.

"Can I touch you?" I whisper.

His eyes fly open, and they're hazy and unfocused as he swallows a word that looks like something he normally doesn't say in front of me. "For a second," he says raggedly. "Just a little."

I lay my hand on his leg and as it starts to climb, his eyes fall closed again. He shifts his feet wider apart for me, his cock punching up and pulsing with every heartbeat as it waits for me to get there. My palm is slick as I encircle the base of him with my fingers, and I can't breathe. I can't blink.

I slide my hand up and his hips buck, driving his arousal harder into my grip. My eyelids droop a little. I love the feel of him, but I haven't even explored his entire length before he gasps out, "Stop. You have to stop *right now*."

I keep traveling up another half an inch before I can make myself unwind my fingers and let him go. I bite my lip until it hurts, so it's as swollen and petulantly throbbing as the rest of me.

"Whoa." Jacob drops his forehead to mine as he works to catch his breath. "Okay. Yes. Well. Sometimes experiments get a little...out of control. Give me just one second." He steps back, blinking. "Maybe one more second."

From here, it looks like he's going to need a few hours' worth of seconds, but I don't argue. He casts a reluctant look back toward the door and I say, "I don't want to get out yet."

Which is true. Incredibly poor judgment, but true.

"Right. Maybe safer territory, then." He takes my shoulders and backs me into the fall of water from the showerhead. "Like...hands."

Jacob picks up one of mine and starts to massage my palm. Disappointment flashes through me, but it feels surprisingly great for him to touch my hand. He dips his head, and kisses my knuckles, his tongue flicking out to taste a droplet of water. Porcelain is smooth under my feet as I take a small step forward. He nips one of my fingertips, wringing a gasp from me before he takes my finger into his mouth, soothing it.

Everything is warm and velvety and he's toying with me as if his tongue is on...places that are definitely not my finger. Actually, he might be Jedi-mind-tricking me right now because I can feel everything he's doing in places that are *not* my finger.

He moves on, scraping dull teeth across the heel of my hand, and I moan, the sound just another layer of steam rising between us.

"Jacob, I want you to touch me." The words come out like begging, a groan of agony and pleasure all twisted together as I shift against his chest.

He nibbles down the curve of my neck and I stifle a cry in my throat. "Are you sure?" he asks.

I'm entirely too far gone for speech. Or fairness, or any kind of thinking ahead. I turn away from him so I'm facing the shower, taking his hand from my arm and flattening it on my belly. His dick presses against my lower back, eager and swollen, and I arch my spine to get a little closer.

"Jera, are you sure this is okay?"

"This is what I want." I cover his hand with mine and drag them all the way down until they slip underneath the front of my panties. He sucks in a breath and his fingers twitch.

I abandon his hand and reach to brace myself on the tile, the spray of water too hot on my skin.

He recovers quickly, rubbing in slow circles over my bare flesh, his knuckles straining against the wisp of wet black satin covering them. I whimper and he slows down even more, both of us barely breathing.

He ducks his head and rests his lips against my shoulder, pressing soothing kisses to my skin as his fingers nuzzle closer to the part of me that's so needy, I'm afraid I'll scream when he finally gets there.

The water streams down my breasts as Jacob's left hand sweeps down and hooks beneath my thigh. I lean back against his chest, trusting him to steady me when he lifts my foot up to rest on the edge of the tub. Sensation shouts as this opens me more to him and his fingers dip lower, his breath uneven against my shoulder when he finds how slick I am.

He toys with me, sliding up until I'm whimpering and back down again. By the time one finger starts to press inside, I'm ready to burst into tears from pure, sweet overload.

He kisses my neck, his tongue teasing me as he adds another finger. The stretch of him feels like I've been waiting years just for that. He lays the pad of his thumb on my clit and my hips strain forward when his fingers shifts, stroking deeper.

I should take off my panties to make more room for him, but I love the sight of lace stretched across his big wrist, his fingers disappearing beneath fragile black satin. Every time he moves, my eyes go a little blurry.

God, is this it? Is it finally going to work? He feels *so* good and he's not pressing too hard or too soft, just resting his thumb exactly where I want it and leaving it there for me to rock my hips against.

Except then he takes his thumb away, pressing farther into me and curling his fingers. I whimper, wanting more, and he adjusts again, going quiet as he listens to my breathing.

"That's not good for you, is it?" he finally murmurs.

"Yes," I gasp, then shake my head, my hips rising against his hand. "No. I mean, I like it but not quite enough."

He kisses my shoulder and slowly starts to retreat, drawing his slick fingers up higher to pet me until I start to shiver and quake. He draws lazy patterns on me, and I moan and bite my lip, my lungs clawing for air.

His arm circles my waist, which is good because I'm paying no attention at all to staying upright. I arch against his hand, everything tight, tight, so screamingly, painfully tight and I just...can't get there.

Everything is so sensitive even his lightest touch is starting to hurt and I want to howl and claw at my skin, but instead I drop my foot down off the edge of the tub and catch his wrist, stilling it while I gulp air like I'm drowning.

Jacob brings his hand back up, water pattering over both of us as he strokes comforting circles over my belly, brushing a kiss to my wet hair.

"You okay?"

"Guh." I growl. "No. Possibly dying. I'm sorry. I warned you."

"That was our deal, right? You're doing a much better job of not breaking it than I almost did." He tickles his fingers down my arm. "Relax, sweetheart."

"*Relax*? Don't you feel like you're just going to...freak out or something? Possibly combust into three-foot-high flames?"

He turns me so my back is to the shower, and squeezes my shoulders in his hands until they feel steadier. "Yeah, a little bit." He chuckles deep in his chest. "But I also feel like I'm here, with you, and any way I get to touch you makes me feel so damned good." He drops his voice. "I feel like you want me. I like that."

I let my head fall forward against his collarbone, and his fingers slide in between mine, down at our sides. He's not angry with me, not frustrated, and the relief of his non-reaction washes through me, sneaking a smile onto my lips.

"I like it, too." Even though I still feel like it might kill me. But Christ, what a way to die.

MICHELLE HAZEN

Chapter 21: MAKING MY LIST

The last sunlight of Sunday afternoon falls warmly on my backyard as I come through the patio door with two beers in hand. Danny is already outside in front of the freshly lit fire, sitting cross-legged on the ground amidst a full set of lawn furniture. I roll my eyes fondly but don't comment because he's his own special kind of irrational and I would expect nothing else.

I'm looking forward to hanging with my friends, even though I admit to a tiny twinge of sadness that I won't get to see Jacob tonight. The last three weeks have been incredible: the shine of stolen hours fooling around on my couch and goodnight calls that stretch into the wee hours, all mixed together with the giddy rush of being courted by Amp Records. I just wish I could shake the feeling that everything is too good to be true.

Amp has been saying all the right things, but I'm not missing how vague their phrasing gets about everything that's actually important to me. Rob calls nearly every day, and he even sent concert tickets up for Dad and Mom to go see the Pixies next month. Mom hates punk rock, so Dad will probably take me instead, but it was still a nice gesture.

I'd trade all the concert tickets in the world for a straight answer, though. I'm worried about us getting pushed out of rock and toward EDM, and Jax is worried about getting shunted into backup vocals. That's probably why he's been acting weird around me, especially during last night's gig. It probably didn't help anything that I bailed on one of our rehearsals to hang out with Jacob. As much as I want to spend all my time with him, I've made that mistake in the past. I like my friends, and I don't want to start ditching them for a relationship. Tonight's band-only bonfire at my house is my attempt at an apology to Jax—because nothing soothes male egos like fire and beer, right?

Of course, we're inside Portland city limits, so our bonfire has to be in a metal bowl with legs that looks like an overgrown wok, but city girls can't be choosers.

Jax isn't here yet, so the yard is quiet except for the snap of the fire as I hand Danny a beer, then drop down next to him and swing my feet into his lap. He glances down.

"New jeans?"

This is not a function of his amazing observational powers. This is a function of the fact that I have exactly two pairs of jeans that aren't edged with his tattoo designs rendered in black or silver Sharpie. It's a win-win for me: uniquely decorated pants that more than one person has tried to buy off my body, and the simple fact that as long as Danny's drawing, he'll talk a hundred times more freely than any other moment in his life. It's a trick I've been pulling on him since junior high.

"Yup." I pull a Sharpie out of my pocket and hand it over. "Knock yourself out." I kick out of my flip-flops and release my weight into the grass, enjoying the rare blue of the sky, finally un-muffled by clouds.

The marker cap comes off with a smooth plastic *snick,* Danny ignoring my jeans as he starts on the top of one foot. The ink slicks cool and pleasant against my skin as he begins some intricate design. There's not a word for his style. It's not Celtic, not tribal, not totemic, though he can pull off all three with programmatic accuracy. His creations are smoothly asymmetrical, a little frightening, and uncomfortably beautiful. I could look at them for decades.

"More temporaries for the girl who won't let me come within a mile of her with a tattoo needle," he murmurs.

I cock my head, confused at his tone. Danny loves drawing on me. Sometimes in the summer, I'll lie out by the lake in a bikini and let him cover my entire back with designs, scrolling down my arms and onto my fingertips, my thoughts getting lost in the sweeps of the marker tip. It's why I've never gotten a tattoo: if one of his sketches were permanent, he'd stop drawing on that part of me, stop creating new designs to tempt me. He's offered a hundred times to give me a real tattoo, but I don't think I've ever caught the tiny flash of disappointment I just saw in his eyes.

"Wait, does that *bother* you?"

He shrugs.

I narrow my eyes. "D…"

Just then, my back pocket chimes and Danny pauses, taking the marker away long enough for me to lift one hip up, digging my phone out so I can read Jacob's message. He was busy modeling for a figure drawing class tonight but apparently not too busy to text me. That happens a lot: he'll say he needs to go home to do homework, or do something for his sister, Hayden, but then he'll text me all night. And if it's really homework, why wouldn't we just study together like we do the rest of the time?

Danny flicks a glance at the screen and then goes back to sketching. I bite my lip against the smile that wants to creep onto my face when I read the text.

How's your Boys' Night Out going? Did you finish the keg yet? When's the stripper showing up?

I laugh, smiling as I type my response.

You volunteering to lose the clothes for a different audience?

I drop my phone next to me, trying not to listen for the chime of his reply.

"I thought you were avoiding that guy because you couldn't date him," Danny says.

"Yeah, well, we kind of made a deal." I try to cover my rising blush with a sip of beer.

"Just friends again?" He snorts. "Last I heard, you were awesome at that."

I stick my tongue out at him. "Don't make me smack you when you're wielding permanent ink."

My phone dings and I sneak a quick peek.

Depends. Is anybody over there likely to get handsy?

I refuse to be that girl who's too into her phone to be with her friends but I at least have to answer his question. That's totally fair, right?

Probably Jax. He's got a soft spot for strippers.

Not the answer I was hoping for. In that case, I'll stick with the art students, since they come with a chaperone. You have fun, though, and if there's a tiger in the bathroom when you wake up, be sure to feed it.

I giggle at The Hangover reference.

LOL Will do.

I lay back on the grass as Danny's marker moves down and begins to inscribe some kind of whorl with my anklebone as the center. The only reason I haven't told my best friend that I'm with Jacob now is I can't decide how to explain why I went back on my no-dating ban. After Andy, Danny was the only one I opened up to about exactly what happened. If anybody will understand what I'm doing now, it's him. It just sounds so bizarre to say it out loud.

"Jacob has this idea that we can be together without the sex thing getting in the way." I prop my beer on my stomach, picking at the label. "Crazy, right?"

"Yup."

I groan, propping myself up on my elbow so I can glare at Danny. "Great. I guess it was too much to ask that you'd be supportive and tell me everything would work out."

"Sex matters. But you might be focusing on it too much." He gives me a sideways glance with the hint of a smile. "Some smart girl told me that once."

I flop back, laughing. "The overuse injury in your wrist kept you off the bass for a month. I think I had a pretty solid argument about what was 'too much.'"

"So? I was fifteen." Danny turns my foot so he can sketch up past my ankle.

"Great, so my lifelong sexual dysfunction can be conquered as easily as your teenaged addiction to porn?" I raise my beer in a mocking toast. "Thank you, Dr. Ruth, for that little gem."

"Didn't say that." He shifts my foot to start on the other side.

"You don't say a lot of things. For instance, for almost a month you've been avoiding saying what you really think about the deal with Amp." I watch him, waiting for even the smallest twitch of reaction.

"Your dad thinks if we don't take it, we might not get another chance."

"Yeah, but you know Dad's biased. His career tanked when he quit his label to get full creative license but that was before the MP3, before YouTube, before Pandora. It was a different world."

"Really? Because YouTube hasn't booked us a stadium show so far."

"So what you want is a stadium show?"

He exhales a quiet laugh. "Subtlety, Jera is thy name."

I take a sip of beer, and then lie back and close my eyes, giving Danny a minute to think about what I said. It feels good to be still, to do absolutely nothing for a moment. I wonder if Jacob ever gets to do that, with his jobs and all the credits he's taking.

Danny carries a line from my skin onto the outside seam of my jeans and begins to fill out his design. I don't bother to check what it is, because I already know I'll love it.

"Seriously, Daniel. I want to know what's going on inside that crazy head of yours."

"Promise not to get mad?"

"No," I scoff. "Why, do you promise to actually *care* that I'm mad for once?"

"No." A smile creeps into his voice. He flattens my jeans against my leg and my skin prickles beneath the tracery of the marker. "I want to sign. No negotiation, no quibbling over royalties. I want to show up at their studio and let them turn my bass into magic. I want to walk out on a stage and not be able to count all the people there to hear us."

My eyes pop open and I lift up a little. "What? You do?" I set down my beer. "I thought you didn't want to sign because you didn't want Amp to tell us what to do, but I figured you were just staying quiet so you wouldn't influence me and Jax."

"I *don't* want to influence you and Jax." Black ink knots stretch across my jeans, sprouting like vines that know exactly where to grow. "But you asked."

"What about them wanting to re-package our sound?"

He tilts his head, but his eyes stay on his marker. "If they want us to change things and it doesn't sound good, I won't do it."

"Um, then they might not distribute our album."

He starts to black out the hem of my jeans to provide a frame for his creation.

"If you refuse to *make* the album, they can sue you for breach of contract," I press.

"My car sucks. And they can have my futon."

I flick his leg. "Don't play poor with me, O'Neil. I know what your family's worth."

Danny grew up the kind of upper-middle class rich where you can't just have stuff: you have to legitimize your stuff by putting it in baskets. Somehow, he never manages to do his dishes until they reach the level of the faucet, but on the table, his salt and pepper shakers are neatly contained a basket. On his coffee table, the remote control and rolling papers rest in a woven sea-grass bowl, and in the bathroom the mouthwash and lotion are also in a low-walled wicker corral, as if at any second they might make a break for it and have to be forcibly restrained in their appropriate areas. I can never decide if he's being purposely ironic or endearingly oblivious. Possibly both.

"That's my parents' money. The record company doesn't have anything to do with them."

I roll my eyes. It's not that simple, but I don't expect Danny to get that. He's pretty well allergic to the finer details of the business world.

The sun finally goes behind the trees, and shadows yawn across the grass. I shiver and take a sip of my beer, which only chills me more. Danny sticks the marker between his teeth and leans back, his thighs flexing beneath my legs as he stretches to grab his hoodie off the grass. He passes it over and waits while I squirm into it before he starts to draw again.

"Why do you care so much what I think, anyway?" he asks. "You're flip-flopping all the time: one day Amp is the devil, out to ruin all your songs, and the next you're dying to get into their studio and let them make us rock legends. Seems like you're the one who needs to make up your mind, not me."

I blow out a slow breath. "I can't shake the feeling that they're only telling us what we want to hear. What if once we sign, they want us to change?" I fidget with my beer, the yard so quiet I can hear the Sharpie crossing the texture of denim. "Worse than that, what if they're right? What if our songs *aren't* good enough on their own?"

He finishes the frame of the design on my jeans and glances up at me. "If you don't know the answer to that, Jimi, you're not ready for the big time anyway."

My forehead crinkles but before I can ask him what that's supposed to mean, the side gate rattles and Jax's voice rings out, "You guys back there?"

"Only if you brought beer," I call back.

He swings through the gate, carrying a twelve-pack of microbrew bottles, his hair pulled into a messy fist of a bun. "Yeah, *I* brought beer. But what are you guys going to drink?"

I sit up. "Oh man, tell me that's the variety pack with the lemon ginger one..."

He narrows his eyes at me. "Depends. Am I gonna starve?"

I grin. "Ribs in the oven, just for me and you. Daniel here is going to starve but we're set."

Danny holds the marker threateningly above my face. "You sure you didn't get anything for me? 'Cause I'm thinking when we meet with the label again, you'd look a little more legit with a mustache..."

I yelp and roll away and he jumps up to chase me across the yard.

Jax drops down into a lawn chair and sighs. "Guess I'll have to drink all this lemon ginger ale by myself. Life is hard."

To our credit, we make it through dinner, sunset, and most of a twelve-pack before anybody brings up the contract again.

And of course it is Jax.

"We could just make a pro and con list," he says during a lull in the conversation. "Tonight. Hash it all out. I mean, I know this was supposed to be a night off but we're all thinking about it, right?"

I drop my head back against my chair and groan. "What *is* it with you and the lists, Jax?"

He stiffens. "Lists are useful. You can pretend it's neurotic all you want. But without lists, people forget things."

I snort and tip my beer up, but it's empty. "Like what? Cotton balls? Loosen up already, Jax."

"Like food." Danny leans forward to toss a stick onto the fire. "His mom used to forget to buy food for the house unless he put it on a list."

My head snaps up and I look at Danny, then Jax. His parents are divorced and I knew he grew up mostly with his mom—his super rich, socialite mom. Not usually an upbringing where food is an issue. "Is that...true?"

Jax throws our bassist an annoyed glance and shakes his head, taking a drink. "Way to be a drama queen, Danny. No, I mean, Mom would take me out to eat if I said I was hungry. It's not like I was starving."

I stare at him. "Yeah, but not knowing there was food if you wanted some, late at night or when your mom was busy or something...that would be weird. And kind of shitty."

"It wasn't that bad. Plus, if it wasn't for that, I might not have gotten hooked on performing."

"What? How's that?" I drop my empty beer into the twelve-pack holder and pull out a new one, swiping Danny's car keys off the ground so I can use his bottle opener.

"When she'd have friends over, Mom always bought really good food. Fancy cheese and weird shaped cookies and stuff."

"You liked fancy cheese when you were a kid?" Danny lifts an eyebrow. "Snob."

"Kraft singles are not real cheese, you crazy redneck." Jax takes a sip of his beer. "Anyway, this one time I was goofing around and I did this made-up skit for one of Mom's friends, and she loved it, laughed her ass off. Probably because I was like, a really little kid and being dumb but I didn't know that. Mom ended up having another party that same week because her friend told her other friend about my skit. I thought that was cool, plus she ordered a cupcake tree for that one."

This, I can picture. Little blond Jax, hamming it up for a bunch of society wives? Pass the camcorder, please. I smile and hook a knee over the arm of my chair, swinging my foot a little as I listen.

"Pretty soon I was doing these plays with elaborate songs and dance routines and everything. They didn't have much for plot, but the songs were epic and I'd make up all the lyrics on the spot. Sometimes they were just nonsense words, but if I sang with enough emotion, they'd hang on every word." He blows out an amused breath through his nose. "Her friends started meeting at our house more often, bigger groups of them, because they heard about me and I was this fad for about five minutes in between the Pilates craze and Guatemalan Algae facial masques. We had crazy sandwiches and fruit platters and cakes and sometimes tiny individual pies, like the kind that fit in a coffee cup, you know?" Jax chuckles. "I had a great time."

My foot isn't swinging anymore. I dodge a quick glance at Danny to see if he's hearing this, too. If I'm the only one who thinks this is a lot more sad than it is funny. His eyes are quiet and he's already watching me when I look over.

"So what happened?" I say softly.

"Yeah, did you eat all the pies and become the chubby kid?" Danny asks, and I doubt Jax realizes how calculated the lightness of his tone really is.

"No, the novelty wore off after a while and they moved onto other stuff." Jax smiles. "Plus, I figured out if I just made my mom a grocery list, she'd get whatever I wanted from the store. The plays were still cool, though."

I swallow. "I, um, I'm gonna get some more beer from inside." I push to my feet, taking my mostly-full drink with me.

The reflection of the fire flickers in the glass of the patio door as I slide it open. Once inside, I close the door and duck to the side so the wall of the kitchen will shield me from view.

Holy shit. I teased him for making lists? I might as well have needled Oliver Twist for hoarding oatmeal well into his Social Security years.

I owe Jax an epic apology. At the same time, I'm not sure I want to bring it up, since that will make him think about how sad his childhood actually was.

The patio door slides open. Before I even turn around, I know it will be Danny. He has always been a better person than me, so there won't be an I-told-you-so in sight, even though he's been hinting for months that there was more to Jax than I was giving him credit for.

I wait until the door closes before I speak. "Maybe we should turn down the contract, Danny. For Jax."

He doesn't nod, doesn't shake his head. Just listens.

"If we don't have sole control over our music, and they push me to co-lead the band, it will tear him to pieces worrying about if he's good enough and if people like him enough and if the songs I headline are more popular than the ones he does. If I had control, I could just do a few new songs, stretch my legs a little but without overshadowing him." I spread my hands, itching to pace but not wanting Jax to see my agitation when I pass the glass doors. "Except what if we pass this up and we never get another offer?" I pause, pain rocketing all the way up into my throat with the terror of my music fading away into the silence of my garage, lyrics stopping at my notebooks and going nowhere. "This is one in a million as it is, Danny."

"So what? They're not going to take away your drum kit if you don't sign, Jimi. You'll always get to play music."

That's crap and he knows it. We're the definition of small time right now, and the contract would change all of that. How can I spend everything in me writing songs only a handful of people will ever hear?

I exhale heavily. "Yeah, but we won't have the *time* so we'll never be as good as we could have been without day jobs. Do you really think I'm going to write some brilliant song after pulling a double shift, when I come home and all I want to do is get off my feet and zone out for a while? Besides, we'll never have the time off or the money to tour on our own, so we'll never get heard outside of Portland."

The possible consequences of tearing up that contract are hitting me hard, panic starting to edge in around the pleasant buzz of the beers I've consumed.

I step forward and lower my voice. "I need this, D. Things are going good with Jacob now but how long is that going to last? At least if I have music, I have something I can pour myself into, something that makes me feel like I still have a soul."

His lips press together, and it's almost painful to look into his eyes, so like mine. "Jera..."

"I'm never going to have a family," I whisper. "I *need* this career."

His face hardens. "Sex isn't what's standing between you and a family, Jera. You can be the best lay in the world and it doesn't mean shit. God, if I thought that was really your problem, I'd take you back in your room right now and show you how wrong you are."

My head snaps back. After all the time I've spent spilling my guts to him, I thought he understood. "Actually, Danny, I am painfully, humiliatingly clear on exactly what my fucking problem is." Tears quiver at the edges of my vision.

"No, you aren't. You think you're cursed because dating didn't work out in high school? Fuck high school. We were all a bunch of stupid kids back then, anyway." Danny's eyes flare. "Do the math. Andy left you a year and a half ago, you threw yourself into taking care of your grandma and then she died, too. None of that was because you fucked up, but you think everything is your fault and you couldn't deal. So you cut everyone out except me and Jax, because we're *safe*."

He spits the words at me like an insult.

"And even that's bullshit because before tonight, you've never had a real conversation with the guy. You pigeonhole him and make jokes when there's nothing to joke about, and I'm sick of all the crap you do to keep him at a distance. Jax is part of your band, Jera, and that makes us your family, whether you want to have one or not. You don't *get* to leave us."

"I never wanted to!" I half-shriek, his face wavering through the tears I'm furious to be crying. "I never said that. And you don't know shit about my problems." Danny's always known exactly who he was. His parents are way more demanding than mine, and yet he still doesn't give a damn about impressing them or anyone else. I seriously doubt he's ever had a problem between the sheets. "Have you been in a single serious relationship where sex wasn't involved? Because if you haven't, don't you dare judge me."

Danny's voice is a low, dangerous rumble. "There are so many things you don't know about the people around you. If you'd open your eyes once in a while, you'd realize that no one, and nothing, is as simple as you seem to think it is." He shakes his head with a snap. "This was never about sex. It's about the fact that you don't trust anybody not to leave you."

"Even if that were true, what does it matter?" My nails dig into my palms, my voice dropping to a furious hiss that scrapes my throat. "How do I *fix* that, Danny?"

He just blinks at me, like I've asked the stupidest question in the world. "You don't."

The patio door starts to slide open and Jax's voice says, "Uh, is everything—"

I whirl away. I don't want Jax to see me cry and it's not because I'm trying to keep him at arm's length, it's because I'd like to keep at least a little dignity, damn it all.

"Give us a minute," Danny bites off.

There's a small hesitation, and then the door closes.

"Look at me," he says, very quietly.

I don't turn, but Danny moves closer and when he reaches for me, I swat him away. "Don't you dare try to touch me after saying that shit to me."

Faster than I knew he could move, he spins me and pulls me into his arms. My hands are caught between us and the harder I fight, the more solidly he holds me.

"Someday, Jera, you've got to trust *someone*, whether it's this Jacob guy or just a fucking record company. If you're never willing to risk anything, you're going to be stuck in the same moment for the rest of your life."

At some point, I must have stopped struggling, and he's still holding me. He murmurs the words against my forehead and they lose none of their strength for his lack of volume. Instead, I feel like he's tattooing them on my skin, ripping me open and dropping the ink inside so I can never forget what he said.

"Life has to be lived blind. You don't get to know the answer before you ask the question."

I drop my head until it rests on his collarbone, and he ducks his head so his chin hugs me into him a little bit more.

"You're my best fucking friend, Jimi." His voice goes rough and my hands tremble where they clasp his back. "Tonight, though? You're acting a little crazy, and being sort of dumb. So I'm gonna go."

He releases me and I let out a shaky, incredulous laugh, tears spilling onto my cheeks as fast as I can wipe them away. "What, you're going to accuse me of having abandonment issues and then just ditch me? Thanks a lot, Daniel."

He smiles, and for the first time in a long while, I notice he's beautiful. As beautiful as Jax, actually, if darker. Quieter.

"Your issues have never applied to me, Jimi. And you know why." He turns and with a little two-fingered wave, he's gone.

I know what he's trying to say, but it's not the same at all. Danny's not different from everyone else just because I trust him. He's different because I don't have to try to be anything for him. He just loves me.

Then again, he doesn't have to sleep with me.

I sniff and turn to the kitchen counter. There's an empty beer bottle, so I put it in the trash. Wring out the dishrag and hang it up. Then I brace my hands against the sink and start to cry. Big, ugly, racking sobs that probably carry right through the thin glass of the patio door. But I just can't…stop.

I sink down to the floor, curling against the cabinet below the sink whose door never closes properly, and cry until I can barely breathe. For Jacob, because I don't know how I can live up to what is in his eyes when he looks at me. For how amazing I felt onstage with my voice pouring through the microphone, and how grateful I was all those times Jax stood between me and the uncertain reception of our audience. For my dad, and how his dream slipped away just when he was trying to make it truly his own. For myself, and my future, because I have no clue what the hell it's going to be.

When I finally quiet, I don't know what time it is, but my eyes are sore and I'm painfully sober. I guess I should go put out the fire before I burn down the whole neighborhood. Jax will be long gone by now. He probably snuck out through the side yard so he could get clear of all the drama.

When I slide the door open, I blink to find him still there. He sits by the coals of the fire, elbows leaned onto his knees and an empty beer with a picked-off label dangling from his hands.

He clears his throat but doesn't look up, leaving me the privacy of the dark. "I don't know if that was because of something I said, but I want you to know I didn't mean for you guys to fight."

Fresh tears well up, even though I could have sworn I needed about three Aquafinas and a good night's sleep before I could produce any more. I may be totally lost about what tomorrow will hold, but there's one thing I can set right, and I can't believe it's taken me this long to do it.

I go over and wrap my arms around my friend's hunched shoulders, pressing a fierce kiss to his temple. "I want you to know you're always on my list, Jackson Sterling," I whisper. "I am never going to forget you, or leave you behind. No matter what happens."

He looks over, surprised and maybe a little embarrassed. And then he stands up, and hugs me back.

Chapter 22: LEAPING BLIND

" Jera, this is Rob Righetti from Amp Records. How are things up there in Portland?"

My fingers squeeze my phone tighter as I turn my back on the ivy-draped bricks of one of the university buildings. "Oh good, they're good. Um, nice to hear from you, Rob. What's up?"

Jacob is supposed to meet me here in a few minutes for another one of his mystery dates. I was passing the time playing a game on my phone when Rob's name flashed across the screen and I nearly had a heart attack. I've been dodging the record exec's calls ever since Danny's "trust talk" at our band bonfire, but I know I can't stall forever, so this time I made myself answer.

"I'll level with you," Rob says. "My boss is all over my ass for me to close this deal. We're eager to get you some studio time booked down here, and the lawyers on both sides seem satisfied with the last draft of the contract, but your manager tells me you have some reservations?"

I swallow. Dad said they'd never give me a straight answer, but it's not like I'll know if I don't ask, right?

"I was…" I clear my throat. "It seemed like you guys had some specific ideas about our next album." I pace a few steps down the sidewalk, managing a quick, tight smile for another passing student.

"And you're worried it won't come out sounding like your band, right?"

"Well, yeah." I stop, and a laugh of relief escapes me. "A little bit."

Rob chuckles along with me. "A common concern with new performers. But we chose you for your sound, Jera. You chose us for our knowledge of the industry, because we know what holes need to be filled in the markets, which trends are on the way up and which are already headed out. That's important, but it's not a dictatorship. It's a collaboration."

Excitement tingles in the back of my throat. "So we will have veto power over decisions about the album?"

"It's your album. It'll be your music."

A slight frown creases my brow and I replay his wording through my head, trying to decide how to phrase a question that might get a more definite answer. Rob is the opposite of Jacob in that everything the exec says sounds like a line. I can never decide when he means it and when he's just telling me what I want to hear.

"Look, Jera, you're not a solo artist, so you already know a lot of the magic happens when your ideas come together with someone else's. Within your band, between you and your sound tech, and between you and your label." He pauses. "I think once you get into the studio with me and your new producer, you'll be pleased with how we can enhance your style, keep those classic influences we all love so much and make sure there's a place for you in today's fast-changing music marketplace."

"That's exactly what I was hoping." Except that so far, none of Amp's ideas have enhanced our style so much as obliterated it.

"You know, it's not just our company who will want to be involved in the creative process." He chuckles lightly. "I'm in A&R.

The 'R' stands for repertoire. It's our business to make sure you sound the best you possibly can, and every record company in the world runs like that." Rob pauses. "I mean, you can always go independent, but I think you're already well-acquainted with the struggles of trying to break into the music world with limited resources."

I tip my head back to the sky and close my eyes, glad my dad's not here so I don't have to see the "I told you so" in his expression. "Yes. We're well-acquainted with the limited resources lifestyle." Rob laughs like it's an inside joke between us. And in my head, all I hear is Danny.

If you're never willing to risk anything, you're going to be stuck in the same moment for the rest of your life.

I open my eyes and catch a glimpse of Jacob's long-legged stride as he approaches. When our eyes meet, he smiles with the totally unabashed delight that always warms something in my chest, even right now when my body is as tight and brittle as an old rubber band.

"Just give me a few more days," I say to Rob. "I'll have a final answer soon."

"Would you rather come down for a visit?" he asks. "The band can fly to our headquarters in San Francisco to finalize the contract, meet the team, see the studio. . . Plus, I've been auditioning some amazing keyboardists to collaborate with you guys. I'd love for you to come down and meet them so you can hear how great the future of The Red Letters is going to sound."

Keyboardists. The word hits my stomach like a brick of week-old meatloaf. They haven't listened to a thing I've said, have they?

"Wow, um…" A flare of anxiety tries to close my throat. "That's a very generous offer. I'll let you know, okay?"

Jacob arrives just as I'm hanging up the phone. He wraps an arm around my waist, lifting me off my feet and swinging me in an exuberant half circle before he sets me back down with a kiss to my forehead.

My muscles ache with the stress of hearing Rob confirm my suspicions, but I still find myself smiling because I can't help it when Jacob's around. I don't want to spoil the mood by telling him about my phone call, so I tuck myself closer into his side and say, "Well, somebody's having a good day."

"Somebody has a date."

I smile, rolling my eyes with the hint of a blush. "Jacob, you find a way to manufacture some date-like activity every time we have more than thirty-five free minutes in a row." I haven't even had time to worry if he cares that I'm not into baseball and cars, because he's always distracting me with something spontaneous and adorable that we both like.

"Is this going to be another spreadsheet joke? Because if you didn't think it was useful, you wouldn't always be nagging me for your own copy."

Jacob, in his infinitely nerdy splendor, made a spreadsheet of our respective schedules to show when we had free time at the same moment in the day. It gives him a near-supernatural ability to surprise me at all the right times, but he refuses to give me a peek at it, which seems unfair considering his schedule is even more packed than mine.

Part of me wonders what's on his schedule that he's hiding from me, and the other part of me thinks I'm an asshole for doubting the kind of guy who's willing to utilize Microsoft Excel just so he can get more time with me.

I take a breath, determined to let the rest of my life disappear for at least the next hour. "Okay, I'll bite. What's your special mystery date? Is it going to involve an inflatable trout again?"

His forehead crinkles. "Not sure. It seems possible."

I laugh. "Don't worry, that's not ominous or anything."

He ducks around me and takes my hand, sweeping me toward the art building. "We, Ms. McKnight, are going to an art show."

Pausing, I glance down at my black canvas kilt, knee-high combat boots and tight plaid button-down, topped with a leather

218

bomber jacket Danny outgrew back in junior high. "Um, should I have dressed up?"

Jacob dodges a glance at my legs. "Absolutely not."

Ever since we got together, I've ditched Danny's old concert shirts. I'm still wearing whatever I want, but I've started to skip over the baggy and concealing for things that make me feel more confident, because I don't want to start hating my body again, the way I did after Andy left. The wardrobe change is more for me than for him, though I certainly don't mind the way Jacob looks at me when I wear a skirt.

I elbow him, flushing happily. "Pervert."

He brings our clasped hands up and nips at my thumb, then leaves a kiss on the back of my hand. "I prefer the term '20-20 vision.' Anyway, it's an art show for the seniors graduating this fall. A buddy of mine, Cody, is exhibiting. I thought you might like it."

After that call to Rob, I'm not really in the mood to go out, but I can't resist the glow of excitement in Jacob's face. Besides, student art shows are free, and I suspect that part of the reason all our dates are so eclectic is because he can't afford the more traditional dinner and a movie thing. There's no way I'm going to make him feel bad about that by complaining about our options, even if an art show is the last place I want to be right now. I let him open the door for me, his fingers skimming over the curve at the small of my back as I step inside.

Jacob gets pulled aside as soon as we enter the small gallery, because on campus, he knows absolutely everyone. I smile at his friends, blushing when he introduces me as his girlfriend. But after a minute, I excuse myself and wander off toward the displays, leaving him to talk with the group of baseball players by the table of boxed wine and crackers. I'm a little too distracted for polite conversation right now.

I stop to examine a multi-media sculpture on a pedestal, squaring my shoulders to disguise the strange feeling in my chest. Each artist has their own little section and it's a wild blend throughout the gallery of paintings, photography, sculpture, and things that sort of mix all the rest.

How many of these people will pursue a career in art, and how many will go on to other jobs? How many of them will never have another showing after they graduate?

If I say yes to Amp, it's something I'll never have to worry about again. Just one phone call and I'll know the next stage I stand on won't be in some tiny bar. The half-guilty allure of the thought is still twisting through my stomach when my eyes snag on the Artist's Statement posted on the wall next to me. Each student has a short essay posted discussing their inspirations and creative role models, and they're always my favorite part of the senior shows. Even when I don't like the pieces themselves, I love hearing what drove their creation.

I skim-read the one by a painting of bridge supports, then move to the neighboring exhibit and scan the next statement, smiling. They're mostly bullshit, a lot of words disguising the fact that they feel moved to make something, and the pieces they use are the ones that come first to their minds, the colors the ones their hands reach for over and over again.

It's why people like us talk about a muse. When it's good, it doesn't feel like it's you, making stuff up. It feels like something reaching through you and into the world beyond.

None of the statements claim they made a beautiful sculpture of a raven because their art teacher told them birds were selling big this year. But then again, none of these students are paying their rent with the proceeds of selling their art. Not yet. Maybe not ever.

I hug my arms around myself, chilled though I'm still wearing my jacket.

"Sorry about that." Jacob comes up behind me, brushing my hair aside so he can leave a kiss beneath my ear. "I guess it's been a good turnout, so Cody was really excited and wanted to tell me about the pieces he's sold, and people kept interrupting."

I clear my throat and shove back my own problems. There will be time to talk everything over with the band later, because I know Jax is as conflicted as I am. For now, I'm here to spend time with Jacob, and be supportive of his friend.

"So, which stuff is Cody's?"

Jacob just smiles and turns me until I face a display of charcoal nudes. And I forget all about the band.

"Holy crap!" My hands fly to my mouth and I whirl to look at him. "How could I forget your modeling? I didn't even think to wonder if there would be any sketches of you here."

"There are a few."

"But I—" I purse my lips, taking a step closer so I can lower my voice. "I feel kind of dirty ogling your naked body with all these people around."

He smiles. "Do you?"

I poke him in the side. "You don't have to look so smug about that."

"Actually, I do." He chuckles. "But I don't think these drawings are what you're picturing. It's...I don't know, it's different. Just look."

I toss one more wide-eyed glance up at him, but he just slips a hand under my jacket to support the small of my back and urges me closer to the charcoals.

The one of Jacob is unmistakable. It's the largest, and the best, and it's nothing like what I thought it would be.

The drawing is a square of white, framed plainly in black, and arranged so it feels like you're peering down from an open tile in the ceiling. His strong shoulders hunch under an invisible weight, and he sits on the ground as if he just collapsed there, his thickly muscled arms slack.

"The detail work with your hair is amazing," I murmur. It's spiky and chaotic and somehow exhausted as well, giving the impression with just a few strokes that he hasn't had time to care for it in a day or two. Every line lies confidently. It reminds me of "Out of Order," how every word of that song felt permanent from the first moment I wrote it.

Nearly the entire sketch is of Jacob's shoulders and his hands cupped in his lap as he gazes down into them. They're empty, and tautly helpless. A ragged scar crosses the swell of his right thumb.

My heart squeezes and I take Jacob's hand, my fingers smoothing over the unmarred skin as if to heal the scar the artist gave his picture.

"Cody was on the team with me before I quit. Real good guy. For this sketch, he spent a couple of two-hour class periods standing over me on a chair." He winces. "That slouched posture put a kink in my back like you wouldn't believe."

"It's beautiful," I say, and my voice is broken.

This sketch is the definition of art: pure creativity pouring emotion into the physical world until it feels so personal, the artist may as well have pulled it out of your own chest.

Jacob's head snaps toward me. He frowns, touching my cheek, and it's not until then that I sense the dampness. "Hey, Jera…"

I let go of his hand and take a quick swipe at my eyes. "I'm okay. That sketch is truly incredible, that's all."

"Cody's good, but…" He ducks his head. "Is something wrong? You seem a little off today, or something."

"I'm sorry. I was trying not to distract you from your friend's show, and I think I did the opposite." I peek up at him with a wobbly smile that turns quickly into a grimace. "It's nothing. Just…Amp wants an answer."

Jacob's eyes darken and he blows out a long breath. "Oh."

"Oh?" My brow creases. "What does that mean?"

He stuffs his hands into his pockets and gives me a sidelong look. "So you're still thinking about signing with that one, huh?"

I laugh uneasily. "As opposed to all the other imaginary record companies clamoring for a chance at us?" I glance at Cody's drawings. "I don't want music to be just a hobby, Jacob. My mom's always been scared that I'd end up waiting tables forever to keep my schedule open for gigs. My dad supports my band, but he knows better than anyone how hard it is to make it as an independent. If I took this deal, it would solve all those problems."

Jacob hesitates, long enough that I shift my weight. Is he worried about me going out on the road? Are we about to get into an argument in the middle of an art gallery? My eyes focus again on the sketch of him, on his tortured, vacant hands. Even rendered on a flat stretch of canvas, they look gentle.

"You've just been so worried about everything Amp wanted to change," Jacob says, "and when we listened to the last album they put out, with Karma Puzzle? You said the mixing sucked ass." He watches me while I avoid his eyes. "You don't trust them. I can't imagine working on something like your music with people you don't trust, for any reason."

I look up to the ceiling, blinking rapidly, because that's exactly why I've been stalling this entire time, and now I really freaking want to cry. Both because he somehow knew that about me, and because it's still true.

"But you've got to take a chance on someone, sometime," I say hoarsely. "Or you'll never know what it was you walked away from."

I let my gaze fall until it comes back to his face. The concern in his eyes makes the huge world outside this little art gallery feel more steady, if only for a second. He swallows, and it might be my imagination, but he almost looks...guilty. "That's true. But you should still say no if something is wrong for you."

"I know that." I purse my lips. "I would, if I knew working with them would mean selling out. It's not that simple, though. I won't really know how much this is going to change us until we're already signed in blood and halfway through the new album."

A couple sidles past us in the narrow aisle, the woman's purse bumping Jacob's hip. He waits a second until they move away, and then lowers his voice.

"You know, baseball used to be all I dreamed about. I loved being the pitcher, loved how the whole strategy of the team shifted depending on how I threw each ball. It gave me so much clarity and focus because I knew everyone was counting on me to do it right. After my parents died, though, everything changed."

The corners of my mouth turn down in sympathy. I don't know what about my record deal made him think of this, but I'm certainly not going to interrupt when it seems like he wants to talk about it. And I can't help but wonder if he might slip and give me a clue to the parts of his life he hides in his secret scheduling spreadsheet, and his bedroom. All the places he's never invited me into.

"My parents died when they were forty, and they had so many things left they hadn't done yet. It got me thinking about how most professional ball players retire in their thirties. The schedule was tough on me, yes, but mostly I didn't want to build my life around something so short lived." He shrugs twitchily. "So I quit baseball and changed my major to the always humiliating 'Undecided.' It wasn't until this year that I started to get passionate about engineering."

My chest twinges as I remember how self-conscious he always gets about his major. "Engineering is one of the hardest and most important majors there is. What could possibly be wrong with that?"

He smiles at my defense of his career. "It's not as sexy as business or premed, but engineering is all about working with a team to design a solution for any problem that comes up. It's even more perfect for me than baseball was, and this way I'll get to keep my shoulders and knees intact. But the day I walked into my coach's office to turn down my scholarship—to give up everything I'd worked for—I didn't know I'd find a better career." He swallows. "It's still one of the hardest things I've ever had to do. Quitting a Division I team is nobody's vision of success, but for me, it was absolutely the right decision."

It's all too easy to imagine how terrifying it would be to face a totally undefined future after so many years of focus and hard work. But he's not telling me this just to share—he's trying to make a point and I'm not at all sure I like what he's leading up to.

I hug my arms around myself. "Are you saying there's a career that would be better for me than music?"

His laugh startles me, and when my head jerks back a little, he rushes to reassure me.

"No, hey, I didn't mean it like that. The way you play...You're meant to make music, Jera, in a way few people are meant for anything. But sometimes the best risk to take is walking away from the wrong thing."

My back stiffens. "I don't think you understand how competitive the music world is. There are thousands of musicians out there dying for a chance like this, Jacob, and most of them have way more experience than I do."

"I know that, but—" He stops and blows out a breath. "I'm sorry. I'm not helping here, am I?"

My shoulders slump. I don't even know why I'm arguing with him. "No, I'm the one who's sorry. I know the deal sucks. I'm just afraid it might be the only one we ever get."

"Okay...but if your songs right now aren't good enough to attract another record company, maybe you could use Amp's help to change your sound."

I suck in a hard breath. "You've heard the albums that they've put out lately. I'm not against input, but everything they've suggested has pushed our songs toward EDM, instead of strengthening the core of the post-grunge rock we're good at. Maybe we haven't gotten many bigger shows yet, but our music? Is fucking solid." My skin flushes hot, a heavy, betrayed lump growing in my throat. I thought he liked our band. How can he say my songs aren't good enough? I drop my voice to a hissing whisper to keep from causing a scene. "There hasn't been a new band in years who could match Danny's creativity on the bass, Jax has a voice Mick Jagger would sell his soul for, and I've had people come up in tears after a show, telling us how much my lyrics meant to them. In *tears,* Jacob, in a venue so small I practically had to set up my drum kit under the Coors Light tap. If that isn't good music, then screw being good."

I shake my head, drawing my weight up onto the balls of my toes until I'm all but bouncing in place.

"And not only that—" My voice drops off when I finally see the smile waiting on his face, and I realize I've just given the closing statement to his argument.

Shutting my eyes, I swallow, everything I'd pictured about my future beginning to waver as the conviction in my words echoes in my ears.

The air around me warms as Jacob leans close, and his breath stirs the tiny hairs at my temple when he whispers, "Your music? Is fucking incredible." I startle and my eyes fly open, because he has never said that word in front of me, not once. He straightens to his full height. "Your band is way too talented to commit to working with a record label until you can find one that appreciates everything you have to offer. You guys need somebody who can help you grow and improve, instead of sticking you in some pre-shaped hole they have in their lineup."

Nervousness skitters through me as I picture calling Rob to turn him down, as I try to imagine telling my dad what I've done. But this time, it doesn't feel like the bottom has dropped out of my stomach when I think about all the months—maybe years—of waiting until another opportunity comes along.

Because Jacob is right. In a very quiet place inside me, I know our music is meant to go somewhere. I know the sounds and words coming together in my garage are making something that speaks to people. It's not the kind of thing you say out loud, to anyone. But it's real.

And if I don't start acting like it, no one else will either.

I tilt my head at Jacob. "How do you feel about putting this date on hold for a few minutes? I have a few calls to make." I manage a half a smile, and the longer he holds my eyes, the more genuine it starts to feel.

"I think I would like that very much." He bends down and kisses me, intimacy trembling in the moment between us. This man knew, somehow, exactly what I needed to hear to cut through the fog of uncertainty and do what is right for my band. By the time he pulls away, my back is a little straighter.

"Tell Cody I loved his charcoals, will you?" I hitch my messenger bag up higher on my shoulder. "I'll be back in a minute."

"I'll be waiting."

I hang up my phone and drop it into my lap, the wooden bench cold beneath my legs as my lungs empty themselves in a long, long exhale. In the end, I made three calls. To Jax, to Danny, and then to Rob at Amp Records, for the last time. Jax agreed with me, and so did Danny as soon as he heard Amp was lining up keyboardists without even asking us.

I didn't call Dad, because I know he's going to freak out. Which is fair. His job is to manage my band's career as if we're a business that needs to make sales to survive. At this point, turning down Amp is a bad business decision. Except I don't think I really grasped until today that for me, making it big isn't enough. The only reason I wanted Amp's money was to buy me more time to make my music, and give me a chance to share it with more people. If it were about the cash, I could switch my major tomorrow and become an investment banker, but every dollar would be another reminder that I had failed because my life would have nothing to do with who I am, or what I stand for.

My band is my family, our songs are our soul, and I believe in the music we make together. I believe in us, and I won't compromise that for anything.

I push to my feet.

Beyond the roof of the art building, the bleachers of the baseball stadium stretch to the sky. All those seats used to be filled by people watching Jacob play ball. He doesn't have to be delivering papers to buy groceries. His baseball scholarship came along with a hefty living stipend, and even though that would have made his school years so much easier, he turned it down when he realized it wasn't right for him.

Somehow, it makes me a little more satisfied with my decision to know it's a choice he made, too.

I start toward the art building and as soon as I approach the glass doors, I spot him: head bent and hands stuffed in his pockets as he paces the lobby. My heart expands in my chest, because of course he wouldn't pass the time chatting with his friends in the gallery. Of course he would wait, far enough away that I had privacy, but close enough he'd be right here if I needed him. He always gets the balance just right with me.

As Jacob swivels to begin another round of pacing, he tosses an anxious glance at the doors and spots me just outside. He heads toward me right away, shoving the push bar so fast that the glass in the door rattles in protest. He lets it drop closed behind him without a glance.

He doesn't ask how I feel: he just studies my face, absorbing every bit of the sadness, the relief, the regret and longing, and the smallest hint of pride. "Tell me what I can do."

I smile, even though it's a little wobbly. "Why don't you let me buy you a drink to celebrate?" My stomach feels like I just leapt off the top of a roller coaster, but in a good way. Now, if my band ever makes it big, it's going to be because of who we are, not because we pretended to be something we're not.

Jacob grins. "I would love that."

The admiration in his handsome face echoes guilt in the back of my mind. I wish I could put as much faith in myself as I just put in my music, because with a guy like Jacob, I should be celebrating in bed rather than a bar. In so many ways, I'm better with him than I've ever been with another man. He laughs at my jokes and listens to my band rehearsals over speaker phone when he can't come in person, and loves everything I wear, from nerdy tee shirts to mini skirts. When I get nervous and start trying to impress him, half the time he pulls me out of it before I even realize what I'm doing. But I'm glaringly aware that we still haven't slept together. If sex might spell the end of inflatable trout surprise dates and sharing terrible puns, it's a leap I'm not willing to take. Not yet.

MICHELLE HAZEN

Chapter 23: PERMANENT INK

I tap my hand on the steering wheel, impatient with the heavy Thanksgiving-weekend traffic. It's the first Saturday I've had without a gig since the Bump In The Night festival and I'm eager to start cashing in my free time.

As I predicted, Dad wigged out that I'd blown our big opportunity. He only lectured me for a minute though, because he was too busy getting on the phone to every reporter in Portland, trying to spin the situation in our favor. Thanks to him, we got one newspaper article and several music blog features that praised us for refusing to sacrifice our musical integrity for a lucrative record contract. Not that it was *that* lucrative by industry standards, but whatever. It must be the thought that counts, because the Portland indie scene loves a rebel, and that's been keeping us busy as hell playing shows.

The gigs help, a little bit, with the fact that we're back to being a local band with no real career prospects. What also helps is that whenever I get down, Jacob is there to tell me I did the right thing, and it's only a matter of time until we attract another label. I smile at the thought but it fades when I realize it's going to take me another ten minutes before I can instigate my own surprise date by showing up at his house. I'm not sure I can wait that long to hear his voice.

I've been waiting way too long already. I dial his number, put the phone on speaker, and drop it into my lap so I won't get pulled over.

Jacob answers his phone, a little breathlessly, on the fourth ring. "Hello?"

I flip on my blinker and merge into the turn lane. "I'm thinking of an animal with four limbs, all pointed straight up in the air."

"Let me get this straight. I had to answer my phone with my elbows and my *nose*, thereby endangering the sanctity of my screen and my neighbors' remaining scraps of belief in my dignity, just so we could play I'm Thinking of an Animal?"

"Uh-huh." I grin at my windshield. If his hands are too grubby to touch a phone, that means he's at home working on somebody's car, which is lucky for me since I didn't think through that whole part of the "surprise" plan. Besides, he's insanely sexy when he's all dirty and elbow-deep in an engine. I shift into gear—smooth as silk since he swapped out my clutch—and hit the gas. "I'll give you a hint. The animal I'm thinking of is small, with funky-streaky hair, and it died in the midst of a vast desert of Jacob-less-ness."

He chuckles. There's a creak of something metal, then the whoosh of a passing car, which probably means I'm on speakerphone, too, so he can keep working while we talk. "Is that a hint I need to get up a little earlier tomorrow morning?"

I gave Jacob the code to open my garage door, and every day when he delivers my paper, he'll come inside for a few minutes and slide into bed with me. I've gotten used to waking up to his big hand rubbing circles on my back through my sweatshirt and wind-chilled lips whispering kisses over the nape of my neck. I get a happy shiver just thinking about it. Still, as much as I like the stolen moments, he's been so busy lately that moments are all we've gotten together. "You can't get up any earlier. At this point, you're probably waking up five minutes after you get into bed." I sigh. "Come on, we've only got two more days of Thanksgiving break left. You *have* to be caught up on homework by now, no matter how crazy ambitious your Design and Manufacturing project is."

"Well..." His voice goes tight with effort for a second, and something metallic scrapes as it comes loose. "My family obligations are done as of yesterday. Except now I have a line of broken-down cars that goes halfway around the block and a lot of customers who are pissed that I left them without wheels for the holiday weekend."

I turn onto his street and wow, he was not kidding about the parking issues. I flip a quick U-turn before he can see my car and head for the nearby McDonalds' parking lot. "They should be grateful they can afford to have wheels at all, which they couldn't if they were paying a garage to do the work instead of you."

"Still, if I want to get through the worst of it by Monday, I'm going to have to start pushing them over underneath the streetlight so I can work all night. Look, I'm really sorry, Jera. I know you're probably sick of dating my text messages. It's just been a really crazy few days."

I park and shut off my car, checking my hair in the visor mirror before I stuff my keys in my pocket and get out. "It's not the text messages that are the problem. It's those dirty notes you've been leaving on my newspaper, Mr. Tate. Highly unprofessional." I cluck my tongue disapprovingly.

He chuckles, low and deep, and my scalp goes all tingly at the sound. I roll my eyes at my own reaction and switch the phone off speaker as I get out of the car and take it with me.

"The between-class make out sessions aren't hurting anything, though. Makes me feel like a teenager, sneaking around behind my parents' backs with a delicious little secret." I break off when he yelps in pain. "What was that? Are you okay?"

"Fine," he says, his voice strained. "Barked my knuckles. For about the twentieth time. Engine grease is a sterile wound salve, right?"

I wince in sympathy. "Aww, Jacob..."

"It's nothing." Something drops with a clang. "Anyway, if you don't want to feel like you're sneaking around, you could introduce me to your mother. Just an idea."

I snort. "What, you think your life would be improved by being kidnapped by a cougar? Polite, clean-cut, with flawless math transcripts? There's no way Mom could be trusted around you."

"Ha! You're afraid she'll like me too much. That's one I haven't heard before."

I stride down the sidewalk, dropping my voice because I'm getting close to his apartment and I don't want him to hear me coming. "I barely get to see you as it is. Are you saying you'd rather spend our time having dinners where my mom quizzes you about your retirement planning and my father makes awkward jokes about our sex life?"

"Consider this: maybe we'd have *more* time together if you introduced me to your super mechanic mom, because then I could charm her into helping me out with my backlog."

I don't answer, rising onto my tiptoes as I sneak up on an old maroon Buick. Jacob's got his head underneath the hood, phone propped on the battery so the speaker can pick up his voice as he works. I click off my phone and drop it into my bag.

In his oil-stained, ripped jeans, his ass is purely world class. Grinning, I reach forward to give it a pinch. He jerks with surprise but thankfully doesn't hit his head on the hood when he whips around.

"Whoa, uh, hi." He glances toward his house. "I have to say, I'm really kind of glad you didn't do that five minutes ago, or I might have lost a finger."

"Hey, startling a guy with his head stuck in several thousand pounds of half-dismantled car? What could go wrong?" I prop my hip against the car and cock my head. "You mad?"

"Furious."

"Would you be less furious after a kiss?"

"Yes," he answers without hesitation. "Hold on, I'm pretty sure there's an inch of me here somewhere that's clean enough to kiss." He glances down at himself, hands black with streaks of grease, grit-dusted sweat glistening all the way up his arms until it disappears beneath an old Perfect Circle shirt. "Actually no, I don't think there is. Have I mentioned lately that I hate my life?"

I bite my lip. "Maybe once."

"Yeah." He shakes his head, bending forward to brace his hands against the edge of the open hood. He looks exhausted. I duck between his arms and perch my ass on the grill of the car, tilting my head back so I can whisper my next words over his lips.

"Maybe I like you a little dirty…"

He chuckles unevenly. "Jera, if you're not angling for a public indecency ticket, that may be the wrong approach."

I lean closer until he stops breathing, and I trace the edge of his lower lip with my tongue. It's salty and I think it may be the most perfect curve I have ever found in my life. I nip at it and something metallic creaks as his hands tighten to either side of me.

"I want to go inside…" I murmur.

"Okay! Yes, okay, inside." He stands with a jerk and looks to the left, the right, then leaves all his tools in place as he snatches a rag off the ground and starts to wipe his hands, using it to grab his phone and stuff it in his pocket. I laugh and lead the way, letting my hips sway a little in case he's looking. I open his door, then pause and look back at him. "Don't think you're bringing that shirt in the house. It's filthy."

He claws it off over his head, leaving black fingerprints behind on the grey cloth, and drops it into the bush next to the entrance.

Best. Idea. Ever.

I grin and step through the door.

Jacob kicks something under the couch, and then swoops around in a fast, fluid move. It ends with the door slammed shut, my back touching it and his forearms flat on the door to either side of my head in an attempt to keep his stained hands away from my clothes.

I gulp in a breath that is woefully short on oxygen, and he leans down to my mouth.

"I like it when you get bossy," he growls.

I kiss him with a sharp bite of teeth and deep play of tongues that's not holding anything back now that we're alone. The door is hard at my back, his chest deliciously firm against my breasts, his muscles slick with sweat despite the chilly air outside.

"And *I* like it when you get rough…" I wet my lips.

He exhales a growling moan. I drop a hand to feel his hip muscles flex, and both of us are panting. It's been way too long since we were alone for more than a few stolen minutes, and I don't give a damn whose car doesn't get fixed; I need to touch him.

"I've got to wash my hands," he groans. "Now. I have never felt such an immediate call to hygiene *in my life.*"

I laugh and curl my hips a little, and his mouth dives back to mine. The man can do things with his tongue that are fantastically immoral. I sigh against his lips as I think about what else that might mean for me. Every time we're together it's like this: a flare of pleasure edged with the low grind of longing. We tease and taste and enjoy each other, but I only ever leave wanting more of him than when I came.

He pulls away and drops his head to the door with a faint thud. "Jera, tell me to go wash my hands."

I rake my teeth along his neck just beneath his ear, and he moans like he's suffering. "Don't wash anything. I want you to take off my shirt. And I want to see the mark of every single place where you put your hands on me."

Both his fists thump gently against the door above my head. Now I'm certain he's in some kind of pain, but I'm also pretty darn sure he doesn't want it to stop. It probably makes me a bad person, but I could never get enough of seeing him like this: wanting me so much he can barely string a sentence together.

He pulls back just a little and his eyes flee from my eyes to my lips. "Ben." He exhales a groan. "Ben is going to be home in like half an hour." He catches a glimpse of the clock and chokes back one of the words he refuses to say in front of me. "Or, you know, eight minutes. Have I mentioned I hate my brother?"

"Let's just go in your room." I hook a finger inside his waistband. "We'll be quiet." But before I even get the button undone, he's gone utterly still.

My hand hesitates, then drops back to my side, but he doesn't take his arms away from where they're braced on the door. He lets his head fall weakly on his neck, forehead coming to rest against mine.

This again. I see something in his eyes sometimes, like guilt, or maybe fear. I know he doesn't want me to ask, but we pretty much always hang out at my house, and on the rare occasions I come over here, he's never invited me into his room. Whatever he's hiding in there, it's not going to be good news.

"Jacob," I say, very quietly. "What is in your bedroom?"

There's a movement of his body in all the subtle places it touches mine. A quiver? A shudder? I'm not sure the exact word for it, just that it's not right and it claws a line of pain down through my chest in a way I'd like to forget immediately.

He lifts his head enough to kiss my hair.

"I'm going to wash my hands." He pulls back until his eyes meet mine. "After that, we need to talk. Okay?"

Obviously, nothing is okay. Nobody ever says they "need to talk" unless it's something bad. But his eyes stay with mine, waiting for my assent.

"Okay." I exhale the word.

He steps back and something in the movement makes me think he's desperately sorry he can't touch me right now. He disappears into the kitchen without a word.

I cross the room and sit, the creak of the couch cushion, the only sound in the room.

It was a Wednesday when Granna died. She was in hospice care, which meant different kinds of nurses came to the house, and they had an odd sort of gravity to them. They didn't seem like regular people the way the other nurses always had. They were quieter.

We knew she would die. It was years and months and a lifetime in the making and no one was surprised or unprepared. But when my phone vibrated on that Wednesday, my stomach dropped and I sat motionless with all the sounds in the room fading into a metallic ringing in my ears.

I knew it would not be okay.

That same uncompromising dread is in the air now. I figured things with Jacob were going too well, and for a guy with a personality like an open book, Jacob has a lot of oddly blank pages. The family emergency that had him running barefoot away from my house. Texts from Ben that pull him away at odd hours, and phone calls he takes outside where I can't overhear. His room.

I take off my jacket and set it down along with my messenger bag, as if that simple amount of order will smooth the craziness in my head. Jacob comes back and his hands are clean, though the creases of his fingernails still show black marks. One knuckle wells blood from a torn scrap of flesh. When he sits down, he looks at his oil-streaked jeans, not me, and his face is different. Not distant but maybe older? A tiny thrill of fear runs through me and I wish he would look up so I could see his expression more clearly.

"Listen, Jera. My life is like oil stains. You think you don't mind them, and they can be fun in the moment, but when you're done, they don't wash off." He looks up and I start to breathe again. His eyes are very dark but steady. "My life is my problem, and I will always take care of it. You'll never have to worry about that."

I don't have a single clue what he's talking about, but the way he says it makes me feel safe. But that's crazy. He's lying to me, and I feel safe? I cross my arms and pretend I don't want to crawl into his lap right now and forget I ever asked. "Hey, remember the part where relationships were about trust and communication and not crappy metaphors about engine grease?"

"You're right, and I'm going to explain everything. First, I just want you to understand I'm not asking you for anything." He cocks his head, lines of strain appearing at the edges of his eyes. "You're a worrier, Jera. And I don't want you to carry my baggage for me, okay?"

"A worrier?" I scoff. Maybe I used to be, but not anymore. "I'm an irresponsible musician who can barely remember to comb her hair in any given week."

"You worry about your mom," he says immediately. "If she disapproves of your choice of career, if you're calling her enough, if she feels left out with all the record label stuff you are working on with your dad. You worry if you disappointed him, if you made the same mistake he did with turning down the record label and if your band will pay the price like his did. You worry about your neighbor across the street when she takes her trash out without asking you for help because she fell last winter." His shoulders sag, just a little. "You worry about me, if I'm getting enough sleep, if I'm working too hard, if I'm sacrificing too much to make time to spend with you. You worry about Jax, all the time, about everything." He shakes his head, a rueful smile touching his lips. "As far as I can tell, the only person you don't worry about is Danny."

I snort, trying to lighten the mood. "It's Danny. The day *he's* not okay, you better start watching for four horsemen and a rain of frogs."

"Yeah, well, for my family, I'm Danny. And we all need it to be that way." His head drops. "Listen, Jera, once you know," he says, "I can't un-tell you, and if..." He slashes a look at me and all his steadiness is gone. "If it makes you not want me anymore, I need you to leave today. Not tomorrow, not in a week, and not in a month when we still haven't had sex yet and you're worried I might freak out on you like that idiot on your voicemail."

With every sentence, my pulse speeds until every beat feels like a tiny flinch, protesting everything that's coming. "Jacob, just say it, okay? I was all braced for the I-Have-AIDS or A-Murder-Warrant or A-Pet-Alligator-In-My-Room Talk, but you are scaring the crap out of me right now."

He reaches for my hand. I pull it away, and his face stiffens. He nods and gets up anyway. The floor creaks as I follow him toward the door of his room, my arms wrapped around my middle like I need to protect myself from whatever is in there. Given the way he's acting, I probably do.

My imagination sprints ahead, flipping through scenes in quick succession, representing all the possible genres: horror, comedy, tragedy. When he opens the door, I'm still not ready for what's on the other side.

Chapter 24: THE SECRET

In Jacob's room, a purple border of Dora the Explorer and a monkey strides around the top of the wall. There's a matching nightlight glowing beside a toddler bed with its purple bedspread made homey by a well-loved village of stuffed animals and a battered, man-sized baseball glove. At one side of the room is a tiny purple velvet beanbag chair, some stacked and labeled tubs of toys, and an extra-long twin-sized bed with a plain wool blanket pulled over the top.

I glance up and Jacob is so close, I can smell the warmth of cedar and motor oil on his skin. "You have a daughter? Where is she? Who—" I almost ask who she is, but that's a ridiculous question. She's his daughter, and that in itself is everything. He has a child and that child has a mother. We've been dating for a month and he didn't even trust me enough to tell me they existed. I plant my feet wider, trying to steady myself against the shaft of pain that sends through me. He called me a worrier, said he didn't want me to carry his baggage for him. Which is probably a nice way of saying he didn't think I could do it.

"I have three siblings," Jacob explains. "Ben's eighteen, Hayden's twenty-three and Maya is two. Hayden has Maya for half of each month. Ben and I have her the other half, but we can't afford a three-bedroom right now. I thought Maya needed a room of her own so she would feel at home, even though she's bouncing back and forth between two apartments all the time. Plus, Maya had a lot of trouble sleeping after the accident and I usually had the best luck at calming her down. I think it's because of all of us, my voice sounds the most like my dad's."

I blink up at him. "Oh, Jacob…" I whisper. *This* is why he said at first that he couldn't have a relationship. Not because of Ben, or even all the time he spends helping Hayden. No wonder he thought I couldn't handle what he's up against, because I can barely fathom how he does it. I know how hard he works, and he just lost his parents, and on top of that, he's been raising a toddler. Not only that, he gave up his room for her so he doesn't even have his own space to retreat to.

And then a thought strikes me.

"Was she ever here? Just in the other room when I came over or something?"

He gives me an odd look. "Um, no. How quiet do you think a two-year-old *is*?" I shrug self-consciously, and he gestures to the toys. "I just didn't want you to see all her stuff. Kind of difficult décor to explain, you know?"

"Is this why you took off so fast the day I met you? Did you have to go get Maya?"

He nods. "She choked on a grape. Ben called me, freaking out because her lips were starting to turn purple. I didn't even think to explain to you what happened, I just took off barefoot." His jaw flexes. "I told Ben to call 911 and I knew there was no way I could ride my bike back before they got there, but I *had* to get to her. I've never been so scared in my life."

"Of course you were." I hug my arms over my chest, shivering just to think of it. "She must have been okay, though, right? Did she go to the hospital?"

"Ben tried the Heimlich. He was afraid he'd break her ribs or something, but it worked. By the time I showed up, she was fine and showing her Barbies to the paramedics." He blows out a breath, rolling his eyes. "I even made it to class on time."

"I just—she's so much younger than you." As soon as it's out, I feel like a jerk. "I mean, at first I thought you must have a daughter because the age difference between Ben and this"—I gesture to the toddler bed—"is kinda major."

"Maya was a miracle baby, an accident. Mom had my older sister, Hayden, when she was only seventeen, and she was thirty-eight when she got pregnant with Maya. Dad had a vasectomy years ago, but apparently there's about a one percent chance of pregnancy after that, and Maya was the one percent."

He puts his hands in his pockets.

"It was really hard for them to go back to diapers and being up all night, but they adored her, you know? They were figuring it out. When they crashed their car, they were out on a date night and Hayden was babysitting, or Maya probably would have been with them." His jaw muscle clenches.

I shake my head, no idea what to say to a story like his. I've been venting to him about record labels and creative freedom as if those were the worst problems a person could have, and this entire time, he's been responsible for an entire human being?

"After they got in the accident, none of us were ready to have kids, but we couldn't let Maya go into foster care or anything. Hayden was married, had a steady job, and she was the oldest. She said she'd take Maya, but her husband's kind of flaky and not much help. Hayden, well, she tries so hard to be perfect for Maya that sometimes she wears herself out. She can't do it full-time."

I glance away. I was such a mess after Granna died. If someone would have given me a toddler, I don't know what I would have done, but it might have looked a lot like Hayden. I don't want to be the kind of person Jacob would need to sweep in and rescue, except in a situation like that…I mean, how do you learn to be a parent on the spot?

"Anyway, that's how we all ended up sharing custody," Jacob says when the silence starts to stretch too long. "I had two or three practices a day for baseball and I couldn't do that and keep up with Maya, which helped me make the final decision to quit the team. Working so hard to throw a ball perfectly, after everything that had happened, seemed stupid." He blushes. "Plus, I couldn't exactly say it to the guys, but I was enjoying my time with her more than the hours I spent at practice."

"Do you have a picture of her?" I need to see her, so she feels like a person and not a situation I have no idea how I'm supposed to deal with. I stare at the purple beanbag chair, and Jacob stares at me. I don't dare turn my head, because I can't process my own emotions, much less his.

"Uh, yeah. Of course."

He pulls his phone out of his pocket, scrolls through a couple of pictures of us together, then one of me lying back on the couch and sticking my tongue out at him, my hair all messy from making out when we were supposed to be doing homework. The next picture is of a tiny blond girl, blank-faced with wide eyes like she wasn't ready for the picture to be snapped. That picture was right next to mine in his phone the entire time. If I'd looked, the secret would have been out with one swipe of a thumb.

He keeps going until he gets to a series taken at a beach. "Here are some good ones."

I take the phone. Her hair is curly and barely shoulder-length, a blond lighter than Ben's. In the first shot, Jacob's sitting on the beach with Maya between his knees as they work on building an unimpressive blob of sand. They're adorable together, because of course they are. There's nothing he can't do: fix a car, build a rocket, be a de-facto father *and* a boyfriend so perfect I don't know how he ended up with someone like me.

"It was supposed to be a sand igloo," he says as I flick to the next shot. In this one, she's running away with a stick that's too big for her, the end trailing onto the ground. In the third, he's caught the other end of the stick and she's shrieking with laughter, looking back at Jacob as he takes the picture. She has his eyes.

I try to wet my lips with an utterly dry tongue, and then look up at him. When I speak, I have to say the right thing. To show I can handle this and I'm worthy of the faith he's putting in me.

His brown eyes are narrowed in pain, his jaw clenched. "I always meant to tell you. But then it was so hard to get you to take a chance just on me, and you seemed overwhelmed at the idea of me having to be responsible for Ben, even though he's technically an adult." He straightens. "When you finally gave me a chance, I could feel how tentative it was, how…" He rakes a hand back through his hair. "Hell, Jera, every time we fool around, I feel like if I have the wrong reaction to a single thing, you'll take off. So then I stopped waiting for openings to tell you, and started to lie." He looks as sick as I feel, and my gaze drops back to that little velvet beanbag chair. "Maya's lost so much, and I knew if she met you, she'd adore you. I couldn't risk you disappearing after that, so I decided I'd tell you when I thought you were ready to get serious with me." He huffs out a breath. "But you're not, and I can't wait anymore."

I take a step back. "What?" He might as well be reaching into my body and wringing my guts out right now, and he thinks this doesn't mean anything to me? He's told me everything about the adorable little sister he took on without batting an eye, and he hasn't told me a single thing about what that means for us. "You think I'm not serious about you?"

He drops his hands to his sides with a slap. "You're not, Jera. You won't introduce me to your parents, it took you weeks to even tell *Danny* we were dating, for God's sake. I've been trying to give you all the time you need to get used to the idea that I care about you, and I'm not going anywhere but it doesn't seem to be helping. You don't have to meet Maya if you're not ready. I just can't keep lying to you, Jera." He shakes his head. "I hate it."

I reach for him, and he holds so still, like he has no idea what I might do. I cup his face in my hands, the slight prickle of his stubble rough against my palms. "You're incredible," I whisper, and as soon as I touch him, tears jump to my eyes. "I'm so proud of you, and everything you've done, and everything you are."

His shoulders drop, like invisible strings were holding him up and they were all cut at once. He takes one shuddering breath, and then he reaches for me, snatching me into a hug so crushingly tight that I know he never expected to be able to do it again.

My tears wet his skin, and I can barely breathe, but I say it anyway. "I'm so, so sorry I made you feel you couldn't trust me with the truth."

His breaths are ragged. I don't think he's crying, more that he's gulping air like he's been suffocating and didn't even know it.

I pull back so I can see his face, and I hate that he's afraid right now, because he's not the one who screwed up here. "You were right to protect Maya," I say fiercely. "After losing her parents and bouncing back and forth between your house and Hayden's, the last thing she needs is a parade of girlfriends going through her life. I'm happy to wait as long as you think we need to before I meet her, because the last thing I'd ever want is to hurt your sister."

"Are you kidding?" His voice is rough, his fingers clutching me much harder than he usually lets himself. "I'll take you over there right now if you want. You're it for me, Jera. How do you not know that?"

I push up onto my toes so fast I lose my balance and fall into his chest. His back hits the wall and it's perfect because his hands are pulling me against him and I need to hold him so bad right now. I let him down, and somehow he's not leaving. I'm not losing him.

It hits me all at once: I'm kissing my boyfriend in his bedroom, which he decorated with Dora the Explorer because he wanted his baby sister to feel comfortable here. A tear slips down my cheek, and I had no idea it was possible to *feel* this much for another human being.

"Jera?" His thumb rubs the tear off my cheek, and he tries to pull back but I shake my head.

"I'm okay, I'm just—" I'm not okay. God, he's perfect, every curve of his muscle against my chest reminding me that he's in the gym every morning after delivering papers, before I'm even awake. He's strong where I'm weak and brave when I've been tentative. Where I'm flat terrified at the idea of being responsible for a child's life, he *volunteered*, even though Hayden had already taken Maya and he technically didn't have to.

I kiss him again, taking it slower this time, not biting at his bottom lip the way I always do when I get carried away. Instead, I trace it with my tongue, being gentle with him the way he always, always is with me.

"You're amazing," I whisper into his mouth.

He runs himself ragged taking care of everyone and everything around him, and he hardly ever sleeps. Even now, his every muscle is drawn tight and I want to give him a break, to feel him relax the way I do when he holds me. I grab his hand and tug him with me toward the bed. I skim my shirt over my head and drop it onto the floor.

"Jera..." He follows my every movement, like he's still uncertain of which way I might go. But he doesn't resist when I lay him out on the bed, stroking one hand down his chest until I get to the button of his jeans, flicking it open.

His Adam's apple bobs and he inhales quickly. His gaze comes back to my face, and I know he's looking for a reaction to everything he's told me. But I don't want to talk, not when words have failed us so thoroughly in the past. I want to be close to him, skin against skin, in this room that's designed for everyone else's comfort but his.

"Let me take care of you for once. I want to show you—" I don't finish, because I don't know how to tell him everything I mean. The kisses I whisper across his chest aren't enough, so I tug down his zipper.

I flatten one hand on his stomach as I reach into his boxer briefs with the other, smoothing my hand over every satiny smooth inch of him. His eyes fall closed while a groan aches out from behind his clenched teeth.

"When we're together, you're always focused on me and what I like, and that's not fair. We've been dating for weeks and I don't even know where you like to be touched."

I squeeze his erection as I lift my other hand, searching for some less obvious erogenous zones. Trailing down his arm, I curl my fingers so my nails lightly score his bicep. His hips jerk beneath me and we catch our breath at the same moment, his eyes coming open just a little to watch as my nails change direction to cross his chest. As I make it down to the first swell of his abs, he drops his head back to the mattress with a growling kind of moan.

Retreating a little, both my hands meet at the waistband of his boxer briefs and I pause. "Do you want me to stop?"

"*God,* no." He props himself up on one elbow and catches me behind the neck, his fingers tangling in my hair as he pulls me down to his mouth. He's less careful than he usually is, his tongue delving deep and reckless until my hands clench, my nails scraping on the crumpled denim of his jeans. He smells like clean sweat and metal, and when he lets me go, I want to growl and rip the clothes straight off his body. I settle for stripping them onto the floor and getting rid of my boots before I nudge him farther back onto the narrow bed. It's longer than a normal twin but his shoulders take up most of the width.

He lounges on his side with one knee bent, reaching out for me. I take his hand and leave a kiss in the center of his palm before I move lower, smoothing my cheek against his upraised thigh. My teeth score the inside of his knee, before I smooth over the bite with my tongue. "Here?"

"Where? What?" he asks. When I smile at him, he seems to remember my quest, and his eyes crinkle at the edges with amusement. "No, not there. Though that's at least in the top thirty favorite places."

I follow his strong thigh with my lips, coming to rest at the soft skin just inside his hipbone. "Here?"

This time, he can't manage words, only a strained-sounding grunt. I'm guessing that means top fifteen.

The rough wool of the blanket scratches my elbow as I scoot up a little, laying a kiss on the bare skin of his abs. They shiver under my lips and I continue circling, leaving small, teasing touches in my wake. He's already fully aroused, and he pulses thicker every time I get close. I'm not sure which of our hearts is pounding harder when I finally dip my head and brush my lips over him.

His moan shakes the air of the room as I slide my tongue over him, learning his texture. He flexes against my tongue and excitement thrills through me. I like when I can wring even the smallest sound out of him, and right now I can measure exactly how much he wants my touch. It makes me reckless. I push his dick slowly past my lips, loving the feeling of him thick and swollen against my tongue. I'm finally in his room, in the heart of his secrets, and I love that, too.

I'm drunk on the idea of Jacob out of control; all the lazy confidence he has in bed evaporated into flashing eyes and chest-deep groans of near-painful pleasure. I want him to forget about our deal and taking care of me. I want my touch to be so intoxicating he can't hold on another second.

I steady myself against his leg. His muscles tighten until they're nearly twanging, and pleasure melts through me. I shift against him, wishing I would have thought to take my jeans off, too, so I could enjoy all his skin against mine.

"Jera..." he gasps. "You have to stop. God, you have to stop."

I let my tongue enjoy every inch of his cock as I slowly pull away, and then I peek up at him, my eyes half-closed.

"Why?" I challenge, my voice throaty and brave. "So you can take care of yourself after I go home? Maybe I want to watch." It's what I think about every time he leaves my house and I stay awake to bring myself to the release I can never seem to find with another person.

The pulse in his throat leaps at my words, then settles into a heavy, thudding rhythm.

"Would you like that?" he asks, his voice a gravelly rumble.

In answer, I take his hand and wrap it around his erection. He doesn't look away from my face, but I can't help but glance down to watch when he starts to move, dragging his fist all the way up his length and squeezing the head of his cock so much more roughly than I'd ever dare to.

I am never blinking again.

His hand slides slowly down. I lean forward and take him in my mouth again, following his rhythm as he strokes himself and I trace him with my tongue, his hips rolling freely now as he pushes up into his fist.

Suddenly, his breathing stutters and he jerks away from me, hauling me up over his body, one arm iron-tight around my waist and the other clutching my head to his chest. His lungs heave as he gulps for breath, his whole body trembling so it takes me a second to realize he stopped me before he could finish. Disappointment pings through me, but Jacob's fingers are shaking as he tries to stroke my hair, and that makes it hard to be sorry. For anything.

His heart thumps explosively beneath my cheek, and I'm overwhelmed with tenderness that I did this to him. That he wanted me so much.

I turn my head and press a soft kiss directly over his heart, and he stops breathing. My hair falls across my forehead as I look up, alarmed, but then he just chuckles unevenly.

"That's it. That's my favorite spot."

I lift a teasing eyebrow. "Is that your final answer? Because I feel like we had some strong contenders there."

"Nope. That's it. That's the one."

I leave another kiss to mark the spot, and then scoot up and rest my head on his shoulder. "You didn't have to stop me, you know."

"That's our deal, remember?" He brushes his knuckles down my arm. "I don't want to go there without you."

I prop myself up a little. "I'm ready, Jacob. I know it would be different with you. Everything is different with you." Even as the words leave my lips, I can feel the truth ringing beneath them.

When I was late for the movies one night because rehearsal ran over, he wasn't mad that we missed the show he already bought tickets for, but he was honestly bummed he hadn't heard the songs that made me lose track of time. With him, I still feel the tug of guilt, like I need to be better, smarter, kinder. But Jacob always seems to know just the right way to tease me out of it so before I have a chance to get all neurotic, I end up curled with him on the couch, eating all the blue and yellow M&Ms out of the bag while we leave the reds for Danny to scavenge later.

He fits into my life like it's been holding a spot open just for him, but our sex life is still a giant question mark. We mess around, and pet and play with each other, but we still haven't even had sex. I don't see how I can meet Maya and move into a more permanent phase of our relationship with that "what if" still shadowing our future.

"Does that mean I get to go on a hunt for all your favorite spots?" His eyes gleam.

My heart hiccups, then starts sprinting, and my fingers clench on the blanket beneath me. I nod.

He hooks a finger in the waistband of my jeans and I nod again, my head going light and tingly. The button slips loose, my zipper comes down, and he strokes the denim off my legs, making even undressing me seem like a caress.

Jacob drops my jeans and prowls back up my body, stark naked. He keeps coming until he could kiss me, but doesn't, our lips nearly touching as he props his forearm beside my head without looking away. My muscles clench, way down low. I'm intensely aware of how aroused he is, and how perfectly we're positioned for him to slip inside me. One fragile layer of fabric is all that's between us.

Jacob dips his head and draws a line of kisses along the boundaries of my bra, his jaw scratching the inner curves of my breasts with a faint five o'clock shadow that nearly cripples my pulse.

When he lifts an eyebrow at me, I manage, "Top five. At least."

He smiles. "On the right track, then." He reaches behind me and my bra releases with a simple snap of his fingers. As it loosens and he tosses it away, it feels like I'm letting go of a lot more than a piece of fabric, and my chest goes tight. I remember all the times I put my bra back on while Andy and I swapped terse, painful words, and how much I hated fighting that way. But then Jacob lays his palm on my ribs just beneath my breast and leaves it there, the warmth comforting my skin even as it makes me feel more bare than I've ever been.

He lowers his head so his lips stroke over mine. Not a kiss, just pure texture. From there, he shifts until his breathing is tickling over the skin of my neck, my sensitive earlobe.

"Every inch on the body feels touch differently, Jera," Jacob whispers. "You just have to pay attention."

My…everything…falters then. My heart, my lungs, my brain, my memory. I am focused so completely on Jacob that the walls could have fallen down and I wouldn't even feel the wind.

The first place he touches me is the hollow at the base of my throat, where my blood clamors hot and chaotic in my veins.

The second is the soft crook inside my elbow.

There's not a single place he neglects, and they are all my new favorites.

My panties melt away somewhere in the midst of it with a light whisper of fabric along my legs, a giddy thrill that I have more bare skin for him to touch. When his slow kisses start climbing up from my knee, I can't even remember what it is like to be nervous. To want anything in this world except his full attention on one tiny scrap of my body at a time.

Finally, he settles where I've wanted him all along, his broad shoulders pressing my inner thighs wide apart to make room for him. Even now, he doesn't hurry, doesn't go to the obvious places. He finds new ones until I'm writhing and twisting beneath his tongue, breathing in a way that is stuck somewhere between desperation and pure joy.

I feel it all too early, that edge at the beginning of an orgasm where everything gets too sensitive and I want more but it *hurts*. I whimper in sheer frustration and anger because I don't think I can bear to push him away.

"Shh," he whispers, lifting his head. "You're okay. I know."

In the end it's so simple. Instead of moving more urgently when I'm almost there, his tongue gets softer, slower. He pulls away until there's almost no touch at all, just the tide of sensations that have been building one caress at a time until the pull of them is stronger than I am.

It's happening. Oh my God, it's finally happening. Everything goes fuzzy at the edges as the first ripple of orgasm spasms through me.

This is going to change everything. Jacob was right—I'm not broken and now there's nothing standing between us and forever. I can meet Maya and…shit, what if she doesn't like me? Jacob makes it look effortless to be a great father figure and friend and boyfriend, but I don't know if I can match him on any of those. After college, he's going to design bridges while my band is still playing The Basement. He's amazing, and I'm just…me.

My every muscle is taut, so it takes me a second to realize the wave of pleasure has frozen, quivering right at the crest but not quite breaking. I jerk back, scooting toward the headboard, and Jacob lifts his head.

"Jera?"

"It didn't work," I blurt out, though I'm not entirely sure if that's true. I leap off the bed, grabbing my clothes.

He sits up, at home with his nudity in a way I've never been. "Hey, it's okay. Slow down a second."

"It was never going to work!" I bite off, this whole room full of kids toys suddenly a glaring sign that I don't belong. I don't even know what half those things *are*.

Snatching up a stray sock, I run. I throw on clothes as I go, hopping into my jeans and yanking my shirt over my head, keeping my bra and underwear balled in a fist as I rip open the front door.

"Jera, wait! What's wrong?"

I only grabbed one boot on my way out of his bedroom, and I can't stop to put it on or he'll catch up to me, but at least my keys are in my pocket this time. I abandon the sock and boot and sprint barefoot down the sidewalk.

It would be one thing if my body or my lack of expertise screwed things up again. But if he says goodbye now, he wouldn't be saying it to our messed up sex life. He'd be saying it to all of me. And why wouldn't he? I'm barely learning how to be a girlfriend. I have no idea how to be the mom Maya desperately needs, and I don't dare try because if I do it wrong, I'll hurt the person Jacob loves most in the world. He must have suspected I couldn't do it, too, because all this time, he's been protecting her from me.

When I hear his voice behind me, I only run faster.

Chapter 25: RUNNING BACKWARD

I pull into a spot in front of Danny's apartment complex and shut off the car, trying to get my mind around everything that has changed in the space of an hour.

I wish I could hide behind anger, to rail at Jacob for lying to me, but he was right not to tell me.

If he would have told me when we met that his "family responsibilities" included a two-year-old child, I would have run, far and fast enough to save us all. The only reason I allowed myself to want Jacob was because I figured if he didn't like who I was, he could walk away. Maya doesn't have that option.

My mind keeps circling, studying each piece of my past like it's a tarot card. If Jacob would have told me the truth about Maya, I never would have gone out with him. I never would have fallen for him, never would have started to believe that a guy could like me when I wasn't putting on a show to impress him. Never would have known that I'm not always a cold fish in bed. But what was the point of going through any of that? Even if I'm enough for Jacob, I'll never be enough for his baby sister.

I used to think if I could find the right guy, he'd love me exactly the way I was, and that meant I'd never have to change. I should have known it wasn't that simple. Love changes everything.

Shoving tears off my cheeks, I open my car door, leaving my bra and underwear crumpled on the passenger seat like two more casualties of this shitty day. I limp barefoot across the parking lot, wincing at the gravel that bruises my feet. I left my stupid phone behind, so I don't even know if Danny's home. It doesn't matter. If he's not, one of his roommates will let me in. Jacob will look for me at my house, and I can't face him right now.

I trudge up the concrete stairs to the second floor of Danny's apartment building. Maybe this is why Andy disappeared after we broke up. I'm sure the sight of my face was a reminder of every problem he couldn't fix. Suddenly, it's a lot harder to blame him for that.

My knock is exhausted and off-center, but it must be enough because after a second, Tiki answers. Her canary-yellow dreadlocks are tied back today with something that looks like an old bike chain, a plasticky rhinestone protruding from the crooked piercing in her nose. She stares at me out of eyes ringed with two or three days' accretion of eyeliner.

"Your funeral." She walks away, leaving the door open.

I don't know what that means, and I don't care. I have no idea how Danny puts up with Tiki, and she's the steadiest of his three roommates. The living room reeks of pot, incense, and oil paints, and I hold my breath as I pass through it and head up the hallway.

Letting myself into Danny's room, I pause and hold onto the doorknob, rubbing one foot over the other to brush the dirt off. My eyes are pointed in front of me, but the whole world is kind of a blur, which is why it takes a minute for me to realize what I'm seeing. I blink and glance behind me to be sure I opened the right bedroom door. End of the hall, check, past the perpetually burned out bulb, check.

Instead of Danny's smoothly monastic furnishings, punctuated by pockets of chaos, it's all chaos. The mattress hangs off the futon; the end of it protruding onto his desk, his sketchpads scattered on the floor beneath. The basket holding his charcoal pencils has rained out onto his pillow, and the basket for his shoes looks like someone put their foot through the bottom of it.

His room looks the way I feel.

Danny's huddled half-in and half-out of the closet, knees up and fingers buried in his hair. Behind him is a carnage of black clothes, some of them ripped like he pulled them off the hangers too hard. I suspected he was still dating the girl Jax mentioned at our concert but I didn't know for sure until this moment.

I drop to the floor in front of Danny and wrap my arms around him, even though he's all sharp angles right now and hard to hold. Laying my head on his forearm, I close my eyes. I miss Jacob already, the way his hands never felt like they were touching just my body. It felt like they were touching *me*, like he was drinking my personality in through his skin and he could never get enough. I wish I could know for sure if that's how he felt, or if I wove it all out of how much I wanted it to be true.

"Why does this shit keep happening to me?" Danny whispers.

I shake my head against his too-hot skin, and I don't open my eyes. I hurt everywhere and I don't know how to stop. His pain just expands into mine until it all feels the same.

"I meet a girl and she seems really into me, but then after a while, she wants me to change. It's always *something* and fuck it, Jera, sometimes I want them so bad I almost think I could do it. That I could be different."

I suck in a sharp little breath, new tears hitting my eyes. "I know, D." It's been our problem since junior high. Every breakup is different, but somehow they're all the same. There's always something about us that doesn't fit with other people.

"She hated you," he mutters, and I love him for how confused he sounds, like that's not even possible.

He lifts his head, our arms and knees still all tangled together. The overhead light is off, or maybe broken, and the evening light from the window is fading to a weak gray.

His hazel eyes sharpen when they spot the tear streaks on my face. "Fuck," he says. "Jacob?"

I nod, the knot in my throat growing. I can't talk about it yet, not even to Danny. "You first."

He shakes his head. "She's been jealous of you, ever since she came to one of our gigs and saw us laughing together. Tonight, I was bummed that the Amp deal didn't work out. I was trying to cheer myself up, so I was watching some of our best shows on YouTube. Anyway, my girlfriend came over while the video of 'My Air' was playing. She totally flipped her shit, and then I told her we passed on the record contract. She didn't get why I was fine with it. Said I was going nowhere with my life and she wasn't going to be stuck with some deadbeat."

"Who *is* this crazy bitch?" I burst out, and the corner of Danny's mouth twitches. Not a smile but for a second there, it almost was. "I'm sorry, D, I want to be supportive, I really do, but mostly I just want to slap your girlfriend with a refrigerator, you know?"

"She's not as bad as you're thinking." He drops his head, and I scoot in so it can rest on my shoulder. I can read in the slump of his body how tired he is. "She knows what she wants, and I'm…I don't know, not exactly that. I mean, I'm a tattoo artist. It's not even as if that's in the meantime while I go to school or something, like you. I *want* to be a tattoo artist, and even if we had signed with Amp, I'd still want to ink people. Maybe that's a deadbeat thing to like, or whatever. I don't know."

I mentally upgrade the refrigerator to a school bus. Preferably with teeth. And talons.

"It's not wrong to love art, Danny. Tattoos are a thousand times more permanent than paintings, and way more personal. If people are going to inject *ink* under their skin, they need somebody as talented as you, so it won't get screwed up."

"It isn't just my job she doesn't like. It's you, it's me." He lifts his head, his bright eyes gone dull. "People just don't get us, you know? But you're the *only* person who has never asked me to change and I don't give a shit what she says, Jimi, I'm not giving you up."

My vision wavers and I hug him, his knee caught between us and digging into my ribs, but I wouldn't let him go even if my bones started to crack.

"Is Jacob pissed about us, too?"

I shake my head into Danny's neck. Jacob saw us sing "My Air" in person, and he was crazy about that song, even though he knew it wasn't about him. In fact, the only thing he's ever said about Danny is that he loves to watch us riff off each other during rehearsals. He had some kind of baseball metaphor for it that I didn't get at all, but I liked the shine in his eyes when he was explaining it to me.

"He want you to change?" Danny asks, his voice so raw that I know he was probably yelling when he wrecked his room, before I showed up.

I start to nod, and then stop. He didn't, not really. Jacob's never questioned that music should be my career, never asked me to spend less time with my friends.

The only thing he's ever asked me for is a chance.

I take a shuddering breath. This entire time, Jacob's been so patient, making me laugh when I was wound up tight with stress, smiling when I expected him to scowl, and texting me so I never felt forgotten, even when we couldn't get our schedules to match up for days on end. He's been perfect. That's exactly the problem because I'm not, and I'm just walking a tightrope, precisely balanced but knowing it can't last. There's a catch. There's always a catch.

"He needs me to be something I'm not," I whisper. He needs someone strong, like him, who isn't going to take off when things get tough. He needs a mom for Maya.

I'm just a junior in college, with a band that can barely earn beer money and a house dripping with out-of-code asbestos, lead-based paint, and shag carpet harboring forty years' worth of toddler-killing germs.

"Danny!" shrieks Tiki from the front room. "What the fuck, man?"

I pull back, sniffling. "What is her problem?"

"I'll deal with it. Be right back."

He shoves to his feet and pulls the bedroom door open. He's not moving right. Heavy and angry; nothing like his normal fluid quiet. I hate his stupid ex even more for that.

"I've got better things to do than get up and down off the couch a hundred times," Tiki says, "answering the door for your stupid friends because you're too lazy to come out of your stupid room. Like it's not hard enough to chill with you throwing shit around back there."

Bong water bubbles, and I roll my eyes. I guess she's not having that much trouble chilling. But wait, what did she say about answering the door? Did his ex come back?

I shoot off the floor. I could use a fight right now, and who the hell does that girl think she is, insulting his band and his art?

The front door scrapes open.

"Jera probably told you to say she's not here, but I know she is," Jacob's voice says. "Can I just talk to her, please?"

All the blood in my veins turns to shards of ice and pain, and I jerk to a stop in the hallway just out of sight of the living room. Tiki's bong starts to bubble again, marijuana smoke threading greasily through the incense.

"You told her she had to change for you," Danny says. "Which means you can point your feet the fuck away from my house."

The door smacks into something and then there's a vibrating twang like it ricocheted back off.

"I told her *what*? Are you kidding me right now?"

"You are going back down those stairs," Danny says. "It can be on your feet or on your face. Believe me, I don't care which." His tone is utterly flat. Both times I've heard him sound like that before, he proceeded to get himself arrested.

I scramble across the living room. "He didn't have a choice about what he was asking of me," I tell Danny. "He has a kid."

Sweeping past my friend, I shiver when my bare feet hit the concrete of the landing outside. If Danny has a reaction to that particular bomb drop, I don't look up to see it. Out loud, all he says is, "You want shoes?"

"I have her shoes," Jacob says.

I look up. My combat boots dangle from one of his hands, socks tucked neatly into the tops, my messenger bag and jacket in his other hand. I don't know if I should be comforted or terrified that he gathered up all my things before he came after me.

"Drama stays outside," Tiki says, trying to slam the door. Danny stops her and looks to me.

"It's okay," I promise him, and only then does he let Tiki slam the door closed. Normally, I'd lay into her for that, but I don't know if Jacob plans on staying long enough for us to bother going inside. After a month, there's not a single thing of mine in his house except what I left today. There's something so wrong about the idea that he could walk away right now and leave no trace except the raggedness inside of me.

"How did you know where I'd be?" My house is in the opposite direction from Danny's apartment, and Jacob got here too fast. There's no way he had time to loop around and check my place first.

He exhales, and it sounds funny, like he pushed it out between his gritted teeth. I don't dare raise my eyes high enough to check.

"When the fuck are you going to admit that I know you, Jera?" he asks. I flinch. I'm not used to that word—not from his lips. "I want to know, honestly. What did I do so wrong that you feel safe to run to him when you're upset, but not to me?"

I can't stand the hurt vibrating out of his voice, but I don't know how to answer. I don't even know if there is an answer. I cross my arms over my thin shirt, my nipples uncomfortably tight from the wintery air.

He drops my messenger bag and boots, and holds my jacket out between us. It feels wrong to take it, but he doesn't drop his hand, so finally I have to. I keep my head down as I thread one arm into it, then the other.

Jacob drops his hands onto his hips, then turns around. Under his shirt, his back is stiff. My heart jumps. Is he leaving?

"I want to ask you what's wrong." He turns back to face me. "But it doesn't matter, does it? No matter what I do, you're just going to keep running."

"I just—" I don't finish the sentence, because I don't know what to say. I just know that he and Maya will need so much more from me than I thought, and I don't know if I can be that and stay true to myself, too. But Christ, I don't want to lose him.

I glance away, down the long line of identical apartment doors. Behind me, there's nothing but a cheap iron railing and a long fall to the relentless pavement below. Right now, it feels all too precarious.

"This is why I didn't tell you about Maya." He throws his arms out to the sides. "I knew it. I damn well knew you wouldn't want me enough to stick around after that."

"It's *not* that you're not enough." The words explode out of me, my eyes flying up to his face now. He doesn't even look like himself. His jaw is knotted, his brows clamped low over his eyes and lines of pain ricocheting out into his temples. There's still a smear of engine grease on his forehead where he shoved a hand back through his hair before he washed up. I want to touch it, like a reminder of the kiss he gave me this morning.

I don't get the chance because in an instant he surges forward and I'm caged between him and the railing. He's big in a way he's never seemed before, his wide shoulders practically snarling down at me. My bare toes curl, scraping against the rough, cold cement.

"No," he snaps. "It's not, is it? Jesus, Jera, *I* had to convince you your music was good enough that another record label would want it, or you would have just signed that shitty deal and been grateful." A sound comes out of him like a cough of disbelief.

"Yeah, and that's worked out so fucking great, hasn't it?" I plant both hands in his chest and shove. "Now we're back to being a piddly little local band getting excited because we've got three gigs a month when we could have been recording a real album. I bet that's what you wanted all along, isn't it? For me to turn them down so I wouldn't get famous and leave you behind." I throw the words at him, because he hasn't backed off an inch and I can't *breathe*.

He doesn't even blink at my accusation. "It's been a week. Are you going to give up on your dreams because it's been a week and you don't have a new record label yet?"

I shove him again, using all my strength this time, and he doesn't move. Nerves thrill through my chest. I've never until this moment been reminded that he's six foot two inches of solid muscle and I can't make him do a damned thing he doesn't want to.

He ducks his head until he's right in my face, eyes boring into mine. "It's not me you don't have any faith in, it's you. You don't believe I'll want you unless our sex life is perfect, I doubt you listened to a thing I said today about Maya being my responsibility, not yours, and you're never going to stick around long enough for me to prove any of that, are you?"

He cocks his head, and for the first time since he showed up, I glimpse a familiar tenderness beneath the pain and anger turning his brown eyes cold.

"Where does all that doubt come from, Jera, huh? Is this all seriously about your ex? Because he sounded like an asshole, but I'm really starting to get curious about who gave up first. Something tells me it might not have been him."

I gape at him. "Screw you." I duck under his arm and spin away. He turns with me, but he doesn't stop me this time. Something about how all he's doing is watching makes me pause instead of fleeing into Danny's apartment.

"I love you, Jera." His voice is soft now, so I can hear the thousands of complicated things contained in three uncomplicated words, and every bit of the pain that shadows the joy. "So much that I trust you not just with my heart, but with Maya's." He takes a step toward the stairs. "But if you're not capable of doing the same, please don't call me again."

Chapter 26: AN INTERNET EDUCATION

I do a hundred things after Jacob leaves me. I get rich and famous and super publicly married to a gorgeous philanthropist just to prove him wrong. I have twenty kids, and people write books about my parenting because I'm such an amazing mom. I go inside and punch Tiki in her stupid nose.

I set my boots and my messenger bag on fire, because they were the last things Jacob touched, when he was busy not touching me.

I don't watch him drive away.

A thousand times, I don't watch him drive away. And a million times, I do.

In my head, I do a lot of things. But the only thing that matters is the thing I don't do. Because when he leaves, I don't stop him.

Days go by. I get drunk with Danny, I play my drums until I fall asleep in my garage, I go to class like it's a normal week. Nothing helps. With every second that passes, the Jacob-shaped hole in my life looms larger.

I can't lose him. The words repeat in every heartbeat, the helplessness of them speeding my pulse until it gallops night and day like it's in a race with no finish line.

And yet I know if I can't give up, the only other choice is to do the thing that scares me most. I have to try and be a better person, one good enough to be trusted with a child. I don't know if I can do that and still be the me I've come to like in the last year, but as Danny said, you don't get to know the answer before you ask the question.

So I do what I know how to do: research. I start by reading articles about kids. What they eat, what they do. What you need to do for them.

I was an only child, and I've never even done any babysitting, so I'm pretty much starting at ground zero. I research everything from developmental stages to blogs about bad parenting. I watch YouTube videos of how to install a car seat and do the Heimlich on a baby. I stop going to class and days disappear into my ever-lengthening search history.

I didn't believe Jacob would really like me if I was only myself, but he did. He made dating fun instead of anxiety-producing, and I bet he's just as sweet and playful with Maya. I can picture him reading her stories, doing voices for all the different characters, even the girl ones. He's totally the kind of dad who would make a game out of diaper changing, rather than the kind yelling at his kids to be quiet in the store. Except wait, do two-year-olds still wear diapers?

I go back to my laptop to find out, and every fact I learn leads to five more I need to know. It's more than a little terrifying. If Jacob would give me one more chance, though, I'd do it. He knows me, and he said he trusted me with Maya anyway. In a way, he proved it the moment he told me about her.

But I know if I try this, there's a chance—a big one—that I'll fuck it up, and Jacob will look at me with pain and anger in those gentle brown eyes. That maybe, even if I give it all I've got, there will come a day when he doesn't want to look at me anymore.

That maybe, that day has already come.

When I finally work myself up to putting a phone on my knees instead of a laptop, my mouth is oatmeal-flour dry. My heart is running sprints up Mt. Kilimanjaro even though my body got left behind on the couch, and just as I'm wondering if I have any of Granna's Nitro pills left around, the phone starts to ring.

I fumble it onto the floor, and my clumsy fingers have already accepted the call by the time I turn the screen back to face me and see Dad's name on the screen instead of Jacob's.

Big fucking surprise, and it should not hurt this much. Jacob Tate is a man who keeps his promises, and he promised me he wouldn't call me again. Or implied it heavily. Jesus, he's so trustworthy even his implications are ironbound.

"Hi, Dad."

"You could sound more excited, you know. There are orphaned kids all over the world that don't even *have* dads."

"Everybody has a dad, Dad. Even if they're of the test-tube-and-turkey-baster variety." Do sperm donor recipients still use turkey basters? Maybe I should look into it. My researching muscles are all warmed up, stretched out, and ready to rock. My calling-Jacob muscles, on the other hand, are completely atrophied.

I take a breath. That's doubt talking. Doubt can go take a leap off the Go Fuck Yourself Bridge, because it hasn't done me a smidgeon of good lately.

"Jera, are you listening to me?"

"Yes." Or at least, I should be. Things for my band have really been looking up this week, but as much as I love The Red Letters, that good news hasn't put a dent in the darkness that lives in the pit of my stomach now.

"You know, I understand not listening to your dad when he's telling you to empty the dishwasher, or get a job, or stop dating some dreamy guy who has purple hair and wants to take you to freshman prom in a Mustang with an anarchy symbol sprayed on the side. But when your dad is telling you there's an offer in from Cornerstone International Records, you'd think you'd grow a set of ears at that point."

My eyes bug. "Cornerstone? Did you say Cornerstone?"

"Oh, I don't know. I might have said you should eat your broccoli. Or make your bed. Maybe I said you should call your father and tell him what a great job he did raising you, even though you cried a whole Mississippi worth of tears about how he made you practice the guitar and the piano all the time, because he knew someday you'd be a famous musician."

I leap off the couch and whip in a circle, then two. "Shit! Shit, oh my God."

"Let's hope you can come up with more lyrics than that, sweetheart, because they're wanting that album in the can by mid-January, and we've still got negotiations to get through." He pauses. "If Cornerstone's your final answer. I know they were your first choice, but now that they're on the hook, feel free to make 'em squirm a little bit. Ask the hard questions. We've got some Ivy League safety schools lined up here, Jera, so don't rush it. I can get that album deadline pushed back, no problem."

I shake my head, tingling from head to toe. I know it's wrong to be so excited when everything else in my life is total shit, but I can't even help myself right now. Cornerstone is the label for Ground Delay, and Halcyon, and *God*, they even work with Sintoxicated, and that album's been on repeat in my car for so long it might be stuck like that. "See!" I burst out. "I told you so. You totally freaked out when I wouldn't sign with Amp but Cornerstone is the fourth call we've gotten *this week.*"

He snorts. "I did not 'totally freak out.' I was just worried if I didn't hurry, you'd give up."

"Give up? On music? Are you crazy?"

"No, on record labels. Sometimes, you take things kind of hard, kiddo. I didn't want you to give up on finding the right company just because Amp turned out to be a bunch of superficial suits. And I really didn't want your band to go through the crap mine did, trying to go it on our own. I never doubted you could hook a better label— you're twice the musician I ever was."

I blink, staring at the walls of a living room I don't even really see. "Really?"

"Yes, really. Come on, Jera. You ate a brussel sprout when you were four and hated it so much that you claimed you were allergic to vegetables until fifth grade. I call that taking things a little hard."

I barely even hear the complaint. All this time, he thought I was...*better* than his band? I swallow. Maybe I've been watching so hard for disapproval that I forgot to watch for other things, too. Good things.

I press my fist into my lips and blink back tears. "I love you, Dad."

"What was that?"

I drop my hand. "You were right. I love you for making me eat broccoli, and practice the piano, and for letting me go to the prom with Jesse, even though you blackmailed me with pictures of his ugly car for years after we broke up. I love you for believing in my band. And I really, really love you for getting me this record deal but right now I have to go."

He harrumphs. "What, you think just because you say nice stuff, you can blow me off? Enough with you. I'm calling Cornerstone and letting them know you've decided to go into telemarketing instead, and I'm not even telling you the brilliant idea they pitched for re-mixing 'Curbside Cowboy.'"

My grin stretches my face so much it hurts, and I'm not sure if that's because it's been so long since I've smiled, or just because it's a record deal grin instead of a regular one. "You're so not. You'd dress up in my clothes and play the drums yourself before you'd turn down this deal."

"Nah, I'd do it in my own clothes. I'd just change the name of the band first."

"I love you." I'm practically vibrating in place now. Maybe telling Jacob he was right about the record labels will help my case. Regardless, I'm not about to give up. Not this time. "I'll call you later, I promise."

Dad scoffs. "Who needs you? I'm going to call Jax. Now that boy knows how to have an appropriate reaction to the record deal of a lifetime."

"He so does. Just remember I love you more. Besides, Jax isn't the one whose name is going to make all the industry rags reminisce fondly about your band's old hits." If Cornerstone wants us, there's no doubt. My band is good enough that having Dad's name associated with it is no longer a raised eyebrow: it's proof that talent runs in our family.

"That was just fighting dirty, Miss McKnight."

Now it's my turn to snort. "Pot, meet Kettle. If you hadn't leapt off the high road and straight into the gutter with the publicity spin after we rejected Amp, Cornerstone would have never heard of us, and we both know it."

I hang up. There's something I need to do before I can convince myself of all the reasons it's a bad idea. Before wasting another minute, I dial Jacob.

Chapter 27: THIS IS NOT A TEST

When Jacob gets out of his car in front of the zoo, I'm not nervous. Okay, I am nervous, but I'm also fully braced with the knowledge that nothing on earth can match the awkwardness of our conversation when I called to ask if I could meet Maya.

In person.

As his girlfriend.

It didn't help that his voice never softened. That I had to be the first to break each of the arctic-grade silences that descended on the line. That the anxiety of it all made me have to pee like crazy and after we made arrangements for where and how to meet, I hung up and rushed to the bathroom only to realize I'd never even told him about Cornerstone Records.

I shift my weight, half hidden behind the Oregon Zoo sign as I watch him open the back door of his Ford to get Maya out of her car seat. I can't tell him today. It's so not the time or place. But the news just keeps getting better. I was on the phone with my new A&R guy until midnight last night, talking ideas for our demo songs that had me messing around on Garage Band with one hand while I held my phone with the other, because I couldn't wait until I got into a studio to try them out. If this is how good Cornerstone's A&R department is, what must their producers be like?

Belatedly, I realize I'm standing here like a tourist. What a real step-girlfriend would do is help out. Hitching my messenger bag up onto my shoulder, I step into the street and a horn blares. I startle, staring at the Dodge that nearly had me as a hood ornament, then keep going. Jacob didn't even look up. Granted, he's a few parking spots away, so it's not like he knew that horn was the sound of me being a moron, but still.

Cold rakes down my body at the idea that right now, we are terrifyingly close to being in a world where I could die, and he wouldn't even know. For the last seven days of my un-showered, Pop-Tart-fueled internet researching frenzy, all Jacob knew was that I hadn't called. That I might never call again. If a Dodge hit me during any of those seven days, he would have thought I abandoned him because I chose to. He would never have known how hard I was trying to make it back to him.

I square my shoulders and stride between cars, keeping a sharp eye out for any moving ones this time. All I have to do to ace this first test is impress a toddler. They like soap bubbles and plastic ponies. How hard can it be?

Arriving at Jacob's side, I say, "Here, let me help." I wiggle past him to get Maya out of the car seat. I actually researched a lot of different models of these online, and his is not the highest safety rating on the market. I'm trying to decide on the best way to inform him of that fact when I realize all the straps are already undone. I pull back, my arms getting tangled with Jacob's as Maya goes to climb out of her car seat, trips over my wrist, and goes face-first into the back of the seat.

She sucks in a breath, I freeze, and then she begins to wail.

Jacob mutters something under his breath as he gathers her up. If this were Harry Potter, it'd probably be a spell to light my face on fire.

"Sh—" I cut myself off just in time. "I'm sorry. Shoot, I'm so sorry." I reach over to pat Maya's little back, which arches stiffly as she wails.

"Hey, hey," Jacob murmurs, rocking her. "Hey now, you're okay." He digs a tissue out of his pocket and wipes her little nose.

Oh my gosh, kids can't even blow their own noses. I stuff my hands into my pockets, standing there uselessly. How do any of them make it to adulthood when they might suffocate to death from the common cold?

"Hi, Maya," I say, but it comes out sounding like a question. According to my research, kids can hear high-pitched sounds better, so I try that. "Hi, Maya!" I chirp.

She buries her face in Jacob's neck. Wait, was that study about newborns or toddlers? Because even to my untrained ear, I sound like a crazy person.

"Say hi, Maya." He jiggles her slightly to get her attention.

No response.

"Maya..." he prods, dropping his voice.

"Hi," Maya says to Jacob's neck.

She hates me. Awesome.

"This is my friend Jera," he says. "We're going to play with her today, okay?"

My heart drops so fast it gets stuck somewhere around my stomach. I was supposed to meet Maya as his girlfriend to show I could deal with commitment but apparently I've been demoted to trial run status. Jacob goes around and unlocks the trunk, using one hand to pull out a stroller.

Is this even worth it, when he's apparently already written me off?

I close the car door and hurry back to pitch in, even though it takes me a couple of tries to figure out how to unfold the stroller. Today is all about showing him I have faith in myself, and in his feelings for me. Of course, it would be nice if he still seemed to *have* any feelings for me. Or if, I don't know, maybe I didn't make his sister cry within seconds of meeting her.

The trunk shuts with a slam and Jacob opens the front of the car again, pulling out a plain navy messenger bag.

"Nice diaper bag," I say, trying to lighten the mood. "What, flowers and elephants weren't manly enough for your taste?"

"Ben won't carry it if it has cartoons on it."

I want to slap myself. Right. With biceps like his, it's not like Jacob needs to spend much time worrying about proving his manhood.

"So...how have you been?"

Jacob pauses in getting Maya settled in the stroller, and just stares at me. I shift my weight. I mean, it wasn't the world's worst question, right?

When he doesn't answer, I squat down next to the stroller and wiggle Maya's tiny foot. She's wearing adorable little buckled shoes with glittering daisies on them. "What's your favorite animal, sweetie?"

She frowns at me.

"At home, her favorite is elephants, but the last couple of times we've been here, I don't think she really made the connection between her stuffed animals and the real thing. The size differential, I think." Jacob shrugs.

I stand up. "You guys have already been here?" Crap, of course they have. Everybody takes kids to the zoo—I was just trying to pick something really fun for her, and I wasn't sure what else a two-year-old might like.

"It's okay, she loves animals." He starts pushing her stroller toward the entrance, and I hurry along in his wake so I don't get left behind.

By the third exhibit, I'm not sure if I should be bummed because Maya is the only child on earth who hates animals, or happy because Jacob obviously lied to make me feel better. So far, she hasn't glanced at a single exhibit. She has, however, tried to climb into the bushes, banged her head on a drinking fountain, and shoplifted a stuffed elephant from the front display table of the gift shop when I wasn't looking.

Getting his baby sister taken away in handcuffs is totally going to make Jacob fall in love with me.

"Maybe we should go to the farm section," I suggest. "They're supposed to have stuff for kids." I gesture at the glass wall separating us from the swimming penguins. "More hands-on, you know?"

Jacob glances at me. Why does he look worried about the petting zoo? I resist the urge to open a browser window on my phone to double-check. They definitely said the petting zoo was for all ages.

He squats down to Maya's level. "You want to see the bunnies?"

"Bunny?" she asks.

He takes the blanket out of her stroller and tickles her neck with its fuzzy edge. "Remember the bunnies? They were soft."

She giggles and grabs the blanket. He plays a gentle tug-of-war with her for a second before she throws the blanket on the ground and runs off toward another stroller. I go after her and grab her hand while Jacob gathers the blanket. Her hand is unbelievably tiny in mine, and something twinges in my chest. Before I have a chance to sort out what it was, she yanks her hand away and sprints back toward Jacob.

I straighten my shoulders and check the signs that lead the way toward the petting zoo. It's no big deal. She's two, and I'm a freaking adult. I'm not going to get all teary over being rejected by a toddler.

"Bunny hop hop," Maya says, skipping her way into the farmyard. "Hop hop hop." She tugs at Jacob's hand, and I take the stroller from him, parking it outside the fence. "Hop," she demands, and he takes a couple of little jumps with her, careful to keep his big sneakers away from her feet when he lands. A smile tugs at my lips. God, they're cute together. Taking both her hands, he lifts her up with every step like she's walking on the gravity of the moon.

"Hop hop hop," he says, and Maya giggles.

The gate squeaks as Jacob opens it, then shuts with a slam behind us. As soon as Maya sees the goats, she stops laughing.

I grin and squat down next to her. "Have you seen goats before, Maya?" They are super weird looking, every different size and texture, with their crazy little goat eyes and stubby horns. Wait, horns? Who let horned goats in with the kids? The horns are like, right at eye level.

Maya must have the same idea, because she shrinks back against Jacob's legs, then starts whimpering as she turns and tries to scale his jeans. "Up up up up up!" she screams as one of the goats comes trotting over and pokes his nose toward her hand, looking for food. I push him away while Jacob pats Maya's back and tries to coax her into turning around.

"They're just like bunnies, sweetie, just bigger. You can pet them. Look, Jera's petting them. She's not scared."

I reach out, nabbing the retreating goat by the collar and hauling him back toward us, petting his hard little goat head with one hand while I paste on a big grin. "See? They're nice goats."

Please, please don't let the zoo staff bust me for manhandling their goats. Rough, oily goat hair slithers beneath my palm, but I make oohing sounds like he's as soft as a cloud. He cranes his head around, licking at my wrist, and I try not to gag at the scent of his breath.

Still holding Jacob's leg with one arm, Maya reaches out a hand, her brown eyes wide. Both my hands are busy, but with a knee, I nudge the goat a little closer, keeping a sharp eye out for disapproving zoo staff. Maya's fingers just barely brush the edge of one ear and she gasps.

I smile. "See? The goat is nice."

The goat gives up on my hand and cranes his head toward Maya, licking her fingers. She shrieks and burrows in between Jacob's knees, escaping out behind him. Sweet Jesus, now she's going to have a goat phobia. In twenty years, she'll be telling her therapist how I forced a vicious, hand-eating goat on her and she had to run for her life.

With a laugh, Jacob turns and sweeps her up. "Did that goat kiss you, Maya?"

"Yessss!" she wails.

Jacob frowns. "Did it feel like…this?" He nuzzles his head into her neck and blows a noisy raspberry. In an instant, Maya goes from horrified to laughing and swatting at her big brother with goat-slimed hands while he tickles her waist. When he tries to set her back down on the ground though, she clings to his neck, starting to cry all over again. "We might have had enough zoo for one day," he says to me. "She wouldn't go down for her nap this afternoon, so I was worried it wasn't going to work out so well."

"We could have rescheduled," I say, even though it feels like my lungs are wilting inside my chest, and he just shakes his head.

They're going home. Of course they are: Maya cried like a hundred times and hit her head twice, and neither of them will so much as look at me.

That was it. This was my audition and I just blew it.

MICHELLE HAZEN

Chapter 28: BALLAST

The walk back to the car takes forever, and not nearly long enough. I can't cry when I say goodbye to Jacob, not with Maya here. I'm wrangling with my tear ducts over this issue when Jacob glances over at me. His shoulders sag a little.

"Hey," he says. "You got an extra minute, or do you have to get going?"

"No, I have—" I clear my throat, trying to control my voice. "I've got plenty of time." Actually, I have a metric shit-ton of finals to study for, but my participation grade is already in the toilet thanks to last week's truancy spree, and I'm not even sure I can focus enough to fake literacy at the moment, so studying's already a lost cause.

"Okay." Jacob pushes Maya's stroller past the car and toward the other side of the parking lot.

A sign for the Portland Children's Museum sits on the other side of the road. Of course. Jacob's dad was a professor, and if Maya inherited any of the same brainy genes as her brother, it makes perfect sense that she'd like a museum more than a zoo. I dip a furtive hand into my purse, trying to determine if I have enough money for another set of admission fees today, but Jacob just keeps right on going past the entrance and toward a trail winding through the woods, browning lawn spreading out between the trees. Maya starts to squirm, and he barely gets her unbuckled from the stroller before she wriggles out. She drops her hands to the ground, nearly somersaulting with the momentum of the abrupt stop.

We both watch her as she pats at the winter-dry blades of grass, examining them as they spring back into place, then pushing them down again, holding longer this time before she lets them go. For the first time today, she doesn't run or squeal, or look off to the next thing. She just brushes her hand back and forth over the strands, fascinated.

Jacob slides his hands into his jeans pockets. "Loves grass. Has like two roomfuls of toys, and all she wants to do is sit on the lawn and smack the grass around. She's a pretty weird kid."

My laugh catches in my throat, and I shake my head. "No, look at her. She's experimenting. She's trying to figure out how long she has to smash it before it stays smashed." I dare a glance up at Jacob. "I'm afraid you've got a future engineering major on your hands."

The hint of a smile touches his lips. "I'm going to try to forget you said that." A puff of wind blows through the trees, ruffling his hair.

Heartened by his reaction, I take a couple of steps, then sit down next to Maya. Not looking at her, I pat the grass, too.

She drops to her bottom, curling her fists in the grass as she rips out a handful of blades, then arranges them on the leg of my jeans. I pull up some grass—Sorry, Portland Parks Department—and return the favor, making sure to evenly cover her whole leg in green, leafy shrapnel. Maya giggles.

My skin tingles at the sound.

The little girl reaches over and pats my knee. Or maybe the grass on my knee. Either way, I don't care because I'm not breathing and I might start crying all over again because she's the cutest thing I've ever seen.

Before I can decide how to respond, Maya crawls up to her feet and runs away, pelting toward a little boy who is kicking a ball around closer to the trail. I look back at Jacob, but he's already searched out the mother of the little boy and they're making parental eye contact while she gives him the "totally fine" nod. Her gaze flicks to me, and she smiles. That too-quick, overly polite one like, "I was just checking out your husband and I super hope you didn't notice."

I attempt to smile back, but it's a little weak. That woman has no idea how much I wish this was my family. Which it's never going to be if I don't grow some courage.

I pull myself up to standing and return to Jacob's side.

"Maya, no," he calls and I whirl around. It's been like one-twentieth of a second, what did I miss?

A stick trails grungy looking moss toward the ground as Maya lifts it and tastes the other end. She ignores Jacob, licking it again, and he changes tack.

"I threw it on the *ground,*" he sings in a familiar tune, miming throwing a stick down. Maya's face breaks out into a grin and she hurls her stick, laughing.

"Oh, no you didn't!" I burst out laughing, my hand coming up to cover my mouth. "You trained your sister not to eat trash using a freaking viral YouTube video from The Lonely Island?"

"I taught her the song with the video on mute," he says defensively. "There is a ton of swearing in that thing." I'm still smiling, and a bit of red starts to flush across his cheekbones. "Hey, nothing else worked. And she loves that video. Granted, she's thrown a lot of food on the ground since then to watch it explode, but better a few hot dogs wasted than have her eat a used syringe or something, you know?"

I try not to laugh, I really do, but it's pretty hard, especially when Maya picks up the stick again and flings it to the ground, giggling to herself.

"Good girl!" he calls. Maya's new friend picks up a stick, and he throws it too. "Kid's mom's going to think I'm a freak," Jacob mutters.

It looks to me like that little boy's mom is squinting herself into early wrinkles, trying to see from across the lawn if Jacob is wearing a ring. I edge a little closer to him.

"So look, obviously the first test was an epic fail, but do I at least qualify for a makeup exam?" I dodge a look up at him through my eyelashes. Please say yes.

Jacob stiffens. "No."

I reel a little, then plant my feet wider to combat the dizziness. He can't mean that. He said he loved me, and now he's kicking me out the door after my first hour-long attempt at parenting. Can't I get an internship here?

"It was never a test!" he snaps. Maya looks over our way and he waves at her, pasting on a smile, then lowers his voice. "The point wasn't that I expected you to be a pro at babysitting. Come on, do you think I knew what I was doing when my parents died? I'd been busy in college since she was born—I'd never even been alone with Maya before the accident." He crosses his arms. "I wanted us to be in this together, Jera. In our relationship, as role models for Maya, in whatever. You don't go through life knowing what you're supposed to do, but if you're lucky, you have someone to figure it out with. You can't do that if one of you is going to give up on the whole thing the first time you screw up."

My stomach drops. He's absolutely right, and yet after everything we've been through, my first instinct was to try even harder to prove myself to him instead of trusting that he didn't need me to.

"You know that game where you're supposed to fall and catch each other?" Jacob sounds past annoyed now, and well into upset. "You'd never fall for me. I'd be standing there, mats laid out, hands extended, muscles braced. And instead, you'd fall on *Danny*." He shakes his head. "He probably wouldn't be paying any attention, you'd both end up on the ground, and you'd laugh like crazy and it wouldn't matter."

This time when I see his jaw flex, I want to wrap him in a legs-and-all koala hug. "Wait, are you jealous now?" I poke him in the ribs, starting to smile. "I thought Jacob Tate was way too selfless and mature to ever be jealous."

He scowls. "I'm not jealous that you love him, I'm jealous that you trust him."

My eyes widen. "Hey." I lay a hand on his arm, but he keeps going because now that he's started, he obviously has some things to get off his chest.

"Did you know the professors gave me a key to the art building? I'm not even an art major. Moms from Maya's daycare practically throw their children at me. When I don't have time to babysit for them, or even go for a play date, they ask my advice. Mine." He frowns down at me. "I'm not even old enough to buy my own beer, Jera. People give me their cars even though I don't have a license, I didn't go to school for that, and they have no recourse if I screw it up. One loose bolt, one forgetful moment, and their car could fail when they're on the freeway and kill thirty other people. Everyone trusts me but you, Jera." His jaw twitches as he looks out at Maya. "So yeah, maybe I'm still a little pissed about that."

I squeeze his arm, his PU hoodie soft against my palm even though his bicep is clenched underneath. "For the record, it's not that Danny's more trustworthy than you. It's that he has lower standards. I don't exactly have to worry about impressing a guy whose roommate lit his toothbrush on fire trying voodoo spells on a goldfish."

Jacob does not laugh.

I turn so I'm standing right in front of him. "Hey," I say softly. "You didn't do anything wrong."

He scowls. "That just makes it worse." He sits down, dropping his arms over his knees and grabbing his wrist with the opposite hand so hard that I wince. "Give me a problem I can fix already."

I sit down next to him. "I can't. Because you're not the problem. I am." There has never been a man more worthy of trust than Jacob Tate. That's not news. But what's giving me hope right now is that he's mad because he cares what I think. He wants *me* to trust him, to rely on him. I already do, more than he realizes. I'm just trying to be someone he can rely on, too.

"There's nothing—" He stops himself, swallows.

"There's nothing wrong with me? That's what you were going to say, isn't it?"

He doesn't answer.

It's not that this is going anything like I planned, or even that it's going particularly well. But for a second there, I saw the crack in his defenses. He cares about me, and as long as I've still got that, I can deal with the rest. Besides, I've got a feeling I know why he's still holding back.

I glance over to check on Maya. She's ignoring the little boy now, pushing his soccer ball around while he breaks the sticks she had into pieces.

I hug my knees into my chest. "There's plenty wrong with me, Jacob. It's just mostly in my head." I grimace. "Which doesn't sound so bad, until you realize that's the most dangerous place it could be." After last year, when I exhausted myself trying to please everyone, I thought the only safe thing to do was to stop trying: to have a relationship, to be a better person, to make my parents proud. I got it half right, because that helped me figure out what *I* really wanted. But the answer wasn't to give up, it was to find a man who would love me even when I wasn't perfect. The way my parents do. The way Danny does. The way Granna did.

Jacob stares across the lawn, his knuckles white where they're clamped around his wrist.

"I know you can't take a chance on me," I say. "You're probably biting back a million terribly sweet things to say right now, because you've told yourself you can't do this *for* me. For Maya's sake, you have to wait for me to be ready, or I'll take off on you guys the next time I get scared."

His face is perfectly, absolutely blank, and in that, I read everything I need to see.

"When are you going to admit I know you, Jacob?" I smile, tilting my head. "Or should I say when the f-u-c-k are you going to admit—"

He grabs my hand before I finish the sentence, squeezing it tight like he's afraid, even though he still stares straight forward. I glory in the pressure, hopeful goosebumps appearing all up my arms. This is what I was missing, all those other times. In every relationship, you fall short or they do…until the last one. And then you're stretching so far there's no going back and you can feel the wind whistling against your face as you fall. But if you're both reaching, you catch each other's hands at the very last minute and it makes the perfect bridge.

"You don't have to hang on, you know. I'm not going anywhere." I bump him with my shoulder. "I'm going to stay right here and screw up like crazy, and if nothing else, Maya will grow up knowing that in this family, you don't have to be perfect to be loved."

He finally turns to look at me, his eyes searching my face like he's afraid I'll take it back. And nothing has ever made me feel safer than seeing how much he wants that future, too.

I just smile. "I do admit, though, I could use a lesson or two in playing Barbies."

I follow them home. Which isn't as creepy as it sounds, because Jacob invited me. When we get to his apartment, I jump out and book it over to his car, determined to redeem myself in the area of car seat operation. When I open the back door, though, Maya's asleep with her head at an angle that would send me straight to the chiropractor.

Carefully, I unbuckle her and slide the car seat straps from under her little hands, nearly suffocating myself because I hold my breath the whole time I'm trying to detangle the straps from her hair.

Behind me, Jacob chuckles, low and deep. My scalp tickles with pleasure at the sound I haven't heard for far too many days. "You don't have to be that careful. We could play a game of volleyball over her right now. She won't wake up until the second I tiptoe out of the room."

I glance back, and he holds out his hands to take his sister. "Can I carry her in?" I whisper.

His eyes shade to a deeper brown in an instant, and he clears his throat. "Sure."

I pick her up, biting my lip when her head kind of flops under its own weight. They said you don't have to support the neck after the first few months, but I'm not entirely sure I trust "them" anymore. Once I get her bottom safely propped on my arm, I cradle the back of her head. Her shoes dangle, knees bumping my metal-studded belt. I leave Jacob to get the stroller and bag, because I need both hands to be sure I don't drop her.

Even through my jacket, she's warm, all her weight utterly slack as if there's no question that I'll hold her up. My heart squeezes, and I look both ways six times before I cross the street. If someone tried to take her from me right now, I'd claw them down to their bone marrow. I sneak a kiss to her soft forehead when no one is looking.

Jacob slips around me, carrying both the navy diaper bag and stroller while he unlocks the door for us.

I cup Maya's head into my neck. She's so delicate, like anything could break her. But with her weight in my arms, I suddenly have the strength of thousands. Is this how Jacob felt when he realized Maya was about to be his responsibility? Maybe it's not that he already knew he'd be a good parent. Maybe it's more that when something so innocent trusts you, you expand until you're whatever you need to be.

Jacob opens the door to his room and steps aside to let us in. I tighten my abs, so careful as I bend to lower her to her toddler bed. Maya sprawls across the mattress, her fingers twitching once as she sleeps. Her brother sits on the end of the bed to take off her shoes, his big fingers deft on the doll-sized buckles. I bite my lip, watching.

This is a whole new Jacob I never got to meet in the weeks we were dating. He's got the same quiet confidence, but there's a maturity to him when he's with Maya. Like there's no room for doubt when it comes to being whatever she needs. I was sure I couldn't possibly love him more, but it's like my heart grows to make space for this new side to him. I don't know how I could have thought I knew him without it.

I move aside as he pulls a purple fleece blanket over Maya's legs, tucking it over her hands, which are probably still chilled from being outside so long. He leaves her jacket on, though, so he doesn't have to wake her. He looks up at me, touching a finger to his lips. I nod.

We both draw up onto our toes, creeping in utter silence out of the room. I hold my breath as he eases the door closed without even a click of the latch.

When we get to the living room, all I want to do is grab him and hold onto him for thirty or forty years. Instead I look up, the coffee table still between us when I ask, "Can I see you again? Soon?"

He closes his eyes, and swallows.

I'm not going to give him a chance to say no, and I'll do anything I have to do.

I close my eyes, too, letting all my weight fall forward. There's a stomach pitching moment when I pass the moment of no return and I have to force my legs not to take a step forward to catch me. Despite my best efforts, my arms leap up to break my fall just as my face hits something hard.

"What were you thinking, Jera?" Jacob's arms tighten around me, my nose a little sore from where it scuffed the front of his sweatshirt. "I was on the other side of the table, with my freaking eyes closed! What would you have done if I wouldn't have caught you?"

I smile, but I don't stand up yet, because I know as long as he's supporting my weight, he won't let me go. "Then I'd have a nasty headache and you'd probably feel guilty enough to give me a second date." I gather my feet underneath me and sneak a kiss onto his cheek before he can stop me. "Besides, I happen to know you're pretty fast, Mr. Baseball Star."

He steps back, his brow still furrowed a little. There's a sound from the back hallway like something plastic hitting the floor, and I'm afraid I might have just woken up Maya.

"Listen," I say, "I have to go out of town for a couple of days, but when I get back, I'm going to have a present for you."

"Where are you—Okay."

I refuse to let my smile die just because he's not allowing himself to ask questions yet. I hurt him when I ran out, and it's going to take me some time to heal those wounds. He said "okay" and that's all that matters.

He caught me.

I touch his arm, my thumb sweeping over his bicep. "I'll call you the second I get back to Portland, all right?"

He jerks a nod. His face is stiff, but I know Jacob. I'm almost completely sure he's going to forgive me. The key word being "almost."

Luckily, I still have one last trick up my sleeve.

A CRUEL KIND OF BEAUTIFUL

Chapter 29: TWO GIFTS

I feel like an asshole for making Jacob come to my house, so to make up for it, I wait outside on the porch for him. On the other hand, I'd feel like more of an asshole if Ben walked in on what we're about to do, so there's that. It also doesn't hurt that I'm less jittery when I'm farther away from what waits inside.

I catch myself pulling up the grass at the side of the sidewalk, and fold my hands back into my lap. Less jittery does not equal calm. Especially since I'm about to see Jacob alone for the first time since we were naked in his bed together. I shiver and tuck my jacket more closely around me, staring into the cone of light the streetlight casts in front of my house. It's kind of late now, since he had to wait for Hayden to get off work and come pick up Maya. I got back this afternoon, and it already feels like I've had to wait an eternity to see him again.

As if I wished him into reality, Jacob's car pulls into that spot of light and parks. I check my phone. Three minutes early. God bless that boy and his engineer's mind, because I can't be responsible for the laps my mind would have been jogging if he'd been late. Except, no. I can and will be responsible for my own thoughts, and today, they are going to be nothing but positive.

289

I meet Jacob in the middle of my lawn. I was hoping for a hug, but his hands are firmly in his hoodie pockets. So we're still in this stage, apparently.

Think positive.

He stops without going closer to the house. "How was your trip?"

I narrow my eyes at him. "Did you talk to Danny? Tell me he didn't ruin my surprise, or his shins are going to be in danger of a sincere kicking."

"No, you told me you were going out of town, remember?"

"Oh, that's right."

Crickets don't fill the silence as we stand awkwardly in the middle of my lawn, but that's probably because it's the middle of winter and they all froze to death months ago.

Think *positive*.

I smile. "I brought you back a present! Two presents. Okay, one I bought here in town"—*don't throw up, throwing up is not sexy, oh my God what was I thinking*—"and one I brought back for you from, uh, somewhere." I crank my smile up another notch. "Wanna come inside?"

I may be imagining it, but I think Jacob's eyes looked a little fond. Just for a second. "Okay," he says. "It's still two weeks until Christmas, though. I don't have anything for you."

Don't make a dirty joke. If you make a dirty joke, you'll blush, and if you blush, you might throw up, and throwing up is not sexy.

Instead, I focus on the other part of his statement. "Trust me, you're going to need those weeks to brace yourself for the Christmas Eve dinner my family is kidnapping you for. My mom wants to meet you and Maya like yesterday, but she'll wait until Christmas Eve as long as I don't give her your address, or last name, or anything else she can use to track you down so she can show up on your porch with a fruitcake."

As I chatter, I turn the knob to open the front door for us, and warm air washes over my numbed cheeks. I didn't think I'd been waiting outside long enough to get chilled, but apparently I went out to wait for Jacob earlier than I thought.

"You told your mom about me? And Maya?"

I'm going to try not to be offended that he sounds skeptical. "I told Mom and Dad about you, and Maya, and Ben, and Hayden. All of whom they invited over for Christmas Eve dinner, though I'll understand if your whole family doesn't want to be subjected to mine. Mom's fine, but my dad lives to embarrass me."

I head toward my bedroom, then remember and circle back for the first present, but once I grab it, there's too much energy in my legs to stand still, so I loop once more around the coffee table before I stop in front of Jacob.

"I hope you don't mind—I sent them a picture. Just of you. I didn't take any of Maya when we were at the zoo, because I was too nervous. I have a picture of Ben but his emo bangs were taking over his face that day and he looks all pouty, so I thought I'd wait and not ruin their first impression of him. He really is less moody in person. A little."

Jacob looks down at me, and his mouth still isn't smiling but his eyes are. "You make it really hard to stay mad at you, you know that?"

I blow out a breath and let my head sag until my forehead rests on the front of his hoodie. Because this seems like the physical manifestation of positive thinking, and because his words leave me a little dizzy with relief, and also because he smells insanely good. "There is literally nothing you could say that I would want to hear more. You're off the hook for Christmas presents this year, Tate."

His arms come around me, resting on my shoulders as he pulls me into a hug. "How about I missed you? Because I did."

I grin so hard I might have left a cheek imprint in his shirt. "Okay, you're off the hook for birthday presents, too. Wanna keep

going? I've got a whole lifetime of holidays to pass out coupons for."
I am the queen of positive thinking.

His lips brush over my hair. "No deal. You're saying a whole lot
of right things right now, and it's making me want to give you more
presents, not less."

I pull back and beam up at him. "Like what?"

He smiles, and seeing him happy again is like every Christmas
light in the world shining out of the center of my chest. "You first.
I've got three days of curiosity built up and I want to see my present."

I pull the small package out from between our bodies, holding it
up. I frown a little when I see that the paper got wrinkled. I wrapped
this sucker twice already, because the first time the design on the
wrapping paper wasn't straight. I mean, usually I'm not above
wrapping things in paper grocery sacks but this one was important.

He pauses, looking between me and the CD-shaped package. "Is
this your new album? Can you make a new album in three days? How
many record companies ended up calling?" He grins. "Oh man, I'm
going to sell my story to the tabloids when you win your first
Grammy. I broke Jera McKnight's window. Did you save the
newspaper that did it? Tell me you saved the newspaper. I'm going to
sell that thing on eBay and pay my whole senior year's tuition."

I laugh. All that from seeing I got him a CD? Good thing it isn't
just Pearl Jam or something. "Slow it down, Sparky. I don't think
anybody's going to be auctioning my fingernail clippings anytime
soon. And frankly, that level of fame is normally saved for the lead
singer." I smile. "Aww, Jax would love that. He'd stop biting his
fingernails just so they could auction the clippings." I hook a finger in
Jacob's hoodie pocket, practically glowing at how much he believes
in my band. "Just open it."

He rips the paper off. The CD cover is blank. I had this whole
idea of me laying on top of a piano with my hair spread out around
me—clothed, for the record—but what with flying to San Francisco
and all, I didn't have time to make it happen. He opens the case, and

there's a neat song list inside. His brow creases as he reads, because I know he owns them all already. The crease deepens when he makes it to the last song on the list, which is simply named "Falling."

"Who...Is this your band?"

"Just me," I say. "I covered all the classic Norah Jones songs, and while I was in California, I wrote a new one for you."

His lips part slightly, and he's just staring at me.

I talk faster to drown out the pounding of my heart. "Originally, they were all Garage Band recordings, but as a gift, Cornerstone gave me a little studio time to play with while we were down there taking meetings. Most of them aren't full ensemble, because we didn't have the time to record so many different tracks. So a lot of the songs are unrehearsed, just me and a guitar or a piano. For a couple of the tracks, Jax did the guitar so we could get them all recorded in a single afternoon."

"Cornerstone?" His eyes light up. "They were the ones you made me listen to that put out that grand piano and gritty bass pairing, right? With the electric violin intro?"

I can't hold back my grin any longer, wrapping my arms around Jacob and hugging him again just for remembering that. "Hells yes they are. You're never going to go back to Norah after you hear this—the sound engineer they loaned me is a freaking wizard. He did things with the upper range of my voice levels that you can't even imagine."

"I don't think I want to hear what he did with the upper range of your voice levels." Jacob frowns.

I laugh. "You know, I never thought I'd be into a jealous guy, but on you, it looks a little hot."

"You're just saying that because you saw the boner I just got over this CD."

My eyebrows head for the ceiling. "Did you really just use the word 'boner'?" I snort. "Just for that, I'm revoking your second present."

He grabs me around the waist and hauls me in for a kiss. It's rough and hot, his teeth nipping at my lips right before his tongue sweeps over them. "Not acceptable. I want my second present."

I grab his hand and squeeze maybe a little too hard. "Your wish is my command." I start to lead him down the hall, and he stops us, holding up his CD.

"Wait. I want my second present, but I have to listen to this first. Did you really write me a song?"

"I have written you a lot of songs," I admit. After I kissed him at my concert. After our first date. After my eyes were too tired to read another parenting article, and my fingers were still too afraid to dial his number. "The one on the CD is just the least angsty. Look, you can listen to that CD until it wears out. Later. Right now, you have to open your other present before I lose my nerve."

His hand closes more firmly around mine. "What is it you need nerve for?"

I lead him to my bedroom door, and step aside so he can see. In this world, there are people who could describe my gift to him out loud without wanting to hide under the couch, and those people are not me.

The quilt over my bed folds back to reveal the fresh sheets: light blue flannel with a print of fluffy clouds. The color perfectly showcases the black nylon and shining metal of the ropes snaking out from under each corner of the mattress, the wrist and ankle cuffs waiting in the center.

Someone swallows audibly. I think it was him. It better have been him.

Chapter 30: HAPPY ENDINGS

"**A**re you sure about this?"

The breath that explodes out of me sounds a lot like a laugh. "Jacob, when a girl asks you to tie her up and have sex with her, you're not supposed to ask if she's sure."

"Um, actually, I'm pretty sure you are."

I refuse to smile at that. "I'm pretty sure you should shut up, Captain Obvious. And take off your pants." My hand rises to the zipper of my jacket and I drag it down, spreading open one side of my jacket, and then the other to expose the surprise waiting underneath.

Jacob bursts out laughing.

I grin, peeking down at my shirt, which features a picture of a drum and the words, "Let's Bang."

"You're amazing, you know that?" He kisses my forehead, chuckling. "But as much as I love that pun shirt, I still don't think our first time should involve ropes. It seems…"

"Spontaneous?" I fill in. "Kinky? Symbolic? Are any of these things you have objections to?"

He raises an eyebrow, his eyes dark and soft. "Unnecessary."

"It's not necessary, but it's…something I want to do. I want you to know that this time, I'm not going to run off on you." I squeeze his hand. "I trust you, Jacob. I trust us."

"Does that mean I finally get to bust out the exotic sex toys?" Jacob waggles his eyebrows, and he's so obviously trying to get me to laugh that I want to drop to one knee and propose, right there.

Instead, I poke him in the side. "You're not that lucky."

"I don't know." His gaze traces the lines of my face. "I'm feeling pretty lucky."

I squeeze my eyes shut, and my breath stutters as I try to contain all the emotions that leapt to life at his words.

His lips stroke over my forehead. "You sure you want to close your eyes? You're going to miss all the fun."

My lids pop back open as Jacob pulls off his hoodie and starts unbuttoning his shirt. By the third button, my mouth is utterly dry.

Positive thinking is suddenly coming so much easier to me.

Jacob kicks his shoes and pants aside and takes a step toward me. I realize it's my turn and start to pull my arms out of my jacket, but he stops me with one word.

"No."

I freeze. His voice is different, more commanding, and it sends a tingling thrill through my whole body: excitement dancing right on the line of fear. He doesn't speak again as he undresses me, setting each piece of clothing aside until I'm only in panties, my nipples peaking in the open air of my room. Jacob hooks his thumbs into the sides of my panties and drags them all the way down my legs, waiting while I lift one foot, then the other to step out of them.

"I think we need some ground rules." He stands, resting his fingers on my neck, his thumbs brushing the line of my jaw. My bare breasts tremble a mere inch from his chest.

I'm little lightheaded at his tone. I want to fold myself into his hug and call a time out, but another part of me thrills darkly to the scream of tension between us.

"You can call this off at any time," he says, "including right now. If you get uncomfortable, or scared, or you just don't like something I'm doing to you, you say the word and it stops. Immediately. Do you understand?"

I nod quickly. Agreeing ratchets up my nervousness about four notches, which is ridiculous. I *know* I could speak up right now and we'd get dressed, Jacob would make soup, and we'd be on the couch watching *It's a Wonderful Life* within twenty minutes. And unlike Andy, Jacob wouldn't be all pouty and hurt about it, either.

"But," he says, and I take a shaky breath. "You don't get to tell me what you want."

I blink and tip my head up, but he's still too close for me to see his eyes. He bends so I think he's going to kiss me, but instead his words whisper across my lips like their own caress. Their own tease.

"I want you to let go of trying to make it work and worrying if I'm having a good time. I want you to relax and just be here with me. No matter what we do. No matter where it leads."

My head whirls, and I think I need to sit down. Possibly get some supplemental oxygen. Instead, I focus on his deep brown eyes. "I think I'd like that."

Jacob smiles. "Good." He picks one of the cuffs up off the bed. It is a wide strip of black fabric with a metal ring attached, and it closes with a long strip of Velcro that my fingers can't reach once he winds it tightly around my wrist. I bought them because somehow Velcro seemed less intimidating than knots, but as he fastens the cuffs, it's not helping whatsoever. He may not have been with many people, but I know his sexual repertoire is much broader than mine. Despite everything he just said, I can't help but be curious. What is he going to do to me?

Kneeling at my feet, he wraps cuffs around each ankle, the material soft and firm and blaringly difficult to ignore.

When he stands, he lifts me into his arms without warning, maneuvering my weight with shocking ease as he lays me onto my bed. He leans over me, a whiff of comforting cedar filling my lungs as he stretches my arm over my head. With a click of metal, my right wrist is secured to the headboard. His cock brushes my stomach when he shifts to do my left, and my back arches, thrilling toward every powerful inch of him. But when he snaps my left wrist into the clip on the end of the rope, I flinch a little and realize exactly how firmly my arms are held. My heart gives a panicky leap.

He moves down toward the foot of the bed and I swallow, my toes squirming. This is kinky, and I'm not entirely sure I know how to pull off kinky. Should I be trying to look sexier? I should have bought lingerie.

He snaps in my left ankle, then tugs my legs wide apart, his hand firm as he clips in my right. When he moves up next to me, his chest seems too warm and nearly twice as wide as mine. He smoothes my hair away from my face, and I have the totally bizarre thought that if I need to scratch my nose, I can't.

"Last night," he whispers, right next to my sensitive earlobe, "I caught Ben taking duck lips bathroom selfies."

Houston, could you repeat that?

The sheets rustle beneath us as Jacob pulls back and smiles at me, and it's the smile of the man who bought his sister purple glittery shoes, the smile of the man who attached a flashing safety light to my bicycle for when I ride at night. "When you get nervous, you always change the subject. Thought I'd beat you to it."

I exhale a laugh and start to breathe again, and he bends to kiss me. My hands shift automatically to pull him closer, but when I can't move, awareness runs through my whole body and centers on the slide of his lips over mine, his tongue entering my mouth. I can feel the exact temperature of every place our bodies meet. When he moves away, I swallow a whimper.

"Do you want me to untie you?"

"No," I admit, barely above a whisper.

He leaves the room.

The pillow sags as I drop my head back onto it, gasping as I try to catch up with everything that just happened. I am excruciatingly aware of my nakedness as I wait for him to return. This position is pure sex, and something primitive in me knows it. My body softens, preparing for him as if the ropes themselves are all the foreplay I need.

There's a soft whoosh as the heater kicks on, and Jacob pads back into the room: gloriously aroused, nude, and utterly unselfconscious. "Better?"

I consider all the possible meanings of this word. I nod.

He kneels on the bed next to me, his warmth both a comfort and a tease as I begin to wonder what he's going to do with me.

Jacob touches one finger to my forehead. Deliberately, he drags it down the pert, upward curve of my nose, over my slightly kiss-swollen lips. He traces a line down my throat, between my breasts, along the soft skin of my belly, past the quick dip of my naval.

Is he going to stop? Please, for the love of Gibson guitars and triple chocolate mocha ice cream, do not let him stop. He's probably going to stop. Jacob never takes a direct line to anywhere when it comes to sex.

One more inch.

He's going to stop. I know he's going to stop.

He pauses at the top of the small triangle of manicured hair that points to everywhere I want him to be.

There's no way he's going to keep going.

One fingertip smooths downward, my gasp lost to the thick tension of the room as he crosses the tiny bump of the most responsive place on my body and then strokes down to the slick hollow below. He takes a small breath and traces me, circling my entrance with the lightest possible touch.

Once.

Twice.

Three times, until I'm fatally, uproariously aware of how empty I am inside, how tightly my muscles clench at the very thought of his arousal.

I'm going to die, tied to my own damned bed, if he doesn't have sex with me right now.

"Jacob…" I half-hyperventilate.

He smiles. "You get to say no, Jera," he reminds me. "But if you don't, I get to decide how we say yes."

And he does. With the tip of his tongue, and the warm, broad slide of his palm, the cleverness of his long fingers, and the infinitely brilliant contrast between his smooth lips and the rough hint of a five o'clock shadow.

I hit the first edges of orgasm within five minutes, but he doesn't untie me. He just soothes me and then starts to build me up all over again. The tension is all but unbearable. I can't stop tugging, writhing against the ropes, but then something in me shifts, and I realize this is no different from the rest of our relationship. He's not going to get bored or impatient, because he never does. He's not going to leave or stop too soon, and I trust him to know exactly what I need.

I relax.

Suddenly, every sensation is different. Wider, softer inside my mind. I'm not straining toward an orgasm anymore, I'm just enjoying each time he touches me because it feels *good.*

And then it happens.

It's almost violent and it slaps into me with no warning. My heels dig into the mattress and I can hear myself gasping but my lungs are empty, crying for air even as I can't make myself care if I ever breathe again. Black spots dance behind my eyelids while every muscle in my body clamps down. The only thing I'm certain of is Jacob's hand, splayed across my lower belly, solid and soothing as sheer, electric pleasure bolts through my whole body, again and again and again.

My moans sharpen to yelps and then almost to screams. When everything finally starts to ease, Jacob pulls himself up next to me, his body steadying mine.

"You okay?" he murmurs, and the contentment in his face only heightens the clench of urgency in me.

"Jacob, please. *Please*."

He dives to my mouth, kissing me with such ferocity that the relief pours like cool water over my overheated skin. Except then he pulls back, resting his forehead against mine as he grimaces. "We can't, not tonight. I didn't—I don't have a—"

"Bedside drawer," I interrupt.

He moves with satisfying speed and pulls out the un-opened box, a smile touching his lips as he turns it to read the words, "Ultra Thin."

The muscle in my neck kinks as I try to turn my head far enough to watch while he rolls on the condom. He digs in the drawer and rips the plastic off a bottle of lube, and I actually laugh. "Yeah, I think we can do without that."

"It's been a long time for you, Jera. And with condoms…it's just better this way."

My lashes flutter as he smoothes lube over himself. God, that stuff is worth the sticker price just to watch him put it *on*.

He comes back to my side and unclips both my legs, leaving the cuffs on. I stretch and bring my knees up, enjoying the exotic feeling of the bands around my ankles.

Jacob settles himself over me, leaving my arms tied and spread wide. I am utterly vulnerable and absolutely safe as his chest settles against my bare breasts.

"Is this all right?" he whispers into my neck.

I love you.

The words flow through my mind over and over again, and all I can manage in response is an inhaling moan of assent.

He rolls his hips, rubbing slickly against me, waiting until I'm panting and straining up toward him before he eases my knee a little wider and presses inside.

Oh God.

Even just the tip of him is so thick and it feels amazing, but my body is resisting and I can't quite take him in. I pull against the cuffs, wanting to brace myself against his shoulders. He pauses and reaches between us, laying his fingers over the top of my sex.

There's something comforting about how unhurried the motion is; I relax and he slides in another inch. The arm that braces him is so tight it's quivering, his legs heavy and tensed against my inner thighs. He drops his head and kisses my forehead, breathing three words so low that at first, I think I'm still hearing the echo of my own thoughts.

I whimper, my body curling up toward his fingers, toward *him*.

He starts to push deeper, whispering soothing words within the kisses he leaves beside my ear. I can't make out a thing over the sprinting of my own heartbeat, but I think he needs the reassurance as much as I do. Maybe more.

"Please," I manage, at last.

His hips jerk in automatic response to my plea, and then he stops dead, gasping as he checks my face. In response, I close my eyes, my head falling back as I widen my knees a little more. He sinks all the way into me, his whole body trembling.

There is something sacred about this moment, and I want desperately for him to untie me so I can hold him. He makes a small movement, retreating and then curling his hips sharply. The burst of pleasure erases every word from my mind. He does it again, cradling me to his chest and anchoring me against the short, jagged thrusts that hit like a detonation button, every single one a feeling I have no name for and have never known before.

There's a tug, and a release of pressure and I wonder if I've fainted, or possibly died.

"Breathe, sweetheart," Jacob whispers, and I realize he's freed my wrists. I open my eyes, and he's smiling as he pulls out of me. I make a wordless noise of disappointment. His smile widens before he rolls me over onto my stomach. Bright, small kisses melt across my shoulders and nestle into the secret curve of my neck beneath my hair.

He bends one of my knees up before he enters me from behind, stroking velvety shivers all the way up my spine. He keeps adjusting, tipping me a little up, then to the side and then sweet mother of—

I cry out as he finds the right spot and it's even more intense than before so that my mind bends around the blast of it. Jacob nibbles at my shoulder, driving into me with deep, commanding thrusts. His hand caresses its way around my side until I'm caught between his hips and the heel of his palm and I know I'm making sounds, possibly loud sounds, but I don't know what they are. I don't know where we are.

I know I don't want him to stop.

He shifts me onto my side, one of my legs beneath him and one bent up against his chest. In this position, he can put the full force of his back and legs into pleasuring me and when his thumb dips to press my clit, I claw at the sheets, my back bowing and my mouth opening for a cry that never finds its way to sound.

I clamp down around him and he groans through his teeth. I can feel his cock so exquisitely now and even the tiniest movement sets me off again, so I don't know if I'm beginning to orgasm or finishing, or possibly just falling apart altogether.

"Jera," he gasps, his hips jerking. "Jera, please, I don't think I can…" Except I have no idea what he can't do because a growl rips from his chest, and he finally loses control. My whole body jolts under one rough, incredibly powerful thrust, and then two. His abs clench and his shoulders begin to shake. I want to watch him like this for hours, decades. I want this on an endless high definition loop in my brain every day for the rest of my life.

He falls a little forward, catching himself on one shaking hand. I pull him down until all his weight relaxes into me and I can wrap my arms and legs around him, holding his damp forehead into my neck as his breath saws in and out, tickling my shoulder.

An almost unbearable tenderness spreads through me, its sharpness only tempered by the weight of him. I tilt my head a little so I can kiss his temple.

The house is quiet around us, a chill seeping through the windows and kept at bay by the heat blowing from the vent above the bed. I close my eyes and pretend it's snowing even though it's freaking Portland, so it probably isn't. It's just that the peaceful silence in my mind is just the right match for the fall of snow on grass, white flakes drifting through darkness and coming to rest, crystalline and perfect, on the ground.

Eventually Jacob sits up to get rid of the condom, but he's back before my skin has a chance to cool from the loss of him. He lies down and pulls me onto his chest, my arms draped around him as he reaches up to massage my back.

"Are your muscles sore? Did I leave you tied up for too long?"

I shake my head, hiding my blush in his neck. His fingers knead their way down the sides of my spine, and tears prickle at the backs of my eyes even though I'm still smiling. I squeeze him tighter as he kisses the top of my head.

"What?"

"I love you, just, so insanely much," I breathe.

The hint of a chuckle rumbles in his chest. "That sounds like a line you feed a guy who just gave you two orgasms, hoping for an encore."

I pull back so I can meet his eyes. "It sounds like something I think every time I look at you."

He pulls me close, his hold suddenly fierce. "I have been in love with you," he whispers, "since the day you made me tell you about my parents, one fact for every bite of ice cream while you pretended not to notice when I got tears in my eyes, and you laughed off the ones you got in yours."

I smile at the memory of the day he's talking about. It was so hard not to reach for him as we lay side by side on my living room carpet, letting old records fill the air around us with love songs that spoke all the words we didn't yet dare to say.

I'm still trying to figure out how to fit air around the lump in my throat when his phone rings with my raw, urgent drum solo from "Out Of Order." I tense as I remember that he set it as his older sister's ringtone weeks ago.

"You should probably get that."

At the exact same time he says, "It's kind of late for her to be—"

I roll off his chest and reach down to the floor for his jeans, fishing his phone out of the back pocket and extending it to him.

"What's up, Hayden?" He pulls himself to sitting.

The volume on his phone is up so loud that I can hear Maya crying in the background when Hayden says, "Nothing's wrong." She sighs. "It's just that I've been trying to get her to sleep ever since we got home, and I'm about to lose it."

Jacob's shoulders loosen and he picks up my right wrist, supporting it as he unfastens the cuff.

I blush at the audible rip of Velcro, and Hayden says, "Could you talk to her? Maybe read her a story over the phone like you did last time? I'm sorry, Jacob, I know you're probably busy or jeez, maybe actually sleeping—imagine that—but you're so good with her and I just..." She sounds like she's on the edge of tears herself.

"It's no problem." Jacob's thumb brushes over my skin as he checks for any rub marks from the cuffs.

He dips his head and breathes a kiss over the inside of my wrist. My heart flutters when his lips linger for another moment, then two. His eyes warm on my face as he straightens, clears his throat a touch, and says, "Wait, but I'm at Jera's. I don't have any of Maya's books with me."

"You're at Jera's? Oh my gosh, I'm really sorry. Forget I even called. We're fine, everything's good. I'll see you soon, 'kay?"

He swaps the phone to his other ear and reaches for my left hand. I move to take off the cuff myself, but he aims a frown my way and I give in, letting him unwind the cuff. A smile tugs at my lips when he takes an extra second to kiss the skin beneath.

"No, you know what?" he says to Hayden. "I've read *Rapunzel* so many times I bet I could do the whole thing from memory."

He picks up one of the ropes and dangles it playfully beside my head like a long braid, giving me a wink. Swatting his hand away, I swallow my giggles so Hayden won't hear and think I'm laughing at her.

Hayden exhales. "I owe you, little brother. Like, one million Christmas stockings. I swear, some days I think if you weren't around, I couldn't..." Her voice catches. "I'm okay, really. I'm just so damned tired, you know?"

"I know." He scoots down the bed and lifts my feet into his lap so he can take the cuffs off my ankles. "Believe me, I know. Put her on, okay?"

Hayden's voice fades a little. "Maya. Maya sweetie, do you want to talk to Jacob?"

Maya's sniffly voice comes on the phone. "Hi."

"Hey, Shortstop. You want a story?"

"Yes," she quavers, like she might be starting to cry again.

"Well, then you have to lie down and put the covers on, okay?" He drops the cuffs onto the floor and rests his hand on top of my feet, giving them a gentle squeeze.

He tosses me a wincing, apologetic look, pulling the phone away from his ear.

"I'm gonna go in the living room, okay? This'll only take a few minutes."

"What, and miss you trying to recite an entire book about medieval hairstyles from memory?" I scoff, pulling him back towards me. "No way."

He settles in next to me, reaching up to adjust the pillow beneath his head. I kick the ropes off the edge of the bed and pull the sheet up around us, wriggling until I can lay my head on his shoulder. In my head, an image forms of Jacob reading Maya bedtime stories in my spare room down the hall, the old rose trellis wallpaper replaced by Dora the Explorer. Longing grips my heart, the throb of it quivering with nerves. *Maybe someday.* It's not so far-fetched: Ben and Jacob have been needing a three-bedroom, and thanks to Granna, I just so happen to own one.

"Once upon a time," Jacob says, and begins the story of the nasty little bait and switch by which Rapunzel's mother coveted a plant and ended up losing her newborn baby to a witch.

I snuggle a little closer into Jacob's chest. I don't know if it's the endorphin-fueled afterglow, but I find myself extra sympathetic toward Rapunzel's bereft parents, who didn't know that a happy ending and a prince awaited their lost daughter.

I know my parents have worried about me, too, because especially in the past year, there have been a lot of days when my life seemed like an ugly joke. Still, even after all the witchy bad luck and lonely towers, I must have had a fairy godmother somewhere who made sure my first big career break wasn't necessarily my only one. And she must have given her wand a serious workout to ensure that my vandalism-prone baseball star would turn out to be the kind of guy who could—without a trace of self-consciousness—put away our sex toys while telling his little sister a bedtime story.

In the end, my hero isn't some guy smirking down from a gorgeously-lit pedestal, taunting me to climb up to him. He's the one right beside me on flannel cloud-print sheets, dropping a kiss to my forehead in between the sentences leading to the happily ever after.

It's this moment when I finally start to understand: the world isn't cruel. It is, actually, kind of beautiful.

The End

Dear Reader

Hello! Thanks so much for reading, and I do hope you enjoyed your time with Jera and Jacob and her weirdo bandmates. If you can, please consider leaving a review on Amazon or Goodreads. It doesn't have to be long, and it doesn't have to be Shakespeare—even a sentence will do. It really helps other readers find my books, and I just really love hearing what people thought about my stories. Good, bad, or ugly, it's all valid. It just means so much to me to know you took the time to read my work.

If you're dying for more of Jera and her band, you can hop on over to my website and sign up for my newsletter at:

http://michellehazenbooks.com/newsletter/

I got my start as a fanfiction writer, so there's nothing I love more than to write little unseen moments from the books, or secret peeks into the character's lives, character interviews or bonus stories. If you're the type with a hankering for extras and deleted scenes, my newsletter is the place for you. Plus, I usually announce new releases and whatnot a little early on my newsletter, along with exclusive peeks at whatever I've got coming next. I also like to chat a bit about my travels and what continent I'm currently writing from. Come on over and join the fun! http://michellehazenbooks.com/newsletter/

You can also keep up with me on Twitter @michellehazen where I chat about writing, drool over Norman Reedus, and shamelessly post pictures of abs or puppies (or abs AND puppies), because the world needs more of that.

If Facebook is more your jam, find me at:
https://www.facebook.com/MichelleHazenAuthor/

You can find me on Goodreads and ask any questions you have at my Ask the Author page:
https://www.goodreads.com/author/show/6559289.Michelle_Hazen

Come on over and let me know what you're hoping will happen in the rest of the series, share pics of your dream cast that you pictured for each character, or just say hello! Chatting with my readers is my most favorite thing so don't be shy.

Thanks for being here,

Michelle

Curious about what the band was like before Jera met Jacob?

Fill Me

AVAILABLE ON 1.4.18

A garage band drummer who can't keep her boyfriend satisfied.
A bassist who's performing on darker stages than the musical kind, and can't tell his BFF.
A lead singer who can't seem to hold the headliner spot in his own friendships.

It's just one more dive bar gig, but tonight, all the secrets are coming to a head for the members of The Red Letters.

Take a peek at our three favorite rock stars back before it all started. This prequel is a short-story-length introduction to the band The Red Letters. It takes place before the books about each of the band members. Though if you ask the author, it's the most fun to read after Book 1.

Turn the page for a sneak preview of the prequel to

A CRUEL KIND OF *Beautiful*

SNEAK PREVIEW: *Fill Me*

BOOK 0.5 IN THE SEX, LOVE, AND ROCK AND ROLL SERIES

Chapter 1: ALMOST PERFECT

Jera

L aughing at your neurotic lead singer is wrong.
 I know it, everybody with a heart knows it, so I clamp my twitching lips closed and try like hell to be a good person.

"Do you think anybody saw me?" Jax hunches his shoulders, his back to the busy bar room as he whips off his shirt, balling the UPS logo to the inside.

"Uh, yeah, dipshit," Danny says. "They did."

"Shut up, or I'm not getting your underage ass any drinks," Jax growls at our bassist. "Now where's my shirt?"

"Don't worry, Jax, I'll shield you while you change so nobody notices." I step squarely in front of him, giving a smile and a wink to a guy whose eyes drift toward us. Danny reaches over and tugs down the already-low V-neck of my Ramones babydoll tee, doubling the amount of cleavage I'm offering. I slap his hand. "Hey, jerk!"

"Just protecting our chances of getting drinks," Danny says. "The only way something as tiny as you makes a decent shield is if you show some skin."

"I thought big brother types were supposed to be protective." I put on a scowl, but my eyes slip away to check the front door before I can stop myself.

Nothing.

"Not your brother." He crosses his arms, hazel eyes gleaming with mischief even though his face, as always, is relaxed. "As your bandmate, it benefits me to get some eyes headed your way. Longer they're staring at you, the longer they'll watch us play."

"Then I guess you should have built me a drum riser, because nobody's going to be able to see me behind my cymbals."

Both men ignore me. Jax smacks Danny, knocking his black beanie askew. "Dude. Shirt."

"What shirt?" Danny pulls off his knit hat, black hair in wild chaos before he tugs the cap back on.

"It was on the list I gave you when I left you my truck so you could load while I was at work."

Danny wrinkles his nose. "List?"

Jax pales, his blue eyes flaring brighter as he stares down our bassist. "The list with *all our equipment* on it. Including my good shirt." He flaps the offending uniform top at Danny, while I stifle a laugh into my fist.

He shrugs. "Play in what you've got."

Jax chucks it in Danny's face instead. "Nobody sees a brown UPS polo shirt and thinks, 'Step aside, panties, there's a rock star in the house.'"

"If you need a shirt to drop panties, man, you better hightail it back to that gym you're always dragging me to," Danny drawls.

Jax's jaw twitches and he straightens to his full height, carefully cultivated muscles bunching.

Danny looks bored, his lean body looking just plain skinny beneath the black hoodie and old jeans he threw on before we loaded Jax's truck.

I step between them, because they like a friendly fight a little too much, and last time Jax's mouth ended up so swollen and bloody he couldn't sing. No matter how many times I explain it to him, Danny doesn't get the concept of pulling his punches.

"He's screwing with you, Jax," I say. "We have everything on the list, and your shirt is on the front seat. I'll get it for you, if you want to make a little refreshments run." I nod toward the bar, my eyes flickering past it to the entrance.

Still nothing.

Jax's hand lands on my arm, squeezing gently. "Was Andy supposed to be here?"

"Nope." I force a smile, though I can't wrench my gaze higher than the tribal swirls of the electric guitar tattoo on Jax's forearm. Somehow, seeing Danny's artwork settles some of the fizzing in my stomach. "He couldn't make it."

"Oh, was Douchefest 2012 *tonight*?" Danny asks. "Too bad. I know he couldn't possibly miss that."

Jax throws him a warning look, then turns his attention back to me. Not long ago, having this much focus from him—plus his hand, his actual *hand* touching me!—would have sent me into a blushing, stuttering mess. Our band had its first anniversary and I graduated high school before the sheer beauty of our lead guitarist became commonplace enough that I could do more than pant in his presence.

Thank God he never noticed. If we had ever ended up between the sheets, he'd probably strain something making sure I was fully inducted into the local chapter of the Jax Is A Sex God Club. I'd be exhausted before we got past the making out part of the scheduled programming. And considering how *I* get in bed? Jax and I would be each other's own private hell.

I smile up at him, his model-perfect jaw and the chin-length strands of his wavy blond hair nothing more than pretty packaging on the concerned face of a friend. "Andy had to study." I shrug. "He's got a lot of big tests coming up this week. It's no big deal." Over Jax's shoulder, a lanky blond guy passes his two bucks to the bouncer, and I push up on my toes to see better, but no, it's not my boyfriend.

Jax lets me go, his brow furrowed. "He'd seriously rather do *homework* than see his hot girlfriend wail the shit out of her drum kit?"

"He's stupid," Danny says. "What else did you expect?"

I ignore my best friend, because arguing with him will just egg him on, and I don't want to risk him dropping something too revealing right now. He insists my issues are all Andy's fault, because Danny is terminally loyal.

I point at Jax. "Don't think I don't notice your sneaky little compliments to cheer me up. And it's fine, seriously. His grades have been slipping because we've been spending too much time together and I don't want to be the reason he loses his scholarship."

My heart squeezes at the thought. I've been waiting my whole life for somebody like Andy. Somebody who yanks the breath out of my chest. Somebody who can distract me from anything, even music. But instead of filling me to overflowing, the way music does, he makes every part of me echo with the need for something that's not quite within reach.

I give Jax a little push toward the bar, his muscles even firmer under my fingertips than I remember. Has he been killing himself at the gym again? I make a mental note to ask Danny if Jax's mom has called recently. His socialite bitch of a parent never fails to set off one of his self-improvement tailspins. "Go!" I tell him, backing away. "Or you're not going to have time to triple-check our set up and Danny's tuning of your guitar."

His eyes narrow. "Talk about sneaky, Jera. That was seriously below the belt."

"Oh, I can't look below your belt," I say, my hand poised on the push bar of the side exit to the parking lot. "Because if I do, I'll see your hideous work khakis and my libido will start cashing in its social security benefits."

I shove the door open before he can come after me, Danny's chuckle sounding low from inside the bar. No way am I telling our singer I packed jeans for him in the truck.

I blink away the glare of the inside lights and take the long way through the parking lot. Who knows? Maybe "homework" is just an excuse for Andy to surprise me and he'll be waiting out here. He's given to cute gestures like that, and that's the only thing that could make tonight's—actually paid!—gig even better.

Besides, if he really isn't coming, then I have a sinking feeling I know why. And it has a whole lot to do with last Saturday.

Fill Me

AVAILABLE ON 1.4.18

Are you curious about what kind of woman is going to steal Danny's heart?

PLAYING THE *Pauses*

AVAILABLE 3.5.18

Independent woman meets her Dominant rock star kryptonite

Kate is a globe-trotting tour manager who can't be tied down.
Danny is a Dominant rock star and tattoo artist who needs her help to explore his true kinks.

Kate just got her big break, managing an international tour for a rising band. Her job is everything to her...at least until she meets the band's enigmatic bass player. After they collide in one unforgettably erotic night on a hotel balcony, he comes to her with a proposition. As a former BDSM club performer, Danny's spent so long fulfilling other people's fantasies that now he wants to reclaim his own—and he says she's the only one who can help.

Getting caught in bed with her rock star boss could cost her career, and yet there's something about Danny's quiet intensity that she can't resist. He steals her heart, hard. But the end of the tour is approaching, and their jobs are headed two different directions.

To be together one of them will have to stop touring, but the only thing they crave as much as each other is music.

Turn the page for a sneak preview of the sequel to

A CRUEL KIND OF *Beautiful*

SNEAK PREVIEW: PLAYING THE *Pauses*

BOOK 2 IN THE SEX, LOVE, AND ROCK AND ROLL SERIES

Chapter 1: LET THE GAMES BEGIN

Today I find out what kind of person I'm about to become.

Mommy, dominatrix, cheerleader, pharmacist, or even servant, bowing and scraping at motorcycle-booted feet. Whatever it takes over the next six weeks, that's what I'll be, because I'm not just a tour manager—I'm a walking life support system for rock bands.

I turn away from the check-in desk and hit the shoe-scuffed tile of the airport lobby at full stride, the worn wheels of my carry-on squealing a tiny protest as they try to keep up. Waiting for me in Terminal 2 are The Red Letters, a rock band teetering on the vomit-slicked gate to true fame. Their heads are bigger than their record sales, their eyes are bigger than the moon, and their every personal failing is about to be mine to manage.

Concert tours are evil bitches. The performers get depleted fast, rocketing from the euphoria of the shows straight to the boredom of mundane travel. They're one in a million on that stage and they are the million again the next day: getting herded barefoot and beltless through airport security, raising their arms to show their pit stains to the body scanners.

Yes, stressed-out musicians can be a pain to deal with. But then there's the moment when they go out on stage, the bass hits me straight in the chest, and I see a thousand people start to dance. To me, that is God. And I will never abandon my religion.

I blow a kiss to the TSA guards as I fast-track it through the pre-screened lane and stride past shops offering kitschy sweatshirts, tiny packets of peanuts and Stephen King's latest.

I recognize my targets before I even double-check the gate number. The lead singer is a long stretch of pretty shoulders, Italian shoes, and dark blond hair. He leans against a wall of windows while he talks to a girl who can't keep her eyes off his pecs. The petite drummer is curled up against a pillar, texting while her feet play a very backseat-of-the-minivan game of kicking footsie with the bassist, who slouches in a chair at the end of the row, his black beanie pulled low over stray chunks of hair the same color.

I throw a quick wave at the crew arrayed throughout the waiting area. I'll catch up with them later, but they all understand the talent pays the bills, so the band gets my attention first. I start forward with a professional smile and the drummer glances over, and bounces up off the floor to greet me. The bassist closes his eyes and leans his head back against the chair, completely uninterested. Great. That's not going to be a pain in the ass or anything.

"Are you the new tour manager?" She sticks out a hand with a big smile. She's cute, with some high-dollar sun-streaky highlights, and curvy as all hell: a combination the fans are going to love. That teacup-sized Marilyn Monroe body is topped off with loose, country-singer curls and a punk-rock wardrobe. Perfect.

"It's so great to meet you." I shake her hand. "Kate Madsen."

Normally, by the time we've made it to an airport, I'm besties with everyone from the lead singer's mom to the light tech's third nipple. But this tour isn't mine. It's a hand-me-down I lucked into from a fellow road wrangler who is currently in a hospital bed, drugged up to his toupee to help his body forget that until this morning, it had an appendix.

Which means I've got to cram four months of prep work into the eighteen hours before the curtain rises on the first show. No sweat.

The problem, as always, will be convincing the band to go along with changes proposed by a twenty-five-year-old tour manager.

"I'm Jera McKnight. The uh, drummer."

Weird name but interesting. I remember the story from talking to the band manager, who just so happens to be her daddy. It's an acronym, some guitar aficionado's pot-smoke-scented idea of a moniker made from the four great namesakes Jimi Hendrix, Eric Clapton, Roger Waters, and Art Garfunkel.

"How is Bill?" Jera asks, sounding genuinely concerned for the previous tour manager she probably only met once.

"He's resting comfortably, but the surgery recovery is going to put him out of commission for at least a week or two." I give her a sympathetic smile. "Tours aren't a great place to recover your strength, so he probably won't be able to join you guys on this run. But he had a friend send me all the relevant documents so we should be able to avoid most of the hiccups of a last-minute change-out in management." Okay, that statement was so optimistic it should have come out spangled with fairy dust, but as long as I don't sleep until I have everything in order, Jera will never know what kind of a whopper I just told her.

"Of course. So what can I do to help you get up to speed? Our first show is tomorrow night, and the next one is in…" She bites her lip and reaches for her phone.

"No worries." I flash her a smile. "I've got the logistics handled." The show tonight is in San Diego. We're meeting up in San Francisco, where their record label is based and also where I live when I'm off work, but these guys just flew down from their home in Portland. I'm well-used to keeping up with the geographic musical chairs of a concert tour, but it gets confusing for the musicians, who are already overloaded with the stresses of performance and publicity. It's why I try to simplify for them whenever I can.

"We've got some, ah, details we need to discuss." Their last tour manager left me a cleanup job more on the scale of a HAZMAT team than a Swiffer, but if I don't build rapport before I break out the bad news, they'll probably just give me the boot in favor of someone with a decade-longer resume. "But that can wait. Right now I'd just like to get to know you guys."

I especially need the scoop since this band is two guys to a girl. Chances are, she'll fall into bed with one or both of them when the pressure gets to be too much and I'll have to talk everyone out of their Jerry Springer moment before they cancel their show dates and flee for home.

"Oh, okay. Well, this is Danny…" Jera gestures at her motionless bandmate. He's thin, with the slouched posture of a pre-teen and apparently the manners of one too, because he doesn't open his eyes even after she says his name. Maybe he can't hear through the noise-cancelling headphones, but I doubt it. He's sharply handsome, dressed in worn jeans and a black discount-store hoodie, and the only interesting part about him is his hands.

Long, agile fingers sprawled on his knees, with a man's thick knuckles and an artist's delicate bones. On the lowest joint of his index finger is a midnight-colored tattoo of a bass clef and that finger taps restlessly while the rest of him is quiet. I've always been a sucker for hands and those ones I can picture all too clearly: deft on the frets of a guitar, or sliding into a pair of panties. Awareness trickles beneath the cups of my bra.

I pull my gaze back to Jera, letting her make the unnecessary introductions because I can never manage to say "I know who you are" without feeling like the star-struck autograph hound I used to be.

She tips her chin toward the window. "That's Jax."

I follow her gaze in spite of myself. A lot of celebrities look like shit in person. Take away the Photoshop and the photogenic and you come to the realization that the camera loves some people the naked eye would never look twice at. Jackson Sterling is not one of those people.

Jera doesn't look impressed, though, rolling her eyes as Jax laughs, shaking his chin-length hair back. "I'll squeegee his fan club off a little later so you can meet him," she says.

I smile. "No problem. So what about you?"

"Me? Ah, I'm easy. Give me my drums, my band, and my boyfriend and I don't give a shit about anything else." Her eyes brighten. "Want to see a picture?"

"Sure, I'd love to!" I brace myself for a photo tour into the foreign dimension of domesticity. In a good year, I spend three hundred plus days on the venue circuit. No relationship can keep up with that, even if it could compete with the thrill of living and breathing music.

Jera steps toward an empty seat just as a woman with a fedora pushes past us and the handle of her stroller bumps my purse, sending it swinging. The bag drops from my shoulder to my elbow, ricochets off the stroller hood and bursts onto the floor in an explosion of this-is-not-fucking-happening. I hit my knees and Jera drops beside me, the harried mom's apologies disappearing into eyebrow-raised silence when she catches a glimpse of everything that's on the floor.

There's no good way to explain that it's not mine, because only addicts and felons ever try that excuse.

In my case, though, it's true. A tour is a war, every venue is a battlefield, and my purse acts as my primary weapon. Forty-five calibers of drug-dealing nanny, dispensing aspirin and wet wipes, vitamin-boosted energy drinks, three shades of foundation and two of eyeliner to save face before the predictable paparazzi ambushes. Condoms. So many condoms. And lube, because really? We all know that one-night-stand sex is a little dry and more than a little disappointing, and the last thing I need is my lead singer wince-dancing because he has groupie-burn on his johnson.

Jera dumps a double-handful back into my purse: tampons and miniature pliers, plus a tube of Super Glue that's stuck to a tin of breath mints. I give her a little half shrug and a smile, because it could be worse. On the bus tours, I carry whiskey to keep musicians' hands from shaking on guitar strings, and I've got a secret pocket to hide the harder stuff, but I don't take that shit through airports.

All appearances aside, I *have* morals. I just apply them to myself, not to the musicians I work for. I don't touch drugs but I can produce just about anything, on cue and under the radar, thanks to the second piece in my personal arsenal that should be safely velcro'ed into a side pocket right over—

My heart tries to climb up into my throat. "Oh God, where is my phone?" I duck my head to peer under the stroller, glance behind Jera to the oblivious bassist, and dump my purse out all over again. My fingers frantically mine the pile.

My iPhone is pistol and bullet, trebuchet and tommy gun. It's the whole damn armory and it is worth more than the GDP of most developing nations. It holds contacts for everyone from record label execs to escorts, diplomats, and cocaine slingers from sea to shining sea. It video chats to the family back home for when I find the backup singer from Kansas in the ladies' room, clicking her heels together and sobbing into the single-ply airport toilet paper. Plus, its microphone records the brilliant song idea somebody had in the alley of a club on Day Sixty of the tour. The idea that becomes the anchoring single for their next album and without my intervention, would have been lost in the haze of the hotel-tile-print hangover memorialized on the drummer's cheek the next morning.

I finally spot smooth black plastic under the chair next to Jera, leaning past her to snatch it up. No bedazzled rubber case for me, *thankyouverymuch*. Otter Box. Waterproof, mosh-pit-proof, blood, sweat and tears proof—and fully tested on all five claims. I'd chain it to my spleen if I could.

I start to breathe again. Give me a smartphone and an overstuffed Michael Kors purse and I can make live music history without ever playing a note.

"I'm so sorry," Fedora Mommy apologizes again. "I love this stroller but it's terrible to try to get through an airport."

"No problem." I climb to my feet and smooth back my hair, tossing her a smile. "Hey, I needed to clean my purse out anyway."

Jera coos over the baby while I check our flight boarding time— we've still got an hour—and then we claim a couple of seats next to her dozing bandmate. I lean in to watch while she scrolls through four billion pictures of a little blond kindergartener and a guy with a Calvin Klein body and Mr. Roger's gentle eyes.

"So this is my boyfriend, Jacob, and this is our daughter, Maya." She laughs self-consciously. "Well, I mean, she's not really. I never know what to call her. She's Jacob's little sister but we share custody of her with his older sister."

I already had my game face on and a whole symphony of appreciative coos queued up, but actually I could look at pictures of this guy all day, and the kid's not half bad either. "He *is* a little bit gorgeous, isn't he?"

"I know, right? It's kind of ridiculous." Jera beams, blushing.

"Yes. Absolutely ridiculous," I say, trying to keep a straight face. Considering the looks of the two guys in her band, it's no wonder she ended up with some crazy high standards.

"It's going to be really hard to be away from him, but we're prepared this time. When we did the last tour, opening for Abyss, it was just..." She sucks in a breath and shakes her head. "But we're ready this time. We've been preparing Maya for months, and we're going to have a visit halfway through, so..."

I smile back, mentally scheduling her for a breakdown, circa Week Three, and probably another during Week Five. I make a silent note to check the budget for airline ticket money for Jacob.

Just then, her phone rings and another picture of the same guy pops up. This time he holds up Maya, who wears a bright red pea coat and a reindeer antler headband. Both siblings are flipping devil's horns at the camera, tongues out in full KISS style. Jera's face lights up like somebody just plugged her in.

"Sorry, I gotta take this." She jumps up and slaps the headphones back off Danny's ears. His head comes up—finally, signs of life—and she hisses, "Warn her about Jax."

I brace myself. Off his meds? On his heroin? Stage fright? Brand-new herpes diagnosis? I try to remember if I packed any Valtrex in my luggage. If not, it's gonna be a bitch for everybody when Jera falls into bed with his soulful smile and bimbo-worn dick.

But then Danny opens his eyes and I freeze as their intensity crackles down my body and nails me straight in the panties. He is pure, dark sex appeal, full-strength delicious kink.

He'll be the man Jera breaks for. Week Three, Week Five, and possibly tonight as well, cute boyfriend and fake stepdaughter be damned.

He shrugs himself straight in the chair and everything that looked wiry before transforms itself into a lean pull of muscle with that single, lazy movement. The edge of his hoodie rucks up to reveal a languid hipbone and in its stillness, I sense the tension that gathers right before the thrust.

I cross my legs. Mental note: Get laid. Preferably before we go wheels up in the next city.

"And you are?" Danny asks without inflection.

Another artist who couldn't give a shit about his support staff. What a surprise. Unfortunately, I kind of need him to respect my professional opinion and that might be a hard sell for this guy, even though he is—for once—even younger than I am.

"Your new tour manager." I hold out a friendly hand. "Kate Madsen."

He ignores my hand. Only his eyes move, flicking dismissively over my face and only bothering with the most cursory of circuits below that. My lips tighten. Even if I *could* sing, I know I'd never make it to the evening gowns and golden gramophones of an award ceremony. I'm nightclub pretty: good enough body and bone structure that with low light and a push up bra, my dark brown hair and gray eyes can rank a seven, even though under the fluorescents I'm more like a five and a half.

I've made my peace with that math. But no girl likes a look that judges her and records a "no score." I drop my hand.

"Your job seems very complicated and intensely boring," he says.

Keeping my smile in place costs enough energy that my blood-latte levels are starting to register in the critical levels. "I believe people have said the same to Stephen Hawking."

His lips quirk.

I straighten up and dig deep for my customer service voice. "Besides, a tour's a monster with a lot of moving parts. Somebody's got to keep them all cranking along."

"Yeah, so that's the problem with Jax. He just quit UPS and he's jonesing for something to organize. To him, the world looks like one big algorithm of moving packages and we're all just glorified cardboard boxes."

I peek over at Jax, who bends to kiss the hand of a blushing redhead while her friend shamelessly takes pictures with her phone. *That* guy used to work at UPS? Jesus, I'm way overdue to sign up for Amazon Prime if that's what comes with my two-day free shipping.

I shrug and turn back to Danny. "I've dealt with backseat drivers before."

"Not like Jax. He'll break into your hotel room just to peek at your day planner." Danny shakes his head and I can't help but snicker.

At the sound of my laugh, his vivid eyes flare with pleasure and I have to admit I don't know if I've ever seen irises like his before. They're a secret, mossy green that melts to caramel at the center, rimmed with something dark and dramatic that makes me want to lean closer to identify the shade.

"Here's what you do." Danny leans back and props an ankle across his opposite knee. "Give him schedules, lists, whatever you already have on paper for yourself. Just bury him in triplicate and when he starts asking questions, flirt."

"Um, what?"

"Don't worry, he'll stay out of your pants because you're a tour employee, but if you flirt, it kicks his brain off and turns on his..." A lazy smile crosses his face. "Well, it breaks the cycle."

His lips are the most X-rated thing I've seen in twenty-five years of pornography, erotica, and a very healthy sex life. What cycle is he talking about again? Krebs? Addiction? Spin?

Screw it, I couldn't care less. I want to set my iPhone to silent, drag him into a storage closet and fuck all the languid sprawl out of that lean body of his. By the time I got finished with him, his face wouldn't even remember how to form the irritatingly dismissive expression he greeted me with.

I wonder what kind of instrument he's packing behind the fly of those worn jeans.

My gaze doesn't dip below his chin but he reacts as if he heard my thoughts loud and clear. His eyes spark and then narrow slightly, his focus pricking my nipples like he just locked them into steel-banded clamps.

This is so not good. My personal Kryptonite comes in two flavors, and the first and most strictly forbidden is musician. The notes of a rock song slide into my heart faster than any pretty eyes or wide shoulders, but I can't afford an affair that might turn messy when I'm still trying to build my career. Still, I won't let this guy think he can use his sex appeal to throw me off my game.

Instead of backing off, I let the sudden chemistry between us sizzle and allow the silence to grow, the air gaining weight until it feels like a sentence. Danny remains completely still but behind his eyes I can see exactly how fast his mind is moving. Finally, he blinks.

I don't.

He leans forward, the movement so tight that it takes everything in me not to react. "Look. I want you to understand something," he says.

I arch one eyebrow and wait.

"You're a travel agent," he says. "And a manager of everything from hours to pennies to roadies."

I tick my chin up a fraction of an inch in reply, though I'm a hell of a lot more and if he took off his headphones once in a while, he'd know that.

"And you're a babysitter. You work for us, but our label sent you, and it's the labels that keep you in business when the bands fade away."

My attention sharpens but I don't respond. Apparently he doesn't have those headphones on all the time. I know twenty-year veterans that don't understand the complex, under-the-table interplay between tour managers and A&R execs.

"I don't need a babysitter, and I've got no use for a spy," he says. "I'll take care of my band. You do the paperwork, forget I exist and we'll all be very happy."

His eyes linger on the line of my throat, and then he's the first to look away. The leather cuff on his wrist flexes along with the muscle beneath in the first unguarded show of emotion I've seen from him.

A pang of totally unexpected sympathy drops down through me at how protective he is of his band. They're in foreign territory now, but he still thinks they can do it all on their own.

"Deal." I stand, refusing to dwell on his reaction, or mine. Neither are as important as the endless scroll of the to do list waiting on my phone. "You make the music and I'll make everything else happen."

This time, he offers *his* hand. My eyes flick over it without reaction.

He takes it back, eyes crinkling slightly at the corners in something that could be amusement, respect, or possibly anger. And then, quietly, he smiles.

Every part of my being squeezes and then goes totally, wordlessly limp.

Turning my back on him before he can see my response, I head toward the crew in my best, no-I-don't-need-to-change-my-panties-I'm-a-professional-woman stride. Whatever he'd like to think, Mr. Sexy Tattooed Fingers will need my particular brand of managerial magic if he wants this tour to get past its first date without devolving into chaos. And I could definitely use his band's rising popularity to jumpstart my career.

But I'm not going to convince anyone that I've got ten years of experience packed into seven years of resume if I can't keep my hands off the damned bass player.

PLAYING THE *Pauses*

AVAILABLE 3.5.18

Acknowledgments

Thanks to Hoku, for being a shimmering beam of light into every single one of my days, including the ones where you're working 36 hours per day being everything to everyone. Your enthusiasm for this project was...yeah, I don't have a word awesome enough. *makes note to learn more foreign languages* And besides that, I couldn't have written it without you because Every. Music. Reference. Would. Be. Wrong. Thank you so much for being awesome and talented, and also my friend, and also for making my song more like a song and less like a dictionary threw up into my laptop, with a refrain.

Thanks to Muse Baby, for thinking grass is funny, and for convincing me that babies can be cute.

Thanks to Sandra, for saying that some books need to be written, no matter what's on the to-do list, and *screaming* for Danny's book. Thank you for refusing, when I asked you to talk me out of self-publishing. There's a darn good chance this book wouldn't exist without you.

Thanks to Alf, for showing me all the good rock moves, letting me play roadie for a day, and not laughing when I asked why no one ever played an acoustic bass. Also for not kicking me out when I wore a cable knit sweater and slacks to your heavy metal show, and that weird couple humped in my lap. Because that shit was awkward.

Thanks to Jade, for loads of useful self-pub knowledge.

Thanks to Layla Reyne, for all the useful business advice and recs for so many things I needed, including my incredible cover designer.

Thanks to Stephen Morgan, for pushing me to write the new climax of this book. It fits so much better.

Thanks to my husband, for truly endless support and understanding of the insanity that a writing career wreaks on a life. If it weren't for him frequently feeding me like a pet goldfish, I might have wasted away at a computer by now. And if it weren't for him making me laugh when I really was not at all in the mood to laugh, I'd likely be a much sorrier person.

Thanks to Andrea, for deciding to stick around in my life after reading the first chapter of this very book, and being my rock when I was not so very rocklike myself. You are amazing at being my better nature, and telling me the correct thing to do (and being annoyingly right!) even when I don't want to hear it. Thanks for always being around, and for editing with supernatural speed, and for the years of your life that you've given up in exchange for not sleeping and working on my stuff instead. My words are glad you are my CP, and I am glad you are my friend.

Thanks to Katie, for editing a million versions of this book, and formatting it, and for knowing exactly the right name for my character (because really, no other name but the right one will do, but how on earth would I have guessed *Jera* on my own?). Thanks for accepting my Modest Proposal. Thanks for fanfic and Macomber and always caring about what I'm doing, even when it's dumb, and also when it's quite possibly crazy. You've been here for every day of this book, for all the joys it brought me and the many many tears. It's taken me more places than any other book I've ever written, but I couldn't have gotten to any of them without you.

I may not have a Danny, but I have an incredible group of people in my life. I have a mom who said there were more fish in the sea until she and I were both sick-unto-allergic of fish, right before I married the king of the damned ocean. I have a brother that I love unreasonably much, and if anybody said I couldn't hang out with him anymore, I would snip their fingers with something dull and awful. And then he would come up with something better that I could have snipped their fingers with. Because he's like that. I have, literally, the best sister-in-law on the planet. Case in point? The fallen pizza. Off the deck. With crackers. Enough said. I have a critique partner with whom I've mind melded to the extent that we cook the same thing and write the same sentence on the same day (the Plagiarism Police are, unsurprisingly, horrified). I have a best friend who has known me through every version of myself I have ever been. She is 90lbs and packs 180lbs of punch. Mean reviewers, take note. Also, I'm sorry about your noses. Really. At least a little sorry.

A non-comprehensive listing of people who have helped me along the way, whether they knew it or not: Julie Mianecki, Maggie Stiefvater, Becky Hazen, Kelly Siskind, Heather VanFleet, Michelle Iannantuono, Gwynne Jackson, Holly Stubbs, Becca Wolf, Colleen McCoy, Michael Mammay, Jenna Goldstein, Colleen Halverson, Michelle Fairbanks, Sheila Athens, Author Accelerator, Keyanna Butler, Naomi Hughes, Inkslingers Publicity, Barclay Publicity.

And to my fanfic readers, who started everything.

About the Author

Michelle Hazen is a nomad with a writing problem. Years ago, she and her husband ducked out of the 9 to 5 world and moved into their truck. She found her voice with the support of the online fanfiction community, and once she started typing, she never looked back. She has written most of her books in odd places, including a bus in Thailand, an off-the-grid cabin in the Sawtooth Mountains, a golf cart in a sandstorm, a rental car during a heat wave in the Mohave Desert and a beach in Honduras. Even when she's climbing rocks, riding horses, or getting lost someplace wild and beautiful, there are stories spooling out inside her head, until she finally heeds their call and returns to her laptop and solar panels.